FASHION
JUNGLE

*Thank you for reading!!
Enjoy xoxo*

KATHY IRELAND
AND
#1 *NEW YORK TIMES* BESTSELLING AUTHOR
RACHEL VAN DYKEN

Fashion Jungle

Kathy Ireland
Rachel Van Dyken

FASHION JUNGLE
ISBN-13: 978-1-7336680-7-1

Editing by
Oxford Comma Editing, Theresa Kohler
Kay Springsteen
Chelle Olson

Cover Design by
Jena Brignola

Formatting & Editing by
Jill Sava, Love Affair With Fiction

For Greg…
Because of Love…
we're forever on The 4th Watch.
~Kathy

To every person who reads these pages
may you feel acceptance and love,
may you find your happily ever after
and realize you ARE enough.
Hugs, RVD

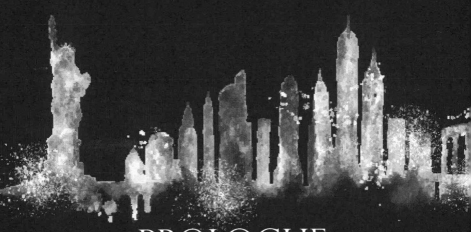

PROLOGUE

It happened too fast.

She wouldn't listen to reason.

They'd tried everything.

One movement, large enough for her to stumble.

Big enough to set the universe into action.

One movement.

One decision.

A scream.

And then, nothingness.

"Nobody has to know," a voice said from the left, and they listened because the alternative was unimaginable.

"It was an accident."

"And the evidence?" A finger pointed to the notebook next to the blood that trailed down her chin. "What do we do about the evidence? What if there's more?"

"You better hope to God there isn't… because all of it points to you."

Nobody has to know.

Nobody has to know.

The blood was cleaned.

Nobody has to know.

The future was set.

Nobody has to know.

And somewhere in the distance, a clock chimed.

Time's. Up.

Rain slid off the umbrella.

Dane counted the drops.

One.

Two.

Three.

Why did it always rain at funerals? Maybe because the world was painfully aware that it had lost someone good—someone incredible. Perhaps this was the Earth's way of mourning while Dane couldn't.

He was too livid to mourn.

Familiar faces locked onto his. The entire fashion world had come to pay its respects, even politicians and people who feared him as much as they loved her.

And all of them seemed altered.

A chill ran down Dane's spine as he locked eyes with Frederick. The man was married, and yet he cried as if he'd lost more than a friend, more than his wife's best friend—almost as if there were something hidden behind the depths of his dark gaze.

Her best friends surrounded Dane, each of them staring at the ground in disbelief as the casket was lowered.

It was a nightmare.

Dane had done nothing but dedicate his life to collecting secrets so that he could protect those he loved.

His eyes locked on Zoe.

She refused to look at him.

Maybe because he looked so much like *her*.

He was the darkness to Zoe's light.

He had done everything to protect Danica.

And still.

Still, he'd found her with a crumpled-up note in her hand that said simply: *I'm sorry*.

The police said suicide.

But Dane wasn't stupid.

His sister had been murdered.

Because she was a fighter.

Because he couldn't bear to think he hadn't seen the signs.

Because he wouldn't survive if suicide was her truth.

His gut clenched as he squeezed his gloved hands together. The leather tightened around his knuckles.

Somebody would pay for this.

Dearly.

Somebody standing around that casket knew the truth.

And he was a patient man. He searched the faces once more and imagined the number of secrets, the amount of deception, and how each and every one of them was drowning in it.

The land wept.

He did not.

Because he chose to focus on revenge... on collecting trust, secrets, money, power. He would amass it all, and then he would bring hell down on this city.

On these people who had somehow made Danica feel less than worthy.

On the plastic faces with their plastic bodies.

Dane would destroy them all.

He stared down at the three women again and pressed his lips into a grim line. He would destroy them all.

And he was going to use Danica's best friends to meet that goal.

A man wrought his revenge not in seconds, minutes, or even days. No, he found his revenge in years, by planning, building, brick by brick.

Thunder boomed.

An omen, perhaps.

Not that it mattered. The devil owned his soul the minute Dane had handed it over in exchange for one thing.

Power.

"Let us pray." The pastor lowered his head.

Everyone but Frederick did the same.

Dane narrowed his eyes.

The last person his sister had been seen with refused to pray.

Dane lowered his head with a cruel smile on his lips. Dane would kill Frederick as a bonus.

Because beneath the sadness etched in *his* eyes, Dane saw something he knew all too well.

Guilt.

ONE

It was impossible not to notice him. His height alone dominated half the people in the room, and the other half, well, the other half didn't pack the same amount of muscle, did they?

Zoe sipped her champagne and fought to keep her attention on her friends, Everlee and Brittany. They'd fought tooth and nail for this moment. Twenty years in the modeling industry had a way of leaving a woman jaded, and they'd shed enough tears between the three of them to create a tropical storm.

But it was worth it.

For this moment.

Zoe flashed a smile at Everlee, who thrust her champagne flute into the air. "To the new fall line."

"Hear, hear!" Brittany's laugh was easy and carefree. The woman was walking, talking sunlight from her long, golden brown locks to the freckles dusting her nose. She'd been America's sweetheart for so long, it would be impossible to think of any other model—retired or not—taking her place. She was still the *it girl*, while the rest of them clawed to stay on top. It seemed that Brittany didn't need to lift a fingernail to stay there. Editor at one of the most sought-after magazines in the world, and they still asked her to pose for pictures because they had to do additional reprints every time she graced a cover.

See? Lucky. Sunshine. If Zoe didn't like her so much, she'd want to strangle her with the strap of her purse or at least set all her heels on fire.

Brittany winked at Zoe. Brittany was chugging champagne like it was water. Uneasiness settled in Zoe's gut; she knew why her friend was overindulging.

All of them were painfully aware of what day it was. They just didn't know why Brittany let loose on this day every year. All they knew was that she'd been hospitalized and had lost some of the light behind her eyes. Dane had been there then.

He was always there. Rescuing, making the world think he was its savior when he was the devil himself.

And then there was Zoe.

Kohl-lined cat eyes.

Long, lanky legs.

Brown-skinned.

Short, ebony hair. Zoe.

She and Brittany couldn't be more opposite if they tried.

"He's staring." Everlee sipped her champagne and smiled into her glass. Her lips were stained a dark purple hue that brought out her flawless porcelain skin. "When are you going to put him out of his misery, Zoe? I mean really, the guy's had this torch for you since… I don't know, the day you took the subway for the first time and ended up in the Bronx."

Zoe glared and tried to settle her racing pulse. Stay calm. Appear indifferent. "Okay, first of all, I came from California. We don't do subways, we drive cars. Remember what those are?" She snapped her fingers and hoped nobody saw the tremble in her hand. "Oh, right, Miss I don't have a license and would probably have to ask a homeless person to parallel park for me."

Everlee shrugged and winked her long, elegant eyelashes in defiance. "Frederick has a driver for me."

Brittany let out a dreamy sigh. "Must be nice to have a world-renowned photographer in your bed—"

"Ladies." Frederick chose that moment to wrap his bulky arm around Everlee and press a kiss to her neck. "I missed you, sweetheart."

The guy had a smile for days and a body that young models whispered about whenever he was on set. The better half of Hollywood had been begging for years to put his face on a movie poster. Who needed to know how to act when you looked like that?

"Cute, I just saw you five minutes ago. What do you really want?" She patted his chest lovingly.

Zoe gritted her teeth. While Brittany smiled at them adoringly as if their happiness was her happiness. See? Perfect. She was perfect.

He sighed and then pulled Everlee against his chest. Her champagne sloshed over the glass and ran in a tiny bead down her pointer finger as he leaned in and whispered, "A couple of the guys wanted to head uptown. Dane has a new club where everyone has to wear masks and use secret names. Sounds fun. Plus, it's good for business, you know how it is. Networking."

Everlee made a face that basically said she'd answer yes to whatever he asked. "Sounds like a really good place for infidelity." She shook her head with a teasing smirk. "Thanks, Dane."

As if he heard the private conversation, Dane nodded in their direction.

Zoe scowled. She felt that heated look all the way down her slim thighs, past her toned calves and elegant ankles, and into her new Jimmy Choos. The guy had always been bad news.

His sister had started in the industry the same week the three of them had, and they all became fast friends—which happened when an agency forced models to basically sleep on top of one another until their big break. Most girls ended up moving back home.

The conditions at fourteen years old were more like summer camp than making it in the big city.

"Frederick?" Dane's voice cut through Zoe's memories like a knife. She mentally cursed. Did he need to have such a rough, exotic voice? Like he couldn't help the rasp that always accompanied his magnificent presence. The entire city worshiped the ground he walked on. Maybe that was why fat decided that it couldn't attach itself to his body—it was actually offended by the idea of upsetting him.

"Sweetheart." Frederick gripped his wife's right hand and then kissed her palm. "I promise I won't be out too late."

Everlee let out a sigh that Zoe knew was coming. She was definitely going to say yes. Then again, when did Frederick

Grassi ever hear a no? That would be a big fat never. He was almost as intolerable as Dane. Beautiful men like that had no business standing so close to one another. Zoe's right eye started to twitch with annoyance.

"Fine." Everlee smiled warmly at her husband. Zoe ignored the ache in her stomach and didn't miss the flash of pain in Brittany's eyes as she took another long sip of what was soon another empty glass. Not that Zoe was counting. At thirty-four, both women were single, still trying to find their person who understood the darkness of their pasts and the way it clung to them like armor in the present. Not to mention, it was nearly impossible to find a man who wasn't intimidated by a woman who knew both her mind and her body.

Finding a man like that in New York was basically the equivalent of finding a unicorn. They were either intimidated or narcissistic sociopaths who would need a magnifying glass to locate their tiny hearts—if they even had them.

"You're too good to me." Frederick kissed her and then turned and wrapped an arm around Dane. "Shall we?"

"Car's out front," Dane said in a bored tone. "I'll be right there."

Why wasn't he gone already?

Zoe finally lifted her gaze. And there he was in all his arrogance. Sharp, clean-shaven jawline, crystal blue eyes, and hair that any woman would feel compelled to run her hands through. His silky, black tendrils lay perfectly against a face that had graced Page Six way too many times to count. No wonder he was one of the city's most eligible bachelors.

It didn't matter that he had a dark side.

That he fed it well.

All that mattered was what was on the outside. Zoe'd had to learn that the hard way. The girl with stars in her eyes and longing in her heart had been replaced by a reality that even the most glamorous lifestyle couldn't shake.

Regret.

Mistakes.

And a heavy dependence on the one man who could ruin them all.

"A minute, Zoe?" Dane held out his hand. She had to take it. There were photographers, investors, peers. The mayor nodded his greeting as they walked by.

She knew what Dane wanted.

Zoe wouldn't give it to him, though. Not yet. Hopefully, not ever.

They walked in silence until they were in one of the back rooms reserved for private parties and events like this one. He shut the doors.

They clicked with finality that gave her heart a jolt.

How did they not see?

He was a wolf in sheep's clothing.

A cunning. Sexy. Devouring wolf.

"The designs look good." He crossed the room and walked toward her. She gulped and met his gaze. "Any buyers yet?"

"Saks, Bloomingdales, Nordstrom." Zoe fired off the department stores. "Then again, you already knew that."

He reached out and caressed her face with his knuckles, his lips parted as if he were going to lean down and kiss her. He didn't move.

She fought to keep her mouth from trembling. Battled not to show her fear, her desire, her confusion, and her very human need for more than just his touch. She refused to let him hold all the cards; it was all she had to work with, her defiance to being with him, to becoming one more *thing* he could control.

"Yes. I already knew that," he said in a harsh whisper. "I found out from Brittany when you refused to answer my fifth phone call yesterday."

She had known he would be angry.

Not enough to corner her.

But angry.

"I was busy." She shrugged like it wasn't a big deal when even her heart knew the danger she was in. It thumped loudly against her ribs, making it impossible to hear her own thoughts as the air buzzed in her ears, her throat thickening with a choking tension that made it nearly impossible to swallow.

"You were at lunch."

He was right.

She gulped.

"I don't like these games, Zoe, and I would hate for it to get out that your dead aunt never gave you a cent… that your *trust fund* was a pillowcase and an old piece-of-crap car that your parents were upside-down in the day they died."

Zoe squeezed her eyes shut. It was fine. Too many people were here. He wouldn't do anything. "I need to get back to my friends."

The only thing Zoe had been able to give back to him in the past had been her secrets; it was their currency, and now, it was a ticking time bomb.

"Yes. You do." He moved out of her way and then pressed his hands down on her shoulders. A mixture of fear and something else ran through her body. She ignored everything but the fear. She had no choice.

"I don't like being lied to, Zoe. I've known you since you were fourteen. I know you better than you know yourself—and you owe me more than just your life. Never forget who pulls the strings." He removed his hands.

"I paid you back." She stared straight ahead at the doors, at her escape from this nightmare.

"No." An arm wrapped around her waist. "You paid back the loan. We had interest…"

"Never again." It came out like a hiss.

"Never again, what?"

"I won't make the mistake of *you* again, Dane. I don't care who the hell you are. I'll get your *interest* money."

"I know why you haven't paid it yet," Dane said once Zoe reached the door and pulled it open. She waited for him to continue. "It's the only thing that still ties us together, besides my dead sister. It's the last part of your past you aren't willing to bury. My bet is, it will be a cold day in Hell before I see anything because if there's anything I know about you, it's that you'd rather torture yourself with the past than face any sort of future where you could be happy."

She snorted out a laugh. "In what world could you ever make me happy?"

"Careful," he warned.

And then he swept by her in a flurry of cigars and fine whiskey, leaving her drained before the party was even over. She held her breath until she saw him disappear through the front door of the restaurant and then rejoined her friends.

"What was that about?" Brittany tugged at her black Gucci dress and grabbed another glass of celebratory champagne. Zoe tried not to frown at her friend. "He looked... angry."

Zoe shrugged to hide the trembling in her hands. "When is Dane not angry? Don't you have an early appointment?" She pointed at the champagne as Brittany resolutely ignored her and lifted the glass to her red pout.

"Ain't that the truth?" Everlee scrunched up her nose. "Another toast!"

Zoe quickly shoved her dark thoughts away and grabbed a fresh glass of bubbly from a passing waiter and lifted it into the air. "To friendship."

The girls all shared a smile and a toast, but sadness still hung in the air. Because their other friend was missing, the one who'd wanted nothing more than to become the face of their new line—her dream since she was fourteen.

She had taken her life a year ago.

Leaving things altered.

"Don't be too hard on him," Brittany said under her breath once Everlee excused herself to use the restroom. "We all deal with grief in different ways. Dane lost his sister. We lost our best friend. And he turned into a sociopath. We're going to see to it that our dream happens and share it with Danica's memory."

Brittany squeezed Zoe tightly.

Zoe hated the tears that welled in her eyes.

Just like she hated how much she needed the hug that would tell her everything would be okay.

It had to be.

Something good had to come from such a pointless tragedy.

Especially since had Danica not done it first, Zoe was petrified it would have been her they were mourning.

TWO

The ceiling fan whipped around in circle after circle—and with each pass, anxiety pressed down on Everlee's chest, making it nearly impossible to breathe, holding her prisoner as the blankets weighed heavily against her ribs. If she focused hard enough on the whooshes of air, she could almost hear bone shattering, her heart stuttering to a stop with each breath she sucked in through her teeth.

It hadn't always been like this.

But it was a reality now.

A constant reminder.

A nightmare she couldn't see past.

Always the same.

Never different.

The only thing that had changed was her. And the only reason she had changed was because of him. She checked her phone again—three a.m. She had to be up early for a photo shoot, and then she was meeting the girls for drinks later. If she could just focus on the positive, on work—on the fact that she was still working in the industry—she would be okay. Not thinking about him, the past, about how each year seemed to add more time that they spent apart rather than together. How each time they were together, he became a little more aggressive, a little more violent, taking pieces of her heart with each passing day and refusing to acknowledge he was doing it in the first place. Like a sick game that she didn't know the rules to.

She swiped at a tear under her right eye.

Nights had once been filled with laughter, sex, and late-night TV. She even used to get crazy and talk about her dreams with him.

And now?

Now, he was late.

Again.

And he'd apologize while smelling like alcohol, cigars, and perfume.

Again.

And she'd forgive him.

Again.

Because she'd forgotten what life was like when she wasn't counting turns of the ceiling fan; when she was so poor, she heated up Chinese takeout two days in a row and prayed she'd get a stomach virus so she'd drop another dress size and look willowy for her next runway show.

Life had seemed empty then.

Filled with so many rules: restrictions on what to eat, what to wear, how to act. Everlee had seen Frederick as her freedom. Her dreams had shifted.

She'd had no idea that she would merely be exchanging prisons.

And handing off another set of keys to an equally punishing guard.

She only wondered what was worse?

Punishing herself.

Or letting someone else do the honors.

The door clicked closed down the hall.

She squeezed her eyes shut as the flicker of the flat-screen in her pristine master bedroom caused shapes and colors to dance along the wall.

Footsteps neared.

She bit down on her bottom lip... and held her breath.

The bedroom door clicked as it closed.

He stumbled.

She exhaled in relief. He was too drunk to pick a fight. This was good; it would be fine as long as he slept it off.

A string of angry curses had her flinching. Another stumble as it sounded like his pants got caught around his ankles, and then more cursing until finally, his body bounced onto the mattress. It didn't matter that she was huddled in the corner.

Or that she had the covers pulled up to her chin.

It never mattered.

Because as her husband, he had certain expectations, certain... rights. *Please pass out, please pass out.*

Everlee's upper lip began to perspire as Frederick tossed and turned, and then she felt it, his hand creeping along the silk sheets. The linens he'd bought after she complained about the cotton ones causing her long hair to knot at the back of her head.

She stayed stock-still as a warm hand cupped her hip. With one pull, and in record speed, he had her body jerked across the mattress. Never let it be said that Frederick wasn't inhumanly strong. He was the opposite of what everyone expected a photographer to be in the fashion industry.

It's what had drawn her to him.

His strength.

Masculinity.

His alpha-male tendencies that made her feel like the most important woman in the world—that was until she'd aged.

Now, this alpha male would never forgive her for not stopping the inevitable.

Getting older.

"Mmm." Frederick kissed down her neck, his mouth hot and eager. She wanted to respond to him, she did. He was, after all, her husband, and that was her job. To honor him, even when he smelled like Chanel when she'd always worn Gucci.

Even when his skin smelled like sweat.

It was her job to love him unconditionally.

And love him unconditionally she would.

Besides, that was just the life they lived.

The parts they played.

Lies they believed.

He pushed her onto her back and hovered over her, his cold, drunken gaze unfocused as he pulled up her favorite Victoria Secret pajamas, the ones he said were too domestic for a supermodel. She refused to let him know how much his judgment of her, and his emotional attacks, wounded her heart. He controlled everything about her... even down to demeaning her choices in intimate apparel. She realized she meant no more to him than any other object.

On good days, he called her basic.

Plain.

On bad days, he called her washed-up and pointed out every flaw with ridiculous precision, even after she'd given him whatever he wanted.

"These again." He gripped the silk shorts and pulled them so hard, the fabric dug into her skin before they ripped off her hips. He dangled them in front of her. "You're so much better than this."

He meant it as a compliment.

He was smiling like she was his world.

Then why did she feel sick?

He dropped the shorts onto the floor and lowered his head, kissing her soundly on the mouth, parting her lips with his whiskey-infused tongue. He moaned like he couldn't get enough.

She held her breath so she wouldn't have to smell the perfume.

She closed her eyes so she wouldn't see the lipstick smudge under his right ear.

And when they joined in those brief drunken moments...

She pretended it felt amazing.

When all she felt was empty.

And resentful.

"We have the perfect life," he whispered when he was finished. "Everyone says so."

"Yeah, sweetheart," she agreed. Because things could be worse, right?

He moved away from her and fell asleep with a snore.

He missed the tear that slid down her cheek as she very calmly crawled out of bed to shower.

He missed the toilet flushing to cover the crying.

And he missed the pills she took to make the pain go away as she tossed them back and fell asleep with a smile on her face. Because she was free.

At least, in her dreams.

THREE

That extra glass of champagne had been a horrible idea. How many did that make? Two? Three? Clearly one too many for someone who only drank when the occasion asked for it. Brittany pushed up her tortoiseshell Tory Burch sunglasses and pulled open the doors to the hospital.

You can do this.

It's just a building.

It means nothing.

Hands shaking, she made her way down the hall toward outpatient care. If anyone noticed her, they were polite enough to make it look like they didn't. Then again, it was a hospital, not a runway, and people only saw what they wanted to see—she knew that all too well.

"Code blue!" A female voice came over the intercom.

Brittany sucked in a breath and pressed her back against the wall as a flurry of nurses rushed by.

She squeezed her eyes shut. One breath, two. *It's just a building.*

The walls she could handle.

The smells, however, reminded her.

They reminded her well.

Haunted.

Dug their razor-sharp fingers into her skin and held on tightly as they twirled her lifeless body around and around.

"Play with me, Mama!" A young voice sounded from down the hall.

Brittany didn't move as she watched the little girl with big, bouncy, black curls twirl and twirl by her mom's feet. "Come on, Mama!"

A dizzying sickness stabbed Brittany in the stomach as tears filled her eyes, tears of anger, outrage. And worst of all... Loss.

"Where is he?" she yelled. "I need to see him!"

"He never came," the nurse whispered.

And Brittany knew... she would never forgive him for it.

For choosing something other than new life.

For not choosing her.

"Miss?" A deep voice interrupted her heavy thoughts. "Miss?"

She blinked up and smiled. It was forced but believable. After all, wasn't that what she was paid to do?

Make it believable.

Make them want.

Make them desire.

The American dream.

Right.

The happiest girl alive…

"Yes?" She found her voice as the man in blue scrubs grinned down at her. He was at least six-two and looked like he belonged in an MMA ring not in the hall of a hospital with its antiseptic smell and fluorescent lights. "Can I help you?"

His laugh was smooth as his eyes crinkled at the corners, and a dimple formed at the corner of his mouth that drew her attention more than it should. "I think you stole my line."

"Oh." She tucked her hair behind her ears and smiled, a real one this time. "Sorry. I was just… I'm here to see a friend."

"Lucky friend," was all he said as he motioned for her to follow him. He stopped a foot away at the nurses' station. "And your friend's name?" He signed some paperwork, didn't look up. No wedding ring, no tan line either.

"Ummmm." Great, now she'd forgotten the name of one of her best friends, her agent, all because she was checking out the doctor's left hand! Stupid champagne. Her head was fuzzy, her mouth dry. Coffee would probably save her soul right about then. That and a re-do with Dr. Dimples. "Roger Maxwell," she said smoothly.

"Perfect." He turned his megawatt smile back to her, right along with that body, and held out his hand. "I'm his doctor, he's just resting. Surgery went as well as can be expected when you have your gallbladder removed. You'll have to remind him to take it easy. Will there be any family visiting or—?"

"Me," Brittany said quickly. "I'm his family." They all were—his girls, his tribe as he liked to call them, though they were minus one member.

Emptiness settled in Brittany's stomach as her eyes searched the doctor's for any information other than that Roger was going to make it.

"Okay." The doctor drew out the word slowly and then smirked as if he were trying to figure her out. The dimple reappeared. "He's in recovery room nine. I'll take you over there. Just curious, is he always so...?"

"Dramatic?" Brittany laughed. "I think that's the word you were going for."

"I was going to say excitable, but dramatic works, too." He chuckled. Laughs were insightful. If the eyes were the windows to the soul, then a laugh had to be a door cracked open. Every intonation, the way someone held themselves, said all there was to know about a person. A laugh was a tell. And Brittany knew by the doctor's that he was a good man. After all, she'd been surrounded by the most powerful men in the world, and most of them laughed because they had to. This man did it because it was instinctive. "Your friend asked me if I copped a feel during surgery then offered to let me while he was awake. He's a pretty interesting guy."

Heat flooded Brittany's face. She'd never quite been able to navigate how someone she loved so much was so continually inappropriate. She could no longer keep track of the times there had been incidents or comments. She wasn't judging, but she quickly moved into apology mode.

"I'm sorry he—"

"Miss…?" The surgeon seemed to be waiting for her to say her name, strange since it was so rare people didn't know who she was.

"Brittany," She rasped, "Please, call me Brittany, everyone does." She found her gaze lingering on him again.

"Brittany," he continued, all business. "I wasn't offended. I, for one, thought it was funny. He's quite… chatty about his girls." His smile was warm, sexy. "However, not everyone shares your friend's sense of humor. The one thing I do know is that he cares about you and loves you so much more than he's able to love himself. Maybe his humor, his double entendres are a way to keep everyone laughing so that, hopefully, they won't notice the pain."

She let out a brief sigh and smiled. "You sure you're a surgeon and not a shrink?"

His soft, answering chuckle warmed her clear down to her toes. She sighed again, falling into easy conversation, even though he was towering over her and smiling at her the way men did when they were about to ask her out. She'd naturally tell them what she did for a living, they'd connect her to the family that shall not be named, and that would be that.

Because there was one true thing about the so-called American Dream.

You didn't go up against those who built it from the ground up.

She had.

And she had the scars to prove it.

Throat dry, she pressed a hand to her stomach. The movement was brief, the pain not so much as she was yet again reminded—it was empty.

"Ah, right here." He grabbed the chart from the door and pushed it open. "Mr. Maxwell?"

"Back for seconds, Doctor?" Roger said in a teasing tone that had Brittany exhaling a sigh of relief and speed-walking toward the side of the bed.

She reached for his hand.

Roger tsked. "Too much champagne last night?"

"Mind reader," she grumbled, not wanting to talk about the anniversary of what had happened or the fact that she could never make it through the day sober. "How are you feeling?"

"Who, me?" He grinned and ran a hand over his bald head. "Incredible. I'm on drugs. They gave me a button but then took it away." His mouth narrowed into a pout.

"Monsters." Brittany laughed.

"Exactly what I said. And then they refused to give me red Jell-O. You know how I rely on red Jell-O to get through the day."

"Weird, since yesterday it was chocolate pudding."

"She exaggerates." Roger waved her off and eyed the doctor. "She's pretty, though, so I keep her around."

"Yes." The doctor cleared his throat, his eyes burning a hole through her. "She really is."

Alrighty, then!

"So." Brittany squeezed Roger's hand. "Ready for me to break you out of this prison?"

Roger gave her a saucy grin. "What if I like my jailer?"

She gave him a look that said, *set me up, and I leave you here without Jell-O, drugs, or your favorite slippers I stuffed in my bag.*

With a sigh, he leaned up. "Fine, take me back to my lonely apartment."

"Penthouse," she corrected. "And you know you hate hospitals. You say they make you feel like you're one bad decision away from death."

The doctor let out a low chuckle behind her.

She locked eyes with Roger.

A warning look.

"So." Roger completely ignored her and peered around her body. "No wedding ring, right, Doc?"

"That's right." The surgeon held the clipboard close to his chest. Ah, a shield. Nice. He was figuratively protecting himself from what was coming next.

Would he see if she kicked Roger's bed? Held a pillow over his face? Pulled the fire alarm?

"Me, too," Roger said a few beats later. "This one..." Apparently, she was *this one* now. He squeezed her hand, making it impossible for her to hide under the bed or beat him with her new Chloe bag. "...lives all by herself, too. Won't even adopt a cat—"

"Okay!" Brittany interrupted loudly. "So, is there anything I need to sign to get him out of here?" Far, far away from the attractive doctor with his knee-buckling laugh and dimple. At this point, she'd sacrifice a kidney. Her love life had been the one thing she kept to herself.

Until *him*.

And then it became the only thing people wanted to discuss, and it still haunted her, everywhere she looked, no matter what she did. It never went away, and it probably never would.

KATHY IRELAND and RACHEL VAN DYKEN

"Yeah." The doctor stepped forward. "My nurse will be by with his discharge papers, but the only way to get him out of here is to go to dinner with me."

Brittany's eyes bulged as panic set in. "Um..."

"She'd love to!" Roger beamed as if he hadn't just tossed her under the bus and waved goodbye at the same time. "Though her schedule's a bit messy tomorrow. Plus, I think you have drinks with the girls tonight, right?" Of course, he had her schedule memorized; it was probably what he had done pre-op. Roger's light reading was work. Always would be. It wouldn't surprise her at all if he'd solved world hunger during surgery.

While high on drugs.

Sleeping.

"*She's* right here." Brittany waved her hand in the air. "And I actually have that gala tomorrow night with—"

"Oh, that's right!" Roger's eyes narrowed. And then the bastard coughed.

God save her.

"Sorry, I think maybe all this talking has been bad for my lungs." He grabbed his throat.

Brittany internally rolled her eyes, dirty little liar.

A confused Roger lowered his hand to his chest and nodded. "I knew they were here, poor lungs. Like I said, drugs. I can't be trusted to be in civilized company in less than twenty-four hours. So, for that very reason, I'm volunteering to stay home so you kids can have a nice meal, dance under the stars..."

Was he still speaking?

The doctor smiled over at her. "He really is always like this?"

"Exhausting, isn't it?" she said through clenched teeth, though Roger didn't seem to notice.

"You don't have to take me." Doctor GQ moved closer. He smelled like a mixture of good and bad choices, all wrapped up into one enticing yet forbidden package. Lovely.

"No, I um, that would be…" Perfect. Because at least he'd see her in her element and that would be that. No awkward: *Oh, yeah, so the president's son, he saw me naked! Spoiler alert: it wasn't enough for him to stay. Oh, yes, that's his new wife. They were sleeping together six months into our relationship.*

Compliments of his mother.

Oh, look. She's here, too.

Kill me now.

"So?" Roger cleared his throat.

Had he really been talking that entire time?

She really needed coffee. Fast.

"So…" Brittany flashed a smile. "Give me your number, and we can just meet there."

Roger groaned into his pillow.

She helpfully shoved it over his face while he kicked his legs up in the air as if he were dying.

"You'll live," she hissed under her breath as the hot doctor laughed and walked over.

And in true meet-cute Hollywood style, he grabbed a pen from the front pocket of his scrubs and very slowly wrote his name and number across the back of her hand.

Was she shaking?

Was it him?

Why did it feel like a sauna in there?

She gulped when he blew on the ink, his thumb caressing where he'd just touched, his eyes meeting hers in a way that didn't allow a person to look down but see right through.

"It's a date," he whispered.

"I'm hungry." This from Roger, who apparently, was done setting her up now that he remembered that he wanted his red Jell-O.

Hot doctor dropped her hand. "See you tomorrow night."

"Yeah... see... you," she said a bit breathlessly.

He left the room.

She exhaled, earning a stern stare from Roger. "What?"

"You need to get out more," he grumbled. "I want a burger."

"Seconds ago, you wanted Jell-O. You'll eat what they tell you to eat, and why are you still looking at me like you're disappointed in me?"

He sighed dramatically and put his hands behind his head. "You don't even know his name."

"Of course, I do. It's Doctor..." She nodded and wanted to smack herself with the hand that had his name written on it, Roger would see so she just waved him off. "There was a name tag, right?"

Roger shook his head slowly, and then pointed to the whiteboard. "Lucky for you, I knew it was written down on both the chart and your hand, good thing I intervened. By the way, he gave me two smiley faces on my pain board. Isn't that sweet?"

"True love." She rolled her eyes. "Imagine if he had given you three?"

He put his hand on his chest over his heart. "Don't toy with me. I sacrificed myself on the altar of friendship so you could at least go to one of those magazine parties without a gay man on your arm."

Brittany sighed and sat down on the hospital bed. "I see nothing wrong with that."

"I'm single. I see everything wrong with that." He patted her hand and then leaned in. "So, where are we on the whole food situation?"

With a laugh, she bent down and hugged him, held him close and relished the smell of him, distinctly Roger; no matter what he always smelled like Dior, and his skin was a perfect mocha color that reminded her of warm autumn days and walks in Central Park.

Without him, she was nothing.

But everyone had their secrets.

Why did she feel it was only a matter of time before hers were out, and the looks he gave her weren't ones of admiration but disappointment?

"Something wrong?" He patted her head.

"No. Everything's fine." Smile back in place, she pulled away then stood. Happiest girl in the world.

Just… the happiest.

And possibly, the emptiest.

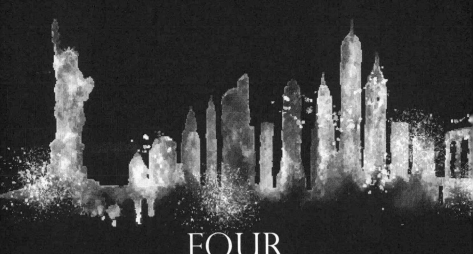

FOUR

The music pumped in cadence with his heart, the aggression of blood pumping through his veins, of the company he kept, the men who sat around him while he snapped his fingers in the air.

It was seconds before someone brought him a drink.

Three to be exact.

His club had been one of the hottest tickets in the City since opening, with its dark, intimate atmosphere and mostly VIP seating with splashes of red, the pillows etched with a single *D*—a personal touch to remind the patrons that he was the dealer of the darkness they would partake in. The devil himself.

And they were surrounded by beautiful women. Women who would make them forget. Women who would help Dane get answers.

"Have I told you how much I love this place?" Frederick sent Dane a smug grin. "Like Heaven and Hell all wrapped up in one sexy package."

The women all wore gold masks that covered their entire faces, only showing their lush mouths and their penetrating eyes. No identities, just sin.

The cover charge was a thousand dollars.

And people paid it.

Because Dane knew the first secret of big business—make it expensive, make it exclusive, make them curious.

But there was a reason for everything, wasn't there? A motive for him handing a shot of whiskey to Frederick and clinking his glass against it, downing the burning liquid in one gulp as Frederick ordered another. As the blond woman ran her red fingernails down Frederick's chest, nearly tearing his shirt with their razor-sharp trail.

Frederick tilted his head back as she pressed an open-mouthed kiss to his neck.

Another rule.

Kissing was permitted anywhere but the mouth.

It drove the clients crazy.

Yet again, giving them something but not everything. There was something very sexual about no sex.

And this city had forgotten that, hadn't it?

Married men wanted something more than sex, they just didn't know it. They didn't realize that the addiction was in the touch, in the fantasy. The addiction was in coming back for more and hoping that it would be different.

So, night after night, they paid.

They craved.

And they went home wanting more.

This was Frederick's third time. And Dane knew it would only worsen from here on out. He would make sure of it.

"Business must be good." Frederick stretched out his legs while Jauq, another photographer, made his way over. His slicked-back, gray man bun stood out among the crowd. Two women hung on his arm, and his eyes were dazed. The guy was clearly high as a kite.

"It's not bad," Dane said slowly with a knowing smile as he clasped his hands together in front of him.

An ex-president walked by and nodded.

Dane may as well be sitting on a throne.

A district court judge followed.

CIA.

FBI.

Police chief, sans wife.

So many pieces of a puzzle that still refused to right itself in his mind. So many faces that had haunted him since Danica's death.

Since her light had left this Earth.

He gave his head a shake and pulled the mask back over his face. Indifference was his friend; sadness would get him nowhere.

"Stay as long as you want." He leaned in toward Frederick and smiled. "I know it's a busy few weeks before the shows start."

Frederick rolled his eyes. "Everlee will want to go to all of them."

"Must be nice to have a supermodel as a wife."

Frederick's eyes narrowed. "She's great."

The guy's tone held no enthusiasm.

Perfect.

"Well, if you're bored…" Dane lifted a shoulder and winked at the woman wrapping her arms around Frederick's body. "We have ways to fix that here."

"Obviously." Frederick burst out laughing clearly enjoying all the attention, ignorant to what Dane was doing. Frederick grabbed the woman's hand and pressed a sloppy kiss on the inside of her wrist then pulled her closer. There was something very twisted, sick even, about the way Frederick treated the women around him, devoid of any sincere feeling. It was mechanical, and Frederick being debased in this ugly transaction was certainly not sexy. It fed his inner demons well. "I think I may come here every night."

"Be my guest," Dane said, looking away as if he were bored; when in reality, his heart was racing.

Frederick would crack. His shirt was open now, his eyes closed. The habit would continue as it always did. Wouldn't it?

He would self-destruct.

All men eventually did when it came to Dane.

The ones who didn't, well… they weren't alive to say otherwise, now, were they?

"Have fun." Dane stood, patted Frederick on the back, and shared a knowing look with the woman currently straddling the man's lap. "Make it worth his while but remember our rules."

Dane shoved the guilt aside as he walked off.

The guilt of what this would do to Everlee.

Then again, Everlee didn't know what he did.

She didn't know the secrets Frederick kept.

That he wasn't who she thought he was.

Then again, nobody really did.

Only Dane.

Because he'd collected everything he could on Frederick for a year and was less than impressed by the sort of man he was.

"Interesting club," Ronan said once Dane reached the bar. He was flanked by two bodyguards.

"They aren't necessary," Dane said in an unemotional voice, pointing to the security. "No weapons allowed, no fighting, only pleasure."

"And yet, here you are, talking to me." Ronan leveled him with a glare. "What do you want, Dane?"

"Is that how you speak to an old friend?"

Ronan let out a snort. "We've never been friends. We've only tolerated each other because of the girls."

The girls.

It was how they all referred to Brittany, Everlee, Zoe and Danica. Pain sliced through Dane's heart, he couldn't even say her name in his head without feeling it everywhere, all the way down to the marrow.

Shake it off.

They were women now.

Women with secrets.

Insecurities.

Girls who'd grown up too fast.

Females who were still fighting their way through the jungle of New York, barefoot and bleeding with fake smiles and deadly secrets.

"I need you to keep him in jail," Dane said under his breath. "They say he's getting out on good behavior."

Ronan muttered a curse. "Let me guess, you want me to go have a golf game with the DA?"

"If you think that would help." Dane tilted his head and narrowed his eyes on the politician, the man he used to trust as much as everyone else before Dane's world came crumbling down around him by way of his sister's death. "Then, yes."

"Fine. This makes us even." Ronan tried to walk off, but Dane grabbed him by the elbow and held him there, whispering in a low voice, "I will never be done with you... tell the former first lady hello. I loved what she was wearing while shopping on Fifth Avenue yesterday, the white made her look so innocent."

Ronan let out a filthy curse and walked off.

And Dane?

Dane stared out across the club as a feeling of calmness washed over him. Chess pieces had been moved.

Now.

Now, he would wait.

FIVE

"Beautiful, just beautiful." Jauq always said that whenever he worked with Everlee, but it wasn't like her vanity didn't appreciate the compliments. He'd been in the industry for thirty years, he knew good angles, and the way he worked with natural light made him one of the best in the business—next to Frederick, of course.

It was a big shoot.

So, unsurprisingly, Frederick was there.

And, naturally, he was ignoring her because one should never mix business with pleasure, right?

She tried not to look annoyed. The pinched expression on her face wouldn't sell this handbag. Neither would the fact that she kept looking over her shoulder every single time she heard feminine laughter coming from the corner.

The studio was set up for a multi-layer shoot; handbags, gloves, scarves, and earrings.

Fall accessory madness for *Trend*, the magazine that Brittany worked for. Speaking of Brittany… she was supposed to show up after she grabbed Roger from the hospital.

"Everlee, sweetie." Jauq snapped his fingers. "Over here. Yes, loosen your fingers a bit from the strap, push your neck forward a bit. There you go."

The fact that he even had to coach her would be insulting if it weren't for the fact that she was distracted. Her stomach rumbled with emptiness as more laughter came from the corner.

"Sorry." She managed a small smile for Jauq, "Last night was a long one."

"I heard." He clicked another photo. "Zoe's line's supposed to be a huge hit at Fashion Week."

"Yes." Everlee beamed over the safe topic. She'd be fine as long as he didn't ask when she was going to pop out some kids. Any sort of family topic was off-limits. "We're all so proud of her."

"Well." Another click. "She deserves it. All of you do."

Jauq lowered his camera and looked away, then ran his hand down the graying ponytail that fell past his shoulders. His black-rimmed glasses slid off his nose, and he pushed them up. "Why don't we take a break?"

Ah, she'd been too focused on her safe topics to remember his.

Talking about the three of them always made Jauq remember her.

Danica had been his favorite out of the four of them.

Dane's sister.

Their best friend.

"You guys, I met the most amazing photographer today!" Danica swirled around the small, cramped room, her skinny arms outstretched as she let out a giggle and then pulled her long, chocolate-brown hair into a ponytail.

A new shipment of trainees had just landed in their cramped apartment, making it around sixteen girls in less than six hundred square feet.

Yeah, they were living the life.

"Come on!" Brittany pulled Danica's hand as the four girls giggled and made their way to the fire escape.

Danica pulled out a cigarette for each of the girls. Everlee took one greedily, hoping to God it would help keep her appetite at bay when all she wanted was pizza, heavy on the cheese.

On command, her stomach grumbled.

"So. Hungry." Everlee waited for Danica to light her cigarette, took two puffs, and blew out the smoke. "All right, spill, who is he? Have I worked with him yet? God, some of the photographers are sexy." One in particular. Frederick. But that was their secret, right? Just theirs.

"His name is Jauq." She grinned. "He's older, but his ponytail..."

"Eww!" Zoe scrunched up her button nose. "He's old? Like as in your dad?"

Danica lifted a shoulder. "Who cares? He said we should hang out sometime."

"That's code for he wants to see you naked," Brittany said softly. "You should be careful."

"*Easy there, Bible thumper,*" *Zoe teased, earning an answering smile from Brittany, who honestly didn't mind the nickname. She was good.*

So crazy good, it was annoying.

"*What's he look like?*" *Everlee tried to change the subject. "Tall? Dark? Handsome? Does he meet the checklist?*"

Danica pulled a piece of white paper out of her tight Levis and unfolded it. They had a master list and had made copies for each other for when they each found their happily ever after. "Well, he just did a cover for Vogue, *so he's well known at least. Rich?" She went down the list and read. "Big apartment? Well, I guess I don't know yet. New Yorker through and through? Absolutely, the guy has the accent and everything." Her eyes fell to the bottom, and then it was like they all went silent. "Would he love me?*"

It was a stupid thing to put on the list.

Everlee had been the one to add it. Brittany had encouraged her because after one year of modeling in New York, it was impossible to know if people loved you for you, or only for your face and your body. Was any of it even real?

It didn't feel that way.

And their agent didn't make them feel like anything more than glorified objects that made her money. And if you didn't, well... You were gone and sent a lovely bill in the mail with an itemized list of what you owed her for having to put up with you for a summer.

It wasn't what people saw on TV.

In ways, it was glamorous.

But a lot of it was like a really competitive summer camp where you weren't given food, and cocaine addictions were encouraged.

"I bet he could," Danica said in a dreamy voice. "He looked at me like... like he saw past everything else."

They all sighed with her.

Because that was the dream.

Look past the face.

See the woman beneath.

Brittany clutched her worn black Bible to her chest. Everlee gave a small shake of her head.

Brittany just smiled with everyone else. "It will happen for you, Danica, I know it will."

"Yeah, wish I had that faith," Danica said with a half-smile. "For the record, thank you."

It was one moment in years of them, where they would confess and dream with the sounds of sirens and yelling and the smell of trash lining the street in Hell's Kitchen.

"Friends forever," Zoe said in a cheesy voice as the girls all shared a group hug, only to be interrupted by a new girl, who poked her head out the window with a snarl.

"Who put their crap on my bed?"

Everlee sighed.

While Zoe said in a sarcastic voice, "Fairy tales really do come true!"

"Everlee!" Brittany stalked into the room. She was tall, but her high heels made her even taller—everyone took notice.

But that was exactly what happened when you were Brittany. People stared, and they had trouble looking away. With gorgeous hair that had strands of every color of brown in the world, blue eyes, and legs for days, she just... commanded a room.

Everlee used to be jealous.

But Brittany had never been anything but supportive and wonderful. Beautiful. She was the perfect woman and smiled at everyone, including their old agent, who had basically been trying to shove them into prostitution every single time they went overseas. They'd learned their lesson really quick when several of their friends never made it back and were still considered missing.

"Hey." Everlee grabbed a bottle of water while Jauq switched lenses. "How was Roger?"

"Oh, you know." She looked flushed. Why did she look flushed? Her cheeks had a pink hue that wasn't normal for her. "Did you sprint here or something?"

"Hmm?" Brittany pressed her lips together, her eyes wide.

"Okay, we both know you can't lie to save your life. If the world was going to end based on your ability to lie, we would all die." Everlee laughed, feeling the stress of the day dissipate. It was like Brittany took it all away with one single conversation, sometimes even with just her presence.

"So?" Brittany crossed her arms and then uncrossed them. Her fidgeting was her tell, mainly because she was always so composed that Everlee sometimes wanted to mess up her hair and run away just to get a rise out of her.

"Who is he?"

"He?" Brittany's voice had a high pitch to it. "Oh, um… Roger, yes he's great. He's not going to die, and after I fed him, he was in a much better mood."

"Right." Everlee waited.

Brittany stared her down and then slumped. "Okay, fine, there was a doctor."

"Ohhhhhhh." Everlee clapped her hands. "Tell me everything. Was he hot? Did he ask to have sex with you during his break? Please tell me he used a cheesy pick-up line like, 'I'm a doctor...'"

Brittany gave her a confused look. "How is that cheesy?"

"If he said it in a low voice, puffed out his chest, and gave you a smolder... cheesy, all of it. That's like you walking up to some poor soul and going, 'I'm a supermodel,' then waiting for them to faint."

Brittany shook her head. "It is not!"

"Is." Everlee sighed and took a seat in one of the chairs while Brittany did the same. It wasn't lost on her that the laughter was getting louder from Frederick's corner, as if he were throwing a frat party.

The girls worshipped him.

"You're so funny, Frederick!"

"You're so hot!"

"Do you work out?"

Everlee squeezed the water bottle so tightly, the cap almost popped off. It wasn't helpful that Brittany was giving her a look of concern either, as if to say, "*hey, should I go over there and kick him in the nuts?*" Though knowing Brittany, she'd just politely tell him that he was a jerk, smiling the whole way through it before telling him that he needed Jesus.

Taking her cue, Brittany started talking. "He was Roger's surgeon."

Everlee gasped. "A surgeon!"

"Shhh!" Brittany hushed her. "Not so loud. Besides, you know how I am with dating now that..." She just shrugged. Yeah, now that her love life had exploded with blood and gore for the world to see. Train wreck? Absolutely. Life-altering? Even more so. Though nobody could ever figure out why it was so devastating.

It felt like the only part of herself that Brittany kept from her friends. Everlee chose to ignore it.

They all had their secrets, didn't they?

"I know." Everlee put her hand on Brittany's, noticing her new Rolex and freshly painted pale pink fingernails. See? Perfect. "But don't you think it's time?"

"Maybe." She crossed her legs. "I guess. I don't know. What if he's there?"

"The surgeon, or the man who shall not be named? And where?"

Another sigh. "Roger sacrificed himself on the altar of friendship and convinced the hot doctor to go with me to the gala."

Stunned, Everlee just stared.

"Yeah." Brittany fidgeted with her purse as if she needed something to do with her hands. "He couldn't just start with coffee? The poor doctor's going to get thrown into a den of hungry wolves."

"Eh, more like thrown into shark-infested waters with a severe head wound and blood all over his face. But, yeah, basically the same thing." Everlee flashed her friend a smile. "Look at the positive, you won't get attached over coffee and a quiet dinner and then see him run for the hills. This way, it's like a Band-Aid. He can either take it and stay, help you heal"—she elbowed Brittany and did a little jig—"or he'll run out of the gala screaming."

"Sounds like a great first date. The doc runs out screaming, I hide in the bathroom and try to stay far, far, away from the family."

"I swear it's like they put a homing device in your purse—where you are, they are."

"Tell me about it." Brittany grabbed her phone and scrolled through it. "Are we still on for drinks later?"

"Yup." Everlee stood as Jauq motioned for her to get back to work.

"'Kay." Brittany kissed her on the cheek. "See you at Domino!"

"Bye!" Everlee watched her friend leave in a controlled flurry of perfection. She shook her head and relaxed as she moved effortlessly in front of the camera once more.

See? Five minutes with Brittany, and she was already calmer.

And as if sensing her peace—

Frederick shouted out some profanity at someone, which had everyone roaring with laughter and telling him how funny he was.

Yes. He fed his beast well.

It hurt to think that after years of marriage, she was only now seeing that it would always be about him.

And what she could bring to the table for him.

She wondered how much longer he would put up with someone who refused to feed his need for attention and compliments. Because every time she gave, he took, leaving her emptier than before.

"One minute." She smiled at Jauq, then walked over to her purse, popped a pill that looked like aspirin, and then returned. "Okay, ready."

"Headache?"

Heartache. "Yeah, sorry, you know how the lights get me."

Jauq grinned. "I do, but they must be bright to capture your perfection."

"Thank you." She relaxed again into another pose and let the numbness wash over her.

It was fine.

It would be fine.

After all, she was living the dream.

Wasn't she?

SIX

She was early.

She hated being late.

It was the exact opposite of what people expected when they saw Zoe for the first time. She dressed in bohemian colors, a mixture of Dolce and Michael Kors that always made people do a double-take. Bold colors paired with extravagant textures and patterns all tied up with one dazzling pair of Stuart Weitzman boots.

Her clothes represented her life.

She wanted it to be colorful.

Free.

Beautiful.

Maybe it was her way of controlling something, just one thing. She eyed her cell with a worried look.

Seven missed calls.

All from Dane.

One text that had a nice little clock emoji on it as if to remind her that time was running out. Perfect, just perfect.

He always got what he wanted.

Always.

Even her.

"I'll make it go away," he whispered. "I'll make it all go away."

"What do I do?" Zoe wailed. "I can't have this go public. My parents will disown me!"

"I told you, I'll take care of it, and I will."

She exhaled. Only nineteen, and already she had a sex tape that would make any porn star proud. The video hid nothing, and it had been done on purpose.

That was the worst part.

She'd been set up.

But who would do that to her?

"I've got this, just promise me you'll let me take care of you. Promise me, Zoe." He begged, he pleaded. Dane was not a man to do either of those things.

He'd said he loved her.

She wasn't sure he loved anyone more than he loved himself. She checked her cell and put it back down on the table just as the waiter brought over four glasses of water. They always ordered four.

It was a way to keep Danica's memory alive.

That and the tequila shot that sat near the empty seat until it was one of the girl's turn to take it and make a toast to the fourth friend who had found life too hard to live.

"You're early." Dane's low, hypnotic voice had her jumping in her seat. Of course, he'd probably gotten her schedule from their secretary, who was never good at saying no to handsome men with fat wallets and most of New York dangling from their wrists like one half of a handcuff.

"And you're not invited." She grabbed her old Kate Spade, the very first purchase she had made when she landed her first cover, and hooked it around her chair, still not making eye contact.

He sat.

"Please, sit, join me," she said sarcastically.

"I will, thank you." His grin was wide, menacing, sexier than it should be, and too powerful to continue staring at. It was as if the sun were beating down on her face, threatening to burn her alive if she kept looking. "We should probably discuss Fashion Week."

That got her attention. "I'm sorry, what?"

"I own half your company, don't I? Isn't it typical for business partners to meet for drinks, go over plans? I just want to make sure you have everything ready to go."

"Okay, first of all, I bought back your half."

"You still owe interest and one tiny debt."

Tiny debt, her ass. "Second, you wouldn't know how to plan my runway show if I held you at gunpoint."

"You're welcome to try." He tilted his head in amusement then raised his hand.

The waiter stumbled over his feet to make it to the table. "Mr. Saldino, the usual?"

Naturally the poor kid was shaking. She knew that feeling well. It's like Dane couldn't help himself.

Was there any restaurant Dane hadn't ruined for her?

"Yes." Dane nodded his head. "And a whiskey sour for the beautiful woman scowling in our direction."

Zoe gritted her teeth. "You know I hate whiskey."

"You don't actually hate it. You just despise that it reminds you of the taste of my kiss."

He had her there.

She would die before admitting it. "The runway show has already been planned. I stayed up late for months, agonizing over the order of the designs and making sure that everything was ready from the coloring to the background music. I've got this."

"You always do." He leaned in, his tan forearms pressed against the tabletop, and ducked his head. "You're prettier when you're not glaring."

"I'm glaring because you make me angry."

"I make you angry because I'm right, which makes you…" His voice trailed off as their drinks were delivered in record speed.

He tilted back his scotch on the rocks, his eyes never leaving hers. "Say yes."

She gulped against the dryness in her throat. "No."

"Well, then." He stood and pulled something out of his jacket, then slid it across the table, one massive finger still holding it pinned to the wood. "I guess you've left me no choice."

"But to pass me a note and ask me to circle yes or no?"

"Don't be cute when I'm being serious. That makes me angry." His voice deepened. "It makes me remember what it was like between us before Danica died. We were a team."

"She was what tied us together."

"You smile when you lie," was all he said as he pulled out a crisp hundred-dollar bill and set it on the table.

His footsteps may as well have been a countdown as he left the restaurant. With shaky fingers, Zoe lifted the piece of paper he'd slid toward her.

It was a bill.

For seventy grand.

And at the bottom, the added interest: her hand in marriage.

SEVEN

Dane slammed the car door behind him and leaned back against the warm, plush leather of the Escalade as Brittany and Everlee made their way into the restaurant. He watched like he always did.

Made sure there were men following them as per his promise to his sister back when the girls had still been modeling full time.

They'd had more stalkers than they realized.

And they had no idea how many of them he'd dealt with.

How many of them were now at the bottom of the Hudson with horror-filled faces and bodies weighed down with cement.

He looked down at his phone, ready to text Zoe, ready to tell her he needed her answer.

Not just for him.

For her, too.

Because she wasn't safe.

Wouldn't be safe if Ronan couldn't magically rein in the district attorney. Dane's worst fears would be realized. And he'd made a promise that he'd protect her, that she'd never have to be afraid again.

The problem with love was that you expected your other half to see you at your worst and accept it.

Zoe had seen him at his worst and ran screaming the other way. She saw his monster, and instead of embracing it or chasing the demons away, it was she who had bolted—in the opposite direction.

She was afraid of him.

But he would accept her fear if that meant he could attempt to take her love. Maybe that made him sick.

But it was the only way he knew how to be.

A headache throbbed at his temples as he turned on the tracking device for Frederick.

He fired off the address to his driver, a few blocks away. The photographer could be at a shoot. Or not.

The car rolled up to an empty warehouse.

The door opened. Dane stepped out and buttoned his coat against the wind and then walked over to one of the side doors.

Voices filtered out from inside.

He pressed his ear against the door and listened, trying to make out the muffled sounds.

"Are you sure?" a female voice asked. "I mean, my agent said it was fine but…"

"Don't you trust your agent?"

"Of course! I'm living the dream!"

Dane almost rolled his eyes.

"Then just take off the blouse. You still have your bra on, but the shot will be a lot sexier with the light in here. Trust me, this is my job. All right, sweetheart?"

Silence. Then, "Okay…"

Dane had heard enough. He walked back to the SUV, got in, and dialed a number he hoped one day he'd get to lose. "Frank?" He drew out the name. "I'm going to give you an address. Make it quick, get some pictures and any information you think might be useful."

"Am I doing cleanup?"

"No," Dane said thoughtfully. "Not yet."

But soon. Very. Soon.

EIGHT

"What's that?" Brittany plopped down next to Zoe and hung her purse on the back of the chair. One didn't just drop a Chloe bag on the dirty floor. Even though she made an incredible living, she always respected the merchandise. The clothes, the purses, the scarves, everything had a place, and that place wasn't next to some guy's spilled beer and a few peanuts.

Zoe jumped in her seat, folded the paper, and stuffed it into her bright pink Kate Spade. "Oh, you know, just notes."

"Still going over Fashion Week?"

Zoe took a sip of her drink and drummed her sharp, black fingernails on the wood tabletop. "I just want everything to be perfect."

Brittany leaned over and placed her hand on Zoe's. "This is your moment, enjoy it."

"Ugh." Zoe fanned her green eyes as they started to mist. "I needed to hear that, thank you."

"Love you." Brittany squeezed her hand. "Now, what are you drinking?" She waved down the waiter, who took one glance at her and blushed.

She smiled wider.

He looked like a recent college graduate.

"Hi." He swallowed at least five times before blurting, "What can I get you?"

"Not that." Brittany made a face at Zoe's drink. "Since when do you drink whiskey?"

"Never." Zoe shoved the drink to the far edge of the table while Brittany looked over the menu.

"Hmmm, how about three Moscow mules with Tito's and a tequila shot for right here." Brittany softly patted the chair that had been empty for a year—and would remain empty, never to be filled again.

A feeling of loss swept over Brittany. It was painful. It always hurt when her past reminded her of things she'd rather forget.

Of choices she wished she could make again.

But that was the cruelty of humanity, wasn't it?

Once you made a choice, you rarely got a second chance.

And if anyone asked her what she wished every time she found a penny and threw it into water…

It would be that.

For a second chance.

"Coming right up." The waiter beamed.

"Thanks." Brittany glanced at his name tag. "Brock."

"Not a problem," he said, still lingering, his eyes drinking Brittany in like she was on the menu right next to the cocktails.

Zoe cleared her throat.

He seemed to realize that he was still standing there, blushed harder, and then skipped off toward the bar.

Zoe made a face at Brittany. "Could you at least *try* to make it so another waiter doesn't fall in love with you and then cries out of rejection?"

"One time." Brittany threw her head back and laughed. "And he'd just gotten dumped. He was already sensitive. Plus, I gave him a huge tip."

"Too bad, since I'm pretty sure all he wanted was your—"

"Sorry I'm late!" Everlee tugged at the chair, creating a screeching noise as she dragged it across the cement. "Whoops! Okay, what'd I miss? And why aren't we drinking yet?"

"She was drinking when I got here." Brittany outed Zoe. "And nothing important."

"We're about to lose another waiter," Zoe grumbled.

Everlee dug around in her purse and pulled out a twenty. "Here you go."

Zoe jerked it away. "Thank you!"

"Wait, are you betting on if I'll get asked out? I thought we stopped doing that when we grew up." Brittany looked between her friends with a soft smile.

"She's too pretty," Zoe said, ignoring her. "We need new friends."

Brittany kicked her under the table, earning a laugh from Zoe just as their drinks arrived.

A moment of silence passed between them as the waiter placed the shot in front of the empty chair. It was always tense, filled with laughter and conversations that lasted for years, only to stop suddenly just when they'd seemed to climb out of the dark pit that was the modeling industry.

"Whose turn is it?" Everlee asked in a soft voice that completely matched her blue-and-white yacht dress and pink lips. She always looked like she just stepped off the cover of *J. Crew*. She was the epitome of a Hamptons wife, who had never visited the Hamptons long enough to claim the role.

"Mine." Brittany eyed the tequila, not her favorite, but maybe it would make the pain of yesterday and the horror of tomorrow a little less severe. She grabbed the glass between her fingers, lifted it into the air, and whispered, "To Danica, we miss you." The glass felt cool against her fingertips as she tilted it back and downed the entire drink. The alcohol burned the back of her throat and spread through her chest, settling like a bomb in her stomach as she reached for her Moscow mule to try and make the feeling go away. "Why did we pick tequila again?"

"Because." Everlee smiled. "Danica was rough around the edges, the badass of the group, and she said she wanted us to take shots every girls night as a testament to the rest of the world that we'd made it, that we were successful enough to order top-shelf shots and drink on a weekday at a fancy bar."

Brittany held her glass close as memories of Danica hit her hard in the chest. Their friend had been the wild one, and yet it was Brittany who'd gone and done the unthinkable, and Danica who had been there when she had nobody to turn to.

Miss you, friend...

She took a long sip of her drink then looked up. It was silent—too silent. They were talkers, so it was quiet enough for her to wonder if something was wrong.

And it was.

In a big way.

She almost dropped the drink as she set it on the table. As it was, she reached for both Zoe's and Everlee's hands underneath it and squeezed them tightly. "The nerve of that psycho."

"I have other words to describe her," Zoe said through clenched teeth while Everlee went white as a ghost.

Their old agent was in the corner with a group of five girls. A group of five men soon joined them, including Marnie's right hand man and ex-lover an Arnold Schwarzenegger look alike who was fully prepared to do anything she asked. It was almost alarming how much they looked alike. His massive presence almost made Brittany want to cower as he pulled up a chair and started sliding small packages of drugs toward the girls like party favors. Nobody knew if he was the dealer, a bodyguard, or just the man who distracted the young models with his good looks and charm.

"We should go," Everlee said in a hollow voice.

"No." Brittany shook her head vehemently, disgusting that they had a daughter the same age as some of the models they were trying to get hooked, then again, that was the life wasn't it? Her body gave an involuntary shudder. "She can go. This is our spot. Plus, you know she just likes to parade herself in front of us like a freaking pageant mom with too much access to hairspray and red lipstick."

"Brittany said 'freaking,'" Zoe repeated triumphantly, earning an eye roll from both women. "What?"

"I heard that the last girl Marnie booked on a shoot ended up crying in the bathroom because the photographer asked her to take her clothes off. Apparently, it was for some nude shot, but she was never told. Mr. Universe over there had to almost break down the door to get her out." Figures.

Marnie never told any of them anything. She just expected her models to keep their heads down and work. Her response to everything had been, "This is your job." And the muscle over there was the right hand that enforced it.

"Marnie," Zoe said like a curse.

"I know." Brittany shook her head in disgust. "Bad enough that she sends her girls overseas to get hooked on drugs during the after-parties. 'This is the lifestyle, this is what you wanted,'" she said, mimicking their ex-agent's Italian accent perfectly as she tossed her hair over her shoulder. Classic Marnie. "She makes me sick."

"Same." Zoe downed the rest of her drink.

Brittany followed.

"Guys," Everlee stood, "I'm going to use the restroom really quick."

"Just don't get caught in a corner with the crazy." Zoe nodded to Marnie's group.

"No worries." Everlee lifted a shoulder and weaved through the crowd.

"Look at her," Brittany said in disbelief. "The doppelganger literally just copped a feel and handed the same girl a package of cocaine!"

"Stay skinny," Zoe said mockingly.

"Stay awake," Brittany added. "Keep them happy."

"Never say no," Zoe finished in a harsh whisper.

"Back!" Everlee announced, looking like the bathroom was the place to be if you wanted to experience a revival.

"That was quick." Brittany reached for her drink again, twisting the straw between her fingers to keep herself from waving the waiter over for another. It was exactly what she needed, especially with Marnie making a scene. Brittany didn't hate people. Not really. At least, she tried not to. But, Marnie? Marnie was the sort of person who was easy to hate because she was selfish to her core. Everything revolved around her. And it all came back to money. She asked for your soul, and if you didn't give it, she was through with you. She manipulated, she lied, and she had no qualms about seducing the younger male models into her bedroom.

Something Brittany had only found out about after one of them had confessed to her that he had been forced to stay over at Marnie's house for a shoot in the morning. He'd had no money, and after taking him out to dinner, one thing had led to another.

He had been raped.

He *said* it was consensual.

When Brittany asked why he lied, he said it was because Marnie had fed him.

He'd lasted about four months before getting sent back to Oklahoma with a bill for all the expensive dinners Marnie had paid for, plus interest.

The woman was an emotional terrorist with too much power and way too many influential friends.

Except for Dane.

Dane hated her.

Which made Dane a friend, even though Zoe would probably disagree.

Then again, that was a situation Brittany never truly understood because it was the one thing Zoe refused to talk about.

"Food?" Everlee grabbed a menu. "I haven't eaten yet."

Brittany cleared her throat.

"Oh, stop." Everlee set the menu down. "I've been starving all day, believe me, but the shoot went long, then I had to change, and I had time for one Starbucks stop before my next call."

"For what?" Zoe asked, changing the subject.

Everlee's face lit up. "Oh, you know, just *InStyle*."

Brittany's jaw dropped. "But they usually only put celebrities on their covers."

"Not that you aren't famous..." Zoe added, giving Brittany a scathing look.

"You know what I mean. Actresses." Brittany glared right back and then flashed a smile at Everlee. "We need details!"

"Well..." Everlee clapped her hands. "Sadly, our friend here is right. The last cover was Jennifer Aniston, and the one before that was J-Law. Point is, they like actresses, but they're doing a three-page spread for their Winter Wonderland shoot, and I got a callback!"

"That's amazing!" Brittany cheered. "You'll get it, I know you will."

"Pray for her." Zoe winked.

"Always do," Brittany said sweetly, meaning it down to her core. "How else do you think we escaped that?" She nodded her head toward Marnie, who was currently draping her arms over two male models who looked like they hadn't yet hit puberty.

"Amen," Zoe said on a laugh.

"And cheers." Everlee lifted the menu. "Now, let's eat!"

"Let's." Brittany eyed the menu and then grabbed her drink and downed the rest of the watered-down ice.

The alcohol should have helped by now.

The pain was still there.

The fear.

The hollowness in her stomach that matched her chest, where her heart *should* beat with excitement.

Roger was healthy and fine.

Her friends were with her.

She had a date!

Her stomach sank even lower.

The waiter came back. "Another round," she said as casual as she could looking back down at the menu. Her eyes always gravitated toward the fries. She imagined what it would be like to dip them in ranch and then let the grease from an accompanying burger drip down her chin onto her tan legs.

"Shrimp salad," she said instead. "Dressing on the side."

"Same," the other girls said in unison.

She'd had enough shrimp salads to last a lifetime.

In the corner, Marnie laughed louder.

It seemed no matter how hard they tried, some things just never changed, did they?

NINE

Everlee couldn't stop shaking as she flipped through the channels. Late-night TV took over the apartment as the lights from their floor-to-ceiling windows displayed an incredible view of SoHo.

She flipped to Jimmy Fallon and grabbed a pillow to hug. It made her feel like her hands weren't shaking as much when she held something. Especially since Frederick had gone long on another shoot.

She sighed as the TV buzzed in the background.

Lonely.

After happy hour, she'd stopped off at Walgreens and made the purchase she'd been putting off for five days.

Now, dark shadows danced around the walls, mocking her, making her feel like she wasn't so alone. At least she had noise from the TV, right?

How was it possible to be so lonely when she was married? Famous? Money bought her things. Fame got her Frederick. But her heart? It needed more than a pillow to hug, didn't it?

She chewed her lower lip.

She wouldn't take another.

She didn't need the pills anyway.

They just helped her relax.

She was shaking for another reason entirely.

The timer went off on her phone.

With a jolt, she stood on shaky bare feet and walked for what felt like an eternity to the master bathroom.

"It's probably nothing," she said to herself. The lonely silence seemed to crackle around her like lightning had manifested itself inside her room, within the walls of the expensive, white tile.

Only the best for Frederick.

For the couple that had it all.

She eyed herself in the mirror.

Beautiful, flowing, blond hair; wide, brown eyes; perfect lips compliments of Dr. Ajaya.

Breasts that were high and full.

Not too big.

Not too small.

Four hundred fifteen ccs on the right, and four hundred fifteen on the left.

Toned muscles from hours of Pilates.

A spray tan that cost more than most people's weekly food bill.

It was fine.

Everything was in order.

Focus on the positive.

Maybe it was the stress that had been making her paranoid. After all, her husband had come home smelling like skank—and not just once.

It seemed to be getting worse.

The violence.

The sickening kisses that tasted like someone else's lust.

"I'll love you forever, you know that," Frederick teased as he chased her around the studio. "Come on, just take off your shirt, nobody has to know."

"You're bad." She giggled then pulled her shirt off.

He snapped a photo, then another. "Gorgeous." His hair was slicked back, muscles flexing beneath his plain white T-shirt; his low-slung jeans hugged his thick thighs.

The guy was a walking sexual deviant.

Everyone said so.

"Now what?" she asked with a coy smile.

"Now, I kiss you." He took two steps toward her. "I'm tired of looking through the lens. I don't want anything between us, not now, not ever."

"I'm not old enough for you to be saying things like that to me."

"Our little secret," he whispered, capturing her chin with his forefinger and thumb. "Besides, you turn eighteen in what? A few years?"

She nodded dumbly, already under his spell, captivated by the way his massive presence commanded the room.

"Nobody has to know," he encouraged, pulling her into his arms. "Right?"

"It's none of their business," she agreed.

"None." His mouth touched hers. She wanted it to be soft, she expected it to be romantic. Instead, it felt rough, aggressive. Wrong. It was her first real adult kiss.

It should be better than modeling.

Better than anything.

Powerful.

He loved her. This was how he showed his love, right?

She clung to his shirt just as his hands moved to the jeans she'd just been modeling. One button. It was on the tip of her tongue to say no, to ask for more time, but she knew he wasn't a patient man. Plus, he wanted her, right? Right?

"You want me," he said.

She was always frightened that he could read her thoughts; it was part of their push-pull dynamic.

All she could do was nod and imagine a life where they didn't have to hide. Where they could start a family and throw their love in everyone's faces. Where he'd kiss her tenderly on the mouth and tell her she was everything he'd ever hoped for in life and more.

Everlee stared into the mirror two seconds longer as memories washed over her. And then she looked down.

Positive.

It was positive.

TEN

"Stop slouching," Roger said from the corner of the living room just as Zoe and Brittany sat down.

"You call it slouching, I call it sitting," Zoe fired back in a haughty tone, but she managed to sit a bit straighter while Roger tied his silk bathrobe around his toned body. The guy was in his fifties but took his nutrition and exercise regimen extremely seriously, which was why it was so surprising when he started having gallbladder attacks. Roger was an anchor for them, and Zoe knew she wouldn't have survived without him.

Without Dane.

Why did it always have to come back to Dane?

"I take it you both thought I was dying and wanted to know if you were in my will?" He brought a cup of tea to his lips and grinned over it, all white teeth teasing them like always.

Brittany was the one who grabbed a blanket and rested it next to his thigh and then sat down on the plush, white leather couch. "Yeah, we just wanted to make sure that we were still your favorites. Bet none of your other clients bring you soup."

"At midnight, too. Color me intrigued." He eyed the soup then both girls. "Why did you wake me up again?"

Zoe was the first to speak. "We saw Marnie."

Roger set the cup down and nodded. "I see."

"Why can't we say anything again?" This from Brittany. "We have proof that she's been abusing some of her girls, and she's slept with I don't even know how many of the guys she represents. She was flaunting them at the restaurant, and it just kills me that we can't do anything."

"Won't," Zoe corrected, feeling sick. Then again, she knew someone who could make the problem go away. He'd probably ask for her spleen or something equally horrifying in return, or maybe just impregnate her and tie her to a bed.

Not that there weren't worse ways to go.

But it was Dane.

Dane, of all people.

Dane, who wanted her only because he couldn't have her. It would be great, for maybe a few months. Then he would get bored as most men did with Zoe when they realized she didn't live the lavish lifestyle they'd seen painted in magazines during their teen years.

And off they went.

Never to be heard from again.

At least she could invest something in her work—her heart, her time, her body.

"Zoe's obviously thinking about killing the witch. Shhh, I think she's burning up brain cells faster than I'm losing them," Roger joked, bringing Zoe back to the present.

With a glare in his direction, Zoe sat a bit straighter. "It's frustrating, that's all."

"Frustrating, yes." Roger seemed to choose his words carefully. "You live in a world full of secrets, ladies. If we start telling Marnie's, then they start telling yours."

Brittany jolted while Zoe tried to hide her reaction. "That's the price you must pay, and no stone will go unturned. She owns her own agency. On top of that, every major photographer goes to her first when they have a campaign where they need a fresh face. You know this since that's how all of you were discovered."

Zoe snorted. "You mean during that one hot New York summer where we slept on the fire escape because one girl had to be hospitalized from heat stroke? I would have given anything for a job just so I could move out."

"Bingo." Roger rubbed a hand over his bald head. "You would have given anything, and that is how Marnie deals with young girls who move into the city. Young boys, as well. She finds your weakness, uses it against you, and then gives you exactly what you wanted all along. Then she seems confused as to why you don't adore her." He let out a sigh. "Do what you want, but my opinion on this is the same. As your agent, as your friend, and more importantly, as your family."

Zoe gulped back the rock lodged in her throat.

"I don't want to see you hurt, and she is the sort of woman who will stop at nothing to hurt you." Roger turned to Brittany with a knowing look in his eyes. "All of you."

Brittany paled and then leaned her head on his shoulder. "What would we do without you?"

"That's easy, you'd be really pretty waitresses," he joked.

Zoe narrowed her eyes. "Very funny."

"You don't need me, but it does make me feel good that you think you do." He kissed Brittany on the top of her head then stood and did the same to Zoe.

What would they do without him?

Zoe's parents were gone.

Brittany, lucky girl that she was, still got visits from hers. She'd grown up with an incredible, loving family, a mom who called her every week, and a dad who told her she could be anything she wanted.

Whereas Zoe? Zoe had grown up with a drunken father, a drug-using mother, and no money whatsoever. She'd had to claw, bloody and beaten, to the top. And nobody—not Marnie or Dane—was going to take it from her.

"She's got that look again," Roger said without even looking in Zoe's direction. "Planning world domination, sweetheart?"

Zoe twisted toward him. "Always."

"Uh-huh, just remember, I want to be queen."

Brittany burst out laughing. "We'll make sure to get you a nice crown."

"It's really all I ask for. Now, go home, sleep. And, Brittany, try not to scare off your date."

"Oh, that's right, the date." Zoe grinned. "I don't suppose you would wear one of my designs?"

"I was thinking the strapless white leather, sweetheart bodice, hand-stitched with love?" Brittany fired back like she was already planning on it, which just made Zoe feel less guilty about using her friend's body and impeccable manners to get more attention before Fashion Week.

"Love that dress." Zoe almost jumped up and down. "You should pair it with the—"

"You should pair it with the black Valentino sling-backs, the studded ones," Roger added in a bored tone as he hid a yawn.

Brittany frowned. "I don't own those shoes."

"Silly me, must have slipped my mind." He walked into the large entry and came back with a black box. "Here, thank you for taking me to surgery and picking me up, you were a lifesaver." He jerked the shoes back when she stretched out her hands. "Honestly, I should just take them back. I already did my good deed for the year and got you a date—fingers crossed you get some action."

"I second that." Zoe grinned.

Brittany rolled her eyes. "Hard pass." She took the box from Roger's hands then leaned in and kissed him on the cheek. "Why don't I dance with him first?"

"Brittany, you're beautiful, and he's gorgeous. I love details about everybody's intimate lives... except yours. Because I know all about the mantra. You won't sleep with anyone until you're married. But please be reasonable for once. Don't shut him down completely. Give the guy the opportunity to get to know you, the *real* you that we all love. He needs a reason to hang around, so if you can't dangle yourself as the carrot, dangle your shining personality." He grinned. His kind words made Zoe's chest ache, maybe because it was true, perhaps because she envied the perfection of Brittany's life just a little more than she was willing to admit. After all, Zoe had had no issue jumping into bed with Dane early on, and look how wonderful that'd turned out. And just like that, it was as if a loud ticking noise started in her head.

Time was almost up, wasn't it?

"Why?" Brittany asked. "Roger, what's so different about the guy? Usually, you tell us that men only want one thing and to run in the opposite direction."

"True." Zoe snorted.

"Ah." Roger grinned. "Chemistry. You have to account for chemistry. And you guys had it in spades. Think about it. If you open your heart, you may even find yourself falling in love."

Brittany shook her head then leaned in and pressed a kiss to Roger's cheek. "You're pushing it a bit for a first date. I'll call you in the morning."

"I want you to call me tonight. If you don't, I'll hold my breath and turn into a puffer fish."

Zoe and Brittany both burst out laughing.

"As if you could go that long without talking," Brittany teased while Zoe made a knowing face. The guy could talk anyone out of or into anything. That was why he was so good. She was surprised that he still had a voice after all these years.

As if to prove a point, Roger sucked in a breath and puffed out his cheeks, then pinched his nostrils.

"Good to know those drugs are working," Zoe teased.

"I think that's just him." Brittany laughed and gave him a brief hug. "I love you, silly. Goodnight."

Roger exhaled and then jabbed a finger into the air. "Just remember what I said!"

"She's got it." Zoe winked. "I'll make sure to knock off the rust before we send her out."

"I'm leaving now." Brittany's melodic laugh made Zoe smile as she leaned in and kissed Roger on the cheek.

"Sweetheart," he said in a soft voice.

"Queen." She winked and then added, "Oh, and next time I get to drop you off. I have my eye on a pair of Yves Saint Laurent pumps."

"Scout's honor." He put a hand over his heart.

The girls slowly exited the apartment and made their way down the short hallway to the elevator.

The doors opened before Zoe could press a button, revealing Frederick and a young model who looked exactly like Brittany.

Zoe frowned. "Late shoot at Roger's?"

Did she just hate all men? Was that her problem?

Frederick held out his hands, one contained his camera. His black bag was slung over his left shoulder. "I stopped by to show Roger the shots, yes. Easy, girls…" His smile was too pretty.

Maybe that was why she wanted to stab him in the throat.

"I'm sure they're lovely," Brittany said, smoothing over the situation and then giving the young model a pretty smile. "First shoot?"

"Yeah." She gulped and then shook her head in disbelief. "I'm sorry, it's just… you're my idol. You're Brittany Nicole, right?"

"That's right," Frederick said with a grin that almost claimed he'd discovered her. The creep.

Zoe clearly needed a nap.

"Wow, I mean, you're so beautiful up close. I grew up with posters of you on my wall." The girl squeezed her eyes shut. "And that sounded way creepier out loud than it did in my head when I practiced it just in case I ever met you."

They were the same height and had the same pretty blue eyes and luscious hair, though the girl's hair was darker, shorter.

"Why don't we take a selfie really quick?" Brittany offered.

"You would do that?" the girl screeched, making Zoe's ears ring.

"Actually"— Zoe held out her hand for Brittany's phone—"I'll do it. She's horrible at selfies. She always cuts off body parts. Last selfie, I had one eye so…"

"My arms were tired!" Brittany laughed it off. "Okay, fine." She handed Zoe the phone and wrapped an arm around the girl.

The smiles were beautiful, broad.

Zoe almost felt wistful as she took the picture and handed Brittany her phone back.

"What's your name? I'll tag you," Brittany said politely, the smile still in place.

"Chrissy!" the girl all but shouted. "Sorry, it's Chrissy Mendoza."

"Found you." Brittany's fingers moved rapidly across her iPhone screen. "Just followed you. Have fun tonight." She put her hand on her shoulder and then pressed the elevator button.

"I will!" The young model seemed more excited about Brittany than her shoot.

"Hey." Frederick jerked his head in their direction. "My wife didn't come with you?"

"No, she said she was too tired." Zoe shrugged. "You know her and late-night TV, though..."

He snorted. "Yeah, she's a homebody through and through."

"Nothing wrong with that," Zoe said quickly.

Frederick frowned and then flashed another camera-ready smile. "Never said there was..." He turned and put his hand on Chrissy's lower back. "See you girls later."

Zoe watched with narrowed eyes as his hand lowered until it was right above the girl's ass. The elevator doors closed. Zoe was still staring daggers.

"Hey." Brittany nudged her. "You all right?"

"Yeah..." She licked her lips and gripped her purse tighter in her hand. "I know it's the job, lots of late nights, and I know Roger will take care of her. I just... Something about Frederick lately is... off."

Brittany tilted her head. "Yeah, I noticed that the other night. We're both single, though, so what do we know?"

"True." Zoe shot a quizzical glance up at Brittany. "Fair warning, I may be into girls."

Brittany wrapped her arm around Zoe and squeezed. "You're not my type."

"Gross, not my friends. I mean like, girls..."

"Yeah, do me a favor and let's have this conversation again in front of Dane. I want to see a man that size pass out."

"Very funny."

"He loves you, you know?" Brittany said once they were at the lobby level and walking passed security.

"Dane isn't a man who is capable of loving anything more than himself," Zoe said in a harsh whisper.

"He loved Danica."

"Yeah." Zoe gulped, thinking about the times she and Dane had snuck away from the group to make out at the movie theater when she was young. How he'd wiped her tears away and told her he would save her when she needed to hear it the most. "He did."

"So, why can't he love you?"

He already does.

But love… was a dangerous, fickle thing.

And Zoe was sure that if she got too close…

It would destroy her completely.

ELEVEN

In the limo, Brittany wrung her hands together. Her fingernails were painted a pale pink. Her studded Valentino's were, in fact, a perfect match for the leather cocktail dress with its curve-hugging fabric. The only problem was that she couldn't take a deep breath to save her life.

Because she had hips.

Something she was always desperate to hide.

Yes, she was thin.

Fit.

Flawless.

But a size zero felt snug.

Women who wore a size zero had the added challenge of pulling it over hips before it could settle, and because of her wider hips, fabric tended to pucker slightly enough for her to notice if she weren't careful with what she wore.

The leather hid it well.

Black hid it even better.

Her posture ramrod straight, she drummed her fingertips against her bare thigh. Her left hand gripped her Lana Marks Cleopatra clutch. The bag personally designed for her over sixteen years ago. She never attended a gala without it. She viewed it as both armor and a reminder of what happened when you thought with your heart rather than your head.

Never again.

A date.

Was she actually going to do this?

Meet a man she barely knew outside one of New York's most sought-after galas?

The car stopped.

Apparently, the answer to that question was a glaring yes because there he stood, just outside the red-carpet area. Yellow daisies in hand.

How did he know they were her favorite?

Her heart squeezed painfully as she watched his eyes skim the growing crowd, along with the celebrities, politicians, and CEOs who came in a steady stream of expensive cars.

Brittany's driver opened her door.

Several cameras flashed.

This was the part that she was used to, people yelling her name, inquiring about what she was wearing, asking where her date was, telling her how beautiful she looked.

Smokescreens.

Suddenly uncomfortable, she gave a shy smile that the photographers went wild over if their cheers were anything to go by.

The doctor slowly walked toward her then, dressed in a custom suit that looked designer, not that she was going to ask or make things weird by checking the tag of his jacket like someone's mom.

Whatever it was, he wore it well.

Were his shoulders always that broad? The stitching looked hand-done. The charcoal color somehow brought out his white smile even more. And then he was standing before her.

And she couldn't speak.

The world was shouting at her.

And all she wanted was the courage to say something.

Maybe even a warning.

An apology?

"You look beautiful," he rasped in a deep voice as he leaned over and lightly kissed the air by her ear. His breath tickled her skin as he whispered, "My name's Oliver Desmond, just in case you forgot. And, tonight, I'm officially the luckiest guy in the world."

He held out his elbow.

She gaped. "You're not nervous?"

He gave her a funny look and then smiled. "Why would I be nervous?"

"Because." That was all she had. And then she laughed at herself. "Good reason, right?"

"The best." He let her direct them back toward the red carpet and the few stairs that led up to the Whitney Museum of American Art.

"Who's your date?" someone shouted.

Brittany didn't answer. What would she say anyway? *Oh, my agent's surgeon. I saw him in his scrubs and was forced into a date in order to get Roger out of the hospital. Isn't he sexy? You really should see his scrubs, though...*

Oliver smiled right along with her; that same grin that had her wondering what his story was; the one that looked real in a universe full of fakes.

By the time they made it up the short steps and into the building, she felt as if she'd just finished a five-mile jog and was getting prepared for two hours of Pilates.

"Champagne?" A passing waiter held out a tray.

Oliver grabbed two flutes and handed her one.

"Thank you." She was about to take a sip when he clinked his glass softly against hers. "You look beautiful."

She lifted the flute to her lips and swallowed a sip. "You already said that."

"And I'll keep saying it because it's true." His eyes crinkled with another smile that lit up his entire face. "So, what exactly is this gala for?"

Oh, right, she had to talk to him.

Because he was her date.

And talking typically took place when getting to know another human.

She could do this.

Focus.

Don't think about the past. Don't let it define your future.

"I actually work for *Trend* magazine. I'm one of the fashion editors. Part of my job is writing about fashion trends." She smiled. "I mean, obviously."

"Hence, the name." He chuckled.

"Exactly." She didn't even realize they were walking, that's how easy he was to talk to. Incredible. "And for every issue, I'm in a six-page spread, modeling the fashion trends and showing readers different ways to mix accessories and piece outfits together. It's the best of both worlds. Though I wish—"

"What?" He stopped walking and faced her. The sound of conversation buzzed around them, yet she felt like they were alone.

"I don't know what I was going to say," she lied. She didn't know Oliver, and she had been about to tell him something that even her closest friends didn't know. Roger did, but her agent knew everything. Probably because she couldn't keep anything from *him,* even if she tried.

Oliver's eyes narrowed. "I know you just met me, but I'm a pretty good listener. I mean, it's probably one of my best talents outside of ping-pong."

She covered her mouth with her hand and laughed. "Ping-pong? Really?"

"Doctor." He held up one massive hand. "We're good with our hands."

I bet he is...

She felt herself blush. "Fine, but if this ends up on some gossip magazine—"

"Right next to the ping-pong confession, you mean?"

"Yes." She grinned widely. "All right, so I've been wanting to do a monthly column on politics."

She waited for the laughter.

The judgment.

The, "*Oh, honey, but you're too pretty to think that hard.*"

She waited.

But instead of the typical male or human response of, "*Why stop doing what you do best?*"

"*Look pretty.*"

He looked... impressed. "I bet you'd be incredible," he said softly, a smile of admiration crossing his perfect features.

She almost kissed him.

She was already leaning in.

She hadn't realized that she needed someone—*anyone*—to tell her that she wasn't crazy. That she was smart even though she knew it. To have someone who didn't even know her... agree.

Then again, he could just be trying for something physical, right?

Wasn't that what all guys wanted? No matter how much she tried not to judge the opposite sex based off of one horrible experience, she did. Because, in her eyes, she'd had what everyone viewed as the perfect guy—and look how that had turned out.

Fresh guilt swept through her body as she eyed Oliver up and down, waiting for something to crack in his perfect facade before she finally mumbled, "Thank you."

"Why?" he countered quickly. "Politics, I mean."

Did he really not know? Before she could suppress it, she gave him a funny look and then bit down on her bottom lip. "Because... of my past."

That was all she was going to give him.

He could Google the rest.

"What I wouldn't do for a computer right now."

"That's what your phone is for," she teased with a wink.

"Not when I'm with a beautiful woman. Not when she's telling me secrets and leaning into me like she's wondering if she could get away with telling me one more."

"Maybe I was just going to fix your tie." She arched an eyebrow.

"Doubtful," he rasped. "But if you want to fix my perfect tie as an excuse to get closer, you won't find me complaining." As if he wanted her to touch him, he quickly tugged it to the side.

"Wow, so blatant." She laughed, reaching her free hand up to his silk tie and pressing her fingertips against it, almost feeling the warmth of his chest seep into her palm. She wondered what it would feel like to touch his skin, to hear the sound of his heart, to see if it was racing like hers.

He grabbed her hand, the one touching him, and he held it there, in front of everyone.

And for once, Brittany didn't care.

She'd sworn she wouldn't have another relationship in public, not again.

And yet, she found that she was incapable of pulling away.

"Brittany?" A cultured, feminine voice from her past pounded in her ears. "Brittany, I had no idea you'd be here!"

Brittany dropped her hand and turned. "Mrs. Kampbell, hello."

Next to her, Oliver stiffened a bit as Nancy Kampbell, former First Lady of the United States gave him a once-over, nodded, and deemed him unworthy of her notice.

"I was wondering if you would be attending. It's such a lovely event," Nancy said through clenched teeth as she slowly eyed Brittany's outfit as if she'd picked it up at a yard sale for half price. It was long, painful, and familiar. It had happened at every single dinner.

At least, *he* wasn't here.

Brittany clung to Oliver like a lifeline.

"And you are?" Nancy finally turned her attention back to Oliver.

"Dr. Oliver Desmond," Brittany answered for him, not wanting to subject him to the questioning she knew would inevitably follow after Nancy deemed yet another human unworthy of her company. "He's a surgeon."

If she were impressed, Nancy didn't show it.

"Mrs. Kampbell!" someone called in an excited voice as they approached.

Brittany exhaled in relief and almost jerked Oliver into a statue as they made their hasty exit.

But the universe was against her.

Because she turned directly into the smell that still haunted her night and day.

The same one she had clung to when she was alone in that hospital room with nothing but the buzz of the TV to keep her company, and a note that said everything and nothing all at once. Her dreams crushed between her sweaty hands, and a nurse telling her that God had a plan; when for the first time in Brittany's life, she questioned it all.

Slowly, she raised her gaze.

"Brittany Nicole." His voice was just like she remembered, commanding yet warm.

It was Oliver who spoke next. "Aren't you Ronan Kampbell?"

"Senator," came the correction from their left.

Brittany didn't look at the woman. Joy—Ronan's wife.

But she did stare at the five-karat diamond blinding everyone in the room. Brittany's stomach lurched as she tried to keep her posture relaxed, and her face calm.

"I thought you might be here." Ronan reached, and Brittany reacted, taking a small step back, giving herself some space between his body, the memory of his smell, the thought of those hands on her. They shook hands awkwardly, and as always, he pressed his palm flat against hers for longer than a few seconds before pulling away.

Thankfully, Oliver had his arm wrapped around her waist, making it possible for her to keep standing. Had he not been there, she probably would have face-planted against the nearest statue or, God forbid, fainted in Nancy's arms. And the psychotic witch would have probably moved out of the way while Brittany chipped a tooth on the hard marble floor.

That was the type of woman the former FLOTUS was.

The type of woman Nancy Kampbell would always be.

American royalty through and through, with blood blue enough to get away with anything and wield the control of the world with her freshly manicured hands.

"Yes, well…" Brittany finally found her voice. "I do still work for *Trend.*"

Not the best response, but also not the worst.

Her stomach sank when Joy held out her hand. "It's good to see you."

"And you." Brittany tried for a warm smile, but the frosty woman only gave her a curious stare in return, as though she had a set number of facial expressions given by her surgeon per day and didn't want to waste one on one of Ronan's ex-flames.

Imagine how she would react if she knew.

If any of them knew.

Ronan locked eyes with Brittany again. "How are you doing?"

"Great." She swallowed against the dryness in her throat. "And you?"

"He's up for re-election." Joy patted his chest with her left hand, the one that probably needed a crane to help lift the sheer massiveness of the rock that rested on it.

"That's great," Oliver said with a wide smile, saving Brittany yet again. "I'm sure it's a very busy time for you."

"Very." Joy grinned up at Ronan. "But he always makes time for his family. Don't you?"

"I always say my son is the best of them." Nancy joined them again beaming, then turned her evil smile on Brittany. "Have you settled down yet, dear?"

And there it was.

Dear. Sweetheart. Honey. All words spoken as a way to make someone feel warm, important, unique. Nancy wielded them like weapons as a way to cut someone down. Every time she used them against Brittany, it was as if Nancy stole pieces of confidence put there by her parents. Like bricks stacked up around Brittany's heart, Nancy took it upon herself to deconstruct them one by one. She found joy in others' pain.

"Not yet," Brittany said with as much confidence as she could muster. Why couldn't the building just burn down and save her from this conversation? Where the heck was a fire alarm when she needed one?

"But you never know the future, do you?" Oliver beamed down at her and kissed her temple. "When you're as beautiful as Brittany, it takes a special sort of man not to be intimidated. Not all of us can handle it."

She bit down on her lower lip to keep from cheering as Ronan narrowed his eyes at both of them.

Oliver was quickly turning into one of her favorite people, all because he knew how to fight with words and secret smiles, something that Brittany had never mastered because it would be the final nail in her coffin, wouldn't it? Sinking to their level of passive-aggressiveness.

"Well." Brittany smiled one last time. "It was great seeing you, all of you, and good luck with the re-election, Ro."

It slipped.

His nickname.

Nancy narrowed her eyes, while Joy looked ready to rip out Brittany's throat with her bare hands.

And Ronan?

He just looked sad.

Like he always did when surrounded by his mother; by people he allowed to control him in order for him to one day win the presidency.

His life had been set out for him by his mom, his family, and by rules that Brittany refused to follow—because that wasn't living.

Funny how she shared the greatest mistake of her life with the one man who the media said was perfect.

Then again, they said the same about her.

They didn't see the other side.

The emptiness.

The shame.

The love shared between two people who just wanted to be seen, for once in their lives, as more than their names and faces.

Ronan slowly nodded and then flashed her a smile, one of his real ones, not one saved for Joy or his mother, not even one he used for the cameras. "Thank you, Britt." And her nickname, great! Maybe next time, they could try for a Guinness world record of the most awkward conversation ever! "You look great, as always."

Brittany smiled in return and dug her fingernails into Oliver's arm.

He jumped a bit as they side-stepped the growing mass of people.

And when they turned the corner…

Brittany grabbed one full flute of champagne.

Downed it.

Reached for another.

Then finally looked up into Oliver's questioning eyes. "So, ping-pong, let's talk about that."

"Do you need me to talk about that?" he asked softly.

Already, her eyes were filling with tears. She gave Oliver a jerky nod. "Yes. I do."

"It's all in the wrist," was his answer as he leaned down and wrapped his arms around her in a hug.

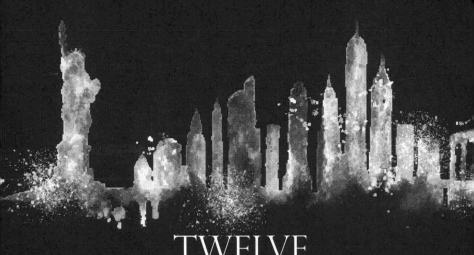

TWELVE

If Oliver were ready to cut and run, he sure didn't act like it. In fact, he walked with her, talked with complete strangers about art and his job as if he had been born to work a crowd. Brittany had always been the sort of person to feed off others' emotions in public then go home and feel completely spent in private. She thrived on life, the energy of conversation and laughter. But behind closed doors, it took a toll. Because she couldn't *not* feel.

It was impossible.

So, she collected emotions like a person collected shells on the seashore. She held them close and realized that maybe not all people were born with the ability to separate themselves from the world.

And maybe that was okay. Perhaps the world needed more people to feel, even if it was painful and ugly.

She smiled as Oliver leaned over and kissed her on the cheek. "You look exhausted."

She narrowed her eyes at him. "First rule of dating, you never tell a woman she looks exhausted."

"Still beautiful," he added with a wide smile. "And maybe someone who didn't have the luxury of standing so close to you wouldn't notice, but you've lost at least a half inch on that wide, bright smile of yours. Which tells me that it's almost time to call it a night, regardless of what you say."

Her jaw nearly dropped to the floor by her shoes. "Um…" Did he notice that minute detail? Really?

"Um… I'm right?" He spread his fingers where his palm rested on her lower back and brought her closer. "It's okay to let someone take care of you."

No.

It wasn't.

Because that meant he wanted something more from her.

And, at some point, she would lose herself, wouldn't she? Because she was complete crap at keeping her heart protected when it needed it the most. And this man, this very dangerous male, was a risk that she wasn't sure she could take.

Not with her secrets.

Not with her past.

How did a person even have that sort of conversation?

She wasn't sure.

Because she'd never had it.

"Fine," she found herself saying in a confident voice. "Let me just go have a word with my editor, and then we can go do whatever surgeons do on a Friday night."

A suggestion of heat danced in his eyes as he offered an apologetic shrug. "Oh, we read medical journals."

"Ha." She bit down on her lower lip. "Incredible how sexy that actually sounds when you say it while looking at me like that."

"My mouth said, 'medical journals,' my brain was somewhere else entirely." He leaned in and whispered in her ear. "And my eyes? Well, they were too focused on you."

She felt a breath escape her lungs. "I can't decide if you're a complete manwhore with an agenda, or if you just can't help being charming."

A lazy smile spread across his face. "Let's go with charming. My mama taught me never to say whore out loud after Grandma, the one with the hearing aid, yelled about sweating like a whore in church… while in church."

Brittany winced.

"Sitting in the front pew."

"Nice." She burst out laughing. "So, no whoring for you."

"Sadly, no." He winked. "But Grandma's clearly all about it."

"Great mental picture, thanks for that." She beamed and then grabbed his hand again as they walked through the crowd of people, all of them wanting a piece of her, all smiling with expectation and admiration.

It never bothered Brittany.

At least, it hadn't in the past.

It was part of the job.

And Ronan? Well, he'd been all about public appearances, so they talked to everyone, posed for pictures, and when she begged him to leave, he just said, "This is what we signed up for."

Not Oliver.

No, Oliver looked like he'd much rather be doing other things, even if it meant that nothing happened. It was just a feeling she got from him: that he was just as happy with a solid conversation as he would be having a one-night stand. Maybe Roger was right. Maybe.

A shiver ran down her spine as she finally reached the Editor in Chief of *Trend*, Grace Wingate. The last thing she needed to do was get her hopes up.

"There you are!" Grace was decked out in head-to-toe Yves Saint Laurent, black, always black, with a long string of black pearls hanging from her neck, and oval-cut diamond earrings sparkling in her ears. Her red lipstick was drawn on with perfection, ideally complementing her pale skin. Exactly six honey-colored highlights blended in with her brown, shoulder-length hair. Not a split end in sight. The woman touched her thick, black spectacles and grinned up at Oliver. "And who are you?"

Grace was confrontational, to say the least, but she had to be. It was part of her job, part of the persona. As the most successful editor—not to mention the most influential—she didn't have time to hold someone's hand.

She was more likely to slap it.

Brittany would know.

Tough love would describe Grace well. She was the sort of woman who threw people into shark-infested waters while sipping champagne with one hand and dumping blood over their heads with the other.

Sink or swim.

And because of that, Brittany had learned a very important lesson in the fashion industry early on. It wasn't a mistake that she worked for Grace.

Brittany had been one of the first supermodels on the cover of *Trend*.

And she knew that Grace was grooming her to be more than just a pretty face.

For that, she respected her.

Even loved her.

"Dr. Oliver Desmond." Her date stuck out his large hand and, rather than shaking Grace's, he brought her heavily ringed fingertips to his mouth and kissed.

Grace's eyebrows arched as she glanced over at Brittany. "Where have you been hiding this one?"

"She only lets me out on good behavior," Oliver joked, releasing Grace's hand.

"Pity. Brittany needs a little bad in her life." Grace winked, making Brittany wish for the floor to swallow her whole. "What kind of doctor are you, Oliver?"

"I'm a surgeon."

"Is that so?" She shared a look with Brittany, smiling behind her champagne. "How lovely for you."

Oliver wouldn't know, but that was like getting the highest praise from the Queen of England; Brittany would have to tell him later.

The fact that Grace was even having a conversation past a greeting was a miracle. Everyone who knew her, knew that.

"We were just leaving." Brittany smiled at her mentor. "Did you need me for anything else?"

"Go, go." Grace initially waved Brittany away but then pulled her in for a kiss on the cheek, whispering in her ear as she did. "We'll talk Monday about the article you wanted to do."

Excitement coursed through Brittany's body. "I would love that."

"Yes, yes, I know you would." Grace rolled her eyes and gave her a dismissive nod. "Now, leave with your well-trained surgeon before I change my mind. Oh, and make sure the ridiculous intern realizes that soy milk and coconut milk aren't the same. And if he shows up one more time with the wrong Starbucks, I'm going to flip that pathetic thing he calls a chair toward the corner for the next six months while he watches paint dry and thinks about all the ways he's failed me."

"How about I just get your coffee?" Brittany offered softly. The woman did not perform without her soy milk latte, one Splenda, a half-inch of room from the top, double cup.

"You're an editor, it's beneath you. He's an intern. We pay him to get coffee. If he can't do his job correctly, then I'll find someone who can," she said simply. "Last chance, you'll tell him?"

"Absolutely." Brittany actually liked Tom, but he was the sort of intern who got distracted by the clothes, beauty products, and celebrities walking in and out of the building. He was basically a human raccoon when it came to jewelry, but while he did a wonderful job with organizing things, he wasn't as good at doing the easy stuff like coffee.

Coffee, the simplest job in the world.

"Lovely." Grace beamed and then turned away like she did whenever she was done using words. The conversation was over.

And Brittany was excused.

Free.

Excitement thumped in her chest. They were going to talk about the article! Finally! Something other than the beauty spread, something other than her face. She would get to write beyond fashion.

"Smile any wider, and I'm going to get jealous I'm not the reason," Oliver said once they were out the door and walking down the stairs.

"Maybe you are," Brittany offered, turning to him.

"Hmm, I think she lies." He knelt down.

"What are you doing?"

"Grabbing your heels. You keep shifting your feet. Are they new?"

She nodded. How did he notice something so trivial? She was a pro at smiling through the pain, but they'd started to rub her little toes on both sides.

Ugh. Roger.

At least walk in them before gifting them!

"So, I'm just going to walk barefoot?" she mused as he undid the buckle on the right foot and slid the expensive shoe off.

"I'll have you know..." He smirked up at her. "I work out."

"Do you now?" She giggled.

"I would flex, but this shirt is really tight. I don't want to kill it. Having that on my conscience may destroy me."

She put her hands on her hips and laughed. "Yeah, think about the sleepless nights."

"See, you get me!" He grinned, his eyes zeroing in on her mouth before he grabbed the other shoe and then turned. "Hop on."

"Hop where?" She frowned.

"My back."

"But my dress…"

"Easy fix." He turned back around and, before she could protest, his hands were on her hips, slowly sliding the dress up her thighs, making it so indecent that she was suddenly aware of the wind rushing between her legs ready to kiss her rear at any moment. "Now, hop on."

"If you say so," she said in a shaky voice, jumping onto his back and wrapping her legs around him.

Her shoes dangled in his right hand as he held her tight and started walking.

"Did you have a destination in mind?"

"Yup."

"Are you going to tell me?"

"Nope."

"Are you always like this?"

"Guess you'll just have to find out." She could hear the teasing, the confidence in his voice as he walked down the street and then stopped at one of those tourist shops with a selection of graphic T-shirts and key chains in the window. He set her down on the cement. "Be right back."

Frowning, she watched him jog into the store with her shoes and then jog right back out about a minute later with a bag in hand. She hadn't even straightened her dress yet.

"Let me guess, you got me that *I heart New York* hat I've been eyeing?" She grinned.

"Even better." He pulled a pair of fire-engine-red flip-flops out of the bag. They said *New York* on the sole and probably cost five dollars. "I got you comfy shoes."

"My hero." She swallowed, suddenly nervous as he bent over and slid the shoes onto her feet, tossed her expensive ones into the bag, and then offered his hand. "Thank you."

"Now, the date can start," he said, not looking at her.

"Excuse me?"

"A date is where you talk to someone, where you get to know them. I was your plus one. Now, I want to be your date—if you're okay with that." His blue eyes flashed as he grinned down at her. Why did it feel like she was the only woman in the world? Why was his stare so... penetrating?

She gulped and then gave him a slow nod. "Yeah, I would like that."

"Good answer... I think I'll feed you."

"Ha-ha. And if I said no?"

"Then no food. I call it positive reinforcement."

"Don't you know you're not supposed to feed the models?"

"Nope." He stared down at her as they stopped at the crosswalk. "You're not the type of person to say no to good food. I don't think you have the heart to reject a good steak."

"Maybe I'm a vegetarian."

"Maybe I'll convert you to meat..." He winked.

She squeezed her eyes shut and shook her head. "Yup, totally asked for that."

"You really did. I had no choice. And please tell me you don't eat some weird soy burger with a side of grass."

"No." She laughed. "I love a good burger."

"What about... a hot dog?"

"Ohhhhhhh." She twirled in front of him and then reached for his hand as they crossed the street. "Sounds like you're trying to spoil me."

"A good hot dog is better than flowers any day."

"The way to a woman's heart."

"I'm glad *you* get me." His emphasis on the *you* started tingles along her spine, and then they were on the corner near a hot dog stand and ordering their food, hers with extra ketchup, and his with extra pickles.

They laid their food out on the steps of the business building next to the stand while the city continued its constant onslaught of noise and lights.

"I love it here." He handed her a napkin. "It's always so alive."

"And loud," she added without thinking.

He tilted his head at her. "Which makes me assume you grew up in a place that was very... quiet."

"Very." She scrunched up her nose. "I grew up on a farm, with the most amazing family... dogs, pigs, goats... When I came to New York, I was horrified that I couldn't just walk barefoot down the street."

"Well, you can... it is New York, but a nice Staph infection would most likely be in the cards if you made it a habit."

"True." She laughed. "Which I quickly discovered after everyone lined the street with their trash." She shuddered. "I learned shoes were probably a better life choice about two months after moving here."

"How old were you?"

"Fourteen," she said quickly, reaching for her hot dog and taking a medium-sized bite. It tasted like it could save her soul, that hot dog. And Oliver was looking at her like all he wanted was for her to keep talking. It was terrifying, mainly because it meant he was interested. Right? And if he were interested, was it in the conversation? Her body? His assumption of what retired supermodels did? See! This was why she didn't date! She had trust issues and questioned everyone's good intentions. Maybe because most everyone had an agenda.

Even Oliver.

"Young." Oliver wiped his mouth with his napkin, his dazzling smile bore down on her. Seriously, the man was good-looking. How was it possible that he was single? There had to be a story. She suddenly wanted to torture herself with every detail of his past, his dating history, the women he'd been with, all in order to find out where she fit into that puzzle. He was at least thirty-five, but he had this playful yet protective attitude about him.

"Very young." Memories assaulted like they always did when she thought about her first day in New York. How wrong she had been about what it would be like to be discovered and launched into the modeling industry. She grabbed her Star of David necklace and twisted it with her free hand.

"What's that?" He asked gently.

She held the necklace out. "Early on in my career I had an opportunity to go to Israel, it changed my life," She was cautious on how much she said. After all, this was date one. And she didn't know him well enough yet. Brittany turned away. "Anyways, it's a reminder of the life I want to lead even when it's hard."

And because memories were cruel, she suddenly saw her parents' faces before she was ready to confess all the things she'd been put through, all the trauma, the horror, the shame.

But her parents had been so proud of her, so she let them believe the lie she swallowed every single day. Perfect. Life.

"You look sad," Oliver whispered. "I didn't mean to pry, about the necklace, your past, I just want to know you."

"Not sad." She took another bite, chewed, and then shrugged forcing herself to relax. "It's just… this city has a way of hurting you in ways I don't think most cities do. Like you said, New York is a living, breathing thing, isn't it? A monster if you let it be. Or a savior. An escape. It can be whatever you want it to be, and I came here thinking it would be this great adventure. And it was, but everything has a cost, you know?"

"What was your cost?"

She didn't answer at first, emotions jamming up her words. With a sigh, she finally admitted, "My innocence."

He was quiet for a few seconds, maybe thinking about his response before asking, "Did you ever want to leave? Pack up and go home?"

"No." Her smile felt bitter. "That's not how things are done in this industry. If you're successful, you get paid. And every time you get money, or you get more notoriety, it's like this… drug, this addiction you can't quit. My parents were so proud of me, I couldn't tell them the truth. I couldn't tell them that I was bunking in a room with no air conditioning with at least a dozen other girls. I couldn't tell them about the girls who didn't make it, the ones who wanted it so bad that they were willing to sleep with photographers just to get a spread in a magazine. The same girls who would cry rape if they didn't get the job. And the horrible thing was, they truly thought that they had gotten taken advantage of if they didn't get the job when they were the ones who offered their body for a price. No promises, not in this place."

"Hmmm." Oliver took another bite of his hot dog and stared at her. "Your parents would have probably understood."

"Maybe." She looked down at her lap.

"Brittany, are you all right? Isn't it late there?" Her mom sounded worried. "I just had a feeling I needed to call you."

"Yeah." Brittany tried to smile through her tears as needles lined her vision. As she looked to the right and saw one of the older models give a younger girl cocaine for the first time. "I'm fine, Mom, just tired."

"You sound tired, but that must be good, right? That means you're getting work and you're happy. Honey, we just want you to be happy."

And there it was.

Happy? Brittany was thrilled. She was successful, but something just felt... off. "I am happy, Mom. I promise."

"Good. I've been praying for you."

Not this again.

Brittany released a sigh. "Thanks, Mom."

It wasn't that she wasn't thankful.

It was that it just seemed... wrong.

And Brittany felt so distant from it all.

She had grown up in church.

And now, she was surrounded by sex and drugs, stuck overseas in a place models referred to as "The Dungeon." It didn't help that earlier that day she was asked to do a topless shoot and wasn't really given a choice. She was new, after all.

She shuddered.

Welcome to reality.

It was like a sucker punch.

And she was still young, trying to figure out where she fit into such a big world.

She dug around in her duffel bag and hit something hard, then pulled it out.

Her Bible.

She almost put it away.
And then she hesitated.
What else was she going to do?
Drugs?
With a roll of her eyes and out of sheer boredom, she picked it up, only to have it slip out of her hands and fall open to the gospels.
Why did it just remind her that she needed saving?

"You look far away again," Oliver commented, taking his trash and hers.

"Just thinking." She drew in a soothing breath.

"Maybe one day you'll tell me."

"Maybe."

"Are we going to talk about the Kampbells?"

"No," she said quickly. And then felt bad. "At least, not right now, not when you're smiling at me like that, not when I feel happy with you. I don't want to bring in the ugly."

"So…" He moved to sit closer to her. "Tell me something true."

"Ahhh, pulling out the big guns." She looped her arm with his, staring down at her flip-flops with a grin. "I used to go to bed so hungry—completely by choice, mind you. I was tall for my age, but I wanted to make sure that I looked thin enough. We all did. It had been pounded into us from day one. I remember passing a hot dog stand and wondering what it would be like to have freedom."

"From the industry?"

"Ha, no. Freedom to take a bite."

"Poor, starving model." He elbowed her. "I promise to feed you… always."

"I believe you," she whispered as he leaned down, pressing a kiss to her cheek, and then cupping her head between his palms. She let out a shaky exhale.

"I'm going to kiss you now." His voice was so confident, it made her smile.

"Are you trying to prepare me?" she asked, her voice shaky. It was happening. It felt both wrong and right. Oliver must have sensed her hesitation because he wasn't quick about it. He lingered in that space between *will he or won't he*. He breathed her in like a kiss would be his undoing.

A small gasp slipped out as he slid his tongue along her lower lip and then brought his hand behind her neck to ease her closer. Her heart thundered in her chest as he deepened the kiss, only to suddenly pull back. "Go out with me again."

Her emotions were everywhere. Guilt that they were already kissing, shame that she was that same girl just older, never wiser, and excitement because, somehow, it still felt safe. And she needed that.

She smiled as he kissed her again, softer, stealing her breath with each coax. "Not..." She grinned against his lips. "Fair."

"I never said I played fair." He tilted her chin toward him. "Please?"

"Only because you fed me."

"Totally understandable." He ran his thumb along her lip and shook his head. "We won't talk about it, but it needs to be said. He's an idiot for letting you go."

Her breath hitched. "Thanks."

"I'll pick you up tomorrow night" he said without even hearing her answer.

"What makes you think I'm saying yes?"

"Your pulse jumped the minute I asked." He ran his hands down her neck and then pulled her close. "I'm a doctor. I notice these things... You want to say yes, don't let your past hold you back. Not with me."

How did he even know?

She found herself nodding her head.

And then he was leaning in again, and she was reminded why it was both a good and bad idea to be with him.

Men like him were dangerous.

He would ask for everything.

And, one day, she would have to tell him the truth and hope he accepted her.

Or live with another broken heart.

Only she wasn't sure how many pieces she had left after Ronan, after their situation. And she refused to be that woman again, the one who would sacrifice every moral left standing, in order to keep someone who wasn't even faithful to her.

The sad part came in the fear that she didn't have anything left to give and that, one day, everyone would find out what a complete fraud she was.

"Let's get you home." Oliver threw away their trash as they walked hand in hand down the street.

Fraud.

Fraud.

Fraud.

The city seemed to scream the word at her, and Brittany was reminded yet again why she only let certain people in.

And why she had decided to live a lie.

Because the truth cut too deep.

And she still hadn't found a way to stop the bleeding.

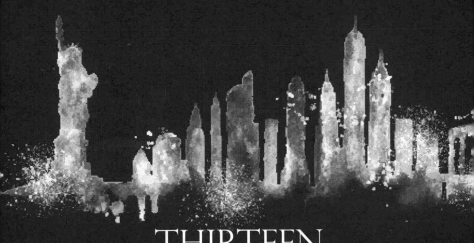

THIRTEEN

"How'd it go?" Zoe asked as she breezed into her office, cell phone practically glued to her ear.

"It was… really good." Brittany sounded as if she were smiling so big, her penthouse apartment might explode around her.

"Oh, was it? Super good? He still there? Be honest. Tell me you got naked. It would make my entire day." Zoe grinned as her best friend made a choking noise. "Tell me you went all Song of Solomon on him, please, God, please."

"I regret the day I showed you that chapter," Brittany muttered. "Second, who sleeps with someone on the first date? You know me, Zoe."

Zoe laughed and then released a long sigh. "You can't see me, but I'm raising my hand—and Everlee's, even though she's not here and hasn't answered any of my texts. I know,

I know, Miss I refuse to sleep with anyone unless they go all Beyonce and put a ring on it and even then, I still worry. Speaking of Everlee, have you heard from her?"

Brittany sighed. "No, actually, I haven't, not since happy hour. I'll call her during my lunch... And he's not still in my apartment, but your concern and enthusiasm are both alarming and noted."

"At least, don't freeze him out. Maybe if you just explain that you have morals, unlike the rest of New York, he won't have bedroom expectations." Zoe sighed. "You know how men get."

"Yeah." Why did Brittany sound so sad? "Hey, I gotta go, I have an appointment with Grace in an hour."

"Winter is coming," Zoe teased. They all said that behind Grace's back, but it was out of love. The woman was harsh, but she was the best of the best. She earned her title as the Ice Queen and wore it like a badge of honor. Zoe liked women who didn't care about pleasing men.

Who runs the world? Girls.

That was Grace's motto, one that Zoe wanted to adopt and live by.

"I'll tell her you said hi." Brittany laughed. "We still on for dinner later?"

"Yup." Zoe blew a kiss into the cell. "See ya."

"Bye!"

She dropped her phone onto her messy desk and hit the trackpad on her MacBook.

"Well, that was an interesting conversation," came a dark voice from the far corner. Zoe nearly fell out of her chair as Dane made his way to one of the seats in front of her desk and sat his massive, beautiful body down. "The way I remember it, you made me wait, what was it? Two years before I got to see you naked?"

"You saw me naked plenty." And so would have everyone else, had he not saved her, protected her from that tape. Zoe narrowed her eyes. "Is there a reason you're creepily eavesdropping on my conversations and lurking in the corner?"

His grin was too sexy. It wasn't helpful that he was in a suit that made him look like an editorial piece on mob bosses. Ha, how close to the truth would that be? "I wasn't lurking."

"You were quietly watching from the darkened corner of the room. If that's not lurking…" She crossed her arms.

"I want to take you to lunch."

"It's eleven."

"You skipped breakfast."

Son of a—did he have some of his men on her? "I had a granola bar."

"Don't lie to me, I hate liars."

Ha, most of them were probably at the bottom of the Hudson. Point proven. "Let me just grab my purse."

"You don't need it, not with me."

And there it was. Just another reason Zoe couldn't be with Dane; why she put as much distance as she could between them.

Had he saved her? Yes.

At one point, had she loved him? Yes.

But when you loved Dane, you loved the good and the bad. You loved the man and the monster. And Zoe had seen the monster too many times to ever love it. To ever allow the man to overshadow the darkness that truly did lurk beneath that black soul of his.

He'd saved her because he was selfish. Because he saw, he fell, he wanted.

"Fine." She pressed her lips together in a firm line and stood. He waited. He'd always been clear about how they were to leave a room and enter. He wanted to be close enough to protect her, as if some psycho supermodel killer existed.

But Dane, powerful as he was, couldn't protect her from himself. And that had always been the problem. It wasn't the physical.

It was the emotional.

He hurt her, no matter how hard he tried not to.

And she hurt him right back.

She grabbed her Burberry scarf and draped it around her neck, it looked perfect with her black jumper—another of the pieces going into the show in less than two weeks. Nerves hit her as they walked down the small hall leading from her office and out the door while her receptionist, Chelsey, gave her a big smile and a wave.

Dane could charm the pants off a nun.

So, it was no surprise that he had the woman eating out of the palm of his hand. He probably brought her coffee and a donut while asking if he could make copies of their financial records.

A black Escalade idled in front of the building.

Of course.

She knew the drill. Zoe got in; Dane slid in next to her. And the driver took them wherever Dane had already planned, in his masterful way.

They didn't talk business.

That wasn't his way.

Not in the car.

Not when the driver could hear.

Not when they were about to share a meal.

Meals were kept intimate unless otherwise planned to be about business, and since he hadn't specified, Zoe stayed quiet, enjoyed the feeling of the leather against her skin, and tried to ignore the fact that Dane's hand was on her thigh like he wanted to keep her pinned in place.

Or maybe just keep her period.

The car stopped in front of an older building a few miles from her office in Midtown. It looked like an apartment building, but Zoe couldn't be sure. There was a small grocery store near the cement stairs that had seen better days, and there seemed to be a call button near the door.

"This is the restaurant?" she wondered out loud.

"Sort of," was Dane's cryptic response.

She knew better than to argue or pry for more, even though she was rolling her eyes and demanding answers on the inside. She knew that it would just encourage him to be more cryptic, prolonging the torture.

She followed him up the stairs. He pressed the button that said *P*. "Here."

The door buzzed open.

This wasn't Dane.

Dane was about luxury.

Dane was about looking powerful, feeling more so.

His image was almost as important as his need to control every living, breathing—and who was she kidding?—dead thing around them.

If it were possible to control oxygen, gravity, the ocean—he'd do it.

The white marble floor looked new and polished. Her Manolos clicked against it as they walked to the elevator.

Dane pressed the up button.

The elevator gave a shrill ding.

And then they were alone.

In a small space.

Story of Zoe's life.

She tried to look bored.

And probably failed as Dane wrapped a bulky arm around her body and pulled her tightly against him. It was abrupt; her heels stumbled as her thigh connected with his.

He'd always been that way, possessive to the core. And there were never any apologies for it. He wanted her by his side, so he literally jerked her to it. It was his way of protecting her, but she always felt like it was more ownership than protection.

The elevator was either taking forever, or she was having a minor meltdown at the way his fingers danced along her waist, at the smell of cigars mixed with the faint scent of peppermint.

She hated that her body instantly responded to the amalgamation.

It was almost as bad as the memories of his mouth on her, his hands everywhere, his declarations of love.

She shook her head. Not this time. He wanted a second chance—at what? Not being a horrible human being? It was bred into him. He couldn't help it.

The elevator doors finally opened.

She waited while Dane very gently walked forward with her still attached to his side. They walked into a small foyer with gorgeous white marble floors and high ceilings.

The door was red.

She frowned.

He shoved the key in.

Every angry word she'd ever tossed in his direction, every sneer, every tear she'd cried on his behalf became paralyzed in front of her face.

The smell of Chinese takeout filled the huge loft.

It had a gourmet kitchen with Wolf appliances. The range was red and jutted out from the rest of the marble in a way that made it look like art.

Fur rugs covered the dark, Brazilian teak floor.

And in the living room, Haute House couches in a midnight black framed a solid wood coffee table.

The same one she had passed on a week ago.

The one she'd told herself she could afford but had refused to purchase after putting so much money into marketing her first show and finding celebrities willing to sit in the front row.

All of her money was tied up.

You had to spend money to make money.

So, she'd bypassed the coffee table and grabbed a Starbucks instead, all the while wondering about the day she could stop worrying about investments and silent partners.

And, most of all…

Dane.

"Say something." His voice was gruff as he placed his hands on her shoulders and turned her body toward the opposite side of the room where a sleek fireplace with black and white rocks roared to life on the wall. In front of it was a reading nook, and next to that? A desk—a beautiful workstation right in front of another huge window.

"It's…" She shook her head as the weight of his hands pressed her down, almost rooting her feet to the floor. "It's… beautiful."

"You should see the bedroom."

Alarm bells went off in her head as she forced herself not to panic.

"Maybe we should eat first. Besides…" Please, God, let the smell of Chinese food be real. "I probably shouldn't be snooping around some stranger's apartment."

"It's not on the market."

"Oh." She frowned. "Then why are you showing it to me?" Dane had often taken her to different developments, condos, apartments, and the like to get her opinion on decorating. But this one was finished.

And it had her table.

She cursed under her breath.

"Let's eat…" Dane's voice was full of humor. "You need to be back at work in a half-hour."

The nerve of the man.

Knowing her schedule inside and out.

Making purchases that showed her how easy it would be to say yes to someone she swore she'd say no to for the rest of her life.

But they both shared the blame for that, didn't they?

For what they'd done.

What they hid.

But there was no other way, was there?

Their mistakes tied them together like a blood bond that she couldn't escape, not if she wanted the secrets to stay hidden.

Buried.

Literally.

"Right." She cleared her throat and walked into the kitchen. The breakfast bar didn't have stools yet, so maybe whoever the penthouse belonged to was still decorating? She could stand and eat. Zoe grabbed the boxes and started opening. "How is it possible this is still hot?"

"Had someone deliver it just before we came up." He winked.

She scowled. "You can wink all you want, smile, show me your six-pack, it's not going to work, Dane."

"Aw, you remember my six-pack. Am I blushing?"

"You'd have to have a soul to feel shame," she fired back without hesitation.

His gaze narrowed. "You have sauce, right here." He reached for her face.

She smacked his hand away, grabbed a napkin, and wiped the corner of her mouth. "You can't just touch people because you want to."

"I don't touch people—I touch you," was his answer, as her stomach dropped to her knees. His smolder should be illegal.

Zoe wondered what it would take to get the cops to arrest him every time he tried to use it on her, there should at least be room for a citation or something. Anything.

"So." She looked away. She had to. "Whose place are we crashing?" With vigor, she put a bite of fried pork into her mouth and chewed.

His blue eyes flashed. "Yours."

The fried pork lodged itself in her throat, while rice tried to come out of her nose. Coughing and sputtering, she flailed her arms, and Dane hit her on her back so hard he probably dislodged a rib. "You okay?"

"Wait." Voice hoarse, she took a drink of water and then shook her head against the tears forming from all the choking. "What do you mean it's mine? Is that what my life has come to? Sleep-shopping? I'm not even apartment hunting!"

"You pay over five grand a month for a one-bedroom that I could fit in this kitchen." He leaned over the counter, his forearms flexed and stretched with muscle. "Think of it as an early wedding present."

And there it was.

The other shoe.

It had finally just manifested in front of her face and dropped like a rock to the expensive floor.

"No." She shook her head. "No. And you just asked me. You need to give a woman time!"

"Time's up." He smiled like he knew he'd won. "Besides, things are about to get very... dangerous around here."

"Okay, that sounds like a bad movie line." She rolled her eyes. "I have security at my place. I'm fine, and you can't just go around buying people apartments!"

"Lofts," he corrected, still smirking at her movie comment. "And I don't have to remind you who we put behind bars, do I? Because it haunts me every day."

"Again, you need a heart for that sort of reaction, Dane, and I'm pretty sure you gave yours to the devil along with your soul in a two-for-one special!"

He leaned in, lingering barely an inch from her face, his jaw tight, teeth clenched. "I've played your games. I've given you everything. Including time. I want you. I will have you."

"On a cold day in Hell." Heart racing, she tried to suck in a breath that didn't smell like him. After a few torturous seconds, Zoe found her voice, but it wasn't as confident as before. He'd bought her a loft? Who did that?

"Then…" He backed away and ran a hand through his pitch-black hair. "I hope, for your sake, you carry a taser."

Her head jerked up. "What aren't you telling me?"

Dane's eyes roamed over her face briefly before he whispered, "He's out of prison."

"Who's out of—?" She gasped, putting her hands to her mouth. "How?"

"Seems he knows how to behave. But you know he won't stop, not after what we did to his brother—"

"Stop! People could hear you. They could!" Terror gripped Zoe like a vice around her neck as tears filled her eyes. "Do you really think he'll come after me?"

Dane snorted out an ugly curse. "The little creep was at your office last night. Didn't break in, just stared up at the window like he was planning a nice reunion with his most hated ex-girlfriend."

Her knees buckled as she tried to process what Dane was actually saying.

"I'm not capable of the type of love you deserve…" Dane wrapped his arms around her. "But I can offer you the type of protection people would kill to have."

"What's that?" She looked up into his stormy blue eyes.

"My name."

Make it go away! Just make it go away!" Zoe yelled as she ran into Dane's arms. Eyes blazing, he gripped her shoulders. "What happened?"

"A tape he made. I didn't know! Marnie set it up and said it was legit, and then he was filming. After, his friend showed up, and then he said that I had to—" Zoe collapsed against Zane. *"It's going to ruin my entire career! They're going to ruin me!"*

"I'll take care of it," Dane whispered harshly. *"But I'm going to need your help…"*

Dane's arms came around her as he leaned down and whispered in her ear, "Tick. Tock."

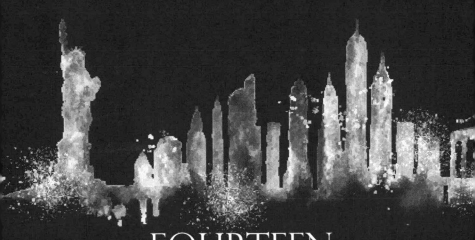

FOURTEEN

Everlee stared at herself in the mirror for a solid five minutes. She would know, she'd counted. The bathroom at *Trend* used to make her feel special, like she was finally making it in an industry that was so cut-throat, she felt like she had lasting scars. She looked the same.

Nothing had changed on the outside. Not yet. She expected the self-loathing to show under her eyes, the hatred to shine like a homing beacon every time someone spoke with her.

So far.

Nothing.

Frederick had come home too late to touch her, thank God.

And had left early that morning for another shoot.

Fresh Faces of *Trend*.

Everlee was the lucky one who would get paired with the new Fresh Face—also known as someone who had yet to get hips and boobs—and mentor them.

Or, at least that was what the magazine wanted. Everlee wasn't quite sure how much mentoring could go into telling those *fresh faces* that life as they knew it was over. And that if they were really lucky and made it… they'd never actually make it.

It was one big, fat lie.

Because success was always measured by an ever-growing yardstick, and you never reached the top.

Ever.

The door to the bathroom swung open. "Everlee?"

"Hey, Britt." She smiled widely. "Sorry, I was just exhausted and thought what better way to cheer myself up than to count my wrinkles? Bonus points for stretch marks."

Brittany rolled her eyes with a grin, looking flawless in a chic, white Calvin Klein dress that hugged every perfect curve. Those legs. Everlee inwardly shook her head.

"You look amazing. You always do." Brittany walked to the other sink and made a pout, lining her natural lips with red. "I'm sorry you're tired, though. The shoot shouldn't go too long, and if you're too tired to count wrinkles, you can always go to my office and take a nap."

"Ahhh, a nap sounds incredible right now." Everlee exhaled loudly. "First the show with my new wide-eyed model friend, and then I'm taking over your office and requesting coffee once I wake up."

"Deal." Brittany laughed. "And funny you should mention your new model sister. I met her a few nights ago. Roger had Frederick do a few test shots."

Everlee felt her stomach clench. "Oh? How'd they look?"

"Not sure, but Frederick seemed excited." Brittany stared at her through the mirror, her wide, blue eyes asking questions that Everlee wasn't at all ready to answer. Her friend always saw too much, and Everlee was afraid if she said one thing, she'd say it all.

And that would leave her worse off than before.

Alone.

With the entire world calling her a liar.

Why did it have to be so complicated? Why wasn't she enough?

"So…" Everlee looked down at the sink and then back up at Brittany. "How old is she then?"

"Well, most of the models look like they haven't ridden a bike without training wheels yet," Brittany joked. "But she looks like she could be around fifteen?"

The tightness in Everlee's chest dissipated just a bit. The girl was still young. That was good. She could work with that. Frederick was a boob guy, he liked women. Why was she even worried?

Oh, right, because he'd come home twice in the past month smelling like someone else.

And it was getting worse.

And, lucky her, she was pregnant!

"Hey." Brittany put an arm around her. "Are you sure you're okay?"

"Fine." Everlee hoped she sounded convincing. "Now, let's go see all the little starving models with stars in their eyes and tell them what it's like to be super."

"I'm a Barbie girl…" Brittany started singing while Everlee fell into step beside her.

It was hard not to notice the way the girls looked at them as they made their way down the hall.

They were idols to these girls.

Supermodels.

World-renowned.

And yet, Everlee kept wondering when it would finally be done, when her life would feel real again, not like this giant production put on for everyone's benefit.

"You're late," Frederick said the minute Everlee walked on set. He didn't even make eye contact, just adjusted one of his lenses, looked through it, cursed, and then played with one of the lights.

"By two minutes." She'd counted. "And I wasn't feeling well."

"Hmm…" came his very husbandly response, and then he looked up and frowned. "Why are you so pale?"

"I told you, I'm not feeling—"

"Can we get makeup over here, now?" Frederick yelled loudly enough for people to scamper all over the place.

And several of the younger models looked ready to huddle in the corner and start rocking back and forth.

There were five fresh faces, and five old ones, though that wasn't how they would spin it, even if it was the truth.

Brittany was in the shoot, as well as Everlee, but Zoe had turned them down since she was focusing more on her line.

And their old friends, Taye, Ella, and Gia all sat in makeup chairs, scrolling through their phones. Most of them still worked off and on. Gia had gone into acting and had landed a few small roles. Ella had gone and had a family. And, Taye? Well, Everlee was ninety-nine-percent sure she was a vampire and used blood as a way to stay young.

The woman refused to age.

It was like her body was against it, and the universe agreed it would be a pity to give such a pretty face a wrinkle.

"She's pale," Frederick said, loud enough for everyone to hear. "Fix it."

Then he was off, talking to one of the set directors while Everlee was ready to sink into the floor.

"He's always like this during a shoot." She smiled at Brittany, who looked ready to march over there and strangle him with her bare hands, smiling as she did it. Because Brittany did everything with a smile.

Everlee imagined that even if Brittany ever murdered someone, she'd still grin and then say "*sorry*" after the fact.

She was just so polite.

And wonderful.

"I'm fine." Everlee squeezed Brittany's hand quickly. "I'm married to him, remember? I know his moods."

Brittany didn't seem convinced, but she finally gave Everlee a slow nod. "I'll see if Grace wants to go ahead and get started."

As if by invoking the name, Brittany had summoned the she-devil herself, Grace waltzed into the room, Starbucks in one hand, sunglasses perched on her nose. She wore a green leather skirt that hugged her body, accented by camel booties and the new Givenchy pleated bib sleeveless that wasn't even in stores yet, haphazardly tucked into the front of the waistband.

"So?" Grace spread her arms wide. "Did Frederick get hit by a bus, or can we start?"

"Actually, it was me." Everlee took the blame. "I was in the bathroom."

Grace stared her down long and hard, though it was difficult to see through the black sunglasses. "Men should be more understanding of a woman's needs at the toilet. If you were late, it's his fault for not giving you more time to use the restroom in between getting ready. Isn't that right, Frederick?"

Frederick shot a glare toward Everlee then nodded at the editor. "Absolutely."

"Good. Now that we're all agreed." Grace lifted a shoulder. "Go."

Go basically meant stop standing still, move, and don't stop until she said it was okay.

In her thirties, and Everlee was still intimidated by the Editor in Chief of *Trend*.

The woman was a tyrant.

And Everlee often wondered how she would have turned out had she listened more to what Grace had to say than she had her own heart.

She gulped and briefly placed a hand on her stomach before turning toward the set.

"We'll start with Everlee," Frederick said in a clipped tone. "And Chrissy?"

A beautiful girl stood up and walked to him. All legs that one, with wide-set, innocent eyes, pouty pink lips, and hair that looked as if she'd copied it identically from the last shoot Brittany had been in with loose waves draped around her shoulders. She wore a leather crop top and joggers that dipped into a pair of Nike high-tops.

They'd clearly tried to dress her like she was hanging out with her friends at a basketball game, but the girl was too pretty for that.

No, she looked like she just stepped out of a magazine.

And that was a problem.

Wasn't it?

Everlee smiled politely at the girl and took her seat on the white leather couch they were supposed to sit on. The theme was girl-talk.

Yeah, Everlee was supposed to give advice, and while they talked and laughed and painted each other's toes, Frederick would shoot.

"Make it natural," Grace said in a bored tone. "And, Chrissy dear?"

"Yes?" Chrissy beamed.

Grace shook her head slowly. "If you look at the camera, I'm throwing you out the window. You will not pose. Repeat after me, 'I will not pose.'"

"I will not pose," Chrissy said in a serious voice. "I swear."

"Swearing's for sailors." Grace sighed as if the world were disappointing her. "Now, off you go."

Chrissy sat next to Everlee.

"First question!" Grace snapped her fingers.

Brittany read it off. "What's the best advice you could give someone starting out in the industry?"

Everlee ground her teeth together at Chrissy's eager and oh-so-innocent expression. "Oh, good one!"

"Look at the camera one more time, and I'm throwing you out the window and letting the pigeons do the rest!" Grace yelled.

Chrissy ducked her head and faced Everlee.

"Well." Everlee angled her head so Frederick could catch some of the light outlining her perfect jawline. "I think the best advice I can give you is to work hard. And all your dreams will come true!" When had she turned into a liar? "And make sure that you keep your circle of friends close."

Chrissy nodded eagerly. "Wow, it's so crazy you say that because my friends from high school and I still talk every day. I think it's really important to stay grounded."

Everlee's eye twitched with the need to roll a bit.

Her smile froze on her face as she quickly said, "Good for you!"

"Second question," Grace yelled.

"What do you love most about—?"

"Wait!" Grace walked right in front of the camera, adjusted one of the pillows, and tossed it to Chrissy. "Hug this right here. Pull your legs up. No double chin. Neck pushes out, not in—we aren't hobbits. There. Continue, Brittany!"

"What do you love most about yourself?" Brittany asked.

"That's easy." Chrissy grinned broadly at Everlee. "I love my laugh."

At that, Everlee did smile, a real one. "I can see why."

"Everlee?" Grace said in an annoyed voice. "You have to answer, as well. You're better than this. You know the drill, faster!"

"I was thinking." Everlee felt her throat close up as everyone waited for her to answer. Her eyes filled with tears as she realized one sad reality.

Nothing.

She loved nothing about herself.

She opened her mouth and lied. "I love my eyes."

"Oh, you have beautiful eyes, I can see why. I like them, too." Chrissy reached for her hand and squeezed it. And then something changed in the girl's expression. The bubbly girl was gone, and in that moment, she was just another human noticing someone else's pain and trying to do everything in her power—through a stare—to make them feel better.

Everlee squeezed back.

"That, right there." Grace walked up to Frederick. "Ladies, don't move, that's our shot."

The camera flashed several times.

And then Grace's voice yelled. "Next!"

FIFTEEN

"Hey..." Brittany knocked on Grace's door and leaned against it. After being on her feet most of the morning and helping coordinate the shoot, all she wanted to do was toss off her shoes and walk around the office barefoot.

But last year, someone had actually been fired for that.

Grace's cousin.

So... Brittany kept her stilettos on, even though the Louboutins pinched her pinky toe, making it nearly fall asleep every time she put all her weight on her feet.

At least, they were pretty.

"What do you think?" Grace held up the *New York Post* just long enough for Brittany to catch the name of the newspaper. Then she tossed it into the trash can and leaned back, her eyes calculating. "Well?"

Great. Brittany would have to guess. "I always enjoy reading your mind."

Grace's red lips twitched. "And?"

"And, I think that if you're reading the newspaper in the afternoon, there's something in it you would like to discuss."

"I always knew you were the smartest of the three." Grace beamed.

Brittany gave her a pointed look. "Zoe's brilliant, so is Everlee—"

"Yes, yes they're fantastic, so beautiful." Grace waved her off. "I like the idea."

"The idea," Brittany repeated. Exhaustion had crept in so swiftly that her brain had trouble processing. It didn't help that she'd stayed up late the night before texting Oliver.

He was in surgery all day today.

And her phone was burning a hole in her purse.

She refused to check it every five minutes.

And broke that promise to herself ten minutes into her day.

"You know." Grace leaned forward. "The idea. Politics."

"Yes." Brittany breathed out a sigh of relief. Then it hit her. "Wait, really?"

Grace shrugged. "No, I'm lying to you because I enjoy breaking your spirit."

Brittany waited.

Grace scowled. "Really, you should know me better by now. Look, I'll allow this under one condition."

"Anything." Brittany was ready to bounce out of her chair and sprint down to Zoe's office for champagne!

"Ronan Kampbell." Grace's eyebrows shot up. "Rumor has it his family's breathing down his neck—mainly his mother, let's be honest—" Brittany cringed. "—to run for president after his term is up. If he succeeds, he will be one of the youngest US presidents, easily following in his late father's footsteps. I want the story. He refuses to confirm or deny the allegation. I want the story, and I want him on the cover." Brittany felt like she was going to be sick. "With you."

"Excuse me?" Brittany couldn't find her voice as her entire body started to sway. "Why me?"

"Because you're pretty," Grace said in a sarcastic voice as she started riffling through her papers. "He's always been fascinated with you, and now that he's married, it would be nostalgic for the American public to see you on good terms with the family. More than that, the *New York Post* ran a story on you two sixteen years ago, do you remember?"

How could Brittany forget? They'd had to let out the dress she was wearing, and she'd gotten in a fight with Ronan over talking to his mom about the situation. About them.

He'd said that he loved her and that they would figure it out.

And then nothing was ever said about it again, about her, though Brittany did get a check from the family in the mail the next day, along with a restraining order.

Ronan had still visited her apartment, but by then, the trust was broken. So broken. She had given him her heart.

It hadn't been enough.

"Yes." She found her voice. "I do."

"That newspaper sold more copies in one day than it did the entire year, Brittany. That's unheard of! This issue could pay for advertising for the next two years. *Trend* will be in every home, on every bus, every taxi—it'll destroy our competition, and you still get what you want."

She didn't want it that badly.

Not if she had to pose with *him*.

Not if she had to pretend.

She couldn't do it anymore.

Obviously. Since the gala had been a disaster and she had almost passed out a dozen times then nearly got blinded by his wife's giant rock.

Thank God for Oliver.

"The correct response," Grace stood and leaned over her desk. "is, 'Thank you, Grace, for this wonderful opportunity.' Off you go."

She waved Brittany off.

Brittany stood on wooden legs. Her tongue felt thick in her mouth. "How much time do I have?"

"I want it done before Fashion Week. We'll be too busy once that hits. I'll contact Roger with more details—that beautiful man better not have died in that God-awful hospital."

"He's alive." Brittany's vision dimmed as the blood drained from her head. "He just hates having to take it easy."

"You can sleep when you're dead," was Grace's response as she picked up the phone. "Roger, you're alive! I'm so pleased you didn't walk into the light…"

Brittany walked back to her office and stared out at the city. Everlee was fast asleep on her couch.

The woman really wasn't kidding. She'd been so exhausted, Brittany didn't have the heart to wake her.

Her phone buzzed in her purse.

Finally!

With a grin, she picked it up. "Hello?"

"Have you talked with Grace?" Ronan said in that deep voice of his, the one that had sent chills down her spine during her first *Sports Illustrated* photo shoot. He'd walked right up to her, introduced himself, and when he saw the Bible sitting on her lap, sat down right next to her and said, "I could use some saving."

It had made her laugh.

It made him smile.

And she'd lost a little bit of her heart in that grin, in the way he looked into her eyes instead of at her body.

Only the briefest touches.

All the other girls had gone wild that he was even on set. She hadn't.

She'd later found out that was why he'd approached.

And then he'd said that he saw her legs. He was a man, after all.

"Ronan," she croaked. "Yes, hi."

"That's all I get? 'Yes, hi?'"

She ground her teeth. "Actually, I'm kind of busy right now—"

"Bull. I'm a politician, and you never could lie very well, Britt."

She squeezed her eyes shut at the use of her nickname. "Yeah, well, I'd like to think I'm better at it since I was exposed to it on a daily basis, compliments of you and your lovely mom. She didn't manage to fall down the stairs last night or choke on a piece of shrimp, did she?"

"She's not that bad," Ronan said defensively. "And you know she's allergic to shrimp."

"Only more reason to feed it to her," Brittany snapped.

"And everyone thinks you're so sweet..." He chuckled. "Look, I'm going to send you my schedule for the week. I figure we can do the interview over dinner."

"Lunch," she found herself saying. "Dinner looks bad. You're married, remember?"

"Business dinners never look bad. Just try not to look too sexy, and it won't be a problem."

"I love it when you ask for the impossible."

"I love it when you fight with me," he fired back. "It's dinner or nothing at all. And wear red, it's patriotic."

She banged her head slowly against the desk and muttered, "Fine, just send me a"—her phone dinged—"text."

"Done. See you soon."

Brittany sighed.

"Oh, and Britt?"

"Yes?"

"You looked beautiful at the gala. I would have told you had the man on your arm not looked ready to throat-punch me. New friend of yours? Bodyguard?"

"Doctor." She sat straight. "And that's all you'll get."

"Ah, working-class, good for you."

Could he be any more condescending?

"Goodbye, Ronan."

"Goodbye for now, Britt."

She tapped end on the conversation and wrung her hands together as old feelings jumped to the surface.

It wasn't just that he was a beautiful man.

He was a lot like Dane in the way he carried himself, powerful to his very core, and unapologetic about life in an addicting way.

Funny how her parents had warned her about drugs before she moved to the big city—about addictions in every form.

But the one drug nobody saw coming?

Ronan Kampbell.

"Who was that?" Everlee said in a sleepy voice. "You sounded angry, and you never sound that way. I don't think I've ever heard you raise your voice." She pushed herself up on her elbows.

"Ronan," Brittany said, striving for an indifferent tone. "He's just…"

"A politician," Everlee said in an annoyed voice. "Between him and Dane, the devil must be having a heyday."

Brittany let out a snort. "So… true." But inside, all she kept thinking was, *he wasn't always like that.*

So controlled by his family.

By his mother.

It had happened slowly.

And then the Ronan that she knew and loved had been replaced by a shiny new version compliments of Nancy and the image she wanted him to present. The woman told him he couldn't get into acting, that it was beneath him. Flying his plane back and forth to Martha's Vineyard? Too dangerous. The world needed him.

She needed him.

And the sick part? Maybe Nancy was right.

Because as much as it made Brittany's heart squeeze in her chest, she knew. He was a leader people would follow.

And the world needed more individuals like that, those willing to sacrifice everything for the greater good.

Just another reason Brittany had fallen for him in the first place. Ronan would sell his soul to save the world.

Brittany just hadn't thought he would give her up, as well.

"Want lunch?" She stood, shoving the dark thoughts from her head and grabbing her Birkin bag just as Everlee moved to a seated position. "I'm buying."

"I would love lunch." Everlee pushed to her feet and grabbed her purse.

With a cursory knock on the door, Frederick walked in, took one look at her, and frowned.

"Everlee?" He took two steps toward her. "Are you still feeling sick?"

Brittany bit her tongue to keep from saying something she would regret while Everlee melted into her husband's arms. "Yeah."

"Why don't I call a car for you?"

"Really?"

"Yup." He kissed her on the forehead.

"I'll just wait in here. I really am tired." She sent Brittany a relieved look and sat back on the leather couch.

"I'll take care of you," Frederick said in a soft voice as he left the office. Brittany waved at Everlee and followed closely behind.

The first thing the man did was pull out his phone and call a car. And the second? He took a left to where the models waited and wrapped an arm around Chrissy.

Brittany kept walking, a frown on her face. When she finally made it out the door, she hailed a taxi, got in, and looked out the window just in time to see Frederick and Chrissy leaving the building.

Together.

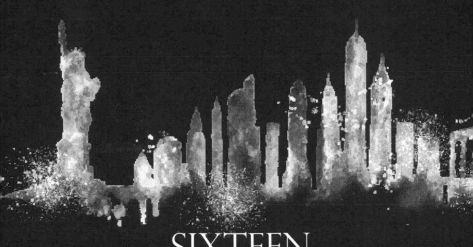

SIXTEEN

Zoe stared at the bill.

Took another long draw of her red wine.

Then stared harder.

She was still at her office.

Blocks away from the loft Dane had purchased for her.

Drinking alone.

And wondering if she should shred the paper and then send him a screenshot of all the tiny pieces.

There was only one problem.

He was right.

And as much as she wanted to throat-punch him, she was petrified. She didn't own a gun, and now she felt trapped in her own office because she'd needed to work late.

Chelsey was gone.

The lights were low.

And every single noise or flicker of light made her tense to a painful degree. Was Aaron here? Would he finish what he started? Was he a changed man? Still angry?

Who was she kidding?

His brother was dead.

Dead.

And he'd gone to prison for rape—they never could prove the premeditated murder.

It had been too easy for her and Dane to fix. Too easy for her to report the story to the police the way Dane had asked her to.

And she'd believed Dane when he said that it was the only way. She'd believed him when he said that he would take care of it all.

And he had.

Until now.

Now, he had a freaking alarm clock dangling in front of her face with a diamond ring and loft attached to it.

The sound of footsteps neared.

She almost dove under her desk until Dane filled the doorway, his massive frame blocking the light, his head of gorgeous dark hair nearly kissing the top of the wood. "You shouldn't be here alone."

"Got that." She sighed. "I lost track of time and trapped myself. Lucky me."

"You're never trapped; not when you have me." He took a step inside, then slowly shut the door behind him. The click was like a gunshot going off in the tense silence as his blue eyes locked on hers with such intensity that it was hard to breathe. Chest tight, she couldn't move as he guided his massive body across the wood floor to stop directly in front of her chair.

Without a word, his smooth hand moved to her chin, tilting it upward. "Be mine."

"If I say yes, I lose myself."

"I think you give me too much credit."

"I think humility looks awkward on you," she said honestly in response to his cruel, beautiful smile as his head descended. He used his hands to grip her arms and pull her to her feet.

It was happening.

His web of darkness and deception was wrapping itself around her inch by inch, and in those moments—the brief seconds when her brain misfired and told her to stay rather than run—he owned a little bit more of her as his lips pressed against hers.

She sucked in a breath at the first taste of him.

Her body seemed stunned by how good it was.

She'd purposely forced all good memories of Dane away. It made it easier to say no.

But now, her body was saying yes without her vote.

She stilled as his tongue slipped past her lower lip.

And then he pulled back, his hands sliding down to her hips, holding her body in place without space between them as his breathing slowed. "I love you the only way I know how."

"By scaring me to death and threatening me?"

"By protecting you."

"Protecting and owning are the same thing to you, Dane," she said in a small voice. "And the last woman you tried to protect still died, didn't she?"

His nostrils flared with anger as his jaw clenched, and rage danced in his orbs. "I swore justice would be served. Trust me."

"That's the thing. I can't. Not when I know what you're capable of."

Knew what he did.

He nodded. "So, it's come to that, has it?"

Fear trickled down her spine. "What do you mean?"

He didn't answer, just held out his hand and said, "Let's get you home."

She took the proffered palm because it was either him or the psycho from her past. With a huff, she grabbed her purse and followed him out of the building and into the waiting SUV.

They were quiet the entire drive.

It wasn't lost on her that they were going in the wrong direction.

Dread pooled in her belly as they pulled up to his Upper East Side apartment, one of the many he owned.

"Come up with me." He made it sound as if he were asking. He wasn't. "We'll talk."

Ha, talk. Right. They would talk.

"So you can use my body in order to find your way to my heart?" she snapped.

His face softened. "So I can make sure I don't wake up and find out that the universe has lost another much-needed light." He touched her face, his fingertips burning her skin. She wanted him, she always did, but he would never give himself to her that way.

They would never have that life.

The one she dreamed about.

A family.

A white picket fence in the suburbs.

Laughter.

His touch led to death, secrets, the limelight. His touch meant she was agreeing to sell her soul in the very same way he'd sold his.

And, suddenly, she wished for Brittany.

For her friend to be there with her ever-present Bible, thumping it over Dane's head and telling him to stay away.

Brittany knew how to keep the demons at bay.

Zoe invited them in.

She stared Dane down. "What do you want from me?"

He was silent, and then he nipped her lips with a slow, persuasive kiss before he whispered against them. "Surrender."

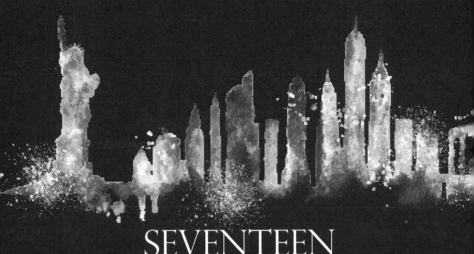

SEVENTEEN

Dane waited for Zoe to move.

She very slowly took off her heels.

And moved around the kitchen, then stood on her tiptoes to grab two wine glasses. She knew his kitchen well.

If only she knew that he couldn't stand being in that room without her walking around it. Well, tiptoeing was more like it since Danica had lived there with him the last time Zoe had treated it like home.

The memories were too hard.

Memories of laughter. Of the girls staying over, eating all of his food and then begging him to order pizza. He'd moved into the city a few years after Danica had started modeling so he could take care of her. He'd left Jersey on a whim, sold two of his estates, and made himself at home in the darkness of the underworld.

And found a home he hadn't realized he needed, playing chess with the demons in his head.

"So…" Zoe's voice snapped him out of his dark thoughts. "If I say no to you…" She handed him a glass and looked up into his eyes. Her mocha skin was flawless in the moonlight. He wanted to reach out, to lick a path down her neck, to kiss her and press his body against hers so tightly she'd have no choice but to touch him back. "Are you going to kill me?"

He tried to hide his shock, and then he tilted her chin with his free hand. "That depends."

Her breath hitched. "On what?"

"Do you want me to?"

Her eyes betrayed her. The way they filled with tears that he knew she'd rather die than let spill down her perfectly sculpted cheeks. She suffered just as he did, but he was able to get the rage out.

Zoe.

Zoe let hers feed on her soul.

Sadness pulsed between them as he set his glass down and gripped her shoulders with his hands. They slumped under the weight. "You aren't her, Zoe."

"I could have been."

"But you weren't."

"People said we were a lot alike," she said in a small voice.

"You were always stronger. You *are* stronger. Don't let her death make you give up. Don't make me the sort of monster who would kill you just because I love you enough to do whatever you ask."

She gulped.

With a shake of his head, he nodded at her purse. "Text the girls, let them know you're safe and that you're with me tonight. Tell them Aaron's out of jail, but nothing else."

"They should know what we did—"

"Great idea, then they can testify in court," Dane said sarcastically as he walked over to her purse and handed it to her. "Text them. They'll comfort you like good friends do, and then you can stay in the guest room."

She took her purse and frowned. "But I thought—"

"I'd rather not get a yes to your proposal minutes after you ask me to kill you. It completely ruins the moment, Zoe." He winked, turned on his heel, and made his way toward the master bedroom. "You know where the towels are. Try not to eat all the Skittles in the pantry."

The door closed to her muffled laughter.

God, he'd missed that sound.

Too bad it was rarely directed at him or with him anymore.

He leaned against the door and squeezed his eyes shut then fired off a text to Frederick. "Club tomorrow night?"

Frederick texted back almost immediately. "Thank God."

Pieces were finally falling into place.

After a year of investigating.

A year of secrets.

Dane would reveal the truth.

EIGHTEEN

The sound of the door slamming jolted Everlee up from her sleeping position on the couch. What time was it? She rubbed her eyes and stared at the blurry phone that she was still clutching in her hand. Midnight? Frederick was supposed to be home hours ago.

She checked her phone and did a double-take. Zoe was with Dane? *Dane*-Dane? The one she wanted to murder half the time? The rest of the text mentioned Aaron. A sick feeling washed over Everlee as footsteps neared.

"You look terrible." Frederick's chipper voice gave her pause. Slowly, she turned to stare him down. Everything looked normal. He was wearing black skinny jeans, a low V-neck vintage tee, and enough man jewelry to choke a person. His hair was brushed back, and he had a scarf wrapped around his neck. He put down his camera bag and then crossed his arms and stared at her. His eyes were cold, indifferent.

Wasn't home supposed to be different?

She stretched her arms overhead. "Where have you been?"

"You my keeper now?" He smirked as if he were kidding, but she heard the irritation in his voice. "You know how it is before Fashion Week."

Maybe for the models.

She frowned as her stomach growled loudly. She pressed a hand against it. The baby inside was already rebelling against her poor diet. And while she knew she needed to eat more, she was petrified of what that meant for her, for Frederick, for the life they had. And for her career.

Getting fat, regardless of whether it was because she was pregnant or not, wasn't acceptable. Nine months of not working, of gaining weight, losing it again, of being exhausted and swollen...

Her eyes filled with tears as Frederick made his way to the couch, sat down next to her, and grabbed the remote from the table.

One bulky arm hung behind her, not touching, just there.

"You still sick?" he asked, not looking at her.

She gulped and then leaned into him, pressing a hand against his broad chest. He stiffened.

What? When had he ever reacted that way?

Hurt, she pulled her hand away as fresh tears blinded her line of vision. "Yeah, just a bug or something... I'll be fine."

"That's a relief." He actually sounded relieved. Huh, maybe he really did care? "For a second there, I thought you could be pregnant." He followed that with a laugh that felt like a million knives digging into her skin. "Can you imagine?

At this point in your career? In mine? Kids." He shuddered. "Not for us, baby." He kissed the top of her forehead. "Besides, can you imagine stretch marks on that beautiful body?"

The guy actually shuddered like the idea of a baby repulsed him so much that he needed to react physically. She recoiled even more as her stomach sank.

And even then, with the disgusted look on his face followed by the loud laughter as he flipped to late-night TV, she knew it was a miracle that she was pregnant at all. Because it had been a secret wish for years until, finally, she realized it wasn't going to happen. Not with Frederick. Ever.

"You're quiet." He turned to her, finally, and reached for her hand. "Do you want me to draw you a bath?"

Like he used to when he said he couldn't get enough of her.

When he said it was their little secret.

When she wasn't yet eighteen.

And he wanted to see what was beneath the clothing.

She shuddered. "No, I think I'm just going to bed."

"I'll tuck you in." He got up before she could protest, and then he walked with her back into their bedroom, turning the lights down and kissing her forehead like it was typical for him to be this gentle with her rather than coming home drunk and smelling like someone else's perfume. He actually seemed... normal.

Maybe he would warm to the idea of a child.

"Love you, baby," he whispered.

He loved her.

He did.

He just needed time.

The problem was that she was going to run out of time. And quickly.

Frederick left the room and shut the door behind him. As luck would have it, she had to use the restroom—again. With a huff, she got up and walked into the room, bumping into the laundry basket and dumping it over before finding the light.

Clumsy while pregnant, too? Fantastic.

She bent down to put the basket back and felt her stomach drop. It was one of Frederick's shirts.

The one he had been wearing yesterday.

There was red.

But it wasn't lipstick.

No, down the arm was a stain in dark burgundy.

Blood.

NINETEEN

NEW YORK FASHION WEEK COUNTDOWN - 11 DAYS

Something about fall and school shopping, kids in their uniforms, and moms chasing after them with their backpacks made Brittany want to cry.

Autumn reminded people of fresh starts, pumpkin spice lattes, Halloween, and the ever-present lure of the upcoming holidays. But today? Today, she saw backpacks and families, she saw people hugging and kissing as they took pictures before getting on a bus for their first day of school.

She saw everything she should have had.

But didn't.

Her childhood had been just like this.

And she'd wanted nothing more than to repeat it with her own family someday.

She sighed, taking another sip of coffee as she made her way into the intimidating building that housed *Trend*.

Everyone was in a hurry. And for some reason, on this day of all days, she wanted someone, *anyone* to just smile at her, say hi. She wanted them to make her feel warm instead of dead inside, wondering and wishing and overthinking all of the mistakes of her past.

"He's really not coming," she said to herself as she held the bundle close. Pink little knit hat. She'd never been a huge fan of pink until that moment. Pink toes, pink lips, a pink little cap covering a pink, wrinkly head.

Tears cascaded down her cheeks as she eyed the bundle in her arms and then glanced up at the clock across from the hospital bed.

Ten hours had passed.

Ten hours.

And each hour she told herself to wait just a little bit longer. He would come through. That's the type of guy he was. Solid. Stable. The perfect boyfriend, right?

"Honey?" Her nurse, Amelia, walked in with a bright smile. "Did you want me to take her?"

Possessiveness washed over Brittany as she held the baby close to her chest. "Just a bit longer."

Amelia nodded slowly.

And then Brittany burst into tears. "Please, could you just... could you just stay for a little bit?"

"I'll do more than that," Amelia said softly before sitting on the hospital bed and putting her hand on Brittany's shoulder. And with awareness in her eyes, Amelia, a stranger... began to pray.

And as the nurse's words washed over her, Brittany continued to weep in both relief and comfort that at least she knew she hadn't been completely abandoned.

The elevator jolted.

To this day, Brittany couldn't recall the entire prayer, only that Amelia had said that all things would turn out for the better. And Brittany had believed her, she'd taken that one simple truth and tucked it away inside her heart.

It had to be okay.

Because the alternative was impossible to digest, to even comprehend. Brittany squeezed her eyes shut as an emptiness stretched inside her chest, and then her cell buzzed in her purse. She hoped it was Zoe updating her on the whole Aaron situation. It was terrifying that someone who'd done such a horrible thing to her friend was somehow now out of jail. Brittany just hoped he wouldn't be stupid enough to talk to them—any of them.

She pulled her phone out and smiled for the first time that day.

> Oliver: *Lunch? Dinner? Snack? I have a few surgeries today, but I'd really like to see you even if it's only ten minutes...*

She quickly replied back.

> Brittany: *Can we do all three?*

Stunned that she'd actually typed that in her current mood and pressed send, she watched the little dots move across the screen, waiting for his response.

> Oliver: *At this point, I'd probably quit my job just so we could. But since I'd like to stay employed so you can always introduce me as the hot doctor, I'm*

going to have to say one out of three. Please don't break up with me.

She grinned.

Brittany: *You mean we're together?!?!*

Oliver: *Don't break my heart. I only have one. Kidneys, however...*

Brittany: *How about dinner? Tonight?*

She briefly remembered that she had to do dinner at some point with Ronan this week but brushed the thought away just as the elevator doors opened to floor twenty-two where *Trend* was housed.

She wasn't able to look at her phone again until she was safely tucked away in her office. And by then, she had five texts from the only man who'd made her heart slam against her chest since Ronan.

Oliver: *Dinner sounds great.*

Oliver: *Want me to cook?*

Oliver: *We could go out too, but something tells me you'd rather stay in.*

Oliver: *I'm overthinking this.*

Oliver: *It's because I want to do this right—you deserve it.*

With a grin so broad it almost hurt her face, Brittany tapped back.

Brittany: *Cooking class. Both a date out and a night in... I know a guy who owns a place. Actually, he's co-owner. Sound good?*

Oliver: *Send me the address and the time.*

Brittany smiled to herself as she fired back the address as quickly as possible and then opened her email to send Roger a quick message. He was one of the owners. Technically, he held the majority, but it wasn't something he talked about. It was his love for food and a desire to find a life partner who shared his same interests that had spurred the idea. It was one of the top places in the city to do singles' night.

Within minutes of sending the email, Brittany had a response. Roger had made room for them and had also invited himself.

Shocker.

With a grin, she rolled her eyes and then started typing back just as a knock sounded at her door.

"My desk is empty." Grace put her hands on her slim hips. Her black pantsuit was tight against her svelte figure, and her cherry red heels added at least two inches to her height.

"Your desk is empty," Brittany repeated, leaning back in her chair. "Because?"

"I need that story, I told you sooner rather than later. Sooner already happened, it's later… today is later. I needed it the minute we chatted. Didn't he call you?" Grace started to pace in front of Brittany's desk, each clack of her heels like a nail in Brittany's coffin.

"Yes, but—"

"No buts. Butts belong in tight jeans or at the end of cigarettes, buts are excuses that I don't have time for. I need that story. And I'm going to move up the photo shoot to this Friday. Don't let me down—" She held up a polished finger. "Lucky for you, he stopped by. I told him to let me yell at you before he came waltzing in with that smile and the dimples and the ridiculous jawline. The man's a monster for not letting me at least touch one of those firm biceps." Grace shrugged. "He had to take a call. Don't mess this up."

And, just like that, Grace stomped out of the office, and Ronan—Brittany's waking nightmare—walked in.

"Grace." He nodded at the editor.

She stopped, looked at him, shook her head, and kept walking.

It was her way.

"Always such a pleasure chatting with the devil herself," Ronan said under his breath, making himself at home in Brittany's office, perching his body in one of her leather chairs.

"Your mother?" she said sweetly.

"Grace," he fired back with a taunt in his eyes. "Though it's safe to say they're on the same playing field. Women like that should come with little alarm bells so we lesser humans can prepare for all the fire-breathing."

"Grace's bell is her shoes," Brittany said with a smirk. "You know how angry she is by how loudly she walks. It's on purpose."

"Clever. Mother's is all in the perfume. I smell her, I know she's circling, and I run. Simple as that." He grinned.

"That must be difficult since the apron strings are still knotted up around your body, hmm?"

He barked out a laugh. "I knew you missed me."

"Hardly." She tried to hide the flutter in her stomach at the way he drank her in. The same way he used to. The way she had dreamed about that night in the hospital.

Her white knight had never come.

Only darkness.

She turned away. "Did you need something other than witty banter, or can I get back to work?"

"Dinner, remember? I sent you my schedule, emailed you a few times, but you never got back to me."

"It's been less than twenty-four hours, and I'm a busy woman," she said through clenched teeth.

"Tonight," he said with a challenging glint in his eyes. He tugged on his black tie and leaned forward, resting his forearms on his expensive slacks. "We can do dinner tonight. The wife is away for the week in Paris anyway."

"How convenient for you," Brittany found herself saying, even though she knew he wasn't the type of man to cheat. No, he just got women pregnant and then abandoned them because of his mother. His family. His name. "I'm busy tonight."

"Are you trying to see how far you can push Grace because it amuses you, or are you really busy?" His eyes narrowed. "I'm busy the rest of the week."

"Your schedule said—"

"I'm in demand, what can I say?"

She almost threw her stapler at him. Did he have to ruin the only thing she was looking forward to tonight?

She clenched her teeth and gave him a firm nod. "I'll meet you at Roma's."

"Michael's," he said quickly.

It had been their first date.

Their spot.

Memories flooded her.

Brittany's heart physically hurt with each thump against her ribs.

"Fine." Was that her voice? That weak sound coming from her lips?

"Great." He stood and walked toward her, and before she could protest, he brushed a kiss across her cheek. "I'll have a table ready at eight. Should I send a driver?"

"No." She shook her head.

"Are you sure?" He was too close, way too close.

She didn't want to back down, though. Didn't want to show fear. "Yeah, I'm a big girl now. I know how to wave down taxis and everything."

"Trust me." He eyed her up and down and then shook his head as sadness flashed across his masculine features. "I'm well aware that you're a woman, a confident, beautiful, incredible woman."

"Please don't say things like that to me."

"I swore to you I'd never lie." He reached for her hand and squeezed. "Don't make me break that promise, Britt."

Tears filled her eyes as he released her hand and walked out.

The worst part of it all had been the sting of his wedding band as it pressed against her skin, as if she needed the reminder that, in the end...

He hadn't chosen her.

TWENTY

Canceling on Oliver had been physically painful. How was she already attached after only one date and enough texts to make a teen blush?

He'd said that he understood, but it was so early, did he really? The worst part was that she didn't tell him who she was canceling to go out with. She didn't want to give him cause for concern, though she had been honest and said that it was for work and that Grace was breathing down her neck.

It wouldn't help the situation if Oliver knew. He'd just worry, or worse, she'd see a side of jealousy she almost always saw when she tried to date, and the fantasy would be ruined. And she wanted to keep it, just a little bit longer, the illusion that a man existed who didn't pressure her for sex immediately, who might possibly understand her beliefs, her morals. A man who looked at her and saw more than a body, more than legs that went on for days.

She toyed with her clutch, holding it in front of her as if it were some kind of armor against attractive politicians who had a habit of breaking hearts with smiles on their faces.

She ducked her head as she walked into Michael's. She was so much taller than most women that she knew she'd most likely get noticed, if not by the people eating, than surely by the staff or the owner who used to reserve the table right by the kitchen just for her and Ronan.

Speak of the devil.

Ronan stood.

He was in the corner at their usual table.

Nostalgia hit fast and hard.

Brittany swallowed against the knot in her throat as lead filled her legs. With each step, she winced. It was like walking into the past, only they were older, wiser—at least she liked to think she was wiser now. But the way he looked at her, and the way her heart responded said the exact opposite, didn't it? Yes, he was attractive, but she'd learned her lesson. She just wished the rest of her agreed because the sick part was that her heart still wanted the happily ever after. It believed, even after all this time, that people could change. That she could have a family with him. It was a sick joke of the universe, toying with her heart.

She forced a weak smile and sat across from him, only for him to abruptly stand and then pull her chair around with her in it until they were side by side, thigh against thigh.

"There." He sat back down and swept his hand toward two opened bottles of wine on the table before them. "Red blend or white?"

"Red," she whispered hoarsely.

With practiced movements, he poured her a glass and handed it to her and then grinned, his full lips spreading into a devastating smile. "To old times."

Old times?

Her stomach dropped.

Old times like when he'd abandoned her?

Like when she was waiting at the hospital for him to show up?

Old times like when he promised her forever and walked away in the same breath?

"To old times." She clenched her teeth and barely managed to touch her glass to his without shattering it in his face and letting out a horrified scream.

A shriek full of sadness.

Regret.

Anger. So much anger toward him.

Toward what should have been but could never be.

"What's this?" Britt had already handed her little girl back to one of the nurses. There was a single red rose and a sheet of paper with the scribbled words, I'm sorry. *She moved the note and started to shake. It was the list, the one she and her friends had built and agreed to make a copy of and give to the man who took their hearts. Each of the girls had one—and she'd given hers to Ronan.*

And just like that, Ronan Kampbell gave something back that she had never asked for.

Shattered. She couldn't even bring herself to touch it.

A deep voice interrupted her thoughts. "I came as soon as you called."

She looked up into crystal blue eyes. "Do you think you could use your connections to help...?" He assessed her for a few minutes before slowly nodding.

She fell into a fit of tears while the devil held her close, and she wondered if she'd had it wrong the entire time. Maybe men like Ronan were evil—and men like Dane? Saviors dressed as sinners.

Maybe everything she believed... was a lie.

"So." She set the wine down and grabbed her phone, kicking all the memories and thoughts from her head. "We should get started—"

"Not yet." Ronan grabbed her hand and pulled it down until it was pressed against his thigh, but he didn't release her fingers. "We have time, Britt."

"We've never really had time, Ronan," she said sadly. Time had been as cruel as his mother. It'd told them that they needed to rush something that neither of them understood, that both of them were too young to possibly grasp. "There's always been a buzzer just waiting to go off. Why prolong it?"

He hesitated. The glow of candlelight on his face highlighted his strong jaw and that stupid grin, not to mention the thick, glossy hair that always looked effortless. "You've changed."

"I have wrinkles now," she said proudly and took another drink of wine. "That and I don't walk barefoot down the streets of New York like a hippie anymore."

"Pity," he said softly. "I was going to say you've lost a bit of the light that used to make every photographer in the world infatuated with you."

She jerked back. "Wow, at least I know you're not trying to seduce me with compliments like that."

"Joy's cheating." He said it softly. "She's been cheating. That's why she's in Paris. It's going to be a media firestorm."

"And the media caught wind, how exactly?" Brittany asked curiously. The Kampbells were notoriously secretive, nothing but good news, things that would win another election—heck, they wanted the world.

He just shrugged. "Some things slip."

"You." She narrowed her eyes. "You let something slip?"

"I did a favor for Dane, he did a favor for me," he said simply, but Brittany knew what it meant to exchange favors with a man like Dane, what it meant for Ronan and what it meant for the position he was currently in, the life he now lived.

Politician through and through, wasn't he? Not that she had a leg to stand on, all things considered. She shifted uncomfortably in her seat. "I'm not the only one who's changed if you're dealing with the devil. No matter how pretty he may be, the man has no manners when he's busy threatening physical violence."

"And yet he calls you friend." Ronan seemed to concentrate on her mouth a little too hard before his eyes flickered to hers. "Because of his sister?"

Her stomach dropped. "We were all friends. And I would rather call him friend than enemy. Wouldn't you?"

Ronan just shrugged. It wasn't lost on her that he knew people in the same sort of underworld that Dane operated in. What was worse? He knew people from the CIA who could make anything look like an accident.

Arsenic in their butter?

Heart attack via a needle between the toes?

Accidental overdose?

Easy.

"We're getting off topic." Brittany cleared her throat. "Let's talk politics."

"My favorite subject."

"Funny, I thought *you* were your favorite subject, and I'm rarely wrong."

He shared a smile with her and then shook his head as if he couldn't believe they were sitting there sharing a meal. Make that two of them. "I think I like you better jaded."

"Who said I was jaded?"

"With me…" he said softly. "You're jaded whenever you're with me."

"I wonder why…" she said sarcastically. "All right, answer the question, Senator. Are we going to see you throw your hat in for a nomination for the Democratic party?"

He grinned like he enjoyed the question, then lifted the wine to his lips and drank, never taking his eyes off her. "What if I told you I was throwing my hat in for the other side?"

She did a double-take. "I'd say you're already drunk and should probably get your head checked before your mom runs you over with her Lincoln."

He burst out laughing, earning the attention of several people in the restaurant, inevitably followed by the whispering that always occurred when they realized who he was, who *she* was.

Ah, lovely. The past was throwing itself into the future. Cheers.

"You never know." He leaned in so only she could hear. "I may enjoy seeing my mom's face turn a shade of purple I haven't seen before…"

"Take this seriously." She found herself relaxing as his cologne created a frisson of memories. "What are your plans?"

"Call me 'Senator' again, and you may find out."

"Happy birthday, Mr. President," she said in a sing-song voice before reaching for her wine again.

"Nice, bring my father into it, well played." He chuckled. "All right, the truth, since I always promised you that."

She waited.

He let out a rough exhale, followed by a curse. "I don't want to, no."

She frowned. "Then why the rumors?"

"That would be my mother thinking I should. That would be the family thinking the apocalypse is coming if a Kampbell isn't in the Oval Office. Personally, I'm not sure I would be the best choice for this country, and that's what it's about, isn't it? At the end of the day, it's not about me or my family name, it's about the country. How's that for a diplomatic answer?"

She swallowed the dryness in her throat and stared at her hands in her lap. "Well, you just got my vote."

"Oh, yeah? Why's that, Britt?"

"Because an honest politician is a good one," she said seriously. "And we need more of that in this world."

"Yes." He lifted his wine glass up. "We do."

She cleared her throat and looked away just as a text flew across her screen.

Zoe: *Staying at Dane's again. Safe.*

Brittany frowned.

"Something wrong?" Ronan asked in that casual way he did when he was trying to be caring. She never could decipher between the tones he used with her and those he used with other people he wanted to placate. How sad.

"Not wrong, no." She sighed and then shared a look with him that felt familiar. He slowly slid his hand down the table and then pressed it to her thigh like he used to when he was concerned.

Back then, his touch had felt like a promise.

Like forever.

Now, it just felt like sadness.

She held back her tears like she always did in his presence and forced a smile. "Zoe's been staying with Dane. Aaron's out of prison. Remember her stalker?"

Ronan's expression hardened, the lines around his mouth tightening before he nodded. "Yeah, stalkers that are hell-bent on killing the people you love are hard to forget, don't you think?"

"He was never after me," Brittany said quickly.

Rage crossed Ronan's features. "You don't know that, trust me. Dane found pictures of all of you girls. The only reason he's even in prison is because, in a fit of anger, he accidentally killed his own brother."

"Accidentally." Brittany tested the word. She'd never asked how it was possible for someone to accidentally fall on his own knife, the same blade that had Aaron's fingerprints all over it, the one that'd lodged itself in his brother's chest minutes before the police arrived.

In a way, she didn't want to know.

Sometimes, the truth was scarier than the lie.

Reality stranger than fiction.

"I tried," Ronan said in a softer tone. "I had a golf game with the DA, but it was out of his hands. The guy says he's saved... found God and all that."

Brittany stilled.

Ronan tilted his head; his laser-like intensity focused solely on her. "Maybe you two have that in common, running around saving us sinners from ourselves."

"That's not fair." She gulped and looked away. "I've never pretended to be anything except myself."

"Exactly." Ronan leaned in. "The reason you're so appealing..." His knuckles brushed her cheek before he dropped his hand back to her thigh. "What would you say if I told you I never stopped loving you?"

"Stop." Tears stung her eyes as her throat almost closed up. "Please... stop."

He shook his head. "Never. I was wrong. You know it. I know it. The world should know it, too. And it's about time they knew the truth."

She tried to stand.

He held her down. "Not that truth. Ours."

"You can't share partial truths."

"I'm a senator. I can do whatever I want."

Ain't that the truth? "Funny, since you did exactly that. I was in the hospital... alone." A tear slid down. "You never came then. What makes you think I would ever trust you again?"

He didn't let her answer, just leaned across the table and brushed a kiss to her knuckles then whispered, "I don't need your trust, just your heart."

She shivered, squeezing her eyes shut. No. She would not go down this road again. She was finally in a better place—older, wiser. But that was the thing about your past. Even when you knew you'd learned your lesson, temptation lingered, and bad habits weren't easy to quit. He'd been one of them, and he'd sucked her into the vortex of his prowess too easily. She'd fallen for it. He'd offered her the world, and she'd believed him. "We're in public."

"I can fix that."

"Ronan—"

He stood and dropped a few hundred-dollar bills on the table, grabbed her hand, and then led her back toward the kitchen and a familiar hallway.

Then outside to the alleyway.

His hands on her hips the whole way.

Her body dying a bit with each step, knowing exactly what he was going to do. She knew him better than he knew himself.

And then those hands slid up and cupped her face, pulling her in for a punishing kiss that was sixteen years too late.

She opened her mouth to protest. He used it as a way to deepen the kiss, to press his fingers into her skin, to pull her flush against his chest and curse against her lips like he was angry that they'd been gone so long.

"No." She shoved his chest with both hands as her chest heaved with frustration. She wiped her mouth with the back of her hand, tears filling her eyes. "Not only are you still married, but you can't suddenly decide that I'm what you want. Not now."

"Britt…" His voice was gruff. "We were good together. We *are* good together. Why can't we start over?"

"You of all people should know you can't rewrite history." It was unbelievable that she could even find her voice as her body trembled like it couldn't handle the onslaught of sadness and disbelief.

"My father tried."

"He was a good man."

"People say that all the time to me, every day of my life, and the only time I ever truly believe it, is when it's coming from you. From the light in those blue eyes, from the goodness of your lips." He reached for her again.

She backed up against the wall. "I'm seeing someone."

"I know. The doctor. Olive?"

"You *know* his name."

"Momentary lapse of memory..." Ronan grinned smugly. Why did he have to have so much charisma?

Addict. Addict. Addict.

He wanted what he couldn't have, but when she needed him the most, needed him to be the man that she always saw—he had run.

Not this time.

"Ronan." She pressed a hand against his chest. "We need to finish the interview." Her purse became a lifeline as she pulled it in front of her body to create separation, gripping it so tightly her knuckles whitened. She prayed he couldn't see her knees shaking, or the way tears swam in her eyes. Too late, he was too late. "Let's go to the bar next door, and you can tell me all about your thriving political career—all without kissing me."

"Fine." He backed away. "I'll do that and more... but I will be kissing you again. Maybe not tonight, maybe not tomorrow, but you're mine, Britt. You've only ever been mine."

"I belong to no one but myself," she said with a shaky

voice, staring daggers at him as he offered her his arm and then walked her slowly down the darkened alleyway toward the bar next door.

"Maybe that's the problem, Britt. You say you belong to yourself, but all you've ever wanted was to share yourself with someone else."

God give her strength.

She was not ready for him.

Not now.

Not ever.

She found herself praying the entire walk to the bar. With each footstep, she asked for the strength to get through this.

Because as right as he'd always felt...

This time, she knew it was wrong.

That lingering sense of dread was like a choking, pulsating smoke column between them.

She suddenly wished her mom was there to tell her what to do, but what would she say? *Hey, Mom, you know that guy I slept with but didn't tell you I slept with because I felt guilty? Well, he got me pregnant and then left me, and now he's going to run for president. Oh, right, and he wants me back. You know, after he divorces his current wife. Surprise!*

Ronan leaned over. "You all right?" he whispered, his lips hitting the curve of her ear. She knew it was on purpose. Because everything he did had a purpose, a reason, and now she wondered if it was something more. If he was using her for his own personal gain.

Gritting her teeth, she nodded, sat down on the barstool, and waved the bartender over. "A Manhattan, make it strong."

Ronan just grinned and said, "Same."

It was going to be a long night.

TWENTY-ONE

NEW YORK FASHION WEEK COUNTDOWN - 10 DAYS

Zoe stretched her arms above her head as she made her way out of the guest bedroom and padded into the kitchen. Coffee was already on, naturally, because Dane wouldn't live in a world where the coffee wasn't programmed to make itself the minute he needed to take over the universe.

She grabbed a black mug and poured herself a cup and nearly dropped it onto the slate floor when Dane walked into the kitchen.

Shirtless.

Mouth dry, she averted her eyes and barely managed to walk in a straight line to the barstool.

"I must be growing on you. Yesterday morning, you only stared for two seconds. I'd like to think this time it was at least four."

Zoe let out a snort. "I never thought I'd see the day where the Great Dane Saldino counted how many seconds a woman stared at him."

"Not just any woman, my future wife." He grinned wolfishly then turned to face her, his ridiculously toned body on display. Silk pajama bottoms that should look stupid only added to the effect. How was it possible that he'd grown muscle on top of more muscle? It was unfair that men aged into themselves, and women were told that wrinkles needed to be managed. His eyes crinkled at the sides, giving him an almost boyish look, which was so foreign that her mouth gaped.

"Out with it." She set down her coffee. "You're in too good of a mood, and you just smiled like I agreed to your terms while shopping for wedding dresses."

"I think I'd like something strapless on you." He leaned his massive body over the counter. His dark hair was unruly as if he'd run his hands through it multiple times. "Why don't you design your own?"

"Nice subject change." She scowled. "And you're still smiling. To be honest, it's starting to creep me out. Don't you have children to scare, puppies to drown?"

The corners of his mouth tilted up into a grin. "I think I'd like children."

"Okay, seriously." Zoe felt her patience waver right along with her belief that the man was incapable of domestication. "Children? You've never wanted children!"

"Maybe I've turned over a new leaf." His face was inches from her. "Besides, I had you in this apartment two days in a row, and you managed not to suffocate me with my own pillow. I'd say that's progress."

"Must have been asleep when I had one hovering over you for a solid half hour last night." Zoe grinned into her cup as she took another long sip.

"Cute." He winked. "And, trust me, if you were anywhere near me, I'd know. You stir my blood too much for me to sleep through your presence. I'd like to think I'd be awake before you even stepped into the room."

"Huh." She gulped, not really sure what to say to that because if she lingered on his current mood and the way he'd taken care of her these past two days by just making her feel safe, she'd waver. She'd start to question all the reasons for not marrying him and do something stupid.

She just needed to remind herself why he was bad news, why he would destroy her from the inside out.

It wouldn't be hard. All Zoe had to do was think about all the people he'd hurt, all the lives he'd destroyed with a smile on his face, and she'd be fine.

But when he was that close…

When he smiled at her.

When he showed her that he could be normal, at least in that apartment, it made her question.

And, sadly, that was probably his plan all along. He never attacked quickly. No, Dane was willing to wait for years to get what he wanted.

"You know I want kids," she said quietly. "Please don't use that against me, it's not fair."

"I'm not." He stood to his full height. "I wouldn't."

His gaze penetrated her as he slowly rounded the corner of the breakfast bar and then reached for something inside his briefcase.

Frowning, she watched him pull out an old, folded piece of paper.

Heart in her throat, she nearly fell out of her chair when he approached, opening the note slowly. It was worn, the blue lines on the notebook paper faded so much they could barely be seen anymore. It was the checklist she'd given him the day he'd told her that he loved her, the one signed by every one of her friends, Danica included.

"You kept it." Her voice shook. "You actually kept this?"

"This"—he dangled the paper in front of her—"is a legally binding contract between two hearts, two souls that recognize their need for each other regardless of what their mouths say."

Zoe pressed her lips into a firm line, not trusting herself to speak.

"I kept it, just like I kept your heart. Just like I've never dishonored your body, even though I've had every right to find another woman. It's only ever been you. You, Zoe."

"Are you telling me you've been celibate for the last year?" She gaped.

"You." Dane leaned in and whispered in her ear. "When I make a promise, I keep it. I told you I was a one-woman man, and I meant every word. I've been celibate since the night you walked out of my life, and I'll stay that way until you walk back in."

Zoe stood, nearly colliding with him and his cup of coffee. She backed up to put space between them. "I don't believe you."

"Yes." Their eyes locked. "You do."

"I need to get to work." She turned and bolted toward the guest room just as he called after her.

"I'll have two of my men tail you today. I need you to stay safe."

She slammed the door shut without answering and leaned back against it. Tears spilled over onto her cheeks.

She didn't believe him.

She couldn't.

She'd given him everything, and he'd... he'd ruined it! He'd ruined her.

She tried to replay all the memories, the gossip in the magazines, the different women on each arm. The lifestyle he led. His clubs alone made him look like the worst sort of person.

And yet she was crying.

Because he'd never once lied to her.

It was one of the only things he had going for him, other than his good looks.

She slid down the door, and her body landed in a heap on the floor. What if she was wrong, though? What if he wanted all of those things? A family? Kids? What if he wasn't the same man?

What if?

Two of the most dangerous words in human history.

She sucked in a deep breath then slowly stood, compartmentalizing that conversation and shoving it into the farthest corner of her mind. Work. Fashion Week. That was all that mattered, not the stupid checklist she had given him when she told him that she loved him.

Not the vow she'd made to his sister when she confessed that it was Dane all along who owned her heart.

"I love him," Zoe said softly. "He keeps me safe. I keep him human."

Danica pulled her in for a hug. "Don't let him lose his humanity. Don't let him turn into the monster. The darkness always pulls at us both." She looked away. "He fights it the way a person should. Sometimes, I wish I was more like him, more willing to face my demons instead of just lying down and taking their punishment."

Zoe frowned. "Danica, you're a good person. I know you are. We all have bad days."

"No." Danica's smile was sad. "Bad days are one thing. I'm talking about bad choices, really bad choices, ones made with equally bad people." Tears filled Danica's eyes. "Insecurity screams louder than the darkness, and insecurity is one of the most terrible beasts I've ever fought. I'm so tired. So, so tired."

"Then quit!" Zoe pulled her friend in for a hug. "You don't need the money."

"It's never been about the money. It's about the high, and you'd be lying if you said you weren't a little bit in love with it, too."

Zoe was silent.

"But—" The girls broke apart. "I'm really happy for you. Truly. I see the way he looks at you. He'd burn down the world if you asked him to."

"Ha. Well, thankfully, I'm the yin to his yang, no apocalypse necessary."

"I know." Danica winked. "Anyway, you know what you have to do now. Hand him the list, and... congrats, you're officially the first girl to hand it over to the man of your dreams." Danica grabbed Zoe's copy of the list and wrote down one final entry. "Number fifteen, never lie. Never go to bed angry."

"Him? Never lie?" Zoe joked.

"I'd be more worried about the second part," Danica said quietly. "He's not a liar, it's his greatest strength and greatest weakness. When he loves someone, he loves them with all the good and the ugly, so promise me that when he shows you the ugly, you'll love him despite it. Because I think you're the only woman in existence who can break him, and that terrifies me."

"I won't break him." Zoe hugged Danica again.

He had kept the list.

He'd kept it.

Zoe didn't even remember getting ready for the day. All she knew was that the stupid list was still on the kitchen counter when she walked by it.

And because she liked to torture herself, she stopped and looked down at number fifteen written in Danica's perfect script.

It was as if she was there with Zoe, reminding her of something she'd purposely forgotten in order to protect herself.

And, sadly, to punish herself for not getting there sooner.

In what world could Zoe save a man like Dane?

She couldn't even save his perfect sister.

And in what world did she even deserve to?

TWENTY-TWO

Her head pounded.

Her heart ached.

Brittany took one look in the mirror and scowled. Not only had Ronan evaded almost every question after the kiss, but he'd kept trying to dig up the past as if it suddenly mattered again.

After two hours at the bar, she still only had an answer to two political questions, and she looked like she'd just gotten run over by a train.

Her phone went off. It was Grace.

Fantastic.

"Hello?" She tried sounding chipper, but her voice was raspy, off, probably from all the talking she'd done last night. Her phone beeped with the sound of an incoming text.

"My email." Fingernails tapped against a keyboard. "I just checked it, refreshed it, checked again, and nothing. Nothing political, and I refuse to count… what's that one intern who sends cat videos? Ridiculous. I refuse to count that as new mail."

Brittany held in her sigh. "It's Marco, and I think it's his way of trying to make you laugh."

A pause and then, "I laugh."

Did she, though? Britt wasn't sure. Her lips curved into an exhausted smile. "I promise I'll have it on your desk by noon."

"That's in three hours."

"I'm aware of the time."

"Good." She hesitated then added, "It might behoove you to get some information on that divorce, as well. News just broke this morning after you two were seen getting cozy at Michael's."

"What?" Brittany clung to her cell with one hand and flipped on her TV with the other. Sure enough, Kelly Ripa and Ryan Seacrest were going through the daily gossip, and she was front and center, smiling at Ronan while he leaned in like he was going to kiss her. And they were speculating about what it meant, and if Brittany was meeting him in secret.

She knew he hadn't kissed her at dinner.

And that when he did kiss her, she had shoved him away.

But the picture looked bad.

Really bad.

She groaned into the phone.

"Cheer up, girl, any press is good press, and you've just magically made our Friday shoot our most important of the year. I knew I could count on you."

"To look like I was seducing a married man?" Tears filled her eyes, threatening to spill over. This wasn't how it was supposed to go! History felt like it was thrusting itself into the present, and she wasn't guilty, not this time. This time, she really had stuck to her morals. She hadn't let him charm her into saying yes when she should have said no.

But the outcome was the same.

Her other line started going off again, this time with a phone call instead of a text.

She pulled the phone away, just in time to see Oliver's name.

"Right," she finally said, sniffling a bit and wiping under her nose. "I gotta go, Grace."

"Noon."

The line went dead. With shaking hands, Britt answered. "Hey, I can explain…"

"You were the one who said you couldn't talk about him." Oliver didn't even seem angry. No, he sounded hurt, which was worse. Anger she could manage, hurt feelings? Betrayal? It was painful. "And I gave you that space. I know you don't know me very well, so imagine my surprise when you cancel on me to go to dinner with him."

"It's not how it looks!" Her chest felt like it was cracking in half as she scrambled for words and sentences that she could string together so she could help Oliver see her side of things. "It really was a business dinner. Grace wants a story on him, she wants us on the cover."

"Unbelievable," Oliver muttered like he was disappointed. "Brittany, you have to cut me some slack. I'm not from your world, but I do know how men think. You were at dinner with him, alone, it's all over the press that he and his wife are divorcing, and you admittedly had a relationship with him sixteen years ago. What am I supposed to think?"

She gasped, and anxiety tightened her chest. "Ah, so you finally did that Google search." Was that it, then? He was done?

"Only after I saw the news this morning," he admitted in a soft voice.

"Find anything interesting?" She felt herself building walls around her heart, and she hated that she was doing it.

"Don't," he said quickly. "Don't do that. Don't push me away. Don't take the easy way out. I was out of my mind this morning, all right? The woman I like, the woman I'm falling for was out with another man. A married man."

"That's not me!" she blurted, hating that her voice was heavy with tears, despising that this was even an issue, that the world was, once again, watching her fail—at least that was how it felt.

What would Oliver do if he knew the truth?

The hospital?

Ronan not showing up?

The lies?

Her stomach roiled.

"Food." Oliver's voice sounded tired. "At the hospital. After my shift tonight, we can talk."

"Okay." She gulped.

"No lies, no omissions. If we do this, you have to trust me."

"Trust you?" she repeated. "When sometimes I don't even trust myself?" She hadn't meant to say that out loud.

The line was quiet; she could hear his breathing on the other end. "Britt, at some point in your life, you're going to have to take a chance, risk your heart again. But you won't ever be able to do that until you move on. Right now, you think you're growing, moving, but it seems to me you're just as hung up on the past as he is. It still has this choke hold on you. And part of me wonders if that's the way you want it."

"Excuse me?" Anger surged through her. "You've been on one date with me, and now you're my shrink?"

He cursed. "That was out of line."

"You think?"

"Look, maybe this is my jealousy talking, but it appears that something is tethering you to him—still. And you aren't the only one risking something here."

"I know." Could she feel any worse? Probably not. "I know that."

"Look, I have to go. Meet me later today, after my shift?"

Get more answers out of Ronan, write her first political piece for Grace, and meet Oliver before the end of the day? Sure, no problem. "Yeah."

"Okay."

She hit end and threw her phone against her mattress then ran around the room, dressed, and for the first time since she was sixteen, put her hair in a knot on her head and grabbed her laptop. She had enough for one paragraph, and it needed to be a cover story—a spread. With hesitation, she eyed her phone again, then with a groan, picked it up, prayed for strength, and dialed Ronan's number, anger pulsing through her body.

He picked up immediately. "Britt, to what do I owe the pleasure?"

"Two answers, I got two answers out of you last night. I need more."

"Meet me for lunch."

Irritation grated her nerves. "After watching the news, you really think that's a good idea?" Her face flashed across the television again, with more speculation as to her being the reason for Ronan and Joy's divorce. "They think I'm the other woman!"

"The media loves drama. Don't worry, my team is on it."

"Oh, good, so your team is on it while my life unravels from one business dinner. Fantastic. And where was your team when—?"

She stopped talking.

He cursed on the other line. "I'm sorry. I can't take back what I did, or what I didn't do, but I'd like to make that up to you."

"You can't make up moments, you can only promise to be there when they happen, Ronan. That's sort of the way the universe works."

"Not being there is the biggest regret of my life," he said softly, making her heart ache in her chest. She rubbed the spot and prayed for it to go away as she squeezed her eyes closed.

"Too. Late," Brittany whispered. "I'm going to email you ten questions, answer them, please. I need to turn in the article by noon since Grace is fast-tracking this for next month's issue."

"Have dinner with me."

"No. We're done having dinners, Ronan."

"Drinks?"

"I think for your political career to not end up in tatters, you should stay away from women for a while. It never works out for your family when the men start dating models and actresses anyway, does it?"

"That was a low blow, and you know it."

Yeah, but she was hurting, and he was the one twisting the knife. "I'll see you on Friday for the shoot."

"Fine."

She hung up and wrapped her arms around herself, wishing it was someone else. Oliver? Roger? Her mom?

If she could send the universe one message right now, it would be: *help*. Just help. A simple request, someone to hug her, someone to tell her that she could handle this, that she could keep it together when she felt like she was in quicksand. What if Oliver walked away? What if this was too much? Would she blame him? And Ronan? As much as she wanted to shove him out of her life, they shared something, they shared an actual person that he'd never met, that she'd—

Someone rang her doorbell.

Either God was really quick, or it was truly the worst day ever.

Brittany jogged to the door just in time to see Roger standing there, coffee in his right hand, a box full of donuts in the other, and a wide grin on his face. "I figured today of all days, you needed sugar."

And then she burst into tears all over his soft leather jacket.

"Can we have Dane murder him yet, you think?" Roger asked, quietly making her laugh.

"Don't talk like that. You know Dane would do it for a price." She grabbed the coffee and shut the door behind him while he did his typical assessment of the place like he was hoping dirt would present itself.

"Everyone has a price, honey." He finally stopped looking around and directed his gaze back to her. His brown eyes were warm but always peered into her, trying to figure her out. "Never forget that."

"I haven't." She took a sip of the coffee and then grabbed a donut. "Thank you for this."

"Well, I saw the news."

Brittany groaned. "Everyone saw the news." Exhaustion hit her again. "I feel like I worked so hard for my reputation, and now this? Really? Oliver's confused and rightfully angry because I was afraid to tell him that Ronan was my business dinner, and now the world thinks I'm the other woman when all I did last night was shove him away and try to act professionally."

"Shove him away?" Roger tilted his head.

"Caught that, did you?" Brittany grumbled.

"As in, he was closing in for a kiss, and you shoved him?"

Brittany winced and took another long sip of coffee. "As in his mouth touched mine, and I shoved him with both hands."

"Good girl." Roger winked. "Though I'm surprised he was that bold. He's not notorious for being the bad boy of the family. I think that goes to dear old Dad."

"Notorious?" she repeated. "He's American royalty, prone to flirting with anything with a pulse. You know this."

"Yeah, well, he's pretty, so he likes to think he can get away with it."

She rolled her eyes and took another bite. The last thing she wanted to think about was Ronan's good looks. Those mixed with his charm were what had gotten her into trouble in the first place, right? He'd been there for her, he'd been solid, larger than life, and he'd let her down. "I hate this, and I have Grace's article due, which—hold on." She held up her finger and grabbed her phone, then quickly sent the remaining questions to Ronan. "He didn't want to talk politics, he wanted to talk about the future."

"Ah, which meant he probably wanted to dig up the past and say he's sorry, blah, blah, blah."

She just shrugged, not wanting to get into the details, mainly because Roger was the only one she'd trusted enough to tell, well not the only one. Her stomach clenched. Like a good friend Roger had quickly sworn to forget the conversation had ever happened.

For both of them.

"If there's anything you've taught me…" He walked over to her and placed a hand on her shoulder. "It's that you survived this jungle because you're a lioness. More than that, you know who you are. Whenever you questioned it, whenever you got off your path, you re-directed yourself."

Brittany gulped as more tears filled her eyes. She didn't deserve those words, she wanted to be the type of woman who did, but how could she see herself that way when she couldn't even forgive her past? "I think you just have a high opinion of me."

"For good reason. Because you're genuinely good, Brittany. You see the world differently. It's why people want to see things through your eyes, why photographers constantly ask me what makes you so beautiful. It's your soul. And, right now, your soul hurts, and I do remember a girl of twenty-two, one time telling me that when the soul hurts, it goes to the only place that sick souls are truly welcome."

"Church," she finished for him.

"A hospital for the sick, not for the well," he said, quoting her younger self. "But since it's a weekday, why don't you do what you did in that hotel room all those years ago? Maybe a little bit of day-reading to center yourself after you write that article. You're my favorite, you know. Not because you think you're better than everyone, but because you genuinely love every single person you meet with your whole heart. Your greatest fault will always be your greatest strength." He kissed her forehead. "Now, go make the politician look good, then remind yourself why you're so unforgettable to everyone who meets you."

Roger opened the door and clicked it shut behind him as he left.

Tears clouded Brittany's vision as she made her way back into her bedroom and noted the small Bible on her nightstand; last night's glass of wine next to it.

He was right.

With determination, she grabbed her laptop and got to work, then cleaned up the wine glass and grabbed the Bible.

To Brittany.

Love, Mom.

And under it all, in her mom's shaky handwriting…

Jesus, be *her center.*

TWENTY-THREE

What Everlee was doing was wrong, but Frederick had blood on his shirt. What was she supposed to do? Approach him and ask if he'd gotten in a fight? Her pregnancy hormones weren't helping the situation, and her paranoia was at an all-time high.

Was she actually hacking into her husband's computer?

He was shooting all morning, and since she was so exhausted and sick, the last thing she wanted to do was leave the apartment. Besides, she didn't have anything until Friday. *Trend* was doing a shoot for Brittany and Ronan, and that meant she needed to be there to support her friend. It helped that Jauq and Frederick were tag-teaming it. Both were being given an opportunity to show the vision they had for the couple.

It would be beautiful.

It always was when those guys worked together.

She typed in another password.

And failed.

She would be locked out if she guessed wrong the next time. Her stomach sank when she realized that after years of marriage, he'd changed all his passwords. The ones for his email, his chat—everything was different, and he'd never told her.

He'd just done it.

He'd quietly shut her out of a part of his life.

One day you're married to the man of your dreams; the next day, he's joking about not wanting kids, you getting fat, and you find blood on his shirt.

Forget Mondays, Wednesdays were now the worst.

She touched her stomach and drummed her fingertips on the table. She did have one idea.

Dane.

He knew every hacker in the area.

The guy wielded power with too much enthusiasm and aggression for Everlee, but he'd always been a friend.

Besides, he owed her a favor, didn't he? Because of his new club, her husband had come home three nights over the course of the last two weeks, intoxicated, smelling like whiskey and perfume. And now this.

With a sigh, she picked up her cell and called Dane's number.

"Everlee." He said her name the way he said everyone's, with expectation, as if he knew she was about to ask him for something. "I'm in a meeting, what do you need?"

"He changed his passwords." That could have come out a lot smoother. "And I just… I'm being a paranoid wife, I know that, but we've always shared everything and—"

"I'll send someone tomorrow morning, but you'll owe me."

"Ha. Are we sure about that? Since it's my husband who's been paying a thousand dollars just to step foot inside your club?"

Dane added, "I give him ten percent off for being such a faithful customer."

"You're the devil."

He just laughed. "People see what they want. They believe things the same way. How about I just do this as a favor from a friend?"

"No catch?"

"A slight catch, nothing huge. But if you find anything suspicious, come to me. Let me deal with it. Especially in your condition."

She almost dropped the phone. "Ex-excuse me?"

"One minute." It sounded like he was talking to someone, and then a door clicked shut. "I'm in my office with the doors closed. And I said a woman in your condition. I didn't stutter."

"How do you know? I haven't told anyone!"

"I know everything, Everlee, don't patronize me with stupid questions. Around seven weeks along, am I right?"

Hot tears stung the backs of her eyes. "Yes."

"You let me know if you need anything else. The last thing you want is to endanger the baby with stress. Whatever you find, I want. And if it's too much to deal with, if your concerns are validated, you come to me. Only me."

A golf ball of emotion lodged itself in her throat. "Dane…"

"Yes?"

"What do you know?"

His sigh was long, exhausted. "I need to get back to my meeting."

"Dane!"

"Deep breaths, for the baby. I'll send over a script for that nausea, too."

He ended the conversation.

She stared at her phone in shock.

Something didn't add up.

Dane keeping tabs on her made no sense.

They were friends, had always been so because of Danica, but for Dane to know that Everlee was pregnant meant that he either had people following her or her apartment was bugged.

That was ridiculous, though. He would have no reason to do that! She set her phone down on the desk and reached for the remote to flip on the TV.

And nearly fell out of her chair when she saw that Brittany was front and center with Ronan of all people.

Divorce?

Dread trickled down Brittany's spine.

No. They were just going through a rough patch, she and Frederick. He was her everything, her dream guy. This was what happened when you got married and lived with someone for so long. You could easily turn into roommates, passing ships in the night. She just needed to remind him why they were so good together, why they had fallen in love in the first place.

Starting tonight.

All they needed was time, right? Time.

And she had exactly six hours to make sure he walked in that door and looked at her the way he used to.

Everlee's feet ached, and she'd had to use the restroom at least five times in the last hour—but it was done. She'd had Amazon deliver enough groceries to last a week and had looked up one of her favorite butternut squash soup recipes. It had some calories, but she figured if they were going to reconnect, why not have it happen over food? She opened a bottle of Prisoner red blend and let it breathe, only panicking a bit over him noticing her not drinking. Then again, if she had one sip and quietly spit it back into the glass, would he even notice? Maybe she would just tell him she still wasn't feeling well.

The salad was made.

And the dining room looked perfect. She'd lit some candles and set out the dinner to look like they were eating out at one of their favorite restaurants instead of dining in, and because Everlee knew Frederick's busy schedule, she'd texted a few times to confirm that he was actually coming home.

Five minutes.

She'd managed to squeeze into her old size-two leather mini-dress. It hugged every curve and was a little tight across her waist, which helped to hold in the small pooch she'd started to acquire over the last two months.

It was hardly noticeable, but because she was so thin, she knew she was on borrowed time. The last thing she needed was to end up on Page Six with speculation about a burrito baby or a real bun in the oven.

She put on a coat of fresh lipstick, arranged her hair in the reflection of the oven, then slid her sore and swollen feet into a pair of Louboutins just as the doorknob turned, and Frederick made his way into the apartment.

"Smells good," he commented. "Did you order in?"

"No," she yelled back, a grin on her face. This was precisely what they needed. Why hadn't she thought of this before? Sure, he had been coming home smelling like someone else, but that was because she hadn't been giving him attention. And now that she was, everything would be fine. "I cooked!"

He rounded the corner. His eyes drank her in as he leaned against the wall. "You? Used the kitchen?"

Heat seeped into her face. "It's not rocket science."

"To you, it usually is," he said in a teasing voice. "It really does smell good, though." He pushed away from the wall and sauntered over to her. "I haven't seen this dress in a while..." She beamed as he ran his hands down her curves, resting on her waist. "You fill it out better than you used to."

"Is that a compliment?" Warmth filled her chest.

"Do you want it to be?" he asked, his lips turning upward. "It's not a bad thing. I'm just saying I notice little things about your body. Technically, that's a good thing." He pulled her in for a kiss, one that tasted like fresh mint.

As if he were trying to cover something up.

She kicked that thought out of her head and kissed him back, wrapping her arms around his neck and tugging on his bottom lip with her teeth. She ignored the pain that started to trickle where her heart used to beat strong and happily. She had no choice.

"Mmm, what did I do right? I think I deserve to know so I can do it again," he whispered against her mouth. "You're wearing a tight dress, cooking…" Frederick's voice lowered, making her belly flutter. "I like it."

"Good." She bit down on her lip as a sharp pain struck her abdomen. She reached for a glass of water and drank a few sips before answering. "It's all for you. I wanted to make you feel special today. We haven't seen each other much, and—"

He burst out laughing. "You're cute. We see each other every day. We sleep in the same bed. But I love that you want more…"

"Always," she said quickly. "I'll always want more of you."

"Hmmm, seems to me like you should follow through with that better when your husband comes home after a long day of work."

Wait. What?

Her smile froze. "I'm always here when you come home."

"No…" He leaned over and sniffed the soup on the table. "I'm saying sexually. It's like you've turned into this giant prude. I swear, last week, I almost asked you if you were cheating."

"What?" she said, a little breathless. "Why would I ever cheat on you? That's ridiculous!" Where would he ever even get that idea? Especially since he was the one coming home smelling like another human!

"Hey, hey." He cupped her face with his hands; she searched his eyes. "I'm just saying you've been off lately. I thought maybe there was some other guy I didn't know about, not that I'd blame you. We both know monogamy isn't realistic."

Her heart stilled in her chest as his words descended between them like a choking, cruel fog. "Well, when you're married, it is."

He just shrugged and dropped his hands like he didn't want to argue about it. "Should we eat?"

"Frederick?" Was she really going to ask this? Was she going to go there? Her blood pressure skyrocketed, she could feel it in the way her head spun, the way her mouth felt dry, and how everything in her body hurt.

"What?" His expression was utterly innocent.

"You haven't been… you know…?"

He chuckled. "Why would you even need to ask? I'm the one who's home with my wife at eight at night, enjoying a wonderful dinner she cooked. I've been giving you space because it seemed like that's what you wanted." He gave her an incredulous look and then winked. "Wow, you even had French bread brought in?"

For the first time in her marriage, she didn't want his wink. She didn't want his laughter or his sarcasm. She wanted to have a real conversation, even if it meant they got angry, even if it meant space for both of them. But she wouldn't get that from him—she never had, and he wasn't about to start now.

Frederick grabbed a piece of bread and broke it off, then sat at the head of the table while she slowly walked to the chair next to him and reached for the bread.

He gave her a judgmental look, his eyes darting from the bread to her face.

"What?" Everlee lifted it to her mouth. "Why are you looking at me like that?"

"Because you're beautiful, and I would hate for that beauty to fade just because you gained too much weight to wear anything in your closet."

She dropped the bread back onto the plate as a heaviness settled on her chest. "I'm a size two."

"You used to be a zero."

Were they really having this conversation? This wasn't the plan. Dinner was supposed to be about reconnecting, laughter, holding hands. Not dietary restrictions because he happened to notice that she was gaining weight!

"Well, you know," she said, flashing a fake smile that made her want to burst into tears. "They say strong is the new skinny."

He smirked at her. "You know who says that, right?" He grabbed another piece of bread. "Girls who like to eat."

"Girls have to eat to live, we aren't robots," she said frostily. "Look, I wanted to do something nice for you. Could we not talk about my body as if I've gone off the deep end because I'm up one size?"

He just took another bite and reached for his wine. "I have to go out tonight."

"But you just said—"

Frederick's eyes zeroed in on her, and then he stared down at the soup and reached for his spoon. "It's for work."

"You've been doing that a lot lately... working." Her voice was quiet, passive. It was as if she were watching someone else's story, not hers. When had she ever let him speak to her like this? When had it become okay? When had things shifted? Her emotions were all over the place.

Slurp.

Slurp.

It was like her ears were hyper-aware of each noise, the sucking, the sound of the chair scraping across the floor, the news in the background, even Frederick's swallows—all like a bomb ready to go off.

He dipped his bread into the soup.

Another slurp.

Her body jerked with each sound, and anger twisted in her gut that he would sit there and judge her small body while he ate whatever he wanted and screwed whomever he wanted.

Jumping to conclusions again.

"Frederick?"

Slurp. "Yeah?"

"Who are you working with tonight?"

He stilled. "New model, the one that looks like Brittany— or at least the hair. I'm taking her to a few clubs to meet some industry people. It should take about two hours. She's underage, so it's more of a 'here's some water and say hi to the person who can make you a star if you play your cards right.'"

He didn't need to explain it to Everlee.

She knew all about that game.

Because twenty years ago, she'd been the one on Frederick's arm as they played it.

"Are you sleeping with her?"

Frederick dropped his spoon into the bowl, scattering soup all over the tablecloth she'd chosen to drape over the dining table so it would look classy. "Are you serious right now?"

She nodded, not trusting herself to speak without yelling, without crying, without blurting everything out to him or worse, without getting down on her hands and knees and just begging him to love her again.

"No." His tone was gentler as he put his hand on hers. "I love you, only you." He leaned over and brushed a kiss across her forehead. "Come on."

His words were so empty. Words without meaning were almost more hurtful than words that held cruelty. She'd rather feel something.

"What?"

"Let's go." He pulled her to her feet and then turned her around and unzipped her dress, jerking it down past her hips.

No, no, no. This wasn't how it was supposed to happen. They weren't supposed to fight and then have sex.

They were supposed to talk and laugh, and he was supposed to tell her that she was beautiful and that he loved her. He was supposed to love her, no matter what.

Tears, ever-present tears sprang to her eyes as he slid the dress down her body. "This is what I want to come home to next. I want to feast on you."

She shook in his arms.

This wasn't right.

They were married.

But that didn't give him the right to touch her. Did it?

"See? You needed this as much as I did."

What he didn't know, and what she'd never say, was that it didn't feel consensual, not then—maybe not for a long time.

A very, very long time.

Images of the 'me too' movement flooded her line of vision. One thing they never included? How it didn't discriminate. Women were bullied even in their own relationships, weren't they?

Everlee forced the bad thoughts away as his mouth touched her skin.

And then her lips.

Wrong. So wrong.

She let him kiss her with her hands pinned at her sides, her heart cracking. Inside, she was screaming.

She pretended again that all she wanted was to have sex with her husband next to the soup she'd spent hours making.

She pretended that her body didn't ache in all the wrong places.

She pretended that she enjoyed herself when all she wanted to do was sob.

And when he left to go back to work…

She pretended to smile as she walked into the bathroom to take a shower—and saw blood.

Only this time, it wasn't from his shirt.

It was all hers.

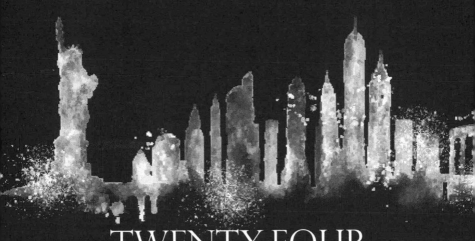

TWENTY-FOUR

He was back. Dane's anger wasn't something that he could control, not when it came to the people he loved—those he needed to protect. He watched from the lobby window of the building as Aaron walked by for the third time. The guy wore a black Yankees hat, jeans, and a blue T-shirt that had seen better days. He stopped once directly in front of the door and looked up as if he were trying to get a better view into the office.

Dane held up his phone and snapped a photo of the creep, and then flicked off the light.

"Hey!" Zoe called from her office. "What was that for?"

"All done for the day," he said as cheerfully as he could, which meant his voice sounded like metal getting run over by a train. "Get your things."

"Please," she said in that bossy voice he loved so much. "Use your manners, or I'm going to work all night and make you sleep in a chair!"

"You're welcome!" he fired back. "For picking you up from work so you don't have to be scared."

Her stilettos pounded against the cement floor as she made her way down the hall and faced him. Her white crop top kissed the brown suede skirt she wore; it made her look downright lickable.

Which was always a problem when it came to Zoe because he would never force anything physical. No, he wanted her to come to him.

Begging.

Promising.

Loving.

Sacrificing.

Surrendering.

Zoe stopped, arms crossed, glaring. She was magnificent, wasn't she? Brown skin, warm, green colored eyes, and enough fight in her to make him want to provoke her daily and then kiss and make up over and over again in an endless cycle. "I wasn't scared."

"Sure." He grabbed her jacket from the rack and then handed her the hanging purse. She turned like she always did when he helped her put her coat on. The funny thing about Zoe was that she didn't realize they were already acting like a couple, already working together seamlessly. Beautifully.

He needed her.

She needed him.

It had always been that way, and part of him knew that his sister had given her blessing. That was why he'd kept the list.

Because every girl in their group had to sign off on it before she could marry her dream guy. It was a pact made out of the dreams and imaginations of fourteen-year-old girls with stars in their eyes; young ladies who still believed that love was the rule and not the exception. That if they just worked hard enough, they could have a happily ever after.

That one day, their prince would come.

Dane was more devil than prince, but that didn't make his heart any less human, did it? Maybe it was the last part of him tethered to his humanity, the fact that he'd given it to Zoe for safekeeping so he didn't destroy it with his own darkness or with what he did for a living.

"I'm not arguing with you." Zoe's shoulders slumped.

With a frown, Dane walked around her and started massaging her shoulders. She leaned back against him, her eyes fluttering closed. "Something I can help with? Other than being your own private security detail late at night and taking you back to the apartment you own? With the man you love?"

"You were doing so good, too." Zoe made a face but didn't leave his embrace. "You know all this pressure isn't helping your case."

"I beg to differ."

"Because you like arguing."

"Only with you."

"Agh!" Zoe turned on her heel and poked his chest. "You're impossible, and I'm starving!"

"Well..." He reached for her hand and kissed it. "Then let me take care of you."

"I can take care of myself," she fired back, but he could see the indecision in her eyes, the want in her heart, the desire to be taken care of. She didn't have family; she had her friends.

And he wanted to give her everything. All of it.

"I know." He cupped her face and kissed her forehead. "That's what I love about you. Fierceness, independence, beauty, grace. But, Zoe, it's okay to lean on people. It's also okay to let them feed you."

"Pasta?" She bit down on her bottom lip and grinned up at him.

"Naturally."

"But without the sauce and—"

He pressed a lingering kiss to her cheek then tilted her chin toward him. "With extra pasta, extra bread, and all the fat you could possibly consume because human bodies are meant to be taken care of. Also because you haven't eaten all day, and because I would rather see curves I know I'm responsible for putting there than ribs people in this industry kill themselves to keep."

She gulped, and her eyelashes fluttered as her gaze snagged on his mouth, her posture leaning.

He met her halfway.

The air was thick, heavy with tension.

And then his cell started buzzing.

She cleared her throat, pulled out of his embrace, and tied her jacket just as Dane heard crying from the other end of the call. "Everlee?"

"You're the only one who knows!" She sobbed. "Dane, they don't know yet, I don't know how to tell them, but Frederick and I got in a fight. Well, kind of. I think he's cheating and—" Guilt gnawed at Dane's gut as he listened to her because he'd been the one to push Frederick, because he required more evidence, because he needed Everlee's trust, because it was a game board for him, and they were all chess pieces without even knowing it. "He left." She hiccupped. "And now, there's blood. So much blood, and cramping, and—"

"I'm calling nine-one-one for you right now," Dane said in a calm voice. "We'll meet you at the hospital."

"We?"

"Zoe and me. Can you make it to the entryway to unlock your door?"

"Y-yes. But Zoe doesn't know—"

"You're bleeding. It's beyond that now. I'm calling right now."

Zoe's face had lost all its color. "Who was that?"

"Everlee." He immediately dialed nine-one-one. "I think she's having a miscarriage."

Tears filled Zoe's eyes as she covered her mouth and shook her head in disbelief.

"Nine-one-one, what's your emergency?"

Dane briefed the dispatcher and watched as Zoe paced in front of him. The minute he hung up, they ran down the stairs and out to the waiting SUV.

All thoughts of Aaron and locking up forgotten.

TWENTY-FIVE

Brittany had barely made the deadline, clicking send at eleven fifty-nine and staring at her computer in awe that she'd actually done it. Ronan had answered every question she'd asked, though he'd purposely made the answers short and so politically correct she rolled her eyes while reading and half-expected him to answer something with "all I really want is world peace."

Hours at the computer hadn't helped her mood, so when she finished, she started sifting through her Bible and followed that up with a nap and some Netflix.

Now she had an hour before she was supposed to meet Oliver, which meant she needed to leave in a few minutes if she was going to make it on time.

Brittany smiled down at the worn brown leather of the book, remembering the day her mom had tossed it into the suitcase and told her that she was never alone.

It felt like a different life.

A different girl.

One who had stars in her eyes and excitement in her blood. One who truly believed that the world was a good place if you just saw past the bad.

And now?

Now, she was jaded, smarter, wiser.

And tired.

So very tired.

She flipped to the table of contents and then just started thumbing through the different chapters. Pieces of her life were held in this Bible.

Moments.

Pictures.

She turned to the last page and let out a little gasp. Two tiny inked footprints stared back at her. She covered her mouth with her hands as fresh tears stung her eyes.

Almost afraid to touch the faded ink, her hands shook as she picked up the small piece of paper and stared down at it.

Born August 23, 2004.

No name.

Nothing but two tiny feet that fit into the same worn Bible that held her own footprints from her birth.

"I'm so sorry." Her body shook as she cried over the Bible and clung to that piece of paper, holding it to her chest. "I was scared, and I couldn't take care of you. I didn't know what to do."

She took a calming breath and looked down. The Bible had opened up to a new page, one that held the paper Ronan had given back to her.

The one that had all of the girls' signatures on it, including Danica's. He'd given his heart back as if she'd never held it in the first place. And next to that, red rose petals that were so delicate, she was afraid to touch them.

How long had it been since she'd opened the Bible? Since she'd faced her past? However raw and painful it was.

Brittany couldn't remember. She'd been so busy with the magazine, but she still went to church, still prayed, still tried to be a good person.

But she'd moved on.

Or so she'd thought.

Because holding these pieces of her past proved one thing—she'd been standing still for over sixteen years.

How did Oliver even know that about her?

About her past?

She swiped the tears from her cheeks and tucked the piece of paper into her purse, not really sure why. It wasn't like she was in love with Oliver, like she could give it to him now. It just felt wrong that it would be in the Bible so close to her daughter's—

Another soothing breath.

No, not your daughter.

Someone else's.

Pink, wrinkly toes.

Small mouth.

And enough hair to style the minute she was born.

Brittany was going to be late if she didn't grab a taxi. She did what she always did, she covered her pain with makeup, wielded her armor of designer brands, and locked up her house.

On the outside, she was so perfect, wasn't she?

And on the inside… utterly broken.

The ride to the hospital was short, and the extra distance from the Bible and the footprints didn't make the pain in Brittany's chest go away. If anything, she didn't feel like herself because she was focusing on the past, not the present. And especially not her possible future.

She paid the cab driver and slowly got out just as a light rain started to fall. It matched her current mood, and honestly, she didn't mind it. She just wanted to explain to Oliver and move on. To work through what she needed to work through.

Maybe it was time to tell the girls.

Maybe it was time to own up to what had happened.

Maybe she owed it to herself, to her daughter, wherever she was, to be brave. To be a good mom, a strong, wise woman if even from afar.

Straightening her shoulders, Brittany grabbed her phone and fired off a text to Oliver.

Brittany: *Here.*

He didn't answer right away, so she walked down the familiar halls all the way to the nurses' station where she had first met him. She was pleasantly surprised when he rounded the corner and stopped.

Had he always been so handsome?

Her stomach flipped.

It was impossible not to compare him to Ronan, but now that she'd reconnected with Ronan in a way, she realized that he didn't hold a candle to Oliver. Not even a little bit.

Oliver was broader.

He had a confident swagger like the one that had attracted her to Ronan, but Oliver's was real, not a skin he put on just to make sure that people paid attention.

And as she took step after step in the doctor's direction, she realized that the last thing she wanted to do was amble toward him. No, she wanted to run. She wanted to wrap her arms around him. She wanted not just his comfort but also more—more than she was in a position to ask for.

Oliver smiled and handed the clipboard to a waiting nurse. Then he met her halfway. His blue scrubs and white jacket fit him perfectly. "You came."

"Of course, I did," she said in a quiet voice. "I missed you today."

"I miss you every day," he said quickly. "Let's go get some food and we can talk. You look tired. Still beautiful, but tired. You can tell me all about the article."

She felt her expression fall. Did she really need to talk about Ronan? About the memories she still held of this very hospital? And its smell? Its bright lights and broken promises?

They walked down to the hospital cafe. Oliver didn't hold her hand. Maybe it was because they were at his workplace, perhaps it was because she was overthinking and overanalyzing everything. Then again, how could she not? She was petrified that something would go wrong. How was it possible to be so attached already? Her hunger for something real in a relationship was making her crazy.

It didn't help that they were walking familiar halls.

She pressed a hand to her stomach as they walked into the large cafeteria. Oliver stopped and grabbed her gently by the shoulders. "Hey, are you okay?" His eyes lowered to the hand that was on her stomach.

"Oh." She dropped her arm as quickly as possible and flashed him a smile. "I didn't eat much today. The deadline nearly killed me, but I did have two donuts."

His eyebrows shot up. "A model who eats donuts. They let you do that?"

"Shhh, don't tell, they could write me up." She winked.

"I like that." He put a hand on her back, leading her to the register to order. "I like that you eat hot dogs and donuts and that I can actually feed you something other than lettuce."

"Who eats just lettuce?"

"My point exactly." His dark hair swept over his forehead, giving him a sexy look that made her stomach feel like butterflies were taking flight. When had she ever been looked at the way Oliver looked at her?

His eyes twinkled as his mouth drew up into a half-smile. "You sure you're okay?"

Great. Next, he would snap his fingers in front of her face. "Yup. Sorry. I just—" Might as well tell the truth. "I was staring. You're really handsome."

He looked down, his smile wide. "And now I'm blushing."

"I like it," she whispered.

"I like you," he said quickly.

"And I like chicken!" The hospital employee behind the register looked like he was ready to strangle them both. "Do you guys need another ten minutes, or we good?"

"Sorry." Brittany shook her head and looked up, ordering the first thing she saw. "Burger and fries."

She'd already screwed herself with the donuts this morning, so today was going to be the first real cheat day she'd had in ten years. Why not? Plus, this conversation required carbs. Lots of them.

Oliver ordered the same.

And Brittany hated the silence that descended as they carried their trays to a table in the corner and sat.

She hated the smell of food and antiseptic.

The way the lights seemed to burn her eyes.

Brittany hated everything about sitting there, explaining herself to a guy she was falling for.

"I was at a shoot for *Sports Illustrated*," Brittany blurted. "Ronan saw me with my Bible and wondered what could be so interesting about it that I wouldn't fawn all over him like every other model on the shoot."

Oliver leaned in. "Can't really blame the guy."

"No." She smiled and wrung her hands in her lap. "He was..." She licked her lips as she searched for the word. "Refreshing, I guess. In a world full of fake people, he wasn't, at least not with me. We fell hard and fast. We were able to keep everything a secret but not for long. And when I say hard and fast, I mean, within two weeks, it was national news. After a few months, things started to shift. Both of our careers were taking off, and we didn't see each other as much, he was done with his masters and already a young congressman. It wasn't on purpose." She took a deep breath. Was she really going to admit this? Out loud? To Oliver? What if she lost him forever? What if he was like every other man out there? What if he was like Ronan? And pressured her? And told her she had to prove her love to him?

"Hey." Oliver slid his hand across the table, his palm up. "It's okay, talk to me."

Their food sat between them, but she couldn't touch hers.

"Well, every time we were together, it felt so good, but rushed, like we didn't have enough time to love each other. One thing led to another. I hadn't had the conversation with him like I should have, but I was young and in love, and I justified every single thing we did because he made me feel good. He made me happy, and I'd never been in that sort of relationship before. It was addicting, and once you're in, it's too easy to keep sprinting until you look back and wonder how everything got so out of hand."

"What got out of hand?" Oliver tilted his head.

"We started sleeping together." She squeezed her eyes shut. "And it wasn't until after that, that I found out his mother didn't approve and was secretly setting him up on dates with girls that would be better for their family."

Oliver cursed and squeezed Brittany's hand. "Ah, so she's a lovely person."

"Right?" Her hand shaking in his, she licked her dry lips as the smell of fries permeated the air between them. Why was this so hard? "I found out about the other women and got angry. Really upset because I'd been brought up in a very different home. One where my parents told me that I needed to save myself for marriage. I—" Her voice cracked. "I gave him everything. Only to find out a year into our relationship that he'd been seeing someone else to appease his mother.

He'd physically cheated on me only once, or so he claimed. And that's when—"

Brittany's phone went off in her purse.

Was that a warning sign?

Not to tell him the rest.

She ignored it.

Oliver nodded. "That's when, what?"

"Well—" Her phone went off again. Seriously? Who was calling her? "That's when—"

Another ring. Three phone calls in two minutes?

"Hold on." She grabbed her cell. Three missed calls from Zoe, and one text.

> Zoe: *Emergency headed to Mercy Hospital with Everlee. Miscarrying.*

"Oh, God." Brittany shot to her feet. "Everlee, she's… she's pregnant? She might have miscarried. They're on their way here!"

It was too close to home.

Everlee was pregnant?

Was that why she'd been so tired?

No, no, no. Don't let her lose the baby.

No.

Brittany didn't even realize she was crying until Oliver pulled her into his arms, offering his strength. "They'll bring her to the Emergency Department let's head over and meet them. And, Brittany?"

"Yeah?" She swiped her wet cheeks.

He leaned in and brushed a warm kiss across her mouth. "I'll do everything I can, but we both know that I'm not God."

"I know." She choked out a sob and gripped his hand as they half ran out of the cafe and into a waiting elevator. "What do I do? What can I do?"

The elevator stopped three levels down. Oliver didn't even look at her, just said under his breath, "Pray."

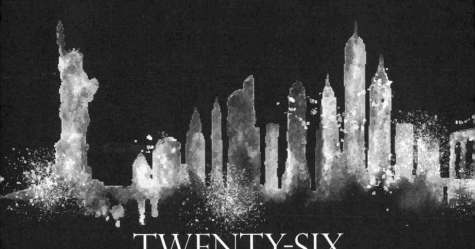

TWENTY-SIX

The ambulance had been quick.

The paramedics were strong and capable.

Physically, they were doing everything they could.

But Everlee felt numb inside.

Numb because she felt as if she were losing the last part of what held her and Frederick together.

She wanted her baby.

She wanted this child.

Tears fell until they suddenly stopped, suspending her in this state of limbo and disbelief as they pulled her out of the ambulance and rolled her into the emergency room.

Zoe and Dane were there, and both rushed toward them. "Everlee!" Zoe's loud voice carried over the chatter from the paramedics as they checked her in.

Could they go any faster?

"She could be miscarrying!" Dane said in a thunderous voice to the waiting staff. "Get her back there and to a doctor, now!"

The paramedic holding the IV bag next to Everlee jumped a foot and paled all at once.

"I've got this." A man with a calm demeanor rushed toward them. "Everlee, I'm Dr. Oliver Desmond. Can you tell me your symptoms?" Paramedics and a nurse rolled her into a private room; her group of friends followed.

"Brittany?" She sobbed.

"Oh, Everlee!" Brittany rushed to her side, and Zoe finally freed herself from Dane to do the same. "It's going to be okay."

No. Nothing would be okay again.

She'd been stressed tonight.

She'd done everything for Frederick.

And he'd raped her.

He'd killed their baby.

This was his fault.

All his fault.

Everlee shook her head violently. "No, no. He did this. He did this!"

Dr. Desmond cleared his throat. "Ladies, I need to treat your friend. I can't do that with you hovering around her. Let me do my job so I can try to save this baby."

Another doctor walked in. "Everlee, I'm Dr. Byrne, I'm—"

"I've got it, Byrne," interrupted Dr. Desmond.

The other doctor frowned in confusion. "Did someone call in a surgical consult? Never mind." He rolled his eyes as if this was normal. "Keep me informed."

"Do you do that often?" Brittany asked. "Just take over other doctors' jobs."

"Actually, no." Dr. Desmond shook his head. "But this is important." He locked eyes with Everlee. "The paramedics who treated you said you were experiencing some sharp cramping and that you saw blood."

Everlee felt like her soul was suspended from her body as she watched everything taking place. Not really participating, just waiting to hear the news she already knew was true.

Hope had died right along with the baby, hadn't it?

"Yes." She found her frail voice, hating how scared she sounded. "I think I'm around six or seven weeks along, I hadn't made an appointment yet for the doctor... I made dinner." Her voice cracked. "I made dinner for my h-husband." As she talked, Dr. Desmond put on gloves and pulled out the stirrups, urging her legs into them while Dane excused himself to get coffee. "And I was..." She squeezed her eyes shut as fresh tears finally made their way down her face. "He doesn't want kids. I just wanted one nice meal with him where we could laugh and love each other like it used to be."

"Oh, honey." Brittany grabbed her hand and squeezed it, holding tightly while Zoe did the same with her other.

"I knew he'd be angry, but I just wanted one last dinner." Why couldn't she stop saying that?

One last dinner.

One last moment.

One last reason to think he still loved her.

That he always had.

"Everlee..." Dr. Desmond's voice was gentle. "I'm going to examine you. Can you tell me what happened first? So I know what we're dealing with here. Did he push you? Did you fall?"

"I wish," she found herself saying, and then she gasped as her stomach cramped again. It was happening. This was happening. "I wish it was that evident. That I could say, 'here's my bruise. Look, I'm bleeding.' God, I'm bleeding!" Her voice shook. "But they're all inside, all of them, every blow, they're on the inside. And I'm so tired. So tired." Another cramp followed by the feeling of more warm liquid trickling down her legs that she knew was blood. "He ate." Her lower lip quivered. "And then he took off my dress. And I didn't say no because you don't say no to your husband. I don't say no to my husband even when it hurts, or when he's drunk. Even when I know he's most likely cheating. So, I stood there and closed my eyes, and I thought about my baby and the life I would have with him or her. I let him use me because I knew that I had something else to live for. And now, I'm losing my baby, and it's his fault. He was rough. He's always rough. And I didn't want it, and... God, why am I so weak? Why?" She sobbed against Brittany, while Zoe rubbed her arm.

"He's the weak one," Dr. Desmond said in a strong voice. "And I don't care if you're married for twenty years, a man never forces himself on a woman." There was movement, and then he said, "I'm going to do a pelvic exam right now and order an ultrasound. I need a nurse in here in order to proceed, though. Do you want your friends to stay?"

"Yes." Everlee sniffed, stared at the white pillow on her side, at Brittany's worried expression, focusing on the pat, pat, pat of Zoe's hand.

Seconds later, a nurse walked in.

And then pain.

Pain because she knew that the doctor was trying his best to be gentle. Pain because Frederick was probably somewhere partying right now while she was in the depths of Hell.

Pain that she'd given her soul to a man who would rather party with models than have a child.

"All right." Dr. Desmond pulled off his gloves. She was afraid to look, to see all the blood she knew was there. "Everlee, it looks like you're having a miscarriage, but I want to be sure. The ultrasound machine should be here in about ten minutes."

"Doctor?" She had to know. "Is it because of the sex? Did that cause the miscarriage?"

"No." His handsome face relaxed. "We can't explain why these things happen. Sometimes, the fetus just doesn't attach properly. Everlee, the reason doesn't matter. Knowing won't make this easier. I don't want you walking out of this hospital thinking that you did anything wrong. If you truly are miscarrying, then we'll discuss options. Until then, I'd like to see the ultrasound."

"Okay," she whispered. Her teeth started to chatter as Brittany rocked her back and forth. "Okay."

"Are you thirsty?" Zoe asked. "Hungry? I can get you something."

"Dane." She sighed. "Can you have Dane text Frederick?" The girls both fell silent.

"I want him to know." Her voice strengthened. Let him know he was a murderer. Let him know that she would never forgive him even if it wasn't his fault because all of the pent-up anger and sadness had suddenly clicked the minute she'd started to bleed. "He needs to know."

TWENTY-SEVEN

Everlee wanted him to text Frederick.

And Dane wanted to strangle the man and then throw him into oncoming traffic. If Dane texted him, the guy wouldn't show. He had no moral compass. To him, being married was like being in prison.

He'd said as much the night before at the club, right after Dane had given him a warning for biting a girl's neck and drawing blood.

He was getting more and more violent with the women, needing more and more of their attention and time. He would snap, and soon. Besides, Dane knew that Frederick had demons that needed to be fed—and well.

Monsters recognized monsters, but there were always different types, weren't there? Frederick's was crazed. Dane's was controlled, solely focused on one thing. Justice.

Dane drove the fifteen minutes to the club, and one of his many bouncers opened the door. "Evening, Dane. Everything all right?"

"Oh, it will be." He patted Mario on the back and walked through a haze of music, smoke, and dancing people.

It was easy to spot Frederick. He was always in the same place, the only thing that changed were the women he wanted around him.

Bastard.

"Dane!" Frederick held his arms open wide and offered a sloppy, drunken grin. "You here to party? Have a drink with us!"

Us? Did he mean the women Dane paid to pretend they actually enjoyed Frederick's company? Idiot.

And then Dane's gaze fell on her.

A face he knew too well.

A girl he'd helped save.

"You're underage," he snapped, crossing his arms. "Why are you in here?"

"Frederick was supposed to take me around, but we only went three places before stopping here." She was slouched over, hugging herself, too young and beautiful to be surrounded by all this garbage, by a darkness that would swallow her whole and make no apologies about sucking her soul dry. "He's also my ride."

"He's drunk," Dane pointed out, and right on cue, Frederick tried kissing the neck of the woman hanging on him while the other whispered in his ear.

"I know." She stood, arms still crossed, beautiful hair hanging down over her right shoulder. She looked just like her mom, not that he would tell her that. Just another secret on top of other secrets, right? "But I just started booking campaigns. I haven't gotten paid yet, and if I ask my uncle for more money, he's going to kill me." Tears filled her eyes.

And Dane knew why.

He knew more than she realized.

With a sigh, he pointed his finger. "You see that man at the door?"

She nodded.

"That's Mario. He's one of my bouncers, and he also drives me around when I need it. He's going to take you back to the model apartments and make sure you make it up safely."

"How can I trust you?" She narrowed her eyes. "How can I trust anyone?"

He tilted his head. "I'm very good friends with the women you look up to, one being Brittany. In fact, I was just with them."

She didn't look convinced.

"Fine, give me two seconds." He quickly dialed the police chief. "Yeah, I need a blue at the new club, nothing serious, just an escort."

Her eyes were wide. "A police escort?"

"Well, I could tell I was getting nowhere with the whole he's safe story." He flashed her a grin and looked over her shoulder just in time to see Frederick try to stand.

"Hey." Frederick reached for her and stumbled forward. "Don't go, we were just starting to have fun."

The guy smelled like he'd taken a bath in rum and then set himself on fire in the beer aisle.

"Frederick." Dane stood between the drunk and the girl. "You've had a lot to drink, and your wife is currently in the hospital."

"Wife?" one of the girls on his lap repeated. "Wait, you said you were divorced."

Frederick glared at Dane.

"Did you not hear what I said?" Dane gritted his teeth. "Your wife is in the hospital!"

Frederick snorted and lifted his glass to his lips. "Probably drank too much or went in for a stomach virus. She's a hypochondriac!"

"I'm stunned you can even say a word that big without stumbling all over yourself. You're drunk, Frederick. Sober up, then go see her, she needs you."

"I'm sober." He swayed on his feet. "Besides, she's got friends for that. Life's too short…" He lifted his glass into the air while the paid women cheered. Was he really that clueless? They had been paid to smile at him. Compensated to make him think he was important. Smokescreens. Frederick tried walking in a straight line. "See? Sober!"

Yeah, so sober that Dane could push him over with his pinky finger.

He motioned to Mario, who made his way over. "Get him home and sobered up once Miss Underage is safely in her apartment." A cop walked in the door. "And there's your police escort, so she trusts us not to kill her then bury the body."

The young girl smiled.

Dane, however, did not.

Because death was never funny.

And he'd dealt his fair share of it, hadn't he?

"Go." He nodded to the girl. She was just starting to walk away when Dane stopped her and whispered, "Who's your agent?"

"Marnie." She beamed. "She was one of my first go-sees, and we just clicked. I've been working with her and Frederick the most."

And just like that, another piece of the puzzle that he didn't even realize he needed, clicked firmly into place. "Be careful. In fact, give me your phone."

She hesitated, chewing her lower lip before handing it over. "If you're ever in trouble or scared or need me to take care of someone or something, dial this number. My name's Dane. You can ask the nice police officer. I'm safe." Complete, bald-faced lie. He wasn't safe, but to her, he would be a knight in freaking shining armor.

Because he knew exactly who she was.

Even if she didn't.

She walked off, and all he kept thinking about was the day he'd held her in his arms and done the hardest thing he would ever have to do.

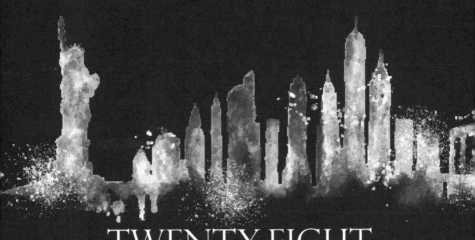

TWENTY-EIGHT

Zoe gripped her phone in her hand as another text from Dane came in. He was returning to the hospital.

Without Frederick.

The results from the ultrasound had come back, and they weren't good.

Everlee cried for a solid hour in both Zoe's and Brittany's arms after the doctor had told her what to expect. She chose to get discharged and handle everything at home.

Brave woman.

In her friend's shoes, Zoe wouldn't have wanted to be anywhere near Frederick.

And that was the other thing she couldn't shake. From the outside looking in, everything had seemed perfect.

But it was all a lie.

And she felt horrible that she hadn't seen even one clue. Was she so wrapped up in her own success and need to prove herself that she hadn't noticed how much her friend was hurting?

She let out a shudder and checked her phone again as if it would magically ring or show another text from Dane.

She was doing exactly what she'd sworn to never do: rely on the monster and fight tooth and nail to see the man beneath it all.

How had he stayed celibate all this time?

Furthermore, what was it about her that he wanted? Really? She wasn't stupid enough to believe that he loved her that irrevocably. That wasn't him, not at all.

She glanced up from her phone as Dane strutted down the hospital corridor toward her, his eyes never once leaving hers.

Nurses stared.

They couldn't help it, could they?

In fact, everywhere he went, people stared, women flirted, men wanted to know his secret. And she always thought to herself, *you don't want to know. You really don't.*

Because he'd built his empire on life and death.

"Any news?" He braced Zoe with both hands. When had he ever been like this with her?

She'd suppressed so much of their relationship. Angry at him, mad at Danica, afraid.

Terrified was more like it.

"Zoe?" He tipped her chin. "Talk to me, sweetheart."

"Um…" Tears filled her eyes. "The baby… the baby isn't there anymore." She couldn't bring herself to call it a fetus. Everlee had had a baby inside her, and now it was gone.

Dead.

She swayed a bit in Dane's arms before he grabbed her, holding her close to his chest while he rested his chin on her head. "I'm so sorry."

"It just…" There it was, the darkness, the secrets they shared, the things she shoved away because it was too painful to think about them. "It just reminded me of her."

Dane stilled.

Zoe was almost afraid to keep talking about it. Danica had gotten pregnant and had lost her baby early on, her child with Jauq—at least that's what Zoe had been told. Things were different then.

"I can't do this." Danica rocked back and forth, hugging her pillow. "You don't even know what he's been doing—what they make him do. And he just lets them! Because money trumps everything!"

Maybe Danica was delirious? Zoe reached for her. "What are you talking about?"

"They're bad people. All of them. I'm going to take them down." Her eyes were fierce, full of pain. "I already have some evidence."

"Maybe you should rest." Zoe sat on the bed and pulled her friend in for a hug. "You're exhausted."

"Yeah." Danica yawned and then laid her head down on the pillow and cried.

Dane saved her by letting out a gruff sigh. "I know, part of me thinks that's what sent her into the depression. But she was doing better, so much better."

"She was sad, Dane."

His grip on Zoe tightened. "She was a fighter, though. You know that. She would have fought."

It was Zoe's turn to comfort him as she held him tight and started rubbing slow circles on his back.

"Why?" Dane asked a minute later. "Can you just tell me why?"

"Why?" Zoe repeated. "What do you mean, why?"

"You didn't walk, you ran from this. From us. I want to know why. I deserve to know."

Zoe squeezed her eyes shut as the conversation between her and Danica played in her head. She'd made a promise to her friend not to run when Dane gave her everything.

But it was too much.

"We fought every day."

"You're provocative. Next."

A touch of a smile formed on his lips as they stared one another down, and then he grabbed her hand and walked her into a waiting room, sitting side by side while the news flashed a picture of Ronan in all his glory leaving a restaurant with his mom.

Zoe almost rolled her eyes. He and his mom rarely got along. Publicity stunt. Then again, she knew he had his reasons, just like he had his reasons for not staying with Brittany.

She'd been so envious of them when they were together, and then everything had just shattered for Brittany. The only person you could count on was yourself. Hadn't she learned that by now?

"Zoe?"

She sighed and leaned forward, resting her elbows on her black leather leggings. "Because you will always love yourself and the power you wield over this city, more than you'll ever love me—"

"That's not—"

"And because the day I came to you for help, you didn't just go to the police, you killed him with your bare hands while I watched and it was just one trauma after another." Her voice shook. "What did you think I was going to do? Run into your arms with thankfulness? You killed a human, Dane, in front of me. You stabbed him, and then told me I had to share the burden of keeping it a secret. That I had to lie in front of..." She lowered her voice as tears filled her eyes. "I lied for you. I lied for us. I wanted you to save me. I didn't want you to damn me in the process! I held onto that for years and when she died it was too much to handle."

Dane was silent, and then he clenched his jaw. "I would kill him again and again and again and relish his screams if I knew I was keeping you safe. Don't you get it? I don't matter. You *do*. You, Zoe, matter. I wouldn't be able to live with myself if I knew that I could have stopped him and didn't just because you wanted justice to take care of the unjust. You want to know why I did it? Why I killed him and framed his brother? Why I forced you to help me?"

She shook her head as dread filled her stomach.

"Because I knew the only way for it to look real was to have your horrified expression in court, telling the story I spun. You're too strong, Zoe. So, yes, I broke you. On purpose. Because that was the only way I could get you to lie to the police."

"Y-you!" She started to shake and stood, then paced in front of him. "I puked three times in that room! Three times! My reaction was so violent, and I got so dehydrated that they almost had to hospitalize me. And now you admit that you did it on purpose? That it could have been avoided?"

Dane's expression darkened. "When you ask for my help, you get it. You don't get to dictate *how* I help you. He was sick, a criminal, and his brother was no better. You helped me take them off the streets. You shouldn't feel guilty about it; that's my burden. Yours is in trusting a crooked agent who told you that you were walking into a safe situation when all she meant to do was cause a viral publicity stunt that would have ruined your career before it even took off."

He had a point.

Not that she wanted to admit it out loud.

She'd been completely traumatized.

Hurt.

And betrayed. So betrayed. Because he'd promised to save her, and the image that she'd always had of him, the pedestal she'd put him on, had shattered in front of her eyes the day she realized that he wasn't her prince.

He was a monster.

She'd fallen in love with the bad guy.

And the thought terrified her.

The blood on his hands terrified her.

He terrified her.

"Zoe." Dane reached for her hands. "I will never apologize for keeping you in this world, for using every ounce of power and money I have to make sure that you succeed. I won't apologize for loving you beyond all reason. Don't ask me to. I'd rather you slit my throat."

She flinched. "Overkill, Dane."

He squeezed her hand and then flipped it over and pressed her palm to his chest. "The only reason I think this still exists, still beats in my body, is because I have you to ground me. You matter. You will always matter."

"Love isn't control, Dane."

"It's the only way I know how to love," he said quickly. "All or nothing. There is no in between. That's not life, and that's not how people should love, with only part of their souls or just when it's easy and pretty. Love is ugly, it's painful, it's full of sorrow, long days, terror-filled nights. Love asks for everything and nothing all at once. I love the only way a person should love. With every part of me that's tethered to this universe."

Zoe could feel his warmth through his shirt, could count the beats of his heart, and still, she wasn't sure if she could trust him. Didn't know if she could trust herself with him. He was the sort of man that would ask for every single part of her. She knew the risks.

She also knew she was safer without him—her heart, especially.

"It's late." She started to shake. "We should go back... home."

It was an olive branch, the only thing she really had as she held out her hand to him.

Dane took it and then kissed her fingertips. "Whatever you need."

She tilted her head at his blank expression. It was so easy for him to confess his love and then pull the mask over his features. In that moment, she wondered if there was more humanity in him than he claimed. Because for a second, it almost looked like he was hurt.

TWENTY-NINE

It was nearing midnight.

Everlee had wanted to go home, and the last thing that Brittany wanted to do was leave her friend, but Everlee had wanted to process things. She claimed she was fine, even though her face said she might not ever be okay again.

And then something shifted in the air as Everlee shot a determined look at both Brittany and Zoe before she got into the waiting car that Dane had called.

Brittany knew that look well.

She'd worn the exact same one the last time she'd been a patient at this hospital. It was the look of a woman changed, but someone who refused to let it alter who she was and what she fought for.

Pain stabbed Brittany in the chest as she took a step toward Everlee. She'd even opened her mouth, ready to confess it all, prepared to tell her that she understood loss, could empathize with the feeling of having something that's yours, only to have it taken away.

It had been Brittany's choice.

It wasn't Everlee's.

What a cruel, cruel world.

Zoe turned to Brittany. "I'll see you at the shoot on Friday?"

Brittany had almost completely forgotten about the shoot with Ronan. Great, just one more thing she had to explain to Oliver. She felt like the weight of the world was on her shoulders, maybe because between caring for her friends, Ronan, and Oliver, she felt like she was barely keeping her head above water.

"Yeah." She found her voice. "I appreciate that."

Dane leaned in and pressed a kiss to Brittany's forehead then grabbed Zoe's hand and led her to his waiting black SUV.

The strange part was that Dane didn't let go.

He held Zoe like she was his.

Which made Brittany wonder if more was going on where they were concerned.

Her eyes narrowed as they got into the car. The doors slammed. A chilly wind picked up, and leaves danced across the pavement.

She squeezed her eyes shut and inhaled the crisp air.

And thought about that day again, one much like today. A day she would never forget.

"Dane..." Brittany burst into tears. "He's not coming, he's not coming." She couldn't stop repeating herself, and the more she heard her own scared voice, the more psychotic she felt.

He wasn't coming.

Not for her.

Not for them.

She had no one.

No peace.

Nothing.

She didn't know what to do.

She was too young.

She didn't even have enough money to support herself, let alone the baby sleeping soundly next to her while she silently cried.

The nurse made her way back in, took one look at Dane, and turned around.

"Wait!" Brittany called. "Stay. You can stay, he's a friend."

She looked at Dane and could understand the nurse's reaction. Dane may seem young, but he was no less terrifying or willing to break every law imaginable for those he loved.

At the moment, he was setting a world record for how many curse words a man could say in less than sixty seconds. The nurse's eyes widened as he paced in front of her and then ran his hands through his hair. "He didn't come?"

"No." She pointed to the note she refused to touch, the paper sitting right next to the list she and the girls all had copies of, the one that she'd given to Ronan the day she'd given him her body and heart.

The list he'd given back.

"He sent this instead."

More cursing.

Brittany squeezed her eyes shut. "Just tell me what to do."

Dane sat down on the bed and reached for her hand, engulfing it in his. "I can't tell you what to do because I'm not you. I can, however, give you options. I can give you as many as you want.

Say it, and I'll make it happen. Just stop crying. I can't handle it when any of you cry. I don't have much of my soul left, but it feels like its clawing at my chest every single time I see a tear fall." He swiped the moisture from under her eyes. "We're going to think about this logically, not emotionally, and then we're going to make a decision."

She nodded as more tears pooled.

"Have you named her?" He stared at the baby as if he'd never seen one before. His eyes lit up with wonder. "Look at all that hair."

"She takes after me." Brittany found her voice again. "And I was afraid if I named her..." She couldn't bring herself to say it.

But she wanted to claim this little girl.

She wanted to be a mother.

But she was so young. Her career was exploding. What would she do? Move home and be a single parent? She had less than a year to get ready for Spring Fashion Week. Less than a year before the catwalk.

"Britt." Dane's voice was low. "There are thousands of people that can't have children."

She knew what he was saying.

"But I'm her mom," she argued. "She'll think I abandoned her. She's used to my voice, and my heartbeat, she's used to my smell, she's—" A fitful sob erupted from her mouth while the nurse watched from her side of the room. To her credit, she didn't move, just waited for them to make a decision.

"Shhh." Dane rocked Brittany back and forth, kissing her head as he held her in his arms. "You will always be her mother. Always. Nobody can take that from you. But are you ready for what that word means right now? As a teenager?"

"No," she admitted against his chest. "I'm not."

He released her and stood, then picked up the gorgeous baby girl and rocked her much the same way he had with Brittany. "I'll take care of the adoption. I'll call my lawyer right now, get the paperwork expedited. You need to heal. I'll give you access to one of the apartments. You can stay there until you feel better."

"Really?" She couldn't believe how easy he made it all sound. Even though her heart was breaking, he was treating it like a business transaction. His demeanor was calm, his voice strong.

"Brittany, it's going to be okay."

"Why does it feel like my heart is breaking?" she asked.

The nurse chose that moment to walk up to her. She didn't say anything, just grabbed her hand and held it. And hours later, when Brittany was exhausted, when everything was finished.

When she was empty.

She looked down into her clutched hand and saw a tiny note.

All things.

Not some things.

All things work together for His good.

And inside the note was a lock of her daughter's hair.

"Hey," Oliver's voice jolted her from the memory. "Sorry, I had to finish up some paperwork. Why don't I take you home?"

Brittany nodded but couldn't move her feet.

And then the tears came.

Tears for her.

Tears for Everlee.

Tears for the daughter Brittany had never known.

Oliver pulled her into his arms immediately. "It's okay, she's going to be okay."

That only made her cry harder.

Because all she'd wanted that day in the hospital was for someone like Oliver to hold her and tell her that everything would be okay.

And as the wind picked up around their bodies, as he held her close and whispered in her ear, she wondered if God was giving her another chance to heal from the past.

"I'm sorry." She sniffled. "It's just been a really long day."

"I know." He leaned in and pressed a kiss to her cheek. "What can I do to make you feel better?"

"The hug was nice." She smiled through her tears.

"It's a well-kept secret that I'm better at hugs than surgery… shhh," he teased. "Seriously, she's going to be fine. I'll give her the number of one of our therapists if she needs someone to talk to."

Brittany let out a sigh. "Thank you for being there for her. For us."

"That's what friends do."

She frowned, tilting her head. "Friends?"

He smirked down at her. "Don't look so insulted… I've always wanted to date my friend. It's actually been a fantasy of mine to marry my best friend. Shouldn't all relationships start that way?"

She gaped. "Uh, yes?"

"Are you asking me?" He laughed and pulled her in for a side hug as they started walking through the parking lot. "I've always believed that when you date someone, you should be looking for someone who sees into your soul and doesn't run away screaming. Someone who gets you for you and doesn't judge you for having weaknesses. It should be a partnership. If you base everything off of attraction alone, you'll end up sorely disappointed in the future. Dating shouldn't be practice for breakup after breakup. So, if I didn't see something I liked in you as a friend, I can assure you I wouldn't already be planning our next date in my head and hoping that I can at least kiss you once."

Brittany almost stumbled in her heels. "Wow, those are some pretty big promises for a guy who hugs better than he cuts into human bodies."

"You got me there." Oliver stopped walking and pulled her against him. "Just in case there was any question, I'm okay with slow. In fact, I prefer it because I don't want to miss the important things just because I can't keep my hands off you."

Warmth rose from her neck and filled her face. "I'm not sure how to respond to that."

"You say something like…" He switched to a falsetto. "'Wow, Oliver, how respectful of you, you're a really great guy. You know what would be fantastic? Another date. Oh, wait, you already have something planned? Great, pick me up at eight.'"

"You would have sold me on that had you not tried to say it in a high-pitched voice." Brittany burst out laughing, tears long gone.

He winced. "Right, but I was already committed, so I had to keep going."

"Are you blushing?"

"Me? What? No. Men don't blush." He teased. "That's not a thing."

"You sure about that?"

"You should get to bed, it's late." He opened the door to his Benz. "Your carriage, my lady."

"The tips of your ears are red."

"Lies." He leaned forward and brushed a soft kiss across her lips. "Oh, look at that, now yours are, too. Guess we're even." He shut the door before she could protest.

And she smiled the entire way to her apartment.

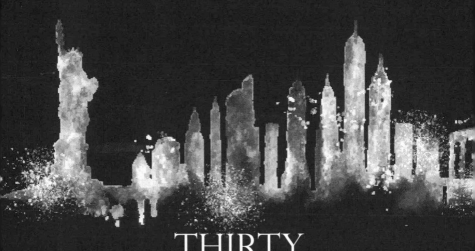

THIRTY

Everlee held the pills in her right hand, the same one that had been pressed against her belly when she found out that she was pregnant, waiting for a flutter, a kick—anything.

She had enough sleeping pills to make it fast.

What was so hard about falling asleep anyway?

You just closed your eyes, and the pain went away—physical, mental, emotional.

She'd taken a shower because even in her death, she wanted to look pretty for her funeral. Nothing but the best for Frederick's wife.

It would be her final way to hurt him.

Let the world know it was fake.

That he didn't love her.

He loved the idea of what they looked like. He liked their appearance. He enjoyed the attention.

She'd seen all the signs and had ignored them because it had been enough... until it wasn't. Until she'd experienced joy for the first time in years.

Joy that he'd still found a way to steal from her.

She blamed him because she had nobody else to blame, and blaming herself just made her shake that much harder.

The mirror didn't lie.

Her skin was pale.

Gaunt.

Her silk nightgown hung loosely on a model-thin frame that still, at her height, looked nothing like she'd let herself go, no matter what Frederick said.

The front door opened and closed.

She stared at her reflection.

Let him come in and see her.

Let him know.

She wasn't sure how long she stared at herself in the mirror, battling demon after demon, wondering if this were how it was supposed to end. Hurting him because he'd destroyed every part of her. It was like she finally realized how damaged and damaging their relationship had been. All the times he'd taken her, and she'd cried herself to sleep. All the moments she'd seen him touching other women, girls.

The signs had been there.

And she'd ignored them.

Right down to the models who hung on his every word. Young women who didn't know that it wasn't normal for a photographer to caress a girl in that way. They'd all had stars in their eyes over him, willing to do anything to get ahead.

Just like she had been.

Footsteps neared.

But it wasn't Frederick that came into the bathroom several minutes later. It was Dane.

He locked eyes with her in the mirror and very slowly approached. His warm hand closed around her wrist as he dumped the pills into the trash can he held up, and then he slowly turned her in his arms.

She searched his eyes. "I hate him."

"Good," he whispered. "Use it."

"What?"

"Don't let him destroy you, too." Dane tilted her chin up. "You can rise above this. You *will* rise above this. We all have our things, Everlee. Life doesn't promise to be fair. We aren't protected from pain just because we have money and fame. If anything, it makes you a bigger target, doesn't it? The mighty fall farther, harder. Don't let him win." He leaned down and whispered, "Choose to live."

"I don't know if I can—"

"Choose," Dane urged and gritted his teeth as he grabbed her by the shoulders. "Don't put your friends through this. Don't put me through this. God, Everlee, don't make me bury you like I did my sister."

Everlee jolted and then burst into tears. "It hurts so bad! It hurts!"

"So, let it hurt!" Dane roared. "Let it burn, Everlee. Scream, yell, destroy your apartment, throw something. Let yourself feel. Because the opposite of that isn't living—you may as well be dead."

She collapsed against him. "I know he's cheating. I know he's been cheating. I think… I've seen some pictures. I've looked at his camera when he's sleeping. They're provocative and, I don't know, I just have this horrible feeling… I saw one of an underage girl, topless. My gut tells me something's wrong. Something's been wrong for a very long time. I was just too scared to admit it."

"Is there a reason for that?"

She was quiet and then said, "Because I was one of those girls, the ones he seduced. Only I did everything in my power to win him over. And when I did, when he proposed, I thought, this is it, this is it. He loves me."

Dane sighed and kept listening.

"But it was just a business transaction to him; it didn't mean anything. I thought it meant a husband, a family, a life. He thought it meant a shiny label to add to his glowing resume: loving husband." She shook her head as anger filled her lungs, burning with each breath. "I'll send you everything."

Dane exhaled. "My hacker's going to put a Trojan program on your system that will unlock any hidden files as well as hack his passwords. It's undetectable, untraceable… we'll see what he's been doing. If he's cheating, you simply serve him divorce papers and take everything you can. If he's… if he has pictures of underage girls, if—"

"You don't have to say it," Everlee said in a cold voice. "Consider it done. I'll be home all day tomorrow."

"For what it's worth… I'm sorry." Dane's voice was heavy with sadness. "I'm sorry that you lost the baby, and I'm sorry that Frederick doesn't realize the treasure he has."

Everlee looked up into his swirling blue eyes. "And I'm sorry Zoe doesn't realize what *she* has."

His lips parted as if he wanted to say something, and then he pressed them together. "Yes, well. We can't always have what we want, can we?"

"No." Everlee suddenly felt exhausted. "We can't."

"I'll be in touch. And, Everlee?"

She looked up.

"My driver's been with Frederick for the last few hours, trying to sober him up. He'll be home soon. When he gets here, I suggest you tell him about the baby. At least then, he won't touch you."

She gasped as tears filled her eyes. That's right. She'd told everyone, hadn't she? About the way Frederick had touched her, wanted things from her even when she didn't want to give them.

"Promise me?"

"Yes." Fresh tears made their way down her cheeks.

The door to her apartment closed.

She slowly walked into the master bedroom, pulled the satin sheets over her body, and counted the turns of the fan.

Only this time, she refused to be a victim.

She refused to be afraid.

Everything hurt.

But in the end, her husband would hurt more.

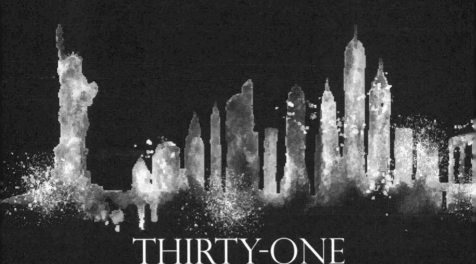

THIRTY-ONE

FALL FASHION WEEK COUNTDOWN - 8 DAYS

Grace hadn't said anything about the article, only, "thank you" and "see you at the shoot." Considering all that had happened, the week had flown by, and when Friday came along, Brittany had the dark circles under her eyes to prove it.

Everyone was getting set up.

And Brittany was holed up in her office.

Not wanting to go through with it.

Not wanting to see him, less than a day after being back at that hospital.

A knock sounded on her door.

She looked up. Zoe stood there with her hands on her hips. "Well, you look like you haven't slept in a year."

Brittany glared. "Good morning to you, too."

"How can I help?" Zoe asked, softer this time as her expression shifted from teasing to serious. "I mean it."

"I just want to get it over with. I can't be with him. I lose my head, but it's not just that, it's—" She almost said it was what they shared, it was what he had done, it was what tethered them together, a daughter he'd never known, one she had given up. "It's just a lot."

Zoe's face softened. "Well, if it makes you feel any better, I'll kick him in the presidential jewels if he does anything to make you upset."

"Oh, yeah?" Brittany smirked. "So, if he offends me, you're just going to walk right up to him and shove your—" She looked around the table. "Camel-colored Manolo as far up as it will go?"

"Basically." Zoe crossed her arms. "Got any other ideas?"

"Nope." Brittany stood. "I guess we should head out."

"Slow your roll, Mary, Queen of Scots. You look like you're ready to be beheaded." Zoe elbowed her just as loud footsteps neared.

"Grace," they said in unison.

Sure enough, Grace rounded the corner in a tuxedo jumpsuit and matching purple hat. "I need you, both of you."

"Sorry, we were just coming—"

"No, no, no nothing like that." She waved them off. "Let's go, faster, keep up." She turned on her heel. "One of the models, the new one who keeps staring at the camera when I ask her not to... Chrissy? Yes, Chrissy. She locked herself in the bathroom. Marnie can't get her out, Frederick can't get her out, Jauq—" She sighed. "You get the point. Nobody can get her to come out of the stupid bathroom, and we have a spread for Guess going on at the Loft in a few minutes. It's none of our business, but Marnie brought her here to meet with the photographers. Long story short, get her out." She turned and beamed. "And don't my girls look lovely today? All right, off you go."

"Well, then." Brittany stared up at the sign for the women's restroom. "Any ideas?"

Zoe's eyebrows shot up. "We can bribe her with food."

"She's not a dog!" Brittany said in a hushed voice.

"You do realize at that age, it would have worked for both of us? I almost sold a T-shirt from a shoot for a candy bar."

Brittany scrunched up her nose. "That's a good point."

"You think?" Zoe was already digging in her purse. "All I have are protein bars, but they have chocolate, so that should do." She knocked on the door. "Hey, Chrissy? It's Zoe and Brittany, can we come in?"

"No." The girl sniffled.

"We have chocolate," Zoe said in a chipper voice. "Please?"

"No!" She yelled this time.

Brittany chewed on her lower lip. "Can you at least tell us what's wrong so we can help you?"

"It's…" Her voice cracked. "It's… I don't know… I don't feel comfortable…"

"Look," Brittany interrupted her. "Just let us in, and we can talk. That way, it can be a private conversation. Plus, I'm sure whatever you're dealing with, we've dealt with it too. All right? Models stick together."

Zoe made a gagging motion, earning a glare from Brittany.

After a few seconds, the door clicked open.

Thank God.

Chrissy looked more beautiful than ever.

How is it possible to look that good after you've been crying?

Her hair hung straight past her shoulders. Her skin was clean from any makeup, and her eyes were wide and terrified.

Brittany and Zoe moved into the bathroom and shoved the door closed behind them.

"It's embarrassing." Chrissy hugged herself. "And it's probably nothing. I just, I don't feel comfortable anymore."

"Comfortable?" Zoe asked.

"Yeah." Chrissy's eyes squeezed shut. "I don't like taking my clothes off. I mean, they say it's normal, that they need shots like that to—"

"Whoa, whoa, whoa." Zoe held up her hands. "Who's telling you to take off your clothes?"

"Marnie." She sniffled again. "I mean, she's been a great agent so far."

Brittany shared a look with Zoe.

"She says to basically do whatever the photographers say, and Jauq was getting really handsy with me. Like he said it was an accident, but he kept touching me and then apologizing, and then he asked me to go topless for a shot. I called Marnie, and she told me not to bother her with stupid stuff, and then Jauq said that I needed to look like I'd just woken up out of bed, so he roughed up my hair and kissed me really hard. I mean, he said it was to make my lips look swollen and pouty, he said it was no—"

"Normal?" Brittany finished, anger pulsing through her body. "No. That's not normal. At least, it shouldn't be. And your agent—" She clenched her fists. "Your agent should have your back. Your agent should help protect you."

"How long is your contract?" Zoe asked out of the blue.

"Another four months. And I obviously have to earn back what she's invested in me. She said I may need to get implants, too, and—"

"No." Brittany was firm. "Let me get ahold of Roger. He represents us. Maybe we can come up with a way for him to sign you once you're out from under Marnie. At the very least, we can get the agency out of the UK to pick you up so you have more options than Marnie."

"You would do that?" Chrissy asked in a broken voice. "You don't even know me."

"Like we said." Brittany smiled. "Models stick together. Plus, we know all about Marnie and her promises. She isn't the most... respected agent in New York."

Chrissy frowned. "But didn't she discover you guys? I mean, that's why I didn't even read my contract. I just freaked out over having the same agent that found you guys."

Brittany clenched her teeth. "Yes, I guess in a way she did, but that's not really what happened. Just promise me you'll text one of us if you feel like you aren't safe or if you have questions, okay?"

Chrissy nodded, and then more tears came. "Thank you. I didn't have anyone to talk to. My parents died in a car accident a year ago yesterday. I just... I think I'm overly emotional because I miss them, too."

"Oh, honey." Brittany pulled her into her arms and hugged her tight as sadness washed over her. "I know what it's like to love someone and lose them. I'm so sorry."

Chrissy clung to her so tightly, it was hard to breathe. "Thank you. Not to sound creepy, but you're the one who got me through it. I'd talk to your stupid poster and imagine you giving me advice like you always do in your columns."

"Not creepy." She soothed. "That's why I do what I do."

"Thank you. I don't think you realize how much girls like me idolize you. Both of you."

"Maybe not me," Zoe teased.

"Please." Chrissy pulled back. "You're flawless, and you have your own fashion line. I would have killed to go to the cattle call for that one."

Zoe beamed. "Next time, just text me that you want in. It's that easy."

"What? Really?"

"Really." Zoe winked. "Now, can we please leave the smelly toilets and get you on your shoot so I can make sure Brittany doesn't puke during hers?"

"You get nervous?" Chrissy asked.

"Yeah, something like that." Brittany smiled through her very real fear of having to shoot something sexy for the magazine with Ronan. "Plus, it's an old flame. Long, boring story."

"Ohhhh, Ronan Kampbell?" Chrissy suddenly looked like a teenager again. "Is he really that handsome in real life?"

"Yup," Zoe answered for Brittany. "Sadly, his soul is dark, and demons feed on his heart every time he closes his eyes."

"Zoe!" Brittany scolded. "He's not that bad."

Zoe just shrugged. Right, this coming from the girl who was secretly in love with a crime boss.

Pot, meet kettle.

Brittany opened the door to the bathroom and nearly turned on her heel and locked it again.

Because standing directly in front of them was the man himself, in the flesh—Ronan Kampbell. "Did you guys get to the part where you gossip about celebrities and paint your toenails?"

"Holy crap!" Chrissy yelped behind them. "You're— you're—we were just talking about you!"

"Were you?" He seemed amused as he looked down at Brittany with a smug expression. He returned his attention to Chrissy. "And who might you be?"

"Huge fan," Zoe said in a bored voice. "I'm gonna go see if they're ready for you two."

"Traitor," Brittany coughed under her breath.

"Come along, tall one." Zoe grabbed Chrissy by the arm. "Let's go get you to Grace."

"Everything okay?" Ronan asked, leaning in far too close. He smelled good. Then again, he always smelled good. But something about him felt... fake. Maybe it had always been there, lingering. Perhaps she just noticed it more now because she'd been spending more time with Oliver. Whatever it was, she was thankful for it because it made it easier to protect herself.

"Oh yeah, you know, teens, emotions." She stopped herself when she realized that if she had kept her girl, she would have been close to that age.

"Hey." Ronan reached for her. "Where did your smile go?"

"I think you killed it the day you didn't come to the hospital," she blurted.

He jolted back as if she'd slapped him.

"Ronan! Brittany! Here. Now. Photo shoot. Lots of people. Come!" Grace was already grumpy.

Brittany flashed a smile and side-stepped Ronan in an effort to not fall apart all over again and say something else that would bring them back to the past.

Because that was what they did. They circled one another. Someone threw a barb, and like a time machine, the hit took them back to that hospital room.

Back to the moment where everything changed.

Where choices had been made.

Futures decided.

Hearts shattered.

"Britt—"

"Not now," she snapped as she hurried toward Grace and everyone else. She would be needed in makeup, wardrobe. At least she had a few hours before she had to face him again.

And with that thought, she reached for the phone she'd shoved into her leather pants and pulled it out.

> Brittany: *I know you're probably saving someone's life... but I miss you.*
>
> Oliver: *Actually... no... I just lost someone in the OR.*
>
> Brittany: *No! I'm so sorry! What can I do? What do you need?*
>
> Oliver: *Your text actually came at the perfect time, I was just sitting alone in my office staring at the wall, wondering where I went wrong, what I could have done differently. And praying for the teen's family.*

A teen?

Her heart broke.

> Brittany: *You aren't God. You're gifted with an incredible ability. But you can't save everyone. Even though that's where your heart is.*
>
> Oliver: *He was thirteen. Can you imagine losing your son at thirteen?*

No, but she could imagine losing her daughter hours after she'd been born. But Oliver was hurting; this wasn't about her. She couldn't make it about her.

> Brittany: *It isn't natural to bury a child. Did you do everything you could?*

Oliver: *Yes.*

Brittany: *Do you trust that there's always a reason? Always a plan?*

Oliver: *As a doctor, it's divided. Science and spirituality rarely meet in the middle, but I've seen too many things, experienced too many miracles to believe otherwise. There is always a reason. Always a plan. But that doesn't make it any easier when you have to tell someone's parents that you failed.*

Brittany: *I know. I'm at my shoot, but I'll say a prayer for you. If you want to cancel tonight...*

Oliver: *No! I'm looking forward to tonight. I need the distraction. It's not the best day of my life, and I feel selfish, I keep thinking about you and him. It's stiff competition, but I'm hoping that at least in the humor category, I have him beat since he destroyed me in the looks and power department.*

Brittany: *Not in the looks department... and power is fleeting. Remember that.*

Oliver: *Did you just call me sexy?*

Brittany: *Ha-ha, I think you're grasping there, Romeo.*

Oliver: *What was that? I'm the sexiest man alive? I should have had the cover of* People?

Brittany: *You're impossible.*

Oliver: *See? Funny. I'm funny. The funny ones always last, we have staying power, the pretty ones just end up in trouble.*

Brittany: *Amen to that.*

Oliver: *Thank you for texting me. Thank you for being you. Just. Thank you. I may have a slight crush on you, but not the type where I light candles and chant, just a normal, healthy, wow she's beautiful, and I want to kiss her endlessly crush. Hope that's okay.*

Brittany's smile was so wide, the makeup artist had to stop doing what she was doing. "Sorry."

Brittany: *Endless kissing sounds exhausting.*

Oliver: *I'll do the heavy lifting.*

Brittany: *Color me shocked.*

Oliver: *I gotta go, see you tonight?*

Brittany: *You can count on it.*

She set her phone down while her makeup artist arched his brows. "Boyfriend?"

She opened her mouth to say "yes" then stopped. Yeah, they were seeing each other, but Oliver was right, it was friendship, but one that could move into something so much more meaningful. "A friend. A really good friend." With gorgeous eyes, an insane smile, and the ability to make even the most stressful days seem perfect.

"Right." The makeup artist laughed. "I have that dopey smile on my face when I talk about my friends, too." He shook his head. "It's all right, keep your secrets. Now close so I can do your shadow."

Brittany had never been the type of person to get nervous before a shoot. She knew it was fun—or it was supposed to be, at least. But this time? The stakes were higher, and she knew the minute that she locked eyes with Ronan, she would have to pretend.

Pretend that it was okay.

Pretend that he hadn't hurt her.

Pretend that they were friends.

Grace gave her a once-over. "Stop pinching your face, you look constipated."

Well, how was that for honesty?

Brittany relaxed her face and made a solid effort to look happy and at ease as she joined Ronan on set.

There was a bed.

Panic set in.

What kind of shoot was this?

Jauq made his way toward Brittany. "The idea is to show the perfect American family. Brad and Angelina did a shoot like it years ago, and it killed. We have a few models who will act like your children. All in all, we should be done in a few hours. Where's your robe?"

She looked down at her silk dress.

Was it supposed to be a nightgown? She hadn't really been paying attention. It was a black slip dress that went down to her knees, and they'd put her hair loose around her shoulders.

Ronan was already sitting in bed. The collar of his shirt was unbuttoned as if he'd just come home from a long day at work, and all Brittany could think of was...

This should have been my life.

Her future.

Coming home to him like this.

Sharing a bed with him, laughing about something silly that their kids had done.

Family dinners.

Thanksgivings.

Christmases.

It was supposed to look just like this shoot.

But reality wasn't the same as her teenage dreams, was it?

She swallowed the sadness lodged in her throat and took a step, then another. Finally, she was standing near the bed while Ronan grabbed the newspaper in his hands and grinned at her. "Hey, wife."

She stilled.

His face softened as he reached for her. "Sorry, I didn't mean—"

"You didn't mean it? It's all just pretend?" she said through clenched teeth.

"It doesn't have to be." He lowered his voice.

"Too late." She took a few deep breaths. She thought of Oliver and, for some reason, that centered her. It took her outside of this fake, happy shoot and into reality where he was literally fighting to save lives on a daily basis. That was reality. This? This was to sell magazines. This was to pay for ad campaigns.

This was to sell an idea to the people.

And she was the person helping to do it.

Her job was to make Ronan look good.

To make the magazine look good.

That didn't mean it didn't hurt like a million knives getting shoved into her chest. Because what she always saw as her plan, obviously wasn't God's.

What did that mean, then?

And why was she suddenly haunted by him? Ronan. By a past that wanted a redo and a future that looked bright.

It felt like she was at a crossroads, and one misstep would destroy her forever.

"Brittany?" Grace snapped her fingers. "Up here, yes, I need you to look happy, can you look like you don't want to murder a US Senator in his own bed with his tie?"

Brittany forced a smile. "Yes, yes, I can do that."

"Lovely." Grace nodded. "Jauq, go."

The camera flashed even as Brittany crawled into the bed. It felt so familiar, though when she was a teenager, it had always been rushed, they were constantly trying not to get caught. It had seemed romantic at the time, very Romeo and Juliet. The older college student and teen romance.

But now? Now that she looked back, she'd always felt... dirty, like she was a secret he wasn't allowed to share with the world.

She put her hand on his chest and smiled as he leaned down and tilted her chin toward him, the newspaper in one hand like it was something they did, lie in bed on the weekend and talk about their perfect lives.

Someone gave Brittany a mug to hold while she laid her head on his shoulder.

He rubbed her hand and then grabbed a pillow and lifted it like he was going to hit her.

Jauq and Grace instructed, and they obeyed.

And soon, she forgot it was Ronan.

It was just another shoot.

Just another payday.

Just another day.

At least, until they transitioned positions.

"Lie down," Jauq instructed. "On your back, Brittany. Perfect, yes." Panic set in as she gazed up at Ronan, who stared down at her with unease. "Ronan, yes, straddle her a bit, make it playful."

Ronan moved and then shook his head. His eyes never left hers as he said, "No, I won't do that."

Brittany breathed out a sigh of relief. While Grace muttered a curse. "Just do it."

"I'm still going through divorce proceedings." Ronan shrugged. "It would look bad."

He was lying for her.

She mouthed a thank you.

He nodded and then squeezed her hand.

Why did life have to be so difficult?

Why did everything with Ronan always feel wrong?

They shot for two more hours.

And when everything was done, Brittany's body was so sore from holding poses that she wanted to take a long bubble bath.

"Good job. I think we got it." Frederick took a few shots then grinned at them.

Ronan held out his hand and pulled Brittany to her feet. "You look exhausted."

"I feel exhausted," she agreed and then crossed her arms. "Ro, do you ever feel like we just weren't meant to be?"

He froze and then lowered his gaze to hers. "Sometimes, it feels that way, like we're dancing around each other, but the universe refuses to let us touch."

She nodded. "I want you to be happy."

"What if you're what makes me happy?"

"Then we're still not right, we're unbalanced. I don't want to be your anchor, Ronan. I want to be your partner. Wanted. Past tense. But can I admit something?"

"Anything." He grabbed her hands.

"I wanted this." Tears filled her eyes. "I wanted this so desperately. I think at the time, I would have given you anything."

"You did," he whispered. "You gave it all. I was just too stupid to see it, too young, too arrogant." He bit out a curse and then kissed her fingertips. "I'm not letting you go yet."

"You let me go the day you gave me back the list."

"Because I knew." He didn't miss a beat. "I knew that the kindest thing I could do was to set you free."

"And what are you doing now?"

"Changing my mind." He lowered his head.

She backed away and gulped. "I'm saying no."

"I don't want you to."

"It's not about what you want, not now. This is about what's good for me, what's good for us, I think—" Brittany licked her dry lips. "I think I'm going to see if I can find our daughter. Just to see her, to check in on her."

He covered her mouth with his hand. "You can't just say that in public. There are voters and—"

Her smile felt sad as he lowered his hand, realizing what he'd just said. "That's why we'll never work, why we never did, Ro, because at the end of the day, your career will always mean more than anything else. And that's okay. We need more men like you in the Senate, more men leading us, those willing to sacrifice everything. But I refuse to be sacrificed."

For the first time in her life, she witnessed Ronan Kampbell give her a look of complete surrender and defeat as he whispered, "You're right."

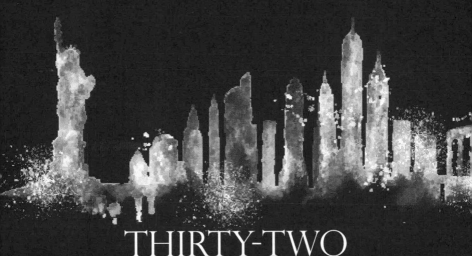

THIRTY-TWO

Dane had access to everything on Frederick's computer. It wasn't pretty, the pictures he had, the things he'd recorded without consent.

But what was worse?

The fact that Everlee had seen it all.

She'd called him bawling again, raging, begging Dane to let her approach him. He hadn't thought she'd be so bloodthirsty, and now he had to worry about her saying something to Frederick and ruining it all.

He continued digging into the past.

And nearly fell out of his chair when he came across photos from a little over a year ago. Shots of Danica.

With Frederick and Jauq.

Marnie in the background.

Roger standing to the side, giving them a look of disapproval.

It looked like they were all at a shoot. Danica was laughing, Jauq had his arm around her. It was candid, everyone appeared happy—except Roger, of course.

Marnie stood off to the side with a scowl on her face, the look directed at Roger.

Who'd taken the picture?

Dane scrolled through more.

Jauq had his hands all over Danica.

There was a video dated the night before.

Dane was almost afraid to press play.

"Danica," Jauq's voice sounded as she danced in front of him. "Stop teasing me."

Why did Frederick have this?

"Teasing you?" She did a little twirl. "I'm not teasing you. You've been teasing me for ten years. Maybe I'll just move on to someone else." Dane's stomach lurched. Jauq was at least twenty years older, which meant that when Danica was in her teens, he would have been in his mid-thirties. "You know you love me."

"I'm addicted to you," he said.

The camera moved, and then he was in front of it with her, kissing her, pulling her into his arms like he had a right to. He stripped her clothes down.

"There's more where this is coming from." He pulled out a stack of cash. "If you want in, just say the word…"

"What do I have to do? Nothing illegal, right?"

"Does it matter?" Jauq laughed against her mouth. "I know who your brother is. What he does. Besides, business is business, right? Think of it as an early retirement from that modeling career. You could have it all, you just have to trust me, trust all of us."

Danica hesitated and then wrapped her legs around him. "I'll think about it."

"You'll do it," Jauq said simply, taking her mouth in another punishing kiss.

The door to the apartment opened. Dane quickly closed the screen, and looked up as Zoe stomped in, throwing her purse onto the countertop in a huff and grabbing the glass of wine he had set out for her when she said she was headed his way.

Amazing how she never realized or even fully acknowledged how easily he'd crept back into her life. She'd gotten used to it, was comfortable with it. If he stayed over, he slept in the other room. After all, it was a gift, her place, and he wouldn't move in until she finally said yes.

At the rate they were going, he'd be eighty, but at least he'd finally get the answer he wanted. "Rough day?"

"No. Yes, I don't know." She took a small sip and then faced him. "It was the shoot for Ronan and Brittany. I know there's history, God knows I'm well-versed in past relationships." She shot him a look, and he held up his hands in surrender. "Anyway, it just seems... sadder, if that makes sense? It seems harder on Brittany, and I worry about her, that's all. Ronan broke her heart."

He'd done more than that, but that wasn't Dane's story to tell.

"You're too quiet."

"Hmm?" He tilted his head. "Am I?"

Her eyes narrowed. "What do you know that I don't know?"

Everything.

"Marry me, and you'll find out."

"Ha, good one. I can't tell if you're being honest or if it's a trick."

"Why can't it just be a proposal where I ask a question, you say yes, and then you kiss me?"

Her smile faltered. "Kisses from you lead to very bad decisions."

"So I've been told." He smirked. "By you, actually."

She nodded to his laptop. "Are you working late?"

"Something like that." He leaned back against the leather couch. "Can I ask you a question?"

"You never ask permission to do anything." She flopped down next to him. "Are you sick?"

"Only for you," he said, the reply dripping with sarcasm.

She swatted him with her hand. "Stop being cute, it annoys me."

"Maybe I like annoying you."

"I think it's our foreplay."

He agreed, noticing how her cheeks pinked, how her breathing almost stopped altogether. Oh, he had an effect on her, she just didn't like it.

Zoe cleared her throat. "What's this question?"

He turned to face her, took in her large, green eyes and flawless, coffee colored skin. "Did Jauq or Frederick ever come on to you when you first started in the industry?"

She recoiled. "No. Never. Then again, Jauq always had eyes for Danica, and as for Frederick, I think we all know how that's going to end."

"That's what I thought." Dane drummed his fingertips against his thigh. "I just wanted to be sure."

"If I said yes, would you kill them both?" she teased.

"Yes." He said it swiftly, with determination. "Then again, you know that."

Her breath hitched. "Why the question?"

"Don't worry about it." He smiled even though his head was strained with all the possibilities, all the information that was now on his computer. Maybe they weren't hiding anything. Then again, perhaps they were.

He wouldn't stop.

Not now.

Not ever.

Danica didn't.

That much he knew.

He needed to put more pressure on the players. Someone would crack, someone would be afraid enough to out someone else. Dane just hoped it would be the weakest of them all. Frederick.

Dane needed to find a slip-up somewhere. From Frederick, Jauq, anyone. The best way to catch a fish.

"Really big bait," he said to himself.

"Did you really just have a conversation with yourself in front of me?" Zoe leaned in and patted his shoulder. "I can't decide if it's creepy or endearing."

"Let's go with endearing." He gave her a wolfish grin. "Why don't I order takeout, and you can tell me all about your long day and the designs that are about to take the world by storm."

Her face lit up and then fell. "It's okay, you don't have to—"

"Actually..." He stood. "Why don't we go out and then stop by your office? You can show me your entire plan."

She gaped. "You're serious?"

"I care. Yes, I'm serious."

"But—"

"It would be a privilege to see the choices you made, the designs you created. In a week, the world is going to know you not just as a model but as a fashion icon. I'm lucky to be a small part of that."

"Now you're laying it on thick. You know you're the only reason I was even able to start this label."

"Now she says it," he whispered, lowering his head.

"Well, she's tired and cranky. She's not really thinking clearly."

"Good." He pressed his mouth to hers, cautiously, waiting for permission, searching for any sign from her or the universe that this was right. She parted her lips, and he tasted Heaven, he tasted her and him the way they were always supposed to be: together.

She wrapped her arms around his neck as he jerked her against his chest, deepening the kiss, relishing each and every second he was given with her in that moment, one that would be over too soon, lost to the evening, never to be had again.

She didn't pull back.

He did.

Her expression was more shock than anything.

"Chinese?" he rasped.

"Food," she repeated slowly. "You want to eat food and leave and…" Her eyes narrowed. "You're not…"

"I can wait for you. I want you willing, not because you're thankful or because you're tired. I want you when you can't think of anything you'd rather be doing than standing in my arms."

"Should have worked for Hallmark," she grumbled, pulling away and reaching for her purse. "And you're buying."

"Deal." He chuckled, following after her.

This was what they could have.

If she would just let it happen.

A life where they teased and kissed, where they argued over takeout and business decisions.

One day.

One day, she would see what he'd seen all along.

That they were soul mates.

With equally needy souls.

THIRTY-THREE

"Here." Oliver didn't kiss her, didn't even ask how the shoot had gone. He just opened the door to his apartment building and handed her a glass of wine then opened the portal wider for her to come in.

They'd planned on dinner out.

But after his day.

And hers.

All they wanted was to stay in.

He'd ordered Thai food and said he'd have wine, and she'd hopped into a taxi, ready to forget about the day.

"I love your place." She did a small turn in the middle of the gourmet kitchen. "Did you have a decorator come in?" It was masculine but still warm, even with all the modern touches. The entire loft was open-concept. The place couldn't have been cheap.

"No, that was ex-wife number three. She had a real eye for color." He shrugged.

She almost dropped her glass of wine. "Wait, what?"

He grinned up at her. "Got you."

"Hilarious." She was ready to throw a pillow at his face. "I think my heart just stopped."

"Never been married, no weird stalkers other than Marissa from third grade, but I think she just wanted a friend who wasn't imaginary."

"Poor Marissa."

"I shared my Cheetos every Friday. She did okay." He laughed as he opened the takeout boxes and spread everything onto black plates. "So, what about you? Any skeletons that Google doesn't know about?"

Brittany froze.

It wasn't like Oliver could find out unless she said something, or unless Roger or Dane said something, but now? She just didn't want to talk about the past, she'd just spent the past few hours reliving what she thought was her future.

No more.

"Nothing you need to worry about," Brittany settled on. "Do you work tomorrow?"

"No, actually, I'm off tomorrow, and I think you should take the day off, too. We could explore the city… go do that cooking class we missed on our first date. What do you say?"

"I say…" She walked over to him and sat on one of the leather barstools, tugging her black Armani dress toward her knees. "After today, that sounds incredible."

His smile was so adorable and sexy all at once, white teeth and a small dimple at the corner of his mouth as his hair fell over his forehead. "Mmm, so I just have to ask you all the hard questions when you're mentally exhausted? Is that the secret?"

"Well, that and I'm starving."

"Must. Feed. Models." He chuckled at his joke. "And just in case you don't get full enough, I also bought garlic bread. Before you say no,"—he held up his hands—"I think the only way for a person to truly feel full is to carbo-load. You got all your veggies and meat here, rice noodles." He made a face. "But garlic bread? It saves lives, you know. Just like me. Lifesaver. Right here."

Brittany burst out laughing. "So, you and garlic bread, same thing?"

"Basically." He nodded seriously. "Only I think I taste better. Shhhh, don't hurt the bread's feelings."

She crossed her arms. "Do you?"

"Do I what?" He was back to putting food on the plates.

Brittany leaned in with an amused smile. "Taste better?"

His eyes narrowed on her mouth. "I'm all for an experiment." He held up a plate between them. "But first, you need to eat. I don't want you passing out mid-experiment and embarrassing us both."

She moaned. "That smells amazing."

"Geez, I give you food, and you moan like that? It's like you just showed me your kryptonite."

"Good Thai food always works." She held out her hand, and he placed a fork in it, and they both dug in.

No cameras.

No awkwardness.

No wondering if people were taking pictures or speculating about what it meant that they were sharing a meal together.

Just. Them.

"This broccoli is amazing." She pointed at her plate. "Did you get any?"

"Nope." He swiped a piece from her plate and chewed.

Stunned, she wondered if he was always this comfortable in his own skin, unapologetically... him.

"What?"

She shook her head and smiled down at her food. "Nothing, I just like you."

"Should I change my Facebook status yet or...?"

"Don't get ahead of yourself."

He cursed just as the oven dinged.

She watched him open the oven, move around the kitchen, and it was eerily... perfect. Today? Lying in bed during that photo shoot with Ronan? That was what she had seen and wanted when she was a teen; that was what her expectations had been.

But she suddenly realized that this—talking and being open and hovering over takeout—felt more normal than anything.

Normal and exciting, all at once.

A grin spread across her face. Maybe she was getting a second chance. Another opportunity to do the right thing.

Which just made her that much more resolute.

She needed to find her girl.

She needed to close a chapter in her life so another could finally, after sixteen years, open again.

THIRTY-FOUR

NEW YORK FASHION WEEK COUNTDOWN - 7 DAYS

Brittany woke up the next morning with two things on her mind: her daughter, and her date with Oliver.

With a deep breath, she dialed Dane's number and waited for him to answer.

Three rings in and his deep voice came over the receiver. "This is Dane."

"Hey." She licked her dry lips. "Are you alone?"

He sounded as if he were walking, and then a door closed. "I am now."

She breathed a sigh of relief. "Okay, this is hard, so I'm just going to say it and get it off my chest." Another deep breath. She could do it, she could say it out loud. Couldn't she? "Do you... do you have any records of where you sent my daughter? Or who adopted her? I just... I don't even need to meet her, just seeing a picture of her with her family, knowing that she's thriving would be enough. I—"

"Brittany."

She squeezed her eyes shut. "Yeah?"

"I'll be at your apartment in five minutes."

The phone line went dead. Brittany stared at it then dropped the cell onto her bed and quickly got dressed and made herself look presentable. Grace was only too happy to let her take a day off, especially since she remembered how good-looking Oliver had been. And Roger? Well, he seemed ready to break out into song and dance when she said they were going to stop by that night for a cooking lesson and a date.

She only hoped that the guy didn't go overboard since he was known for doing that. It would also be a great opportunity for Roger and her to talk about Chrissy and the whole Marnie situation.

She knew there was a very serious no-poaching rule when it came to the models and agents, but Marnie was just the worst. Surely, there was a way for Chrissy to get out of her contract. Or somehow Roger could snatch her up.

The only problem would be if Chrissy were booking a lot of shoots, Marnie would want that money, and she'd want to, yet again, have the notoriety of discovering the next best thing.

Brittany slammed a throw pillow onto the bed just as a knock sounded at the door. It took too long for her legs to carry her down the hall, for her hands to turn the doorknob. Her heart hammered against her chest as she jerked the door open.

Dane was standing there in black Nike joggers.

She did an actual double-take and frowned. "Are you wearing sneakers?"

"I was headed to the gym." His mouth curved into a smile. "I know, it's like seeing an animal outside the zoo."

"Or your first-grade teacher at the bar taking tequila shots," she added, crossing her arms.

"Hilarious." His white T-shirt looked so foreign on his body that she was having trouble focusing. In theory, it made sense that he had a life outside of controlling every possible situation in his universe, but he looked so relaxed.

He placed the large cardboard box he held on the table.

"So, how are things with Zoe?" she asked, trying to break the ice again.

He stilled and then turned his intense gaze to her. "We're not here in this moment to discuss Zoe."

"No." Tears welled in her eyes. "I'm afraid to ask what's in the box."

His face softened. "Don't be, Britt. And you don't even have to look if you don't want. Tell you what, I'll leave that box full of things on this table for one full day. When you get back tonight, decide what you want to do. Open or keep it closed."

"That easy, huh?" she teased, wiping away a stray tear.

Dane leaned back against the wall and crossed his arms. "Facing our truth is never easy, but you don't grow when you stand still, Britt," He pushed off the wall and settled a hand on her shoulder. "You sink."

"When did you get so wise?" She laid her hand over his and squeezed.

"I've always been the wise one. It's you girls who drive a man to day drink. I can't make this decision for you, but

I can give you the opportunity to choose. To see her life for what it is. Beautiful. To close a chapter that has maybe stayed open for too long, allowing that wound to fester over and over again. I don't know, Britt, I think that too often we try to keep things black and white and completely forget about the gray areas."

"You…" She let go of his hand. "You exist in that gray area."

"Oh, I have a flat-screen TV and hot tub in that gray area." He winked. "No pressure either way. And have fun with Oliver today."

She froze. "How did you know?"

He just grinned and shrugged. "I know everything."

"I see Zoe hasn't had a chance to rein in that arrogance yet."

He chuckled. "Probably because she secretly likes it."

He sauntered to the front door and looked over his shoulder at her, then at the box and back to her. "If you do decide to open it, I know you'll have questions. I won't have all the answers because, sometimes, life just happens, and even when we try to control every minute detail, the world still spins however it wants."

With that cryptic comment, he shut the door behind him.

Brittany turned to face the box. It seemed so plain, so nonthreatening, and yet she knew that answers were inside. In that cardboard container, she would find pictures of her girl's face. Inside, she would discover memories she hadn't been a part of. A life that, now, she would have sacrificed anything to share.

With shaky movements, she walked up to the counter and held the box lid between her hands.

She had all day to decide.

Why was it suddenly so difficult?

She dropped her clammy hands to her sides and walked away from the box. A knock sounded at the door.

Tonight, she promised herself.

Tonight.

She opened the door to see a handsome looking Oliver dressed in skinny jeans, combat boots, and a V-neck vintage tee that looked incredible on him.

"You know…" She eyed him up and down. "There's just something about the way a guy leans against a doorframe."

"They teach it to us in first grade. It's the only way to make friends. Learn the doorframe move, and you're in. Fall on your face, and well… it's the lunch table facing the bathrooms where you can time people's flushes."

Brittany laughed. "Wow, both descriptive and a bit personal. I'm guessing you didn't master it until later on in life."

He grinned down at her. "Late bloomer."

"I see."

They stared at each other for a few more seconds, smiles wide before she cleared her throat and closed the door.

Body heat radiated off Oliver and seemed to reach out to her. It didn't help that he smelled warm and spicy. His eyes lit up when she beamed at him and then grabbed his hand.

His palm pressed against hers.

And he held tight.

As if he were afraid that she would slip away if he loosened his grip. Brittany decided she liked it.

And when they walked out into the sun, she took a deep breath and grinned down at her red Pierre Hardy boots.

She'd gone for more of a weekend look with her blue-and-white-striped Ralph Lauren peasant dress and low ponytail. Something about it felt playful. Or maybe it was just Oliver and the fact that she wasn't working on a Saturday when she typically would. She walked toward his car parked on the street, but he twirled her around and kissed her cheek, managing to wrap his arm around her as they walked.

"No driving this morning."

"I like it." She patted his chest. "Plus, it's beautiful out."

"I call it pre-autumn in New York, nothing like it." He grinned down at her. "I figured since you planned the evening, I could plan the late morning and afternoon."

"Does your plan involve coffee?"

He gave her a serious look. "All plans should involve coffee. I'm not a monster."

"Good." She liked the way he felt next to her, the easy steps they fell into like they were already in sync.

"Favorite color?" he quizzed.

"Blue," she answered quickly. "Yours?"

He stared down into her eyes and gave his head a shake. "I think you just converted me."

She had blue eyes.

Was he talking about her?

"Favorite food?" he asked next.

"What is this? Twenty questions?"

"Oh, no. It's going to be about a hundred, but don't worry, you get a prize in the end."

"What's my prize?"

"A really good kiss, the best of your life."

"You know you make a lot of big promises," she pointed out, loving the teasing side of him, the easiness of it. She'd never had that with Ronan, and she hated that she was comparing, but he was all she had to compare to!

"And I fully intend to follow through." He kissed her forehead as they continued to walk. "So? Your favorite food?"

She licked her lips and grinned up at him. "Garlic bread."

"Is it wrong that I want to give you your prize after two questions?"

"God forbid you call me a cheater." She elbowed him.

"Ouch. Okay, fine." He laughed. "Favorite book?"

She almost stumbled when the answer came to her head. "Um… the Bible."

He gave her a curious look. "I had you for more of a Darcy sort of girl. Okay, so the Bible. Can I ask why?"

"When I started modeling, I was in over my head. It was the only thing that sustained me, that made me feel peace, safety." Brittany shrugged. "Plus, it reminded me of home, of my faith, of family. It kept me grounded and focused—not that I'm perfect, not by a long shot."

"Well, that was a pretty perfect answer. My Grandpa was a pastor, I think he would have called that a Sunday School answer, but I'll give it to you because I can hear the conviction in your voice, and I like that you chose the Bible. What I like even more is that you were honest—and you meant it."

Her lips parted in shock as they rounded the corner and he led her into a tiny bakery that smelled so delicious, her mouth started watering. "What is this place?"

"Heaven," he said simply. "Remember? Carbo-loading." He pointed to a flaky croissant, and Brittany's stomach immediately growled. "We'll take two of those and two of those." He pointed to a chocolate éclair. "And five maple bars."

Brittany made a choking noise. "I hope you don't expect me to eat all of that!"

"Oh, I don't share their baked goods. You have to make your own order. I keep a very vigorous workout routine so I can come here and splurge."

The guy behind the register laughed. "It's true, he's here every Saturday."

Brittany's stomach warmed.

Her heart thudded wildly against her chest.

He hadn't just taken her to a bakery.

He was showing her his life.

His spots.

His routine.

The barricade around her heart started to shake with the need to fall, to expose her entire self to him and see if he'd accept her just as she was.

Flaws and all.

"Your order?" the high school kid asked.

"Um, right. A maple bar and… how about a croissant?" She looked to her right. Oliver was staring at her mouth. "What? Do I have something here?"

"No." He held out his credit card to the kid without looking away. "It's just, I've never heard anyone say croissant so sexily. I'm admittedly jealous. You don't say my name like that."

"I'll practice," she joked.

"Wow, you're just earning all the points today, aren't you? Must want that prize."

She found herself nodding and then wrapping an arm around him. "Maybe because I know the prize doesn't come with conditions. You aren't that sort of guy."

"No." He sobered. "I'm not. And for the record, I meant it when I said a kiss. Nothing beyond that. Because, honestly, I don't think I would be able to handle anything more without losing my head and begging you for it, and that just puts you in a bad position where you have to reject me and... bam, friendship over."

Brittany bit down on her lower lip. "Baby steps, Oliver."

"Baby steps," he agreed with a wink and handed over her pastries.

As far as dates went, this one was topping her list. They went from bakery to bakery. Apparently, Oliver liked to eat, and when they were done doing that, they went to the MET.

Something she hadn't done in years; it seemed she was always too busy doing other things.

They had two hours before they had to meet Roger and Grace for the cooking class and dinner.

"So." Oliver twirled her with his hand and smiled down at her. "We've established almost all of your favorites, including your favorite person." He pointed at himself.

"But,"—Brittany held up her finger—"only because—"

"Chocolate bananas. Which I agreed was completely fair this early on in our frelationship."

"Frelationship?" She laughed so hard her throat started to hurt. "You gonna explain that one?"

"That," he said and grinned, "is self-explanatory. Friendship plus relationship equals frelationship."

"And, somehow, I don't think that would pass during a Scrabble match."

"I could get away with it. I'm extremely charming."

"Mmm." They swung their arms as they walked through the park. "I've seen my fair share of charm. How do I know it's not an act?"

"You've been with me all day. Either I'm a really good actor on top of being one of the best surgeons in the state, or…"

She smiled, narrowing her eyes. "Or you were born that way?"

"Just like Gaga, but with less makeup and costumes."

"I think my favorite Gaga costume was the one with the bacon, you remember?"

Oliver stopped walking. "Brittany, there is absolutely nothing wrong with honoring bacon by wearing it. In fact, you should tell your friend Zoe to add that to her lineup for her show."

Brittany beamed. She'd explained the line to Oliver, and he'd genuinely looked excited then asked if he could go. She was only too happy to not only show off her friend's hard work but also show off Oliver.

Everything just clicked between them.

"I'll let her know." She sighed happily. "So, we have some time. What did you want to do? We could always go freshen up if you want."

He pulled her into his arms and then held up his finger. "I think we need to go over that hill."

"Okay?"

He gripped her hand and led her over the hill.

A small park was on the other side.

It had swings, a slide, and a merry-go-round.

"We clearly need to swing. It's abandoned."

"And sad," she added for dramatic effect.

"It would be wrong to walk by." He took her hand again as they made their way to the swings first.

She sat, and he just naturally moved behind her and started to push. "I used to be so terrified of the swings when I was little."

"Really?" she asked as he pushed her higher. "Why?"

"First off, they're really high, and when you're a controlling little kid, you don't like the idea of weightlessness. I was absolutely petrified that I'd fly out into space like ET."

"Logical." She laughed. "But I can understand why you'd feel that way."

"Exactly. You're feeling it now… It's terrifying letting someone else push you. What if they push too hard, not hard enough? What if they stop pushing altogether? And what if they just… let go? You could drop, get hurt, or you could even be stuck…"

She frowned as he stopped pushing and then stopped the swing and pulled it close so he was facing her.

"Life's kind of like that, isn't it? Depending on other people, letting go, allowing yourself to just… fly. It can be scary. Trusting people always is, but I don't want you to think I'm the sort of guy to shove you into a swing and push you as high as you can, only to come crashing back down to Earth. That's not what this day's about, that's not what I'm about."

Her throat felt heavy with tears. "Why me? There're a million women out there who would fight me just to go on a swing with you."

"Well, Roger did vouch for you," he teased. And then sobered. "It's your eyes, the way you carry yourself, the way you look at the world when you don't think anyone else is looking."

"Oh? And how do I look at the world?"

He sighed. "Like you used to look forward to living in it until you were forced to survive instead."

Tears threatened; they stung the back of her throat and her eyes. "I was jaded at a young age. I tried to keep the sunlight, but you know the thing about the sun? It goes down… darkness always descends. I do love the world and everything in it, but some days, when my past comes back to haunt me, all I can do is turn to survival mode and pray to God that it passes."

Oliver caressed her face. "That's why you have friends, relationships, family—that's why you have me. I'm not asking to replace anyone in your past. I just want to exist in the present, with you, here, now."

"On the swings?"

"On the swings," he agreed. "And in a few minutes, on the slide. I want these tiny moments, however brief, because they build into something epic. They become life. And I love seeing it through your eyes, however jaded you claim your view to be."

Heat suffused her cheeks as she turned away and whispered, "Do you just store all these perfect lines, or do they just come out of your mouth naturally?"

"Both." He winked. "Now." He helped her off the swing. "I think it's time you let me push you down the slide so I can chase you and pull your hair."

She burst out laughing. "And why would you do that?"

"Ohhhh, easy. To show you I like you." He rolled his eyes and then drew her into his arms, pressing a chaste kiss to her mouth and then pulling back again to give her space that she didn't say she needed but did. "Let's go."

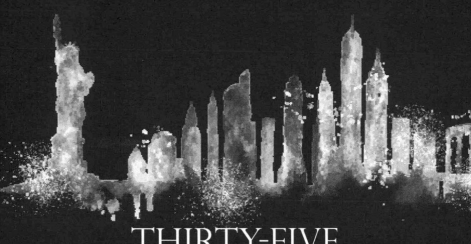

THIRTY-FIVE

It was Saturday.

A beautiful weekend day with kids playing at the park and people spending time outside with friends and family.

Everlee glanced out the window one last time then made her way back over to the computer. Frederick had come home, slept in the guest room, then left again.

He was due back anytime.

He wasn't working this afternoon.

Which meant she was going to get her confrontation, after all.

Her stomach roiled at the thought of him taking pictures of all of those girls topless, some of them as young as ten or eleven.

She shuddered.

Everything she'd found had been sent to Dane.

And Dane had told her he would continue to search and take care of the situation, whatever that meant.

The fact that several of the photo albums had videos and pictures of Danica didn't sit well with Everlee. Had Danica known? Had she helped them? Everlee knew that Danica had been in love with Jauq the same way that Everlee had been in love with Frederick. Had they just been stupid, innocent kids?

She took a sip of coffee and heard the sound of the front door opening. This was it.

Slowly, she rose from the couch and made her way into the kitchen where she heard Frederick humming to himself.

"Hey." Her voice cracked.

"Hey." He didn't turn around; half his body was in the fridge. "Did you get the grocery delivery yet? I'm starving and we're out of chicken." He shut the door and turned. He looked just as beautiful as he had the first day she'd seen him. Messy hair, scarf wrapped around his neck, leather jacket paired with combat boots and jeans that cost more than most people's apartments. His eyes were empty, though. His soul, dead.

"No," she said through clenched teeth. "I was in the hospital."

He didn't so much as flinch.

"Miscarrying."

With a sigh, he lowered his head and then shook it. "Can we not do this now?"

"This?" she raged. "THIS? I'm your wife! We lost our baby! Yes, we have to do *this*! Where were you?"

He gulped and then shrugged. "I was out."

"Did you hear anything I just said? I was pregnant! With your child."

He sneered. "Wow, thanks for clearing that up. Who knows who you've been running around with while I'm at work?"

"You mean at work shooting underage girls topless?"

He cursed and then lunged for her.

She dodged him and moved around the island. "Don't touch me!"

"You don't know what you're talking about! You can't just run around yelling things like that, Everlee!"

"Stop!" She ran down the hall with Frederick chasing her. His hand grabbed her by the arm, and then she was being slammed against the door, right next to the wedding picture she'd paid so much to frame.

It was like a shrine.

It meant nothing.

An empty.

Expensive.

Shrine.

She squeezed her eyes shut as he choked her and then slammed her head back against the wall. "Keep your mouth shut."

He jerked away from her as someone rang the doorbell.

The wedding picture fell to the floor with a loud crash. Glass flew everywhere, and Everlee stared down at it, wondering if she'd ever truly been anything more than a trophy on his arm to show to his powerful friends.

Frederick jerked the door open.

Two police officers and a detective appeared.

"Can I help you, gentlemen?" he asked in a calm, confident voice that Everlee had grown used to. Mainly because he used it on her.

Daily.

She shook her head and continued cleaning up the glassy mess as the detective stepped forward. "Are you Frederick Grassi?"

Frederick leveled the men with a stare. "Yeah. And?"

The detective held up a piece of paper. "I have a warrant to confiscate your computer."

"What?" Frederick hissed out a curse. "There has to be some mistake. I'm a photographer, I need my pictures. It's my livelihood. You're more than welcome to look at my computer, but the hardware stays here."

Everlee's blood ran cold, and her ears buzzed.

Frederick didn't know.

All of his private files had been un-encrypted.

No longer hidden.

No more secrets.

It was all there, plain as day.

She'd seen enough to make her sick and had given Dane the rest. In a way, she didn't want to know because somehow, that made her a part of it.

Frederick looked ready to attack.

And that's when it hit her. The minute they saw what was on his computer, he would be going to prison for a very long time. Regardless of who else was involved, he was in possession.

And she'd helped to reveal that.

Exhaling a sigh of relief, she put her hand to her stomach as she mourned more than just the loss of her baby. She also grieved for the loss of the dream she'd held onto for so long.

The fantasy of a family.

Of them.

"All things happen for a reason." She could hear Brittany's voice in her head. So her baby had to die for this to happen? Her marriage had to crumble? She didn't understand it, but she knew it was the right thing to do. Even though it was hard, even though she wanted to stick her head in the sand, plug her ears, and pretend that everything was okay—that it would always be okay.

It was probably Dane who got the information about inappropriate pictures to the police, though she wished he had told her. It wasn't like *she* had gone to them, though. She had planned to ask Dane what to do next; she wanted to set the thing on fire.

"Sir..." One of the officers held out his hand. "We can have the computer back in twenty-four hours. We're conducting research on a child pornography ring. We've been following a tip and, so far, it's led us here."

"Well..." Frederick changed voices, lowering his head. "I can't imagine my daughter being caught up in something like that. We... actually..." He wiped under his eyes. "We actually just had a miscarriage, and I—"

SERIOUSLY?

Everlee gaped up at the stranger she'd been married to for over a decade and watched as the mask fell and his true colors showed.

Had he loved her at all?

No.

He loved himself too much to ever share that affection with another human being.

"I'm sorry," the detective interjected. "That must be so hard."

Frederick nodded. "Sorry, it's just still so fresh."

"You're a suspect, Mr. Grassi, which means that it doesn't matter if you were just in a head-on collision, we still need that computer."

Frederick sobered. "I understand, you're just trying to do your job." He stepped away from the door. "It's in my office. Can I get you boys coffee? Beer?"

"No." The detective narrowed his eyes. "We'll just get the computer and be going."

Frederick basically took them on a tour of the house. He had a story for every piece, a price for every story. Oh, look, this is the table we flew in from Africa, paid twenty thousand for it, but look how it sets off the room.

Everlee almost gagged.

The detective did a small circle in the living room. "The computer?"

"Oh, right." Frederick flashed a smile. "I'll be right back."

The detective nodded to the officers, who followed Frederick into his darkroom.

Everlee stood and dumped the glass into the trash. The detective walked by her and held out his hand. "Thank you, and so sorry for intruding."

He pressed a small piece of paper against her palm.

"Of course." She shook his hand and slid the note up into the sleeve of her cable-knit sweater.

Minutes later, everyone was gone, including Frederick. He seemed panicked and angry.

Which only made her more resolute in her desire to ruin him.

She unfolded the paper and gasped.

Don't follow him, let me handle this. —D.

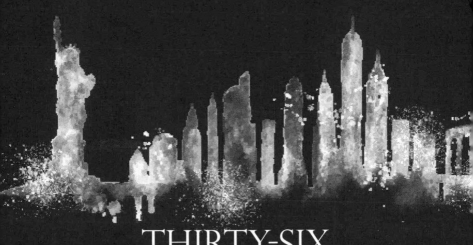

THIRTY-SIX

"Rough afternoon?" Dane asked once he located Frederick in one of his clubs. He was where he always was, even though the club had barely opened for the evening: the VIP section with two of the same girls draped around him.

The same *underage* girls Dane had paid weeks ago.

The same underage girls he'd been protecting.

The ones the cops had given him to use in his own little sting operation. It was coming together perfectly, and yet he still felt guilty. He was destroying a family. Doing something that he couldn't come back from.

His phone buzzed in his pocket.

> Zoe: *I'm at the office, I need to work late, I'm fitting a few new models, and then I have one last design to alter.*

He typed back quickly.

Dane: *I'll come check on you in a few. Text me if you need anything.*

Uneasiness churned in his gut. He didn't like the idea of Zoe at the office alone, but he had more business to attend to.

Dane had set Frederick up in more ways than one, but the man was guilty through and through.

Anger pulsed through Dane's veins as he watched Frederick try to kiss one of the girls spread across his lap. He ran his shaky fingers down her neck and then squeezed, she let out a little squeak.

Dane just shook his head and sat across from him, as casual as he could be. "You were saying?"

"I wasn't saying," Frederick said through clenched teeth, his eyes wild as he stared at his lap and the girl lying in it. "She's young."

"They all have to appear young. It's part of the reason I hire them."

"I'd love to photograph you." Frederick lowered his voice as his hand drifted from her throat and moved lower.

Dane cleared his throat.

More regulars started to filter in.

It was almost too easy.

To catch people in their own darkness, their own sin. To watch them struggle against a web of their own making.

"How's Everlee?" Dane asked, knowing it would trigger Frederick even more.

Frederick glared up at him. "Boring as always. Today she wanted to talk about the baby I never even wanted. The police came."

Dane tilted his head. "Because you got in a fight?"

"No, well, I roughed her up a bit but nothing like that. They took my laptop, which is strange. Apparently, there's some sort of child pornography ring in the city, and I'm a suspect." His eyes cleared. "Know anything about that?" The guy was visibly upset, shaking, and perspiring across his upper lip.

A year of this.

And finally.

A crack.

"A little. Want me to look into it for you?" Dane asked as calmly as he could, even though his heart was thundering in his chest. This is what he needed: more information, more access.

"Maybe." Frederick moved away from the couch, stood, and then sat on the leather chair closest to Dane. "I can trust you, right?"

Dane spread his arms wide. "You realize this is my world, don't you?"

On cue, another younger waitress rounded the corner and dangled an arm around Dane's chest. "Did you need anything… sir?"

Dane focused in on her mouth. "Maybe later, you know how I like it."

She winked and then turned her attention to Frederick. "And you?"

Frederick looked momentarily stunned and then shook his head slowly.

"You know where to find me," she whispered in a husky voice to Dane, playing the part perfectly. For being a rookie at the NYPD, she did a pretty good job of selling it.

"She's new," Dane explained to a stunned-looking Frederick. It helped that she was gorgeous with long, wavy, dark hair and innocent, blue eyes and didn't wear a stitch of makeup.

"Right." Frederick gave his head a shake. "Here's the thing, I may know a little about the ring, but it's not me. It's someone else. If they find anything on my computer, it's not going to lead to them. They may suspect, but I would need to confess, right? So, I guess what I'm asking, is if I rat them out…?"

"Them?" Dane repeated. "How many people are we talking? One? Two?"

"Two." Frederick coughed into his hand. "Two others are involved. Say I go to the police first. Say I confess… what happens next?"

"Well…" Dane waited a few dramatic seconds. "I would then talk to the DA, get you a plea that doesn't involve anything graphic like the death penalty but a nice little vacation in prison, and they go away for life."

"Life." Frederick gulped. "Forever?"

"Yeah, but at least it doesn't fall on you. I would hate for something to happen to you, Frederick, you're a friend. You were Danica's friend. Think of it as a favor, one friend to another."

Please, God, finally confess!

Give me answers!

"I'll think about it." Frederick's usually tan skin went even paler as he got to his feet and walked over to the bar.

It was Dane's move.

He stood, straightening his suit coat, and reached for his cell. Nothing from Zoe. Unease trickled down his spine.

The last time he'd felt it, he'd been too late.

He was only a few minutes away. Who cared if he looked overprotective? He snapped his fingers at Mario and left.

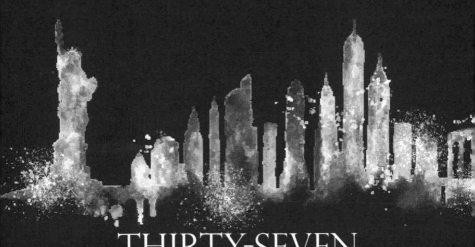

THIRTY-SEVEN

"This place is incredible!" Oliver exclaimed when they walked into the SOHO industrial building. Down into the basement they went until they were in a massive room with gourmet ovens, granite countertops, and workstations for each couple.

Not to mention the wine pairing that the serving staff continuously provided after each dish was made.

It was like Disney for adults.

"I know." Brittany beamed, proud of her friend and everything he'd accomplished just because he wanted something for himself outside of the fashion industry. "He's done an incredible job."

"The name, too." Oliver pointed with a grin. "Meet-cute?"

Brittany sucked on her lower lip and shrugged. "Yeah, well, that's how the best love stories start, right? By accident?"

"Or," Oliver said as he grabbed her hand, "by being semi-hit on by a patient who wants to hook you up with his beautiful client. That's sort of a meet-cute."

"That would have only been a meet-cute if it had been accidental. Like if I had run into you, your clipboard went flying, we touched it at the same time..." Brittany cleared her throat and looked up into his amused expression. "What?"

"Thought about this a lot, have you?" he teased.

"Shut up." She elbowed him.

He spun her around and pulled her into his embrace. "What if I was watching you and trying to get your attention?"

"You were very focused on your clipboard."

"Blank, my blank clipboard, just like my blank brain the minute I saw you strut down the hall."

She covered her face with her hands. "I do not strut."

"Yeah." He grinned, his eyes crinkling at the corners. "It's more of a saunter. I can demonstrate if you want."

She slapped him on the chest just in time for Roger to approach and give them a look of pure joy with a bit of arrogance mixed in—like he was the reason for them meeting.

"Looks like you kids had a fun day." Roger stared straight at her, his brown skin positively glowing with excitement.

Tamp it down, Roger, tamp it down.

"I hope you're ready to feast. Grace is late... which means, she'll be irritable when she gets here and may snap off someone's head. But I've come prepared." Roger handed them each a glass of chilled, sparkling white wine and then whispered, "I poured her two."

"Good plan." Brittany took a sip of her glass as bubbles tickled her tongue. "Do you know what station we're at?"

Roger gave her a look and sighed. "Next to the instructors, of course. And the owner. Special treatment, lucky girl."

"Very lucky." She beamed up at Oliver as he grabbed her free hand and kissed it.

"Not jealous. At all," Roger said in a sing-song voice as he crooked his finger at them. They followed him to the front of the room. "You'll be starting with a nice flatbread appetizer with goat cheese, followed by tomato bisque soup. Don't worry, I have the perfect white wine to pair with it, and it looks like we'll be ending with roasted lamb and garlic sweet potato fries. I'd hold off on the garlic, you know, just in case."

"You done yet?" Brittany said through clenched teeth as Oliver chuckled at her side.

Roger beamed. "Not by a long shot. Good question, though. Oh, look. Grace!" He power-walked away from them, leaving them completely alone with all the recipes and instructions.

Grace sashayed her way toward them, sunglasses on even though it was nearing six at night and wearing a large black hat that made it almost impossible to see anyone behind her. "Traffic was horrible. I don't understand what's so hard about stoplights. Stop, go, stop, go. Oh, hello, you're the attractive doctor seeing my Brittany, aren't you?" Beaming, Grace pulled off her sunglasses. "Tell me, how many surgeries do you do in a day?"

"That depends on my schedule, but typically three to four. I do whatever needs to be done, a lot of cases of appendicitis, hernias, gallbladders, that sort of thing."

"If I had a heart attack right now, could you cut me open?" Grace just had to ask. "Because this wine isn't doing its trick with my stress levels."

"I could cut you open." Oliver smiled. "But I doubt you'd want me operating on you since cardiothoracic surgery isn't my specialty."

"Hmm." She eyed his hands. "Do you cook? An ex-wife? Divorces? How are you with lawn care?"

"I think we should start!" Brittany said a little too loudly, pointing Grace toward Roger so they could gossip together. Then Brittany and Oliver could continue with their date. "She's harmless."

"I know." Oliver picked up the first recipe sheet. "All right, you know your way around a knife?"

"Knife…" Brittany made a face and stared down at the three knives in front of them. She reached for the serrated one, saw Oliver make a face, tried again. He shook his head. Finally, she picked up the right one. "Easy, right?"

"Mmm, you're a natural," he teased and then moved behind her. "Now, watch and learn while you show this piece of garlic who's boss."

His warm breath tickled her neck. Strong arms guided her as she started to cut. Typically, she would have pulled away. It would be too much, too soon. Was she that skittish? But in his arms, she felt… safe, like it was okay to stretch her wings and soar.

There was no reason she should trust someone so early on.

But Oliver made it easy to do.

So, she let herself think about more than just herself. She started thinking about what an *us* would feel like.

An *us* with him.

A relationship.

Something more than just laughter and dates, something passionate and loving. Goosebumps rose up on her arms at the thought.

It wasn't just his sense of humor and strength.

There was something so solid about him.

With a grin, she looked down at his left hand and nearly dropped the knife. On the middle of his thumb was a small tattoo of a cross.

"What's that represent?" she asked, her mouth dry.

"It's the last thing I see before I prepare to cut someone open. I see it when I scrub in, and in the OR, I look down, right hand holding a scalpel, left hand empty. And even covered with a glove, I know it's there, that tattoo of a cross, is my reminder that all the schooling in the world doesn't save lives. He does. I may not have control, but that doesn't mean I'm lost. It's just a startling realization that the universe still turns, lives are still lived, and it makes me realize that I can only give one hundred percent of me, and the rest—the rest, it just is."

"Yeah." She rubbed her fingertips over the tattoo. "Sometimes, it just is."

He nuzzled her neck a bit and then pressed a kiss behind her ear before guiding the knife back.

And she realized that she could stay like this forever.

In his arms.

Near garlic.

Feeling the tempo of the way he showed her how to slice.

Forever.

So simple, so easy.

No banquet, no cameras, just them, cutting up food and talking about life.

Something she didn't even realize she'd been craving until he gave it to her as if he knew what she had been searching for all along.

A friend.

Oliver walked Brittany to her door. She wasn't sure if he was walking slowly or if it was her. Either way, she didn't want the night to end, but she knew it had to. The box had been somewhat forgotten. And now? It was burning a hole in her brain.

She had to look.

Alone.

"Thank you." Oliver bent down and kissed her cheek. "I think today was one of my favorite dates I've ever been on."

"Because Grace and Roger got in a fight, and he accidentally threw flour in her face?"

He burst out laughing. "Yeah, let's just say that moment is tied with everything else."

"What else?"

"Literally every other moment when you smiled at me." He shrugged. "I'm going to kiss you. I was going to ask permission, but then I decided it would give you time to overthink things. I'm not coming inside. I'm just kissing you, and then I'm walking away, hopefully in a straight line, back to my car."

"As opposed to diagonal?"

"Kisses are powerful. What can I say?"

"I think you've built up too much, this kiss."

"Maybe I have, maybe I haven't." He leaned down, his smile so sexy that her knees went weak, and then his mouth was stirring against hers. She wanted more but held still while he gently coaxed her lips apart, massaging her tongue like he was asking for permission to taste more, to own more of her.

Her mouth opened as she arched against him. His hands braced her arms and slid down to her hips as he deepened the kiss, then pulled back and whispered, "Definitely not a straight line." He brushed the hair from her face and tilted her chin toward him. He nipped her lips again. "I'll call you. Soon."

"Okay," she said in a breathy voice as wonder pulsed through her body. She wanted to grab him, ask him for more, but at the same time, it seemed like her past was jerking her back into the apartment. The box was pulling her. It was her past. Did that mean Oliver was her future?

He seemed hesitant; then his eyes flicked to her mouth. He shook his head like he couldn't believe that he was walking away, and then he got into the elevator.

She leaned against her door as he disappeared, and almost sank to the floor from the kiss.

It wasn't just passionate.

Or sexy.

Or possessive.

It wasn't rushed.

She was used to hurried.

Used to having to hide.

But with Oliver, she didn't have to.

No politician mother was breathing down their necks, no cameras waiting to catch them doing something inappropriate. It was just… them.

Brittany touched her lips with her fingertips and smiled as she opened the door to her apartment. Her smile fell when she saw the box. It might as well be a bomb ready to go off.

With shaky movements, she made her way over to it and without giving herself time to think, pulled off the lid, throwing it to the floor.

Inside were hundreds of pictures, folders. All labeled with the year taken as well as the place.

And, finally, one that said, *Recent*.

She picked up the manila envelope and pulled out the first picture.

It wasn't just a snapshot.

It was a headshot.

Of Chrissy Mendoza.

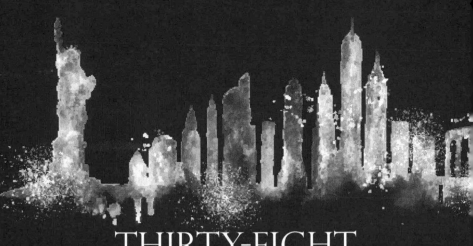

THIRTY-EIGHT

Seven days.

Zoe had seven days to make it work.

To take all the moving pieces and make sure they worked together to launch her line. Every penny had been invested in it being a success. Zoe had even convinced Grace to sit in the front row, though it was more begging and less convincing.

With shaking hands, Zoe sat down behind her desk and inhaled the scent of hours-old coffee and fabric. She could do this. This was what she had been born for.

Her brown skin shimmered with the lotion she'd tested on herself to see how it would look under the catwalk lights.

She wanted the line to look otherworldly, with bright colors and patterns that didn't seem to make sense, but when worn together, looked like a chaotic masterpiece. It was one hundred percent bohemian meets futuristic, and it was a risk. A huge one.

One that Dane had invested in.

She squeezed her eyes shut. Dane. Dane had been everywhere since his ultimatum, but he hadn't asked or threatened again, which almost made her more nervous. How could she make him understand? It wasn't about just him or her; it was them together. Like a bomb waiting to go off. She wanted to make it on her own, away from his influence, from the industry. She owed it to herself, didn't she?

And she was terrified that she couldn't trust him.

Because at the end of the day, it came down to the fact that he ran an empire through the city's underground, and if he had to, he would choose that over her, just like he'd chosen to kill Aaron's brother and force her to watch.

It was all about control.

And after twenty years in the industry, Zoe was done with being controlled. Done.

She wanted to pull the strings.

Just for once in her life.

"You look like you're concentrating really hard," came a dark voice from near the door. Her heart leapt into her throat as blood started to pound in her ears. It was almost impossible to catch her breath as she looked up into the shadowy eyes of Aaron, the guy she'd helped to put in prison. The guy whose only crime was to film underage girls and sell the videos on the dark web, and then, if it made sense, slip them to the media. He did it for a price. Both of them had worked for Marnie.

It was the final straw.

Thank God for Roger.

"Aaron," she said his name out loud. "I heard you found religion, good for you."

He snorted out a laugh. "Yeah, I'm the perfect inmate. Who knew I had such a bright future?" His dark hair and olive eyes used to fascinate her when paired with his copper-toned skin. He was half Native American, half German. She remembered thinking that he had the most intriguing eyes she'd ever seen, and then that was it.

Seconds later, she was being asked to pose. And when she got uncomfortable, she was given a shot of whiskey to relax. Whiskey laced with drugs.

"Did you need something?" she found herself asking in a confident voice, even though she was perspiring in her heels and Nicole Miller dress.

Where was Dane when she actually needed him?

Her phone buzzed on the table again, and Dane's picture popped up.

"Don't answer that. It's rude." Aaron grinned. "I just want to have a conversation, that's all…"

"All right." Zoe's body shook as she sat back in her chair and waited. Aaron pulled out a gun and stretched his arms overhead. *Dane! Where are you?*

"It's her fault, you know… the woman behind all the crazy, the one behind the scenes playing everyone for a fool. She's in her high tower, sipping wine while the rest of us go to prison for what she did." His eyes were wild as he faced Zoe, what was he talking about? Who? "Do you want to know what I did?"

"No." Acid burned the back of Zoe's throat. "I think that's between you and God."

"God." He choked out a laugh. "He has forsaken me." He held his arms out wide. "I'm going to Hell for what I did! HELL!" Spit dangled from his lip. He wiped his mouth and paced in front of her. "I would rather die than go back to prison. And I think I want to take someone with me. Think of it as the ultimate sacrifice, maybe one bad soul and one good one will equal my entrance into Heaven, huh? Worth a shot! After all, you're the one who ruined my life. You just couldn't leave it alone, you had to go to the police!"

"You taped your brother having sex with me while I was high on God knows what, and I'm the one who deserves death?"

"It was a job! You were a job!" Aaron screamed. "She paid us too well! And it's not like you care! You take your clothes off for a living, so we filmed it. Same thing, different audience." He cursed and spat on the floor. "You know, for old time's sake…" He lowered the gun with one hand and started unbuttoning his jeans with the other.

This wasn't happening.

Not happening.

She had no weapons.

Her cell went off again as Aaron finally got his buckle loosened, and with clumsy fingers, jerked his jeans to his thighs. "Yeah, I think I'll enjoy hearing you scream."

One minute, he was glaring at her; the next, he was on the ground with Dane standing behind him, a gun pointed at his head.

"Dane!" Zoe burst into tears. "You're here!"

"I had a bad feeling." He didn't look up at her, just kicked Aaron in the ribs multiple times before flipping him onto his back and pointing the gun right at the center of his forehead.

"Don't," Zoe found herself saying. "Not again. You shoot him, I don't know if we… I don't know about us, Dane, but I do know that I can't let you kill him. Please don't kill him." Aaron's eyes rolled to the back of his head. Maybe he'd passed out from the pain. Perhaps he was faking it. Whatever it was, Zoe couldn't let history repeat itself. She couldn't bear to watch a person suffer, no matter how horrible the human was.

Dane bit out a series of curses and stood to his full height, tucking the gun inside his jacket and very calmly grabbing his cell.

"Yeah, I have a situation. I'll need a detective unit down here." He rambled off the address. "I think we have someone finally willing to talk."

He hung up and turned to Zoe. "Are you hurt?"

"No." She rubbed her arms as tears trickled down her face. "I'm fine. I think."

Dane pulled her into his arms, holding her tight and close. "Then I need you to listen to me very carefully."

She nodded against his chest, breathed in the scent of whiskey and cigars, and exhaled like it was her drug, her safety, her home.

"I need you to start at the beginning and tell me everything, leave no detail out. This is extremely important. Can you do that for me?"

Zoe frowned up at him. "Why is it so important?"

"He's in the pictures."

"Pictures?"

"With Jauq, Danica, Frederick, even Marnie. Aaron's in the pictures on Frederick's computer. All of them are linked."

"Danica would never—"

"I know, I know." Dane narrowed his eyes. "But I guess we never know what people are capable of until it's too late. Human nature is unpredictable, and we're only human, Zoe."

She clung to him and explained what Aaron had said about a woman being in charge. Dane seemed to flinch at that. She looked up into his blue eyes, searching. "Dane, what aren't you telling me?"

Their gazes locked, and his expression went from hard to soft in seconds.

A few policemen made their way into her office loft. "Dane? The chief says you may have more info on the—"

"Be right there." Dane kissed the top of Zoe's forehead. "I'll be just a minute, then we're going home, all right?"

She nodded and waited for him.

Just like he'd promised, after she'd given her statement, after they'd arrested a now-alert and irate Aaron, Dane helped her into the car.

She was still shaking when Dane reached into the center console and handed her a small flask. "Whiskey. I know you hate it. Take two small gulps and see if it helps."

She grabbed the flask, did what he instructed, and then laid her head on his shoulder, her arm resting across his hard stomach.

The ride to the apartment was quick. They walked quietly to the elevators.

In silence to the kitchen.

The buzz of the hush was going to kill her.

"Dane?"

"Yeah?" He shrugged out of his jacket and crossed his arms, concern lacing his features.

She took a step toward him. "Why didn't you kill him?"

He paused and then uncrossed his arms, pacing a small circle in front of her before facing her again. "Maybe because the last time I killed someone in front of you, it was like I killed you, too. And I couldn't bear the thought of letting someone as evil as Aaron ruin what we have, what we *could* have if you'd just let us."

She sucked in a sharp breath. "You listened because of me?"

"Do you really think I like the idea of that guy being in prison? He doesn't deserve to breathe the same air as you, let alone suck dry tax dollars just because he doesn't have a conscience."

Her eyes filled with unshed tears as she reached out to him, pulled his massive body close, and then rose up on her tiptoes. "I need you to kiss me now."

He hesitated. Dane never hesitated, so she grabbed the back of his head and pulled him forward. Her tongue slid past his lower lip in a frenzy to taste him. He lifted her into his arms, deepening the kiss as they clung to one another, her suspended against him, and him rock-solid.

Like he always was to her.

Rock. Solid.

She pulled back, her eyes searching, her breaths coming out in short, small pants. "I lied."

"About what?" he asked softly.

"I need you. I miss her. And I need you. And I don't know what's worse. Knowing she's gone because she couldn't handle the pain, or that I pulled away because I was terrified of what she warned me about."

He tilted his head. "Danica warned you about me?"

"Not in the way you think." Slowly, she slid down his body. "I betrayed her. I betrayed you. She told me that you would scare me, told me not to run. And I did. Because I was so afraid everything else was more important than my sanity, than my peace, than me."

"Zoe." Dane growled out her name. "I made a judgment call, a bad one, but one that put a bad man in prison and the other in the ground. I can't apologize for that. I won't. But I will apologize for forcing you to witness something someone as beautiful as you should never have to see. Something so ugly that I can't bear the thought of you closing your eyes and seeing nothing but blood. That's my burden to bear, not yours. Never yours."

"You have got to stop talking to me like that!" She stomped her heel. "It just makes me want to—"

"Fight? Kiss? Make love?" he offered with a wicked grin.

"I thought the Great Dane Saldino didn't make love... I believe, on several occasions, you said that men like you—"

"I was an arrogant idiot, and I was afraid to show my cards too soon. A man doesn't just cut open his heart on the first date and bleed all over the table."

"Some do," she challenged.

"You're right, teenagers and hipsters. I'm neither, if you haven't noticed." He crowded her space just enough for her to be overwhelmed with his scent, his protective stance.

She was giving in like she knew she would.

But she would give in on her terms. "If I asked you to hold me all night, just hold me, make sure I fall asleep, what would you say?"

He didn't answer. Instead, he jerked his shirt open. Buttons flew everywhere as he continued to strip down to his boxers, and then he was carrying her to her bed and laying her down on it. He covered her with a million blankets and then lay down next to her, pulling an afghan over himself.

"You know we can share blankets, right?"

"No," he said gruffly. "We really can't. You're asking me to protect you from all the things on the outside of this apartment. This is my way of protecting you from the things on the inside."

She gulped.

"Celibate, Zoe. Cut a man some slack. And if you wiggle even once, and I leave, don't panic. I'm just taking one of the very many cold showers that I've been cursed with over the last year."

With a giggle, she turned and faced him. "How cold?"

"Let's just say…" He sighed and started brushing her face lightly with his fingertips. "That I was afraid of blood loss and possible amputation of something greatly needed to have kids."

"Kids," she repeated.

His lips pressed up into a blinding smile. "Kids." He kissed her forehead. "Now, go to sleep. I'll keep the monsters away."

"And what about the monster in my bed?"

"Sometimes, men have no choice but to become monsters to protect those they love from the darkness in this world.

Monster fighting monster is better than monster fighting man."

She sucked in a sharp breath as the reality of his words sank in, and then she was flying, soaring, in the arms of the city's most renowned crime boss.

A murderer.

A thief.

An extortionist.

Funny how the safest place people always expected to find themselves in, was the most dangerous. And the most dangerous?

Peaceful beyond reason.

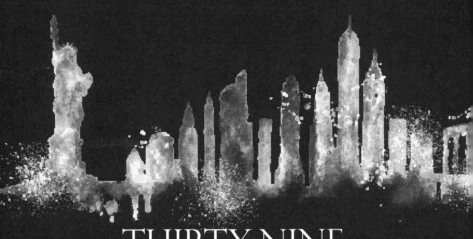

THIRTY-NINE

NEW YORK FASHION WEEK COUNTDOWN – DAY 6

"I needed this so bad," Everlee said the next day as she hooked her bag on the seat and slumped against the wooden chair. They were finally at happy hour together the following day. How had the week gone by so fast?

"How are you feeling?" Brittany asked. Her eyes were puffy, and she looked as if she hadn't slept in a week, but other than that, same old Brittany, concerned about everyone and everything. It was sweet, except Everlee didn't want sweet right now. Her husband was currently getting investigated by the police. And he was a monster.

She didn't want to hate him.

But she did.

"I'm getting a divorce," Everlee blurted. "I just… I wanted you guys to be the first to know."

Zoe chose that moment to breeze in, her face a bit pale, her smile brittle. A chill rippled through Everlee. What was going on with her group of friends? A week ago, everyone had seemed as if they were at least surviving. And now?

"Divorce?" Zoe asked, sliding into her usual seat.

"Yeah." In spite of her supreme effort to remain steady, Everlee's chin wobbled, and then she burst into tears. "He shoved me, and the police came—"

"You called the police on him?" Brittany was out of her seat, her arm wrapped around her as Everlee cried in her friend's arms.

"No." Everlee sniffed. "I mean, they came because of Dane, because… I thought Frederick might be up to something, and I just had this feeling. His computer has all these encrypted files, so I asked a favor."

Zoe froze in place. Brittany kept rubbing her back.

"I asked him to hack Frederick's computer. Guys, it's bad. It's so bad. I don't see how he's going to get out of it, and I don't want him to! If it's true, if what he's doing and has done is true, then I can't believe I ever thought I loved him."

"I'm so sorry." Brittany rubbed Everlee's back more and more. It should be calming, it wasn't. "Sometimes, these things just happen—"

"If you say '*for a reason*,' I'm going to shank you with this fork!" Everlee burst out. "Everything's so perfect. When have you ever struggled in life? What? You're upset because your politician boyfriend didn't love you enough?" She knew she was overreacting, but she was just so angry, so hurt. And it was easier to lash out at family, at loved ones, rather than taking the blame, wasn't it?

"Everlee!" Zoe snapped. "Stop!"

"And you!" Anger and sadness pulsed with every breath Everlee took. "Dane's been in love with you since we were teens, and you just lead him around like some pathetic guy on a leash. He'd kill for you, probably has if we're really throwing down at the table. It's not like half the city doesn't know he's connected to the Italian mob!"

Tears streaked down Zoe's cheeks, but Everlee couldn't stop. They didn't get it. She'd lost everything! She'd lost her baby! Her husband! Her life! Child pornography? Seriously? Could it get worse?

Brittany stood, swayed toward Everlee, then locked eyes with her and whispered in a choked-up voice, "Chrissy Mendoza is my daughter." She squeezed her eyes shut and started to cry softly into her hands. "Mine and Ronan's."

The server chose that stellar moment to stop at the table and drop off the tequila shot for Danica and to take their drink order.

"Alcohol," Everlee said in a desperate, confused voice. "Just… all of…" He gave her an annoyed look. She waved him off. "Just bring us house wine, go!"

"Honey…" Zoe reached for Brittany. "What are you talking about? You've never been pregnant. I thought you were still a virgin!"

"Joke's on you," Brittany said between sobs. "Ronan and I… We loved each other. I thought he was my forever… things just… escalated. It was exciting, and I felt cherished and wanted. And I mean, look at him. His family? When they found out, they sent me away. Roger helped, he didn't know what else to do except lie to Marnie and tell her I got really sick and that if I had a career left, he'd take over. That's why I switched, probably why she still hates me." Brittany slumped against Everlee. "She's perfect. Chrissy is perfect. I held that girl in my arms, I gave her up for adoption. I gave her away!" She started sobbing even harder.

Everlee wasn't sure what to do, mainly because the news was so shocking, so raw that she resorted to doing what Brittany would do, which led them all back to the soothing back rubs and complete shock.

"Britt." Everlee went from the back rub straight into a hug. "Talk to us. How'd you find out?"

Brittany wiped under her eyes. "I only knew I needed to close that chapter of my life, come clean. It felt like I always had this guilt hanging over me, this shame, the happiest girl alive isn't really the happiest. She's just barely surviving. I lost both Ronan and Chrissy that night. But I *chose* to lose *her*. I chose my career over her, just like he chose his career over me. So, I felt like, in some small way, I deserved whatever came next."

"You know that's not true," Zoe piped up, tears in her eyes. "You're one of the best people I know, probably *the* best. You deserve all the good things life has to offer. Abandoning your child and her mother to choose a political career versus ensuring a good life for your baby are two very different things."

"But that's the thing. I gave her a better life because I wanted to still live mine. I was selfish, young..." Brittany shuddered. "And now, I don't know what to do. I thought I would see a picture of some vaguely familiar face and move on. But now I know where she is, *who* she is. I know she idolized me growing up, and she's in the same city as both me and Ronan."

"Creepy." Zoe breathed out what Everlee was already thinking. "What? It is! How does that even happen?"

"Second chances," Everlee said on a whisper as she stared into both her friends' hurt faces, pain she had put there because she was hurting herself and because lashing out felt better than crying herself to sleep. "Maybe you've been given a second chance to do it right this time. Have you thought about that?"

Brittany nodded. "I have, and I want to, I just don't know how to get my second chance with Chrissy while still dating Oliver. I mean, that's a big secret, a huge one. It's like dropping an elephant onto a Maserati and going, '*whoops!*'"

"Nice." Zoe grinned and then sobered as she reached into her purse and pulled out the piece of paper that had Dane's list of demands, including the proposal. "Dane asked me to marry him."

Everlee's jaw nearly came unhinged from her face. "Say what?"

"Marriage. There is no great aunt or trust fund. He gave me every dime I had to start the line… I paid him back, but the interest was me, literally. So, I either give him the cash, or I marry him. Oh, and it gets better. He bought me a loft, remodeled it, put everything in it that I would have put in it myself, and then, last night when Aaron stopped by—"

"Wait! Aaron? Creepy Aaron?"

"He's currently Creepy Aaron to a nice jail mate." Zoe lifted the untouched tequila shot and swallowed it. "Dane saved me, again, and yet I'm still holding back. Why am I holding back? Why am I so afraid of him?"

"Because he sees you," Everlee found herself saying. "And to be seen beyond the glitz, the glamour, the face, it's a beautiful thing. Frederick only saw the outside. He only cared about what it would do for his career. And now look at us. Look at him."

"Well!" Brittany laughed through fresh tears. "We're a mess, aren't we?"

Everlee reached out and grabbed each of their hands. "I'm sorry, guys. It's just everything always looks so perfect when you're on the outside."

"It's the Instagram effect. Perfect pictures on the outside, total mess on the inside." Zoe agreed.

"I need to tell Ronan," Brittany said in a quiet voice. "And Oliver, of course."

"And I need to decide if Dane loves the power he wields over the city more than me, or if it's because of me," Zoe admitted.

Zoe and Brittany looked at Everlee.

But she had nothing.

And then she stared at the empty tequila shot and thought about Danica, about her feisty attitude and easy smile. About the way she had looked at the world, not as a friend but as her opponent, something that needed to be beaten into submission.

"I think…" Everlee leaned back in her chair. "I need to discover who I am again, without Frederick by my side."

"Cheers." They lifted their water glasses and then Zoe set hers down and stared at each of the girls. "I have a favor to ask."

"Anything," they said in unison.

"A few models dropped out of the show. It's not a huge deal, probably Marnie just pulling her models because she hates us and always has, but would you guys be willing to model? At all?"

"Of course!" Everlee was the first to answer. "Plus, it will be fun, walking with both of you again."

Brittany nodded. "On one condition."

"It's yours," Zoe said quickly.

"I want to walk with Chrissy."

"Oh, man, now I'm going to cry." Zoe glared. "You know I hate crying. I have to redo my makeup, and this is perfection." She pointed to her golden-brown skin and perfect eyeliner.

"It really is," Brittany agreed.

"Is that a new eye palette?" Everlee leaned in.

And then the girls burst into laughter despite all the tears that had been shed, despite all the tears they had yet to shed. Despite the still empty seat at the table.

And the now-empty shot in front of it.

They all stared over at the chair.

"You think she did it?" Brittany finally asked the question that had been looming over them for a full year.

"No," Everlee said quickly. "I really don't."

"Me either," Zoe agreed.

"Frederick." Everlee licked her dry lips. "He had a lot of pictures of her on his computer, several videos of her and Jauq."

"Jauq sobbed at the funeral," Zoe pointed out.

"It just—" Everlee stopped talking and thought about it. "It doesn't make sense. She never really hung out with them as much as the pictures show. It's almost like it was on purpose." She shook her head. "I just wish I knew what that reason was. Why would Danica spend any time with Marnie? She hated her."

"But she loved Jauq," Zoe added. "And Marnie and Jauq have always been close with each other and Frederick."

"Yeah." Everlee toyed with the end of her straw. "Maybe?" She grabbed a menu and opened it. "I guess we just need to trust that the truth will come to light."

"Exactly," Brittany agreed, squeezing Everlee's hand and then turning to Zoe. "What do you need us to do to help you get ready for the show?"

"Thank God." Zoe exhaled in relief. "I thought you'd never ask."

FORTY

"Have I ever told you how much I love and appreciate you?" Zoe asked Brittany and Everlee as they were backstage getting ready. The clothing was gorgeous. Brittany knew it was going to be a huge hit.

Already, Oliver was sitting in the front row between Grace and Roger, getting an earful. The guy would probably never forgive her, but every time she looked out, he was smiling, so that was good, right?

Progress.

Because of the show and prepping, they hadn't seen much of each other, but they'd talked and texted. Things were progressing; Brittany just didn't know when she could tell him.

And the bigger issue, she needed to tell Ronan first.

"Speak of the devil," she murmured under her breath as Ronan made his way toward her.

"You ladies look amazing." He leaned in and kissed each of them on the cheek, saving Brittany for last. "Some more than others."

"Dating," she said with a smirk. "Someone else."

"A guy never stops trying." He winked and then turned to Chrissy and did a double-take. "Sorry, for a second, I thought I was seeing Brittany's twin, nice to see you again."

"Yeah, I get that a lot." Chrissy beamed. "It's a huge compliment."

"How long have you been modeling?" He seemed genuinely interested, his smile warm.

"Just this year. And can I say that when I turn eighteen, I'll totally vote for you?" She made a face. "Sorry, that came out extremely aggressive and way too loud."

He laughed and pulled her in for a side hug. "I love the enthusiasm."

"Good."

Brittany couldn't stop the tears welling in her eyes, and when she turned to Zoe and Everlee, both of them were wiping their cheeks as if they were swiping away moisture from their eyes.

"Chrissy! Makeup! Now!" someone shouted.

"That's me!" She skipped off in the direction of the makeup chairs.

Everyone else dispersed, leaving Ronan and Brittany staring at each other.

"How are things?" he asked in that polite tone she was used to him using when they were in public.

She thought about the last few days with Chrissy and then of Oliver. "Good, actually. You?"

"Other than the ex-wife and her inability to stop talking to the media, good. Busy, but good." He smiled down at her. "If I told you I missed you, would it matter?"

"Being missed is always nice, Ronan. Of course, it matters. For future reference, I would love to be your friend. I actually have something to tell you—"

She was cut off by Zoe colliding into her and swiping either tears or sweat from underneath her eyes.

"Breathe!" Everlee grabbed Zoe by the hands. "Just breathe. We have time, we can figure this out, all right? In and out, there you go."

"What's wrong?" Brittany took in her friends' suddenly pale faces.

"The models," Everlee said with a pinched expression and hate in her tone. "A few of the ones that were booked for the show backed out for another one, and basically it looks like Marnie double-booked them on purpose and threatened their careers if they chose Zoe over Marc Jacobs."

Brittany squeezed her eyes shut. "Why? Why is she so horrible?"

And, of course, that would be the moment that Marnie made an appearance with Frederick on one side and Jauq on the other. "Trouble in paradise?"

"How dare you?" Zoe lunged. Everlee was barely able to hold her back. "What have I ever done to you?"

"Plenty," Marnie spat. "Besides, you're all guilty by association. Isn't that right, Frederick?" She patted his cheek.

He kissed the inside of her palm and stared daggers at all of them, while Jauq just looked at the floor.

"You know how this business goes. It's eat or be eaten," said Marnie. "Well, I think I'd rather eat."

With that, she walked off.

"Frederick," Everlee called. "Wait, this isn't you, you don't have to—"

"Wow!" Frederick turned on his heel. "This isn't me? Do you even realize what I'm facing right now? The police are all over me. All over my laptop. All over some encrypted files that apparently were no longer encrypted." He glared and then looked ready to puke. "I'm done with you and whatever the—"

"Enough." Roger walked up to the group, earning a wide-eyed, over-the-shoulder stare from Marnie. "Go."

"Frederick," Marnie called, her tone a bit panicked. "Leave it."

"Wow." Everlee stared dumbfounded at Roger. "Are you telling us that she's actually afraid of you?"

He just shook his head and turned to Zoe. "We need at least three male models and another woman who can fit into that." He pointed to a slinky black number with combat boots and colorful thigh-high stockings with a draped army jacket over the top.

"Okay." Zoe nodded. "Okay, just let me think…" She gave them all a desperate look.

"Ronan," Brittany blurted, earning Ronan's cautious gaze. "Publicity is his thing. He'll do it."

"I will?" Ronan asked, his voice cracking.

"He will," everyone else confirmed in unison.

"Yeah, right, Ro?" She would do anything for her friend. "Anything."

"Suurrre." He shook his head. "I would love to wear…" He glanced over at the men's clothing hanging on the racks and gulped. "That." Another gulp. "In public."

"It's high fashion." Zoe rolled her eyes. "What about the rest of it?"

"Dane!" Everlee snapped her fingers.

"Oliver." Brittany tossed him on the sacrificial altar of friendship and new relationships. "And what if we got Grace up here? She loves trying new things."

Everyone gave her a doubtful look.

"I'll get her," Roger announced. "She owes me a favor." And then he called over his shoulder. "I'll grab your boy toy, too, Brittany. Can't promise I won't ask what he puts in his protein shakes."

Brittany groaned while Ronan gave her a curious look. "What?"

He shrugged. "Just never took you for the type of girl that was into all that bulk."

"Um, every girl likes a solid six-pack." This from Zoe as she recovered and fixed her hair. "I can model the last dress when I walk through. It's not going to be perfect, but…" She took a deep breath. "It will work. Right?"

Brittany wanted it to work, but she wasn't sure. It was extremely fast-paced. Things had to be timed perfectly. For the last six days, they'd helped Zoe work on the show, and now, they were going to help her succeed even if they had to bribe the guys.

"Right." Brittany found herself saying a little prayer as Roger approached with Oliver and Grace. They both looked as though they were being walked toward the figurative plank. "Hey, so we need a favor."

"This one explained." Grace pointed to Roger, subjecting him to a malevolent glare. "I loathe the day I told you I owed you."

"And yet I don't, and probably never will." He grinned. "That's your outfit, mmkay?"

Grace's eyes widened. "At least it's gorgeous, even if it flashes a bit of thigh."

"A lot of thigh," Roger corrected.

"That's not at all helpful, Roger, thank you," Zoe said through clenched teeth, grabbing Oliver by the hand. "And you get to wear this."

His eyebrows shot skyward, and he stared at Brittany, then swallowed hard and shook his head. "Well, I guess there's a first for everything."

"He'd better be getting a really big kiss or something else tonight," Ronan said under his breath.

"Ah, the senator."

Ronan held out his hand. "Nice to see you again. Am I being too optimistic when I ask if your outfit has more... color?"

"Only the best for Ronan." Zoe dangled a hanger in front of them. Ronan looked heavenward and muttered a curse. "How is this supposed to fit me?"

"That should get you a lot of votes." Oliver whistled.

"If I ever live it down." Ronan grabbed the hanger. "Yes."

"We go on in five," Zoe told the room. "Guys, Grace, head to makeup and hair so they can do something really quick, and then line up. Brittany and Chrissy, you walk down first, together. Ronan." She licked her dry lips. "Ronan, you're right after. Once you get to the end, twirl Chrissy a bit, and then lean in and kiss Brittany's cheek, I want it to look… familial."

Oh, God. Brittany tensed but nobody seemed to care—at all.

Within minutes, everyone was lined up and ready to go, and Zoe looked like she was seconds away from puking.

"It's going to be fine," Brittany assured her.

Zoe was bent over, her hands on her thighs, sucking in deep breaths. "How do we know it's going to be fine?"

"Well." Brittany eyed the guys. "Dane's here. He fixes things, right? He won't let you fail. Furthermore, I keep praying you don't fail, so I'm just going to believe you won't. How's that for having some faith?"

Tears gleamed in Zoe's eyes. "I don't know what I did to deserve you and Everlee, Danica, Dane, everyone. But I thank God I have you."

"Same." Everlee grinned, though it didn't quite reach her eyes, Brittany knew it would be a while before Everlee felt okay with the shift in her life, in the future she saw for herself. But Brittany also knew firsthand that just because the window closed right along with the door, that didn't mean there wasn't another window somewhere just waiting for a person to crawl through.

Oliver winked at her; he seemed more excited than annoyed.

And then the music started.

And it was time to go.

Brittany grabbed Chrissy's hand, squeezed it, and they took the catwalk together, as mother and daughter.

For the first time.

The crowd went crazy when they got to the end, especially when Ronan joined them on stage. The cameras were blinding, the chatter and talk insane. Ronan twirled Chrissy then bent low and kissed Brittany on the cheek. Then they walked back, as a family.

Oliver passed Brittany with Everlee soon following.

Within minutes, they all lined up again while Zoe made her way down the middle, proud, beautiful Zoe in a tight, white dress that set off her brown skin so beautifully, it almost hurt to look at her.

Standing ovation.

Brittany's eyes filled with tears as she clapped for her friend, and when Zoe finally made it back to the end, it was Dane of all people who walked down to meet her and hand her a bouquet of white roses.

Then kissed her full on the mouth for everyone to see.

Brittany gasped while Everlee's eyes widened.

And the best part of the entire thing was that Zoe, angry Zoe, kissed him right back.

Dane released her, grabbed her hand, then walked her back through the line. They followed back into wardrobe, adrenaline pumping, so tense it was tangible.

That was what Brittany had loved about her job.

About modeling.

The adrenaline, the knowledge that people weren't just looking at her as a person but as a model for something they wanted for themselves. It was never about Brittany, it was about the designers and how she could make them look good. There was something so satisfying about helping someone else.

Because that was what she felt like she was doing, helping sell something she believed in, and enjoying herself in the process.

"Wow." Oliver pulled Brittany in for a kiss. "I'm not sure I'm ever going to recover from that. Until then, I just got paged, so I'm going to grab my cell and then I'll be back to celebrate." He looked back at Zoe. "We are celebrating, right?"

"Yes!" She hopped up and down. "Absolutely."

He disappeared. Brittany quickly changed and then went in search of Ronan. Maybe they could sit and talk?

"Hey." She found Chrissy instead, wiping off her makeup. "Is Ronan still here?"

"He went to go change." She shrugged and then reached for her purse, knocking Brittany's to the floor. "Oh, sorry!"

She reached to pick up the fallen lipstick and billfold and froze.

Lying face-up was a picture of Chrissy when she was twelve. "What's this?"

Brittany couldn't find her voice. "I can explain."

"Explain why you have my seventh-grade picture?" Chrissy's eyes darted back and forth as if she were trying to figure things out.

"I think you should sit." Brittany reached for her.

"No." Chrissy jerked away. "This is weird. You know this is weird, right? What's going on?"

"You knew you were adopted," Brittany said softly.

Chrissy's eyes widened. "No, there's no way, I don't believe—"

Brittany took a deep breath and blurted, "I'm your biological mother."

Chrissy burst into tears and ran off while everyone else just stared at her like she'd grown three heads.

Ronan and Oliver were already heading toward their dressing rooms when Chrissy raced by them. They both gave Brittany equally concerned looks.

Brittany gave Zoe a pleading look. Her friend nodded quickly. Brittany's eyes welled with tears as she took off after her daughter.

Her. Daughter.

She didn't have to look far.

Chrissy was in the corner, shoving her things into a small duffel bag, tears streaking her makeup, hands shaking. Her cell phone nearly slipped from her grip as she fumbled it and finally managed to get it inside the bag without it shattering on the floor.

"I'm sorry." Stabbing pains shot through Brittany's chest; her heart hurt more with each breath she took. "I didn't know, I promise. I just found out."

Chrissy stood to her full height and turned to her, crossing her arms. Her daughter was beautiful, wasn't she? Fierce. Strong. "How long?"

"Days." Brittany's voice cracked. "And, suddenly, it was like I was back in that hospital room, trying to decide the best future for you, for myself, for everyone." Tears filled her eyes. "I was going to wait until after the show."

Chrissy swiped under her eyes and hugged her body. "And how exactly were you planning on dropping that bomb? Hey, wanna know why we have the same hair and a similar nose? Surprise!"

Brittany squeezed her eyes shut and prayed for strength. "As silly as it sounds, I hadn't even gotten that far. I think I'm still in shock, too."

Chrissy leaned against the wall and then sank down until she was sitting near her bag. Models walked by them, makeup artists passed, racks of clothes rolled by. All of them reminders that the world kept spinning even though it felt like Brittany's had stopped.

Because she was staring at it.

Her world.

Her daughter.

"I loved you," Brittany whispered and then leaned down and reached for Chrissy's hand. "I loved you so much, but I'd just turned eighteen and your father was out of college already working hard—succeeding."

"I'm sixteen," Chrissy said in a wooden voice as she stared up at Brittany, her eyes searching, questions swarming between them like a thick fog. "You were young."

"Yes," Brittany agreed and then joined Chrissy on the floor. "I've never let you go. The memory of holding you in my arms, brushing back your hair, singing songs over you, knowing that someone else would get the honor of doing those things for the rest of your life. It was the hardest thing I've ever had to do."

Chrissy leaned her head on Brittany's shoulder. "My mom and dad died."

"I know." Brittany's throat felt like a ball was lodged in it. "I know."

"I was so mad." Chrissy sniffled. "So mad that God would take them away from me, so mad that they had to die. We had a perfect life."

Something in Brittany's chest eased. "You have no idea how happy that makes me."

"But they left... and then I just felt... empty. I knew I was adopted, but I didn't know anything beyond that, and I honestly didn't care because it was just one more person who didn't stay for me."

"Oh, sweetheart." Brittany reached for her hand. "I've always been here." She touched her chest as tears slid down her face. "And I've prayed for you every single night since the day you were born."

Chrissy burst into ugly sobs as she held onto Brittany.

They held each other long enough that they were starting to gain the attention of people who walked back and forth between shows.

Chrissy finally let out a deep sigh. "What happens now?"

"That's the best part." Brittany squeezed her hand and then kissed her forehead. "Whatever we want, right?"

"You mean it?" Chrissy's eyes were so bright, so innocent. Had Brittany ever been that young?

"I mean it." Brittany would die before letting anything happen to her daughter.

"I would like that." Chrissy finally smiled and then laughed through her tears. "Amazing, the one woman I looked up to all my life, and she's the one who gave me life."

Brittany almost started crying all over again. "It's a beautiful mess, isn't it?"

And, suddenly, it made sense.

All things together.

All things work together.

Brittany sighed. "We have time. Let's go eat before they send a search party. Maybe we can talk about getting you out of those model apartments."

Brittany hoped it wasn't too much, too soon.

Chrissy threw her arms around Brittany's neck. "Yes! I hate it there so much!"

"I figured." Brittany stood and held out her hand.

Chrissy hesitated and then looked up at her. "What about my... dad?"

Brittany hesitated and then took a deep breath. "He knows I was trying to find you. I was going to try to tell him tonight, give him time to process. Are you okay with that?"

"Yeah," Chrissy said quickly. "I think *I* need time to process this even..." She seemed embarrassed over it, though she didn't need to be. "What do I call you?"

"That's another good part." Brittany grinned. "Whatever you want. Just know I'm not going anywhere, all right?"

"All right." Chrissy took Brittany's hand and gave her one last hug.

As Brittany opened her eyes and looked across the room, she saw the devil himself, Dane Saldino, smile.

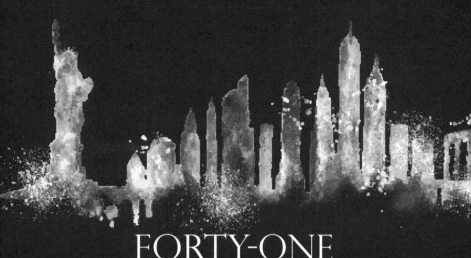

FORTY-ONE

"Well, that went well." Roger lifted his glass into the air and clinked it with Oliver's. Apparently, they were best friends now. At least, according to Roger, who'd decided it a minute ago when they ordered the same whiskey.

He judged people based on their drinks. Brittany suppressed a chuckle. He always had.

According to Roger, a guy who drank good whiskey... well, he was someone you could keep around. Plus, he was easy on the eyes.

Roger winked at Brittany and then gave a warm smile to Chrissy. Strange how things were working out.

Was she really sitting next to her daughter?

Had she really just done a fashion show with her child?

She smiled to herself and then reached under the table to squeeze Chrissy's fingers. She got a tight squeeze back.

Sixteen years of separation.

And the minute she had known, the second they had hugged, it was like part of her soul was knitting itself back together again.

So many tears shed after each of them had taken the catwalk.

And then to hold her hand, to have that moment with her where they were able to stand side by side facing the crowd. Magic.

All Brittany kept thinking was, *let them know, let them see.* She'd given up this special girl because she'd thought she had no other choice. Because she had been afraid. And if she were being totally honest… Because she had believed she would lose the career, the life she wanted if she kept her.

It just went to show that free will wasn't all it was cracked up to be. Neither was adulting.

"So." Oliver sat across from her, next to Roger. "I'm new to all of this. Would we call the whole show a success?"

"He wants to know if he looked good," Roger teased.

"Oh, no. I'm not worried about that in the slightest. I had leather pants on." He nodded confidently.

"Don't forget the vest," Zoe added with a lift of her glass into the air. "Seriously, guys, I don't know what I would have done without you." Her eyes flickered to Dane; the guy still had a smudge of makeup on his face. It would be comical if they were allowed to actually laugh at the guy without getting a violent sneer in their direction. "All of you."

Dane sighed. "I think I still have makeup on my face."

"Oh, honey, that's been there for the last hour. We took bets on how long you would last before you yelled at someone or shot something." Roger just shrugged while Oliver gave Brittany an amused grin.

Dane grumbled under his breath about fashion.

His pants didn't fit very well; they had been tailored for someone a lot thinner. Male models weren't exactly known for putting in gym time, let alone hitting leg day twice a week.

The pants almost split across his thighs when he walked, though Brittany was convinced that was probably what would sell them out in the first place. He made them look good, not the other way around.

In fact, all the men had done a fantastic job.

Even Ronan.

Brittany stared into her wine glass and then stared harder.

When was the last time she'd even drunk alcohol with the purpose to forget and numb the pain?

Weeks ago, she had been hiding behind it.

And now, she was staring at a full glass.

Two weeks ago, she hadn't even been able to think about Ronan, about her past, without wanting to numb it away.

Had she been using that as her therapy? As her way to escape?

"Well…" Everlee still looked pale and a bit fragile, but at least she was smiling again. "I think it was a huge hit." She turned to Zoe. "You're so talented, my friend."

Tears filled Zoe's eyes. "Thank you. I'm so overwhelmed, I think I'm going to sleep for a few years."

Dane made a face like he wasn't quite sure he liked the idea.

And Brittany couldn't blame him.

He was a man in love.

Because only a man in love would walk in a show, last minute, wearing a pink fedora.

Everything seemed perfect. It felt right. Oliver and her friends got along as if they had grown up together, and Dane had already planned an outing with him and a few people later that week for some sort of poker game.

Brittany should be happy.

But she wasn't.

She'd been given a glimpse of what her life could be like if she just came clean, and it was time to do exactly that. She'd already talked with Chrissy. Now, it was time for Ronan.

"Be right back." She stood and flashed Oliver a smile as she cradled her phone in her hand.

The ring tone felt like it would go on forever.

"Britt?"

"Hey, Ro." She cleared her throat. "Thank you for tonight. I know Zoe appreciates it."

He chuckled. "Well, I told her she had to vote for me in the next election, so now she owes me." He cursed. "I doubt anyone will let me live it down, a purple pinstripe suit. Don't get me wrong, it would look good on anyone but a stodgy politician."

She smiled down at the people passing by. "You aren't stodgy."

"A compliment?" He sounded tired. "Did you need something, or did you just want to make sure that my pride survived?"

"Actually..." Her lips felt dry, she licked them, and then just came out with it. "I need to tell you something."

"I'm listening."

"In person."

"I can't meet tonight."

"It's important."

"I'm flying to Martha's Vineyard for a party." He sounded like he didn't want to go. "Family obligations."

She frowned as more rain came down. "You're flying in this?"

"I don't really have a choice."

"Just be careful. We can talk when you get back, all right? It is urgent, but I know you have things…" Her voice trailed off as the door to the pub opened, revealing all her friends and Oliver laughing. The doctor had his arm around Roger, and they looked like they were having the time of their lives.

Obligations.

She wanted to be a part of something.

With Oliver.

She'd been an obligation with Ronan. A thing to take care of, to do. Not anymore, not now.

"Britt? You still there?"

"Sorry, long night. Just call when you get back. And please be safe."

"Always am."

She knew that he attempted it. It wasn't like the guy had a death wish, but he was known for taking risks, for just assuming that everything would be okay, and it hadn't failed him yet. But she had to wonder, how long could a person stay lucky without using their head?

Or having faith to get through.

"My feet hurt," Chrissy complained as she hugged everyone goodbye. "I need to work on my walk, and my—"

"Stop." Brittany pulled her in for another hug. "You were incredible." She brushed a piece of hair away from her face. "I was so proud. I *am* proud."

Tears filled Chrissy's eyes. "Really?"

"Yes." She clung to her daughter harder and then whispered in her ear, "Roger's going to take care of getting you out of the model apartments. That is if you want to live with me." She hoped her daughter couldn't hear the worry in her voice. She hadn't exactly had time to process anything.

"YES!" Chrissy yelled and then laughed. "I mean, you know what those apartments are like. Plus, last night, someone brought in some drugs, and I just… I don't want to be around that. Ever."

"Good." Brittany touched her face. "Oliver needs to know. It's…" She looked over her shoulder as Oliver and Dane chuckled at something. "Give me tonight to talk to him. I shouldn't have kept it from him. Then again, I didn't know you were actually here in the city. Or that the girl who looked at my poster for strength was the same one that I couldn't stop staring at when she was born."

Tears spilled over Chrissy's cheeks. "I'm so happy… so happy. You have no idea."

"Oh, I do." Brittany exhaled and gave her a watery smile then swiped under her eyes.

"You ready?" Roger wrapped an arm around Chrissy. "It seems we have a lot of work to get done. Don't worry, though. I'll save you from Marnie. She's always been petrified of me."

"Oh, yeah?" Chrissy laughed. "Why's that?"

"Let's just say I know enough about her to be very dangerous." He winked. "Now, tell me all about growing up in that small town with the cows. That sounds horrible…"

Chrissy giggled and walked off with him while Brittany stared after them. Longing washed over her.

They were going to be a family.

Oliver made his way over to Brittany. "Let me get you home. You have to be exhausted." He pulled her into his arms and brushed a kiss across her lips. She wanted more. She knew that now. It was as if the flood gates had opened and she realized that everything she could ever possibly want had been given to her, dropped into her lap despite her mistakes, regardless of her insecurity and her need to fix everything on her own.

She didn't hold back as she deepened the kiss, wrapping her arms around his neck, holding him there as she tasted him, the man she wanted to keep forever. The man who saw her for her.

The man she had lied to.

Abruptly, she pulled back. "I have something to tell you."

"And I have something to tell you."

"Really?" She tilted her head. "You go first."

"I'm going to marry you someday."

Her jaw dropped. "How much whiskey did you have?"

"More than you, less than Roger."

"So, a lot?" She let out a nervous laugh. "You can't just meet someone and a few weeks later tell them you're going to marry them."

He leaned in, his sexy smile on full display. "Just. Did." He pressed a kiss across her lips. "And I had one drink. Completely sober."

Breathless, she whispered, "You're impossible."

"That's why you'll eventually say yes." A grin spread across his face. "Plus, we both know I'm patient."

"All right, Romeo." She kissed him again, lingering there in that space between passion and genuine friendship. "Take me home. We can talk in the car."

"Great."

They said their goodbyes to everyone. Dane and Zoe seemed to be in deep conversation with Everlee, though, so through waves and quick hugs, they made their way out to the waiting Mercedes.

Brittany yawned behind her hand, suddenly exhausted.

"Knew you were tired."

"Shut up."

He opened her door, and she ducked in and buckled her seatbelt, vaguely aware of the car starting and the seat warmers turning on.

And then she was asleep. Floating, getting carried somewhere.

She clung to his warm body and smiled against his shirt, inhaling his spicy scent as she was placed on a mattress. Her heels were pulled off, and then a blanket was drawn over her body.

"Sleep," Oliver whispered. "We can talk tomorrow."

She opened her eyes. He was a blurry figure. "No, we should talk now. I can get... up."

"Britt, sleep. Please?" He grazed her cheek with his knuckles. "I'm going to head home."

It was on the tip of her tongue to ask him to stay in her guest room or on the couch or just stay until she fell asleep.

But she wondered if that would be too much temptation. Not only did she really like him, but she'd also gotten an insane view of his abs today as everyone changed backstage.

He was perfect. In every way.

And he was hers.

And she wanted more than anything… to be his, too.

Wait.

She would wait.

Patient, he'd said.

Ha, maybe she was turning into the impatient one. Because when you knew… you knew.

FORTY-TWO

1 DAY LATER

The rain hadn't let up that next day. It matched Brittany's mood. Oliver had been called into the hospital and had to cancel on their date. He'd put her to bed a night ago, and they'd texted, they'd talked on the phone, but she wanted to tell him about Chrissy in person. She'd already nearly had a heart attack when she realized that he'd dug through her purse for her keys.

Thankfully, the picture was tucked into her Kate Spade billfold, but it was too close, and she hated it.

Chrissy had moved some of her things into the apartment but said she had an appointment and was with Roger so not to worry. It was insane, really. Brittany had gone from not even knowing that Chrissy was her daughter to turning into a mom who needed to be texted every hour to make sure her child was okay.

It was a feeling that was both foreign and exciting.

She stared down at the phone in her hand, willing a new text to appear. She still hadn't heard from Ronan, and she needed him to know. With a sigh, she dialed his number again.

"Britt." He sounded stressed. "Sorry, I've been busy. I just got back into the city early this morning…"

"I know you're busy, Ro. I just…" Here went nothing. "I found her."

He was silent, his breathing heavy. "You found her?"

"Our little girl, not so little anymore, and I think you're going to want to know the rest. She's in the city—"

"I have to fly out tonight back to Martha's Vineyard again and then the house. Why don't I pick you up, and we can talk in the car, does that work? Eight?"

She sighed in relief. "Yes. Perfect. I'll be ready."

"I can't believe it," he whispered more to himself than to her, and then he let out a laugh. "I'm… thank you, Britt, thank you for finding her."

Well, she couldn't take all the credit. Somehow, her avenging angel had ended up being one that often looked like the devil himself. "Dane helped."

Ronan swore. "Of course, he did. The man has more secrets than the president."

"You would know," she teased.

"Hey, now. Dad never shared the scary stuff, trust me." He sounded light, happy. "I'll see you tonight, Britt."

"Tonight."

A weight lifted off her shoulders. She inhaled, exhaled, and stared at the clock. She had a few hours to herself, so she started going through a few pictures she knew Ronan would want. He was Chrissy's father, and he deserved to see the things that made his daughter click. And, hopefully, he'd want to meet her. Even though he already had at both the shoot and show, this was different, he would be meeting her with the knowledge that she came from their blood.

And at the time, their love.

Finally.

"Thank God," she whispered to herself before digging into the box once more.

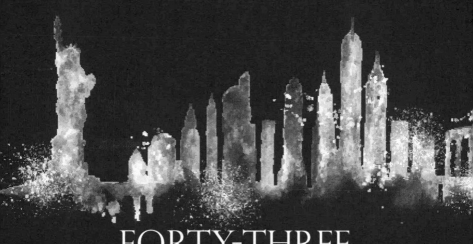

FORTY-THREE

Frederick was slippery.

They had everything they needed on him, close to everything, especially after his outburst at the fashion show.

All Dane kept coming back to was dangling bait in front of him like he'd been doing for the past few weeks, wearing him down, making him addicted.

He needed to catch Frederick in one of his lies, but it needed to be massive, something big enough to put him away, scary enough for him to want to confess whatever needed to be declared.

The videos were enough to get him prison time, but Dane wanted more, he knew there was more, and he knew that it involved Danica.

Dane refused to believe it. Didn't want to think that his sister had been with them, that she was a part of what

Frederick did. Was that what had led to her murder? Because that's what it was, a murder. There was no way Danica had committed suicide. The police were getting antsy, and he could only control them for so long, especially with a still-open investigation.

Dane thrummed his fingertips on the table while Zoe stretched her arms over her head and gave him a confused look. "Are you plotting world domination again?"

"No, I'll leave that to you," he teased.

"So, why the intense face?" She joined him at the table and then reached across and grabbed his hand. "Is it about the fashion show? And being forced to walk because of Marnie? That woman's a curse. What the heck does she have on all these people? It's like she's just as bad as you with trading secrets."

Dane's head snapped up. "What did you say?"

"That she's just as bad as you." Zoe winced. "Sorry, that came out wrong."

"Where's Roger?"

"Huh?"

He stood, knocking his chair over. "Roger, do you know where he is right now?"

"I think he's helping Chrissy move the rest of her stuff into Brittany's apartment, why?"

"He knows something." Dane wasn't sure how he hadn't seen it before. How else could he just pull Chrissy from Marnie? It wasn't done. Not in this industry. And Marnie hadn't even put up a fight. She'd just rolled over and moved on to her next victim. Oh, she was furious, sure, but she didn't challenge Roger for a reason.

Now to figure out what that reason was. Because whatever it was... Dane was convinced it was a piece of the puzzle.

Dane grabbed his keys. Zoe chased after him. He turned to stop her but found himself watching while she put on her favorite Frye boots and a leather jacket.

"What?" she asked when she caught his gaze.

"You don't have to come."

"I'm not letting you do something stupid without me. Plus, I know Roger. You guys are more like... I don't even know what you are. Regardless, I'm coming."

He opened his mouth to protest but then shut it and nodded.

Zoe looked so stunned, he would have laughed had he not been so intent on finding Roger and Chrissy.

"So..." Zoe dashed after him. "Is there a reason we're chasing Roger this afternoon?"

"Because secrets are our currency in this jungle, and I'd bet you my entire fortune that Roger knows Marnie's," Dane muttered. "Which means, she knows his. Full circle. Neither of them can truly attack because the injury would be self-inflicted on both sides."

Zoe grabbed his arm. "Is this about Frederick? Or something more?"

Dane stilled as the video of Jauq and Danica played on repeat in his head. He'd stopped watching; he didn't need to see the rest to realize that he had been filming them together. The timestamp? A week before her death.

"Do you remember how Danica acted before she died?"

Zoe's face broke out into a sad smile as they made their way into the waiting black SUV. "She was the happiest I'd seen her in a long time. Strange, since she and Jauq had broken up."

"Right. They broke up, and she was happy."

Zoe frowned. "Maybe she was faking it? Masking her pain?" Her tone was gentle, soft as if she were afraid to upset him.

"No. Danica was never good at masking pain. She wasn't like the rest of us, she felt it all, and she drowned in it, only to come up fighting. She wasn't upset before she died, Zoe. She looked like she was finally free."

Zoe licked her lips slowly and turned to him as the engine roared to life. "Are you saying she was killed?"

"We know she was killed."

"She was hanging from the closet, Dane." Tears slid down her cheeks.

With a sigh, Dane pulled out his phone, scrolled through his pictures, and held one up to her. It was a photo of the autopsy report. He waited for her eyes to scan it and then watched them widen in horror. The truth, he needed to tell Zoe the truth. "She was dead before she asphyxiated… the investigation has been ongoing, no leads. I took things into my own hands, paid off everyone to keep them quiet, off the trails I needed in order to find out what happened. She died from a brain injury, Zoe. And even if I could suspend belief and think that things had really gotten that bad, it's not physically possible to hit your head at that angle, snap your neck, then crawl to the closet and hang yourself."

"Oh, God." Zoe covered her mouth with her hands. "How long have you known?"

"Since the funeral."

"All this time? All the secrets? The clubs with Frederick?"

"Just trying to catch a rat. It's what I do." Dane dialed Roger's number and waited for him to pick up.

"Dane?" Roger sounded surprised. "Are you drunk-dialing?"

"Where are you?"

"Marnie had one last shoot scheduled for Chrissy. I took her myself to make sure she was safe and felt comfortable, and Everlee tagged along since we had to talk business. We're at the warehouse on Fifth."

Dread pooled in Dane's stomach. "Who's the photographer?"

"Frederick," Roger said in an irritated voice. "Don't worry, I can control him, have for years. Besides, Everlee looks ready to singe him alive every time he looks her way."

"Are you inside the building?"

"No. Closed shoot. It's for a sexy Athleta campaign. They wanted something different for this campaign. Horrible cell service in there, I walked out to make a few calls."

"Go back in. NOW!"

"Calm down, like I said it's fi—" A muttered curse followed.

"What's wrong?"

"The door's locked." The sound of metal crashed and twisted. "I can't get it open, let me see if there's another way to get in."

"Hurry, we'll be there in five." Dane hung up and gave Zoe a look. "Everlee and Chrissy are alone with Frederick."

Zoe gave him a worried look. "How is he even working? After the child pornography scandal?"

"I don't think he's working. I think he's doing what he does best. Lying. And I think Marnie helped him do it."

It took another seven minutes of traffic for them to get to the abandoned warehouse. And things quickly went from bad to worse.

Makeup and hair got locked out when Frederick sent them away because it was making Chrissy uncomfortable.

So, the only individuals inside the building were Chrissy, Everlee, and a very angry Frederick.

Dane dialed the police chief and briefed him on the situation and then started to search for other ways to get into the building.

Zoe and Roger helped.

They tried not to look too frantic. According to everyone else, they were just worried that something had gone wrong, and the three of them were trapped.

But inside, Dane knew it was worse than that.

Frederick had violent tendencies. He'd thrown Everlee against a wall. And in a few days, he was going to be charged with multiple counts of possession of child pornography.

"I think I found something," Zoe yelled at them, gesturing to a door that led to the back of the warehouse. She tried the knob. "Locked."

The window was big enough for someone to fit through. Or something.

He was out of time.

Dane grabbed the scarf that Roger kept perpetually tied around his right hand whenever he was out on a shoot and wrapped it around his fist then punched in the glass. It shattered around his knuckles like a thousand tiny needles.

He reached inside and tried to turn the lock. But it was too far down.

"Let me." Zoe moved in front of him. "Move the glass so I don't get eviscerated through my stomach, and you can lift me."

"Are you sure?" He would die before he let anything happen to her. Her emerald-colored eyes lit up with determination.

"Do it now."

He shoved the pieces of glass still protruding from the window and double-checked to make sure it was seamless, then lifted her in his arms as she crawled through the window, using his body as leverage. "I think I got it."

Something clattered, and then the door opened.

He carefully pulled her back to the ground, tempted to kiss her senseless. Instead, he shoved her and Roger behind him, held a finger to his lips, and moved around all the old equipment until they reached the main part of the warehouse.

Crying. Someone was crying.

"I wonder what it feels like to know that you're being replaced, right in front of your very eyes, by someone more beautiful," Frederick said in a low voice. "Do you remember how our shoots used to go, Everlee?"

Chrissy winced as Frederick wrapped his hands around her neck. "It was so easy to seduce you, to get you to want me, and now, you've ruined everything because you got too curious. All those files, all of them, point to me. Me!" he roared. "My entire career is gone because you got too needy, too jealous."

"I got needy?" Everlee sputtered. "Jealous? I'm your wife!"

"Guess you forgot about those vows the minute you hacked into my files and ratted to the police, huh? What did you think you were going to find? Sex tapes of me and young models like this?" He thrust Chrissy forward. "I keep those under the bed so that when I'm forced to sleep with you, I can imagine I'm with them, over and over again."

Chrissy whimpered.

"Let her go," Everlee said in a strong voice as she tried to approach him. "She's done nothing wrong, she's just a kid."

"You were too, and now look at you," he sneered. "My entire life is on the line because of you. It's only fair I take you down with me, don't you think?"

Everlee froze. "What do you mean?"

"I mean, I'm a liar, it's what I do. I'll make sure they realize that we worked as a team, the girls trusted you, and in return, you lured them to me with promises of stardom. Isn't that right, Chrissy?"

"No." Chrissy tugged at his hands, but he was too strong.

Dane had seen enough. He moved to get up, but Zoe kept him down and shook her head slowly as she pulled out her cell and started to record.

"Frederick, there's no way out of this, and that's perjury, plus blaming it on me just makes you guilty."

"My lawyer says I'm already going to prison!" he bellowed and then burst out laughing. "And the worst part of it? I wasn't working alone! I was told to keep quiet."

"What do you mean?" Everlee asked, clearly trying to keep him talking, buying them time, praying for a savior. "With the pornography ring?"

"Do you know how much money's in the black market? Millions. Do you know how many young girls will do anything just for a chance to be like you and your friends? Even more."

The acidic taste of bile rose into Dane's throat; he was going to be sick if he had to hear much more of this.

"Maybe you should just turn on them," Everlee said in a strong voice while Chrissy still struggled against the photographer's hold. "Instead of me. Sounds like a better idea."

Frederick's eyes were wild. "Don't you think I thought of that? But I can't. I can't. They know too much, we all did... too much."

The guy was starting to sound like a lunatic.

"Too much?" Everlee prodded. "What do you mean?"

"We didn't mean for it to happen." Frederick loosened his grip on Chrissy, then threw her to the floor and pulled out a gun. "Stop talking!"

Chrissy crawled to Everlee and grabbed her legs. To her credit, Everlee didn't look like she was about to pass out.

"What happened?" Everlee asked softly. "If you're going to kill us, if you're going to prison, you may as well say it, get it off your chest. It's obviously been weighing on you."

"Stop." Frederick moved closer to them with his gun. "Talking."

Everlee held Chrissy in her arms. "So, what are you going to do now, Frederick? Kill us? Frame us? Let us go?"

The gun shook in his hand.

"I'm curious, as well." Dane stood and slowly made his way over to them while Roger and Zoe remained hidden in the darkness. "You have so many wonderful choices. Prison, death, blood... Then again, you know all about choices, don't you, Frederick?"

"I didn't do it." Frederick shook his head. "I did nothing wrong."

"You mean other than taking pictures of eleven-year-old girls? Okay, sure..."

Dane lunged for him and knocked the gun out of his hands. They both scrambled for it, but Dane was faster. He hit Frederick in the temple and pushed to his feet. Then he kicked him in the ribs.

Frederick howled with pain, then charged Dane kicking him in the shin before Dane had a chance to shove him backward causing Frederick to stumble to the ground.

"You have two choices." Dane pointed the gun at Frederick's head. "Answer a question, and you live. Fail to answer, and I'll make sure that you get the death sentence. It will be easy to frame you, easy to make things look like a happy accident. You know who I am, you know what I can do. So, I'm going to ask you something, and you're going to tell me."

Blood dripped down Frederick's chin. "No."

"Fine." Dane fired a shot into Frederick's left kneecap and waited until the guy stopped screaming obscenities. "I can do this all night. The police chief and I golf every Sunday, and the DA owes me a favor. Need I go on?"

Frederick stared him down, his teeth chattering.

Another shot, this one into the other kneecap.

"Danica died from blunt-force trauma to the head," Dane said in a calm voice. "You were one of the last people to see her alive, the police proved that. I want to know what happened. I want you to tell me the story once and for all. I have enough proof to put you away for a very long time, I could probably frame you for her murder at this point, especially after your horrible decision-making in trying to put the blame on your wife and using Chrissy as bait…" He trailed off. "What happened that night? Because you're suspect number one."

Frederick paled and then shook his head in defeat. "It wasn't me, it was an accident! We were going to talk to her calmly and you know Danica, she was anything but calm, threatened to expose everything, she tried running past, I shoved her back, we didn't know she would trip and hit her head. You have to believe me, it was an accident!"

"So you say."

"She knew about the pornography ring," Frederick said through clenched teeth. "Jauq, well… Jauq helped build the website. Marnie—" He stopped himself and looked down. "Marnie supplied the models. Some of the ones who didn't make it out here were given other… opportunities to prove themselves. That was all Jauq and Marnie."

"Are we talking sex slavery?" Dane asked in shock.

"It's easy for someone to disappear in the big city, and if someone pays enough…" Frederick winced in pain. "Marnie had an operation in the UK, and it was booming. We were new in the industry, young. The money was good and it was easy! Danica and Jauq were fighting one night and she went to his office and the idiot had his email open, it didn't take her long to connect the dots." He winced, "Like I said, we were younger then, stupid, Marnie's very convincing!"

"Don't blame something like this on stupidity and innocence." Dane dropped the gun to the floor.

"That's it?" Frederick struggled to sit, grunted, his face twisting in agony as he fell back to the side. After a couple of deep breaths, he stared up at Dane. "I can go now?"

"Oh, absolutely," Dane said with fake enthusiasm. "Let me just make sure we have the devil ready to escort you to Hell." Dane pulled out *his* gun, the one he always used, not the dirty, discarded one Frederick had probably bought at a pawn shop while wearing a disguise. He held it up. "Give me one reason not to shoot you."

"Don't." Zoe came up behind him. "Don't do it, Dane. You don't want his blood on your hands... he's not worth it." Her voice wrapped around him.

He slowly lowered the gun just as she touched his arm.

"Roger, open the doors." His voice sounded hollow as adrenaline buzzed through him.

Footsteps, and then the door opened.

"Let's go." He lifted Chrissy into his arms while Zoe and Everlee clung to each other.

"Hey!" Frederick called from his spot on the floor. "Hey!"

Police moved past them as they walked out.

It was going to be a long night.

For everyone.

Chrissy shook in his arms, and he was reminded of his little sister, with stars in her eyes and joy reflected on her face.

She had been killed for doing the right thing.

She had been murdered for being that same young girl who'd moved to the city to pursue her dreams. She had been killed for robbed innocence and the need for justice.

Dane shuddered as Chrissy held him close, tears streaking down her face.

He stopped walking when Roger finally caught up to them. He asked, "Did you know?"

He didn't have to specify.

Roger sighed. "I heard rumors about Marnie, but there're always rumors swirling around her and her models. No, I didn't know."

"Then why? Why is she so scared of you?"

"She's not scared of me. She just knows I know a few of her secrets. She's ten years older than she claims, and she came from Cheyenne, Wyoming. Many years ago, when she was still fresh-faced and new to the industry, she tried to seduce a gay man," He pointed at himself, "And the real clincher... she's Frederick's mother, and Jauq's lover. Take your pick."

Dane's jaw dropped to the floor, or at least it felt like it. "What?"

"It's the jungle, things get wild," Roger said with a hint of sadness. And then he was cupping Chrissy's face. "I'm so sorry, I didn't know—"

"I know." She sucked in a shaky breath. "I know you didn't, I just... I really need my mom."

Dane cursed as he realized he was yet again giving Brittany life-altering news while holding her daughter in his arms.

History.

It had no choice but to repeat itself and beg of you to make the right decision a second time.

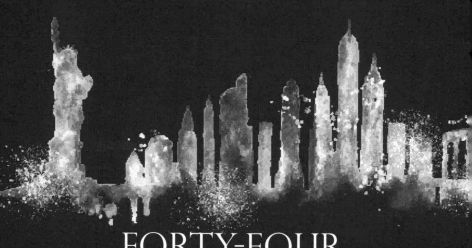

FORTY-FOUR

The limo felt the same, even though Brittany knew it wasn't. Maybe it was that the air hung heavy with those same tense feelings from before? From all of the events she'd attend with Ronan, both political and personal.

The only thing that had changed.

Was her.

She smiled at him.

Finally.

She finally felt like she could give him at least that and mean it. Maybe it was Oliver. Perhaps it was finally reconnecting with Chrissy. Whatever it was, she felt at peace, something she hadn't felt in a very long time.

"She's beautiful, you know." Ronan released a deep sigh as a tear rolled down his cheek and dripped onto the new iPhone with the bright pictures of their daughter's childhood. "Just like her mama."

Brittany put a hand on his arm. "I'd like to think she has the best of both of us."

"Sometimes, I wonder if my best still isn't enough," he rasped, grabbing her hand and kissing her fingertips. "Sixteen years. I lost sixteen years because I listened to my mother. I gave in to the fears, and I left—" His voice cracked. "I'll never forgive myself for leaving you."

Brittany pulled her hand away as sorrow wrapped its hands around her throat and squeezed, making it hard to breathe. "But you did, Ro. And a part of you will always belong more to the people than to me, or to her."

"Don't say that." He shook his head.

"Ro…" Tears filled her eyes. "It's okay to be that person, to be someone that others look up to. We need more people like you in this world, in politics. Don't focus on the lost sixteen years. Focus on the fact that you have time now."

He gritted his teeth and shook his head, sliding his phone back into his pocket. He didn't answer, just stared straight ahead, shutting her out again. He was good at that.

And now, she knew the signs.

He'd only ever let her get close enough to see pieces of him. He never wanted to show her the ugly, the bad, the unloved side that drove him to want to succeed in every area of his life—to prove his mother wrong and his father right.

"Time. Right." Voice heavy with sadness, Ronan turned to her, reaching for her hands. "Is it us? Is it the universe? I'm ready to start over, I need that, I think…" He looked down at their hands. "I think I could be a fantastic father. I want to try, why can't we try?"

Words she'd always wanted to hear from him. But now, they were too late, not just because it had been years, not even because so many hurt feelings stretched between them like a ravine, but because she'd already given her heart to someone else.

The temptation was there, though.

To have that happy family. The perfect house, American Dream. Everything she'd always wanted. Except now when she looked at the picture in her head, it was Oliver's face smiling back at her.

She needed to tell Oliver about Chrissy. It was time. It wasn't fair. And that was a risk she was willing to take because regardless of Oliver's feelings, she had her daughter back.

And peace in her soul.

No matter what, she would be okay.

"Ro..." She squeezed his hands. "You'll be a fantastic father to Chrissy. I know it, and so do you. You're a busy man, just don't make promises you can't keep."

"My father was good to us," he said in a serious voice. "He was busy, but he was fair, he was good."

"I know he was, Ro. Everyone loved him. Your mom lost a part of herself when he was killed. And I think you did, too."

He just nodded.

The limo came to a stop, and all too soon, his door was opened for him.

He put one leg out, and then turned and gripped her face between his palms. "One more chance, please."

Tears filled his eyes and hers. "Ro—"

"I love you."

But he didn't.

She knew what love was now.

He loved the idea of them, the possibility of getting a do-over. He might love her with the pieces of himself he allowed her to see, but he didn't love her with everything he had.

And she wanted it all. Regardless of how painful it might be to lose it—she wanted it, was greedy for it. Needed it like her next breath.

"I can't." The words were painful, her tears felt like knives falling down her face, pricking her skin, causing a river of blood to wash over all of the hurt feelings between them like a baptism. "You know I can't."

"I know," he whispered. "I know. I just wish I hadn't been so stupid to let go of you once, let alone watch you walk away twice."

"I never walked away."

He hung his head and dropped his hands. "He's a lucky man, you know, that surgeon."

"This isn't goodbye, Ronan. We'll figure out a plan for Chrissy, all right?"

"It's not goodbye, but it hurts the same, Britt. It feels like my heart's getting ripped out of my chest, and yet I know it's going to be okay. It has to be, right?"

"Yes." She relaxed and pulled him into a tight hug. "I prayed for you, you know."

"I felt it, you know," he said back just as quickly. "I don't know what I would do without your prayers. I highly doubt God hears mine anymore."

"Of course, he does—because for sixteen years, I prayed that we'd finally find peace between us."

"Me, too." He let out a sigh and hugged her tight again. "I have to go."

"Be safe, Ro."

"Always am." He shot her a mischievous wink. "I'll call you when I land, all right?"

Something twisted in her chest at the sight of him getting out of the limo with his two bags. The plane wasn't big. It was one of his private ones that his mother hated, but Brittany knew Ronan. He was happy in the sky. It was the only place in this world where he had control.

Above the Earth, floating, he could be free.

He was always like a bird, wasn't he? Trapped in a gilded cage of his family's making.

The perfect life.

Ha. She knew it too well.

People saw what they wanted to see, like an Instagram account with only happy pictures. That was the life she lived, the life he'd lived.

Until now.

He waved at her from the cockpit just as the Limo started to pull away. She'd never looked back whenever he flew out. It scared her too much when they were dating, to think it could be her last time seeing him.

But this time, this time she turned around and blew him a kiss, then said a prayer. And she had to place her hand over her chest as more distance grew between them.

Her cell rang as the limo pulled out onto the street.

"Britt!" Everlee was sobbing. She could hear something else in the background. "Hurry, you have to hurry, it's Chrissy!"

"What? What do you mean, it's Chrissy?" Brittany's hands started to shake. "Everlee!"

"She's hurt, long story—Britt, she's going to be fine, but you need to go to the hospital. Oh, God, this is all my fault. All my fault. I'm so sorry, Britt, I'm so sorry!"

"What happened?" Britt tried again, sickness pounding like nails into her heart. "Everlee!"

"Frederick attacked her. He got really angry, he just… lost it. Marnie said that Chrissy had one last contract in her shoot and that she had to be there. Roger came, so we thought it would be fine, but then he got locked out." She choked out another sob. "Frederick had a gun. She's in the ambulance, shaken up. She just… she needs her mom."

Brittany squeezed her eyes shut as fresh tears ran down her cheeks. "I'm on my way. Oliver's hospital?"

"Yes." Her voice quivered.

"I'll be there in fifteen." She quickly jotted off information to the driver, and as they turned around, she dialed Ronan's number.

It went straight to voicemail.

Maybe he was already in the air.

But it would be too soon.

She dialed again. When it went to voicemail again, she decided to wait a bit.

The fifteen minutes to the hospital were the most stressful of her life. She almost got out of the car and sprinted through the congested traffic, but they finally made it. She tried Ronan's number a few more times.

All she got was voicemail again and again. It wasn't like him to turn off his phone, but she knew he'd been stressed, busy. He probably wanted peace, and he could have put it in airplane mode already.

She shoved her phone back into her purse and ran to the ER nurses' station. "Hi, I'm Brittany—"

"Oh! You look the same as when you came in sixteen years ago." Amelia, the nurse from her past, stood and gave her a warm smile. "I'm so happy to see you. I know it was such a hard decision to put your little girl up for adoption. But you look like you're thriving."

As the surprise of seeing Amelia again wore off, Brittany opened her mouth to explain why she was there.

"Little girl?" A man's voice choked from behind her.

Heart thumping against her ribs, Brittany turned. Dread lodged in her stomach like chunks of cement as she took in Oliver's pallor and shocked expression.

"Oliver…" she croaked.

His eyes narrowed, and a mask of distrust settled over his face.

Commotion near the bay doors drew her attention. An ambulance was just pulling up, lights flashing but the siren off. That had to be Chrissy.

Dane's familiar SUV pulled up right behind it.

Zoe, Everlee, and Dane all filtered out, while the paramedics unloaded Chrissy.

"I'll explain. She needs me now. Sixteen years ago, she needed me. And I won't make that same mistake again. I won't let others dictate my future for me. So, if you're going to walk away, please do it now." Hot tears streamed down her cheeks as Oliver shook his head, turned, and did just that.

Britt didn't have time to think about what it meant.

Both men were out of her life.

But she had her daughter.

Her beautiful, brave daughter.

"Chrissy!" She ran as fast as she could in her heels toward the gurney. "What happened?" Bruises lined the outside of Chrissy's throat; they were faint. A bit of blood trickled down her lower lip.

"He had a gun," Everlee whispered. "Apparently, she'd been denying him for weeks. Frederick was angry at me, upset that I helped turn over critical information to Dane about him being involved with a child pornography scheme." She sobbed into Zoe's arms while Dane tenderly held both women.

"Dane?" She covered her mouth with her hands. He had a slight limp but otherwise looked fine, angry but fine. "Did you…"

"He deserved death. I would kill him for looking at any one of you sideways. And I would have, except Zoe intervened. Frederick's in police custody."

"Okay." It was too much information, too much… everything. Brittany reached for her daughter's hand and squeezed it. "You're going to be okay."

"I was so scared," Chrissy admitted, trying to sit up. The paramedic gently pushed her back down. "I prayed, though. I prayed… I think it worked." Her eyes squeezed shut as a tear slid along her bloody lip. "I just thought what would you do, you know? In that situation? What would you do? All I got out was, God."

"Sometimes." Brittany kissed her hand. "That's all we need."

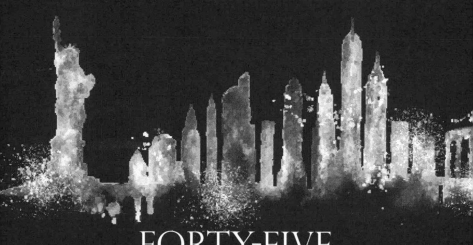

FORTY-FIVE

Chrissy was going to be fine. Right? She had to be.

Brittany clung to her daughter's hand as they sat in the small ER room, waiting for the doctor to show up.

It was taking longer than she would have liked, plus having all of them in that small room wasn't helping. But nobody wanted to leave, and Dane looked too angry to be let loose on the city of New York.

Was it wrong of her to want to set the monster loose? To let him make everyone pay? To accidentally kill Frederick in that prison cell? Fresh anger hit her in the chest as she tried to keep herself calm in front of Chrissy.

"Britt." Chrissy's voice was strong. "You're shaking."

"I know." Brittany's teeth chattered. "I'm just... I keep thinking about what could have happened, and I wasn't there... again. I wasn't there for you."

"You've always been there." Chrissy smiled. "When my parents were killed in that car accident, it was your poster that I stared up at, your image that motivated me to do something with my life instead of wallowing in sadness. It was your ridiculous workout DVD that introduced me to Pilates. It was always you, this person I didn't know but felt connected to despite the distance and weirdness of the situation. You." She pressed her lips together and then burst into tears. "You've always been there; you just didn't know it."

Britt crawled onto the bed with her daughter, kicked off her shoes, and rocked Chrissy while she cried.

And it was then that she realized.

She was on the same floor she'd been on sixteen years ago.

She was just on the other side of the obstetrics unit.

With her daughter.

Rocking her, like she had done the day she was born.

Crying, holding her, praying over her faster than her thoughts could keep up with her words.

Full circle.

Except Ronan was gone.

And Oliver had turned away.

A knock sounded on the door.

Light from the hallway framed a silhouette. It was impossible to make out Oliver's expression, but he leaned against the door like he always did, as if he'd practiced it for her a million times.

Warmth surged through her. Please, let him forgive her. Please, let it be okay.

"Oliver?" Brittany sat up. "What are you doing here?"

He locked eyes with her. "I told you I wasn't a guy who walked away. And I'll prove that to you every single day that you allow me to be in your life. No more secrets, Britt."

"No more secrets," she choked out. Was that it? Just a warning and then things were back to normal? She was used to emotional terrorism, passive-aggressiveness, jealousy. Instead, Oliver simply told her to be honest.

Dane looked ready to intervene if need be, and Zoe was already holding him back.

"You're a surgeon." Dane pointed out the obvious, making Britt laugh despite her tears.

"Thank you, I'm fully aware of my profession. I'm still on shift, and I wanted her to have the best treatment, so I kicked Dr. Byrne out. He'll be fine, he needed a break anyway, and this is a family thing... isn't it?"

Dane seemed to like that answer. He nodded his head and stepped back, Zoe clinging to his side.

"Chrissy." Oliver moved around the bed and squeezed the girl's free hand. "Your CT came back clear along with your lab work. Other than a few cuts and bruises from that maniac, everything looks good. You should make a complete recovery. And I'm happy to announce there will be no scars, at least not on the outside."

Chrissy's eyelids lowered, and then she tilted her head at him. "How much schooling did you go through?"

"Chrissy." Brittany covered her face with her hands. "He's a doctor. Plus, he operates on people, it's a lot."

"Your mom's right," Oliver agreed. If a pin dropped at that moment, the sound would explode through that hospital room. "It's a lot of schooling, but I love what I do."

"And my mom? Do you love her?"

"I see what you did there." Oliver let out an amused laugh.

"I'm sixteen, I'm born to manipulate." She sat up a bit. "Plus, it keeps the focus off of me and what happened." She looked away.

"What happened wasn't your fault," Oliver said gently, walking farther into the room. "And I love your mother very much, but she thinks it's too soon."

Chrissy let out a sigh. "Then you should marry her."

"Chrissy!" Brittany was ready to crawl under the cot and plug her ears.

"Who's getting married?" Roger called from the door. His gaze settled on the bed. "Chrissy, I'm so sorry sweetheart, I had no idea. I never would have stepped outside that cursed building had I known. I just gave my report to the police. Otherwise, I would have ridden with everyone else. You poor, sweet girl." He kissed her cheek and hugged her. "I'll kill that bastard for what he did to you—"

"Took care of it," Dane said in a bored tone. "And when have you ever lifted a finger other than to snap it at a waiter for more wine?"

"Man has a point," Zoe said under her breath while Everlee let out a small laugh.

Roger waved him off and approached the bed. "Dear girl, I had no idea what he had planned, what he was capable—"

"It's not your fault." Chrissy's voice was strong, confident. "Just like it's not mine, right?"

"Right." Roger leaned down and kissed her forehead.

"So," Chrissy interjected yet again, her gaze landing on Oliver. "Shouldn't you ask her?"

"Ask her?" Roger repeated. "Huh?"

"Oliver, you said you loved her."

"Sweetheart, it's been two weeks," Brittany said through clenched teeth.

"When you know, you know," Chrissy argued.

"Any drugs you can give her?" Brittany stood and gave her daughter a serious look that probably came across as more nervous than anything.

Oliver beamed at her. "Actually, I agree with the sixteen-year-old."

"Nobody ever does. I think I like you." Chrissy laughed. It felt good to hear her daughter laugh. It did something to Brittany's insides, made her want to laugh with her.

"Thanks, I like you, too." Oliver winked and then gave her a fist bump. "By the way, according to your chart, you just had a birthday. I think I see shopping money in your future if you can convince your mom to at least think about saying yes."

"I have a good feeling about you."

"You're already dreaming about purses, aren't you?" Roger laughed. "For your mom, it was always shoes. But for you? Purses."

"They hold things," Chrissy pointed out. "And they change an outfit instantly."

Oliver narrowed his eyes at her. "You're going to be expensive, aren't you?"

Chrissy gave him a cheeky grin. Already, her face looked lighter, happier. Brittany let out a sigh of relief, only to suck in a breath seconds later as Oliver dropped to one knee in front of her friends and family and grabbed her hands. "Will you… do me the honor… of marrying me…?" He grinned at Chrissy. "In the near future, you know, once we date a little longer and I get to know the family better."

"How far in the future?" Brittany asked with tears in her eyes, happy ones.

"Two weeks."

"Two months," she fired back.

"Days." He grinned, getting to his feet.

"You're impossible."

"Hey!" He tucked a piece of hair behind her ear. "When you know, you know. Just try stopping me, I dare you."

He leaned in and pressed a kiss to her mouth. She sighed against him, suddenly exhausted. "Yes. Let's save a very near future date… how's that?"

"Perfect." He grinned as if he'd just won when she realized that maybe they all had. "And now that that's settled. Thanks, Chrissy." With a sassy half-grin, he winked. "I'm going to go see a man about getting you guys checked out so you can get some rest."

"Thank you." Brittany clung to him one last time.

"Anything for you."

"Not just for that." She lowered her head.

He tilted her chin. "Never apologize for having secrets. We all do. My only disappointment was in your inability to realize that I always want to help carry the load, however burdensome that may be, all right?"

"She's not a burden."

"I can hear you," Chrissy piped up.

"She's sixteen," Oliver teased.

"That, too!" Chrissy grumbled.

"I do want to love you. I want this," Brittany said with tears in her throat.

Oliver lowered his head, his lips brushing against hers. "Then trust me, trust us, trust this, and if all else fails, trust Roger, he's a genius."

"Knew I liked him..." Roger said from the corner. The rest of the group fell into quiet laughter.

"Be right back." Oliver left the room.

"Dane?" Brittany was going to ask for another favor, but she knew this was one that Dane would do without question. "Can you make sure all of Chrissy's things make it to my apartment? I'm not sure if Roger still has stuff in his car or—"

"Already done," Dane said in a smug voice with an equally haughty smile. "I texted a few of my men in the SUV once the paramedics said that Chrissy was going to be okay."

"Men?" Chrissy asked, her eyes narrowed. "As in like... guys that work for you?"

"Leave it," Roger said through clenched teeth. "Dane, have I ever told you how nice you fill out a jacket?"

"Several times, actually," Dane said, also through clenched teeth, though his eyes danced with humor. "Especially after the runway show when you ran your hands over my biceps for a solid ten seconds."

"Lint. I was searching for lint."

"Right."

"You know..." Chrissy tilted her head at him. "You look like one of those guys in those mafia books that—"

The room quieted.

"Okay, good talk." Brittany broke the tense hush. "What do you say we go shopping and decorate your new bedroom tomorrow? We can get to know each other and try to figure out this crazy fashion jungle together."

"Yeah," Chrissy said through her tears. "I would really like that."

"Good." Brittany squeezed her daughter tightly and thanked God that she was safe, that she was in her arms, that things were as they should be.

The only missing piece was Chrissy meeting Ronan.

Brittany frowned, realizing that he hadn't called her back. It wasn't like him to not respond.

"Good news," Oliver announced as he walked back into the hospital room. "I have discharge papers right here, and my lovely nurse Sarah is going to check you out, all right? Hospital rules dictate that you have to leave in a wheelchair. Other than that, we can get you out of here in about twenty minutes. Sound good?"

"Great." Chrissy nodded. Her smile was so pretty, so familiar. She might have Brittany's hair, but she had Ronan's smile.

He would be so proud of her.

So proud.

Brittany let out an exhale and looked across the room just as Dane lifted his phone closer to his face, then slowly lowered it, and locked eyes with her, giving his head a slow shake.

And then he was running out of the room.

Running.

She'd never in her life seen Dane run.

He didn't need to, did he?

"Dane?" Zoe yelled.

And somehow, Brittany knew.

She knew.

"I'll be right back." On wooden legs, she followed Dane out of the room and down the hall to the nurses' station where patients and staff hovered below a flat-screen TV.

"Breaking News, New York Senator Ronan Kampbell, Jr., son of the late president Ronan Kampbell crashed shortly after takeoff from Teterboro Airport, double engine failure, no survivors."

Brittany gasped, covering her face with her hands just as Dane rushed to her side and caught her.

And for the second time in her life, Brittany collapsed against a crime boss's chest and cried.

For a child lost and found.

For a man whose life was not his own.

And in the end.

Was cut too short.

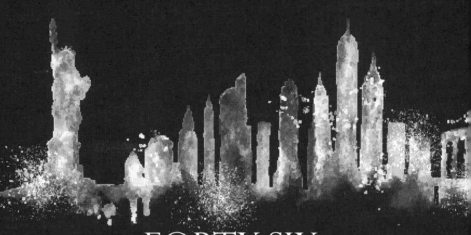

FORTY-SIX

1 WEEK LATER

It was a funeral fit for a king.

The week went by in a blur. Reporters were scattered along the streets with cameras held high, each of them greedy for a shot of the grieving family.

Of them.

A year ago, she had stood there and cried over Danica's death. Now, she was back, crying over Ronan's.

Life could change in an instant, couldn't it?

Chrissy stood silently, crying on Brittany's right. Oliver supported them both on the left.

Roger and Grace huddled next to the small group of people invited to the funeral. Every expression was stoic. Sad.

It didn't matter that there was enough military personnel there to make it a funeral for an American hero, or that three past presidents stood side by side, tears in their eyes.

It didn't matter anymore. Because he wasn't here, he wasn't living, breathing. The pomp and circumstance were empty. They were celebrating a life lived—one cut too short by any standard.

A life that should still be here.

It wasn't a happy ending.

Not for Ronan.

All Brittany wanted to do was ask why.

But the only answer she got was life.

Life.

There was no why in life, only free will, decisions built on other life-altering choices.

And life.

Tears streaked down her face as they lowered the casket into the ground, and her heart broke all over again. Not for herself, though she was in mourning for what could have been.

No, her heart was broken over the fact that the first time Chrissy saw her father with the knowledge of who he was— was while burying him.

And Brittany wanted nothing more than for her daughter to know the good things Ronan had done, not the abandonment, but the fight he'd given on the Senate floor, the way he moved in rooms and commanded a crowd.

His legacy deserved something more than Brittany's sadness over everything that had transpired between them.

And Chrissy deserved to know that her dad, to most people, even most times to Brittany, was an American hero.

"Let us pray." The pastor held open his hands, a Bible in his right, his left palm facing the crowd as if he were blessing everyone during such a devastating time.

Reporters were suddenly stoic.

Dane hadn't blinked, just stared down at the casket as if it weren't real. She knew they'd been friends; he'd helped Ronan get elected, after all. And Ronan had helped Dane gain control of the darker parts of the city.

And now, he was gone.

Dane's gaze flicked to Brittany—it was out of character for him to stare at anyone too long—and then he gave her a two-finger salute.

It was something that Ronan had always done to her when he said goodbye, and it only occurred to her then.

He hadn't done it last week.

Had he known?

Somewhere in his gut?

In his soul?

Had he felt that something would happen?

She'd turned back around.

She'd felt like they had no time; he'd felt the same. The entire conversation had taken place in the past tense as if they didn't have a chance for a future, and she wondered if that was one final gift that God had given them.

The gift of a final goodbye.

Of reconciliation.

That even in the darkest moments of a person's life—there was a chance for peace, for the human soul to find rest, even in pain.

There was always a way out.

An opportunity.

A window instead of a door.

She nodded to Dane, and then she was following the family as they all dropped rose petals onto the casket. She wasn't sure why the family had included her in their seating arrangement.

The same family that had sent her a restraining order.

Her tears mixed with the petals as they dropped in rapid succession onto the casket, one, two, three. Goodbye.

Memories of Ronan's laugh assaulted her.

His kiss.

His promises of forever.

The smell of his cologne.

"If you could do anything for the rest of your life, what would you do?" They danced under the stars, near their blanket in Central Park and the Chinese takeout she could barely afford.

Ronan stilled and then looked up at the sky. "I'd be up there. I'd fly and fly and fly." He spread his arms wide while she hugged his chest. "There's freedom in flying."

"Yeah." She hugged him. "There really is."

Brittany lowered to her knees, probably breaking protocol for this sort of thing, and reached her hand over the mahogany then released the crumpled piece of paper with their daughter's footprints on it and the pieces of rose dust that accompanied it. "Fly, Ro, fly."

She stood, lifted her head to the stormy sky, and imagined him there, happy. Free. Oliver grabbed her hand and held her close while Chrissy did the same on her other side.

"Let's go home." Brittany kissed her daughter's head as they slowly made their way out of the crowd, only to come face-to-face with Nancy.

Out of the corner of her eye, Brittany saw Oliver tense. Both Roger and Dane weren't far away, and Grace looked ready to march over and throw words like daggers.

Nancy held up her hand. "I'm not here to fight." Her expression was softer than normal. She dabbed under her eyes, adjusting her dark sunglasses before turning to Chrissy. "You have his presence."

"Really?" Chrissy asked in a choked-up voice. "I wish I knew..." She shook her head, clinging with a sweaty hand to Brittany's palm.

"I've made a lot of mistakes in this life. God knows that, so does the rest of the world." Nancy held out her hands to Chrissy. "But I would like to know my granddaughter, if her mother will let me."

"It's what he would have wanted," Brittany said, her voice thick with emotion.

Nancy nodded and then leaned in and kissed Brittany on both cheeks, followed by the same gesture to Chrissy.

"We'll set up a lunch." Nancy released their hands, and her fake smile was back, her ungenuine presence, but Brittany couldn't find it within herself to be upset.

It was a small step.

And she knew, somewhere up in the sky, Ronan was smiling.

FORTY-SEVEN

"I can't believe he's gone." Zoe clung to Dane's hand as they walked around the small restaurant everyone had decided to head to after the funeral. Brittany had changed her mind on heading home, and Zoe wondered if it had to do with the fact that they all needed a little bit of normalcy after the past few days.

The flat-screen TV in the corner of the grill lit up with reports of the sex trafficking ring, right along with Frederick's face and then later with video of the funeral they'd just left.

"It's real when it makes the news," Dane whispered and then let out a sigh, pulling her in for a hug. "Do you think people can possibly comprehend the things that guy did for our country? The countless hours he worked through the night on the Senate floor? Do you think they have any inkling of the sacrifices he made? They mourn a man they didn't know. Politicians have a thankless job, if you ask me."

"Hmmm." Zoe turned to face him, still clinging to his massive body, finally finding peace in the faint smell of whiskey and peppermint. "So, is that why you went all Robin Hood?" She adjusted his tie and pressed her palms to his chest. "You would have made a great politician yourself. Instead, you linger beneath the city, controlling every single person, every little thing, using your words, your secrets, your money to wield power."

The corners of his mouth lifted in an amused grin. "You realize I'm taking everything you said as a compliment, right?"

She rolled her eyes, unable to help the smile that accompanied the gesture. "Would you rather nobody remembered you? Would you rather they give you a funeral like that?" The idea of anything happening to him suddenly hit her so hard and fast that she couldn't suck in enough air.

"Hey." Dane gripped her chin with his thumb and forefinger. "I don't need that. I've never needed accolades or attention. Do you know why I moved to the city? Why I sold properties and businesses and fought to build an empire?"

She nodded. "To watch over Danica."

"Danica never needed me," he said softly.

"But…" Zoe narrowed her eyes. "You're not making sense. I mean, we barely knew each other when—"

"When you walked into the Pizza Hut with a backward Yankee hat on, a white T-shirt, and jeans that were so tight I almost covered you up with my jacket? You had the most confident walk, the look on your face was almost as arrogant as mine, and all I kept thinking was that I would never forgive myself if I stayed in Jersey because you weren't even eighteen and already had the world eating out of the palm of your hand. Because when I first saw you, I saw my equal in every way. And then when I got to know you, I realized I would never deserve you, so I wanted to do everything in my power to protect you and be what you needed me to be, even when you didn't know you needed it—"

Zoe cut him off with a kiss, wrapping her arms around his neck as she clung to him for dear life, tears in her eyes threatening to cascade down her cheeks. He kissed her back, tasting like fine whiskey and all man. His lips parted, taking her in, reveling in her, loving her in a way he always had.

The only way he knew how.

"You love me," she whispered against his mouth.

"More than you'll ever know."

"You've always loved me."

"I always will," he vowed and then wiped away a tear from under her left eye. "Next to doing all those dirty and dangerous things that nobody will remember me for at my funeral, it's my only purpose in this life."

Zoe sniffled and then punched him in the arm. "I'll remember you."

Dane smiled and then slowly dropped to both knees. "Marry me. Not because of a contract, not because I'm trying to lord it over you, but because if I die tomorrow, I want no regrets between us, no missed conversations, no missed hellos and goodbyes. Marry me because I love you. Because I've always loved you."

Her friends went silent around her, suddenly realizing that Dane was on his knees proposing after Ronan's funeral.

Zoe burst into tears for the third time in her entire life and yelled out, "Yes!" Just as her friends cheered around her.

And when Brittany walked over to hug them both, she whispered so only they could hear. "He would have loved this."

"I know." Dane nodded. "I figured it was right since he helped me pick out the ring." Overhead lights flashed off a frosty blue-white diamond big enough to skate on. It was perfect.

"What?" Brittany gaped. "What do you mean he helped you pick out the ring?"

"He had connections." Dane shrugged and then winked. "Keep your enemies close and all that. We may have looked like we were in a power struggle, but Ronan knew he owed me a debt for the rest of his life."

Brittany was silent, and then her eyes widened while Zoe tried to figure out what Ronan could possibly have owed Dane.

"What am I missing?" Zoe asked.

Dane let out a sigh. "I was the one who helped put Chrissy up for adoption. Ronan knew that I'd gone to the hospital, put two and two together, and tried to get information from me. I refused to give him anything, but I made him a promise."

Zoe noticed Chrissy start to make her way over to them, along with Oliver, who had his arm wrapped protectively around her. Already, he was acting like a father, the man she needed in her life right now, in this moment.

"What promise?" Brittany put her hand on Dane's arm while Zoe waited. Everlee had managed to make it over with a big grin that she quickly lost when she noticed Brittany's pale face and sullen demeanor.

Dane cleared his throat. "I've always protected you three. At first, it just happened. And then it turned into a part-time job when you all started landing campaign after campaign—luckiest guy on Earth having to keep creeps from stalking all of you." He locked eyes with Brittany. "It was only natural to check on Chrissy, and when her parents died in that car crash, and she had to live with her aunt and uncle, I had my guys send her information on a Fresh Faces contest. I knew she'd win, and I knew that more than anything… she needed her mom."

Brittany covered her mouth with her hands. "Why would you keep that from me?"

"Why does it matter? She's here, safe, happy. Reunited."

"I can't decide if you really are the devil or just a nice person under all of this." Zoe rolled her eyes at Dane. "Seriously? Talk about messing with people's lives."

"I'm controlling, I can't help it." He grinned down at Brittany. "For what it's worth, I apologize for meddling… not that I need to. I know how much you needed this."

"Oh, do you?" Brittany shook her head and sighed. "God finally gave you a second chance, and now you have his ear or something?"

"Nah, nothing like that." Dane grinned. "Because your light's back. That's how I know." He left the group gaping.

Zoe stared at Brittany, who stared back at her in shock.

Everlee wrapped her arms around both of them. "Funny, everyone wants a guardian angel, and God found it within himself to send us… that." They all looked toward Dane, in head to toe black, looking every inch the crime boss who had too much power and time on his hands.

"Well." Zoe finally managed to find her voice. "According to Brittany, he works in very mysterious ways."

"True." Everlee nodded as a tear fell down her cheek. "Sorry." She swiped it. "I'm just… still trying to wrap my head around everything with Frederick, Marnie, Jauq. I just… I feel like I lost years of my life. And for what?" She dropped her arms and touched her stomach.

Zoe's chest ached.

It wasn't fair.

Two friends were dead, Everlee had lost her baby and her husband all within two weeks of each other, and the girl who Zoe had at one point been jealous of was left with an empty apartment and a husband in jail.

"Hey." Zoe nudged her. "It's going to be okay."

"Is it?" Everlee sniffed. "How do I know?"

"Well…" Zoe looked to Brittany for help and almost gasped because Dane was right, her light was back. "I think that's where faith comes in."

"Did you hit your head?" Brittany teased.

Zoe just grinned. "No, but I'd like to think that I've realized something after this year. We never would have survived this without you and your faith. So, maybe there's something to be said about all those prayers, Bible thumper."

Brittany burst out laughing and pulled both girls in for a hug. Zoe rested her head against Everlee's and squeezed her tight.

"It's going to be okay," Zoe said, locking eyes with Brittany as they hugged their friend.

Brittany smiled. "It is. It really is."

EPILOGUE

1 MONTH LATER

"There's something I think you'll want to see." The chief brought Dane into the back room. "There were a few things in Marnie's apartment, one thing in particular we thought was strange. A folder of Danica's things."

Dane narrowed his eyes. "What sort of things?"

"Pictures, notes, journals, all of her findings when it came to the sex trafficking and pornography. She was watching them, obviously, knew what was going on, but that's not what I thought you'd want to see." The chief gave Dane a sad smile. "Just look on top of the first page. I'll give you a few minutes."

The minute the door closed, Dane opened up the folder and stared down at the piece of paper written in his sister's handwriting. A document he knew well.

It was the girls' checklist for their perfect happily ever after.

The one the girls had come up with, the one they had made each other sign when they said they'd found their person.

The name *Jauq* was scribbled in and then crossed out.

And written in at the bottom was: *Myself, I finally love and choose myself. I don't need him, or anyone, to give me my happily ever after. I already have it.*

And taped below that was a picture of the four girls laughing.

Dane knew the picture well.

Because he was the one who had taken it.

"Be well, Danica," he whispered, staring down at her smiling face.

He left the precinct with a grin on his face, though it was a sad one. His sister's case was finally closed, and he liked to think that maybe her spirit was finally at peace.

He made it back to the apartment in minutes.

And then he watched her.

His new wife as she unpacked box after box, cursing when things looked broken, and talking to herself as if she didn't have an audience.

Dane's chest swelled with pride. Zoe was his, he was hers. And even though things would always be messy and most likely confrontational with both of them constantly butting heads—he knew it was perfect.

It was everything.

Love wasn't cut and dried, and if you couldn't fight for something, that meant a person didn't deserve to have it in the first place. At least in Dane's book.

He'd fight for the rest of his life to deserve her.

"Stop staring. It's creepy," Zoe said, not looking up from the photo album she'd just pulled from a large, brown box. "At least your lurking is getting better."

"Lurking sounds… like the least sexy thing a man could be doing. You get that, right?"

"And yet, here you are…" She grinned and then looked up at him and gave him a wink.

"That's it." He took two steps toward her, three. She let out a playful scream as he pulled her to her feet and tossed her over his shoulder, making a beeline for the master bedroom.

"Put me down."

"Done." He tossed her onto the bed and laughed when she bounced up and then launched herself at him. He caught her by the waist and devoured her mouth with a punishing, happy kiss. She moaned against his lips as he tugged the sweater up and over her body and tossed it to the floor. "I love you."

She clung to him, her lips moving against his as she breathed against his mouth. "I love you, too."

"I'll never get tired of hearing you say that."

"Mmm." She reached for his pants and winked. "Talking time is done for now."

"Thank God."

"My poor, celibate husband…"

"Because I was yours, I've only ever been yours."

Tears filled her eyes as they kissed again and again, the minutes fading into the hour, the caresses making his chest ache in ways that were unfamiliar for a man like him.

Maybe it was possible to find redemption.

You just had to look hard enough.

And believe it could happen.

Even for a man like Dane.

A monster like him.

Everlee stared up at the ceiling fan as it whipped around slowly. She frowned and then slowly walked over to the window and opened it as a fresh breeze picked up. After a moment's hesitation, she turned off the fan, put on her favorite pair of pajamas, and flipped on Jimmy Fallon.

The sound of the TV made her smile, just like the flickering light that danced along the walls. Instead of staying on her side, she lay back in the middle of the bed and took a deep breath.

She touched her stomach and then smiled to herself.

Fresh starts came in all shapes and sizes, didn't they?

"It's going to be okay," she said to herself. "It already is."

It wasn't lost on her that the ceiling fan was off.

That she no longer needed to count in order to keep the nightmares away.

Instead, she stared up at it.

And smiled.

"Oliver's pot roast was amazing!" Chrissy skipped into the room. "If you don't marry him, someone else is going to steal him, and you can't cook!"

Brittany gave her a narrowed-eyed glare. "I can cook!"

"You burn everything!" Chrissy laughed and then threw a pillow at Brittany. "Admit it, Mom, just leave it to the pros!"

Brittany's heart still jumped when she heard Chrissy call her *Mom*. It felt so natural, so real, and Chrissy had explained that she felt blessed to have not one mom but two.

Brittany had to agree.

"You ladies ready?" Oliver walked into the massive living room with his coat and gave Brittany a sympathetic look.

"Yeah." Brittany stood. Light flashed and sparked off the engagement ring on her left hand. He'd proposed, for real, a day ago.

She'd said yes through her tears.

And then she'd found out that he'd asked for Chrissy's permission first.

It was a lot of adjusting, but she knew that Oliver was it. Only him.

She'd known it the moment she met him, hadn't she?

"Let's go." Chrissy put her hand in Brittany's as Oliver locked up.

The car ride was slow.

Torturous.

At least, it wasn't raining.

When they arrived at the cemetery, Chrissy hopped out first and walked to the grave marked by the prestigious tombstone. "Hi, Dad."

Brittany barely kept her tears in as Oliver squeezed her hand and then wrapped his arms around her like he knew she needed his strength to keep standing.

She wished more than anything that she hadn't given in to fear, that she had sought out Chrissy sooner, told Ronan earlier.

"No regrets," Oliver whispered in her ear. "Life is life. Sometimes, things just happen. You can't change the past. You can only make choices in the present that will affect your future."

She nodded, not trusting her voice.

"Dad, I want you to know…" Chrissy's voice carried on the gentle wind. "I really like Oliver. I think you would, too, and Mom's so pretty. She told me yesterday about all the late night Chinese food and how you used to say goodbye with two fingers. She said I have your eyes and your smile. I'd like to think I have your laugh, too. Mom said it was the best, then again, she loves laughs." Chrissy's voice lowered. "I miss you, even though I only met you twice. I miss the confidence you had when you walked into the room. But I know that you left me in good hands. Mom said you loved to fly, that you finally felt free, so I figured since you have to be in the sky, I'll have to come visit you and tell you my stories down here until we meet again, right?"

Tears streamed down Brittany's face as Chrissy slowly got up and rejoined them. As a family, they each set a rose on the gravestone.

"I love you guys," Chrissy said in a broken-up voice once they were back in the car. It was a typical Sunday: church, pot roast, and a visit to Ronan.

It was everything.

And when Brittany looked up at the New York skyline and saw her face right along with her daughter's in the middle of Times Square, she knew. It might have been ugly and hard, and she might have felt defeated.

But she had survived.

And while life could be cruel.

That didn't mean it couldn't be good, too.

THE END

If you need to talk to someone, here are some resources that are available all day, every day. Please know you are not alone.

The National Sexual Assault Hotline

RAINN (Rape, Abuse & Incest National Network) is the nation's largest anti-sexual violence organization.
Telephone: 800.656.HOPE (4673)
Online chat: online.rainn.org

The National Suicide Prevention Lifeline

The National Suicide Prevention Lifeline provides free and confidential emotional support to people in suicidal crisis or emotional distress
Telephone: 1-800-273-8255
For Deaf & Hard of Hearing: 1-800-799-4889

The National Domestic Violence Hotline

We answer the call to support and shift power back to people affected by relationship abuse.
Telephone: 1-800-799-SAFE (7233)
Online chat: thehotline.org

loveisrespect

loveisrespect's purpose is to engage, educate and empower young people to prevent and end abusive relationships.
Telephone: 1-866-331-9474
Online chat: loveisrespect.org
Text: LOVEIS to 22522

ACKNOWLEDGEMENTS

KATHY IRELAND

Countless people made this book possible. To those not acknowledged here, please believe, gratitude is written in my heart.

Greg, you are the realization of my dreams as a husband and father. Your courage, wisdom, strength, and beautiful soul are so much more incredible than your handsome face and stellar form. Never believed in "love at first sight." I gazed into your gorgeous, kind eyes. Melting into your arms? Finally, safe harbor. Thank you for loving, leading, and healing. My one true love. Hero!

Gratitude, prayers and "Relentless" love for all listed in these pages and your beautiful families, you give so much.

Our children, Lily, Chloe, Erik, and our daughter-in-love Bethany, for joy each day. Children are God's Gifts… To the best parents ever… Mom and Dad to us, John and Barbara Ireland to the world. Your love, empowerment, and prayers rescue always. Blessed by Phil and Barbara Olsen, father and mother-in-love, and our Utah relatives. My sisters, brothers-and-sisters-in-love and relatives on both sides of our family tree, nephews and nieces: Mary, Sal, Cynthia, Mark, Elijah, Polly, the Neimanns, Grant, Dyan, Wyatt, Dana, Paul, Jacob, Joseph, Daniel, and Sophia. Aunt Dorothy, you're incredible. Thank you all for teaching priceless life lessons. Becca, Larry, Noah and our Childers family. In Heaven, Grandmother Gladys, Granny Polly, Grandpa Gus, Granddad Eric, Mama Eva, Viola, Mary Ann, and Del.

"My Guys," from our *kathy ireland Worldwide*/SWC family. For 30 years, you've always had my back and you know I'll always have yours. Our devotion never wavers, because our love never lessens. Geniuses, Jon and Stephen. Erik and Jason. Steve and Adrian. We're together forever.

Shining stars: Brittany Duncan, Brian Nguyen. Rocco Ingemi. John and Marilyn Moretz, we started it! Elise Kim. Nephew Tommy Meharey, Nic Mendoza, Dee, Maria and Felipa. Andre Carthen, Trinity, Miles Robinson, Rubén Torres, Zulma Ponce, Bialik Benjamin, Dwayne Maddox, Selena Hunter, Mitch Sternard, Albert Bonds, Caitlin Runnels, Stephen D. Hemedes, Deb Brabo, Dave Lewis, Bram and Steve Glick. Vanessa Williams, your family, Brian Edwards, #WORKTODO and MORE! Love.

Glick, for magnificent #1 New York Times Bestselling Co-Author, Rachel Van Dyken. Erica Spellman Silverman and Nina Grinstead. RVD, for honoring my beliefs, voice and your exquisite talent; weaving these stories, truths and histories into Fashion Jungle. You are every type of beautiful.

Miriam Wizman. Sam, Mary, Mary Lane, Sam IV, Mei, and the precious Haskells. Paul, Leah, Natalie and

Stephanie Raps. Clark and Karen Linstone. Alex, Mina and the Peykars. Julie Rosenblum. Abe, Sarah and the Hanans. Michael Amini, Martin Ploy and Chuck Reilly. Marilyn McCoo and Billy Davis, Jr., always present in love. Nicholas and Tamara Walker. Frankie Mayer, you believed, when none did, translating fashion and forged a forever-love. Sports Illustrated Icon, Jule Campbell for beauty and genius.

Elizabeth Taylor, the Joan of Ark of HIV/AIDS, with greater courage. Thank you for mentorship, strength, humanity, humility, legendary jewels and valiant love. Tim Mendelson, we "truly love you." Barbara, Quinn, and fellow Ambassadors at the Elizabeth Taylor AIDS Foundation at etaf.org. My board members and our brilliant players at the NFLPA and WNBPA.

Hartwig Masuch, Andreas Katsambas, and BMG. Janet Jackson, for our untold "Unbreakable" history. Jane Seymour. Anita Pointer. The Marshalls: Joan (Van Ark), Jack, and Vanessa. Anita Baker, my Shero! Ashley Graham, for our beautiful friendship, and kindness to our youngest as your own family grows. Kareem Abdul-Jabbar. Serena Williams. Sharlee, for always bringing "The Stuff," Derek and the Jeter family. Guttman Associates: darling Rona Menashe, Alyssa Marquardt and Dick G. Michael McVean, Bruvion Travel, and Nader Sarkosh.

Randy, Amy, Gabriel and Ava Clark. Providence. Helene and Dr. David Winter. The Bacons, Bohlingers, Stretchberrys, and Morgans. The Stanley, Corbo, Brewer and Van Leer families. Baret, Camille, Jenny, Joy, Missi, Amy, Dawn, Sue, Cheri, Kim, Michelene, and your loved ones, you know what you mean to my heart. Irv, Susie and the Blumkins, you are cherished and loved. Warren and Astrid Buffett, for kind, life-changing lessons. Debbie, for flying Mr. Buffett's office. Telisa Yancy, for teaching all to "Dream Fearlessly." Robert Maricich, because. Terry and Tina Lundgren.

Dr. Anthony Fauci, for non-partisan, brilliant service to our country as Director of the NIAID. Dr. Swamy Venuturupalli, Bryant Uy, and Stephanie Bustos of Attune Health, Dr. Margrit Carlson, Tom and Ellen Hoberman, Marty and Deena Singer, Steve and Judy Wolf, for everything. Physicians and staff who serve Cottage Hospital in Santa Barbara.

Selina Lopez, Graham Nation, Kenny Paves, Darren Stone, Eva Roston, Luis Casco, José Eber, Robert Steinken, Diane Meehan - for honoring Jon's vision, and keeping it a lil' bit cute.

Lord and Savior, Jesus Christ, in the dungeon of Paris, I opened Your Bible, and in fear, found Your Truth! You became the closest Friend I'll ever know. As my Faith grew, I learned of confusion, false words, and those who exploit Your Holy Name. As the Giver of all Life, Your Love is for each human being, *none* superior to any other, for any reason whatsoever! Each of us is able to embrace Your Love, despite our mistakes and greatest sins. Because of Your Word, I realize how much more than Friendship, You offer to all who accept You, Your Love, The Cross, Your Blood, The Resurrection and Eternal Life. Scripture's promise for all? "I can do all things through Christ, who strengthens me." Please believe that Truth. My prayer is that our book will encourage you to please, pick up The Bible, and experience Your Everlasting Forgiveness and receive the greatest Love of all.

Love and God bless.

- Kathy

Acknowledgements are always so difficult for me! How do you even begin to thank all the people who help make this book what it is?

I'm so, so thankful to God that he's given me this job that feels nothing like a job but a passion. I love waking up and creating new worlds. And this project was easily one of the hardest and most rewarding yet! Working with Kathy was an absolute dream come true, hearing her stories and seeing her put pen to paper was so fascinating and impacted me in a huge way. How brave. That's all I kept thinking through this process, not only is she brave, but such an incredibly strong woman and role model. The world would be a better place if we had more people like Kathy in it.

To the incredible Jason Winters, thank you so much for being so available during all of this, I promise I'll keep working on slowing my roll when I talk. It was an absolute pleasure hearing story after story from you, you were such a huge part of this process I think we both would have been lost without you.

To my husband Nate and son Thor, thank you for being patient with me when I was up late writing or re-reading stories and emailing late at night, writing with a co-author is amazing but it's two personalities merging as one, and the material is so sensitive—but necessary in conversation especially this day and age. Having my family, my two best friends by my side during this was everything. My boys truly are the best!

Erica, you are the best agent a girl could ask for, I think we all breathed a sigh of relief when we hit the end, trying to pack so much into one story is hard and I so appreciate you helping not only make this happen but being a sounding board during it. Nina, my publicist, haha, fifty-two, I'm just going to keep saying that and hoping you can laugh now that we are at our release of this project! I don't think I've talked to my own mom (who is literally my best friend) as much as I've talked to you these past few months, multiple times a day, all hours of the night. You are magic and such a true friend. I love you.

Jena Brignola, thank you for the lovely cover art. Jill as always, your formatting is on point and your feedback during this was everything we needed! Tracey, Krista, Candace, Georgia, Yana, and Stephanie, I so appreciate your beta reading and finding things that we needed to fix that we missed!

To the editors who worked tirelessly on this project, Kay, Theresa, Chelle, and Jill again haha, we are in your debt! To the rest of the Trident publishing arm who have helped us get this into the hands of readers, you have been so patient!

Words can't express how thankful I am to the entire Kathy Ireland Worldwide team, Steve, Brittany, Brian, Stephen, Rona, Nic, oh gosh I know I'm forgetting people and it really has taken a village! The family behind KKW is just, honestly words can't express how lovely they are. It's a testament to Kathy how her company truly is a family that I want to be a part of.

Finally, to the readers, thank you for reading, for reviewing, spreading the word and supporting!

I know I forgot so many names of people behind the scenes that have helped us in such huge ways. This is why it's hard for authors to do this haha our brains are tired from all the words so, I'm just going to say again, thank you from the bottom of my heart!

Hugs, RVD

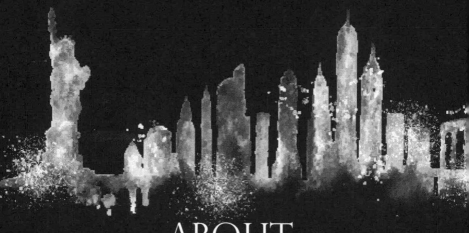

ABOUT
KATHY IRELAND

Kathy Ireland, Chair of kathy ireland® Worldwide (kiWW®), is a fashion and home industry icon, whose unprecedented, American entrepreneurial success, inspired the term, model-preneur. kiWW® is owned solely by Kathy's family trusts. Kathy's first novel, Fashion Jungle, is co-authored with #1 New York Times Bestselling author, Rachel Van Dyken. Kathy entered the "jungle" as a teenager, sheltered by loving parents,

John and Barbara, of Santa Barbara, California. Covers of Vogue, Teen, and Cosmopolitan, led to a record 13 issues and all-time bestselling cover of Sports Illustrated Swimsuit. Kathy is the supermodel turned supermogul, hailed by Harper's Bazaar as the most successful "model in the world." kiWW® launched a single pair of socks, during Kathy's first pregnancy. While selling over one hundred million pairs, retail expanded. kiWW® develops for home, office, fashion, luxury jewels, vacation destinations, weddings, lighting, flooring, furniture, personal care, media and more. After billions of dollars in sales, kiWW®, a private company, was reported on by Forbes. Kathy's story continues in global media, including three Forbes covers (two USA, one Asia), Inc., Wall Street Journal, Cheddar, Success Magazine, television, and online. Kathy's speaking events occur in America, the Middle East, Asia and beyond. Residing in Santa Barbara, California, Kathy Ireland and Greg Olsen are parents to Lily, Chloe, Erik and his wife Bethany, their daughter-in-love. Kathy holds numerous Honorary Doctorates of Humane Letters including one from CSU Channel Islands. Kathy's philanthropy includes: women and children's health, HIV/AIDS, Education, human freedom, life, wars against religious persecution and violence. Kathy is a Board Member of the NFLPA, WNBPA Board of Advocates, an Ambassador and donor for the Elizabeth Taylor AIDS Foundation. Kathy's survival in the jungle is because of a personal relationship with Jesus Christ, His inerrant Word, and The Gospel, which is the Good News of Christ, crucified for all sins. Kathy believes everyone is loved by Jesus Christ, without any exceptions. Please experience Kathy's journey of Faith, at kathyireland.com/fashionjungle/faith.